MAIDEN, MOTHER, CRONE TRILOGY

THE *Curse* OF MAIDEN SCARS

NICOLETTE CROFT

HISTORIUM PRESS
U.S.A.

All rights reserved. No part of this book may be reproduced or transmitted in any form or by any means, electronic or mechanical, including photocopying, recording, or by any information storage and retrieval system, without written permission from the publisher.

This is a work of fiction. All characters, locations and events in the narrative are products of the author's imagination and are used fictitiously. Any resemblance to real persons, living or dead, is entirely coincidental and not intended by the author. Where real historical figures, locations and events appear, these have been depicted in a fictional context.

FIRST EDITION
COPYRIGHT © 2024 Nicolette Croft

All rights reserved. Published in the United States of America. No part of this book may be used or reproduced in any manner whatsoever without written permission except in the case of brief quotations embodied in critical articles and reviews.

For information, contact:

historiumpublisher@gmail.com

www.nicolettecroft.com

thehistoricalfictioncompany.com/hp-authors/nicolette-croft

Hardcover ISBN 978-1-962465-39-7

Paperback ISBN 978-1-962465-40-3

Ebook ISBN 978-1-962465-41-0

Library of Congress Cataloging-in-Publication Data on file

A HISTORIUM PRESS NOVEL

www.historiumpress.com

Cover by White Rabbit Arts at
The Historical Fiction Company

TABLE OF CONTENTS

YORKSHIRE, ENGLAND   7

  AUTUMN, 1795   7
    ORPHAN   7
    WOUNDED CHILD   18
    SAMARITAN   27
    BULLY   34
    SERVANT   41

  WINTER, 1795   49
    PRINCE   49
    PRIEST   59
    STORYTELLER   67
    THIEF   75
    ADVOCATE   82

  SPRING, 1796   91
    COMPANION   91
    WARRIOR   100
    EXORCIST   110
    MYSTIC   120
    ARCHITECT   127

VENICE, SERENISIMA REPUBLICA VENETA   136

  AUTUMN, 1796   136
    EXPLORER   136
    TRICKSTER   146
    TEMPTRESS   155
    PROSTITUTE   163
    LOVER   172

  WINTER, 1796   178
    DON JUAN   178
    QUEEN   188
    HEALER   195
    SABOTEUR   205
    SCRIBE   211

1797 **219**
    KNIGHT 219
    SHAPE-SHIFTER 229
    AVENGER 239
    RESCUER 249
    JUDGE 260

15 MAY 1797
    LIBERATOR 269

AUTHOR'S NOTES
    AND ACKNOWLEDGMENTS **281**

ABOUT THE AUTHOR **283**

THE CURSE OF MAIDEN SCARS

YORKSHIRE, ENGLAND

AUTUMN, 1795

Orphan

Light Attributes: Independent, able to be alone, survivor
Shadow Attributes: Abandonment stifles maturation,
inappropriate surrogate relationships

I rushed through a dense fog toward my evening post outside the Board Inn. The bells of the York Minster clanged through the walled city. Mist hindered my vision, and I stumbled, tripping over two women clinging together for warmth under the low-hanging eaves of a crowded mug house.

Scurrying around them, I settled into my place on the walk outside the Inn. Inescapable dampness seeped into my muscles. I inched my feet aside from a rain puddle—a vain effort to stay dry—and played with my greasy hair. I scratched at the bites on my legs and tried to ignore my aching, empty belly as I watched passersby.

During the day, I plucked cotton. But at night, I was tasked with a different job—Scout out culls for the more seasoned girls. The cotton house matron, Camilla, would hold back my dinner until I completed her bidding. I was grateful not to make a living by whoring and dutifully stood watch.

My story must have begun before life as a stray waif, but I didn't know the tale. The cotton house takes in children as little as three—the unwanted offspring of *criminals, crazies, and the contagious*. By sixteen, we were expected to make room for younger sprogs and pursue meaningful work. It was weeks until my sixteenth birthday, and I didn't have a plan. Choices for a girl like me were limited, so Camilla told me. I had some learning and hoped I might find a maid's position. Whatever I was to become, I didn't want it to include lurking about the seedy, dank Yorkshire streets like a wet cur.

A cackle of laughter echoed from inside the Inn that stood open behind me. A woman's mound of blond hair tied in red, pink, blue, and black ribbons appeared in the window's waving candlelight. She tossed her head back and let out a bright, spirited laugh as a burly man with a beard kissed her neck. I envied their intimacy. I longed to know such love and care.

Deep shivers tightened my sodden dress over my back, and a cough rattled through me. I was prone to illness. My lungs had never been strong. And the wetness only made things worse. I stuffed my head between my knees and swooned in lightheadedness. I closed my eyes and wished myself someplace warm and safe, dreaming of a small bed in a quiet room free of mold, surrounded by soft blankets, the amber light of candles, and a stack of leather-bound books with stories waiting for me to discover. Such a wish was only a fantasy to me—nothing in my real life resembled it.

Boot heels sounded beside me, ripping me out of my daydream. I lifted my head too quickly, and my vision faded darkly. Panic grew from the depths of my belly. Had I missed the opportunity to signal the workhouse strumpets, giving them time to sell their comfort for a copper?

A passerby kicked me and shot, "street rat ." He poured ale over my head and rolled with laughter. There was always laughter. I'd have kicked his feet out from under him if I hadn't felt weakened from illness. I was accustomed to this sort of abuse, having scouted for culls since the age of eight, and wasn't afraid to fight back if needed.

Suddenly, a set of large hands gathered me from the walkway. Brisk air smacked the back of my legs, and I shivered in the chill. My heart felt like it had stopped beating, and I squeezed my eyes shut. A man clutched me against his chest and carried me inside the Inn. My cheek brushed over the rough bristles of his beard.

The door sounded with a thud. Stagnant air thick with the pall of tobacco and the rancid smell of cooked meat made me want to gag. I wasn't sure if I should fight my way free, back to Camilla's expectations, or yield to the man holding me. Lack of will and pangs of hunger chose the latter.

The man consigned me next to a cooing fire. Afraid to confront the faces eyeing me, I pulled myself into a ball. The man hovered near, and without permission, he parted the hair hanging over my face. Daring a glance at him, I was amazed by his bright emerald eyes, rimmed in black lashes and bounded by expression lines from the impress of sunlight and time. A slight grin peeked through his unruly black beard that matched loose hanging hair, which fell in thick ringlets. I sensed great life and beauty in this man but hardness too.

He exhaled a breath of whiskey and pipe smoke. "You have been on the stoop a long while."

My cough rattled. He clapped a large hand between my shoulders, pounding out the rumbling cackle, and passed me a glass. "Drink." My nostrils burned as whiskey bathed my mouth in a brisk fire. "Again." After the second taste, the whiskey boiled away my chill and insecurity. Wrapping my fingers around the glass and inadvertently around the man's hands, I steadied my third drink.

He lingered near me before freeing himself and gracefully easing to his full height. His vivid green eyes stayed trained upon me. The angle of my gaze strained my neck, so I focused on his heavy leather boots, elevated by worn wooden heels. I gulped down the last of the whiskey, appreciating its numbing effect. It might be my only nourishment, especially if I didn't make it home on time.

"You've taken to that quickly." He clasped my wrist. "Up." My tendons stretched, and I imagined him pulling on me like a hunk of mutton, tearing the fibers of my muscles but not wholly undoing them. Side-by-side now, he was almost a foot taller than me. He announced himself with a spirited Irish accent. "I'm Donovan McGuinness."

A woman's squawking voice intruded. "You have no idea what it might have." She floated closer for a punctual quip and retreat. "Such filth."

I knew the reason for her disgust. I'd seen myself this morning before leaving the workhouse. My dark oily hair was worse than my grimy face. I had missed my Sunday bath in the rusted basin, occupied by each successive child, oldest to smallest. By the time the littlest had their chance, the water was thick with debris, even blood. I was usually last, ensuring others' care before my own. Despite the visible filth, my hazel eyes and odd fleck of gold in the right iris glowed when I was sick, angry, or enthralled, so I'd been told. And it always marked my appearance.

"It's here now, I suppose. And what do you plan, pray tell?" seethed the woman.

Donovan donned a sympathetic expression. "I am sure I cannot say. But I know what it is to crouch in a puddle wishing for the cold to finish its job, and the morning street sweeps to dispose of me with the rest of the trash."

His long hair and unshaven face gave him an aged look, but I guessed Donovan to be in his late twenties. He watched me with intensity. I thought he saw right through me. Unlike most men I'd met, he exuded an air of protection, of safety. He caressed my hair behind my ear again and gave me an encouraging smile. His teeth were straight and pearly bright, framed by a broad jawline. Whoever he was, he seemed to understand my struggles. And, yet, he was a man—that alone made his journey through life easier.

Camilla had made clear that my life could only lead to three possibilities if I did not find a proper job in service—I could be a nun, a wife, or a whore. I had little taste for religion. Street life, whether as a whore or vagrant, was the worst option. And I wasn't marrying material. I was too poor and had no real family.

But, oh, how I wished someone might find me worthy. Every night, I dreamt of a lost family that might return for me, or a lover who might rescue me. But those dreams were only fantasies fueled by the many novels lent to warm me on frigid Yorkshire nights. Any future I might have would come from bravely grasping luck and opportunity.

I held Donovan's gaze and tried to echo his sentiment about street life. "Survival requires sacrifice."

"I'll bet she might have a mind," declared a man by the window with hauntingly bright grey eyes who stared me through.

Donovan had softened my defenses, but I felt drawn to this man. And he was right. Despite my tattered, soiled appearance, I was learned.

Years ago, I'd struck a deal with a priest at the Minster. He agreed to steal me into the church library, explaining every question I could divine in exchange for affection. The priest's *tutelage gifted keys that opened doors of opportunity*—so he said. Learning was a privilege granted to few, particularly an orphaned Yorkshire lass. But between my pact with him and Camilla's tenuous guardianship, I at least had an education and was still a virgin.

Donovan asked, "What's your name?"

"I'm Renna." Lingering whiskey burned into the cracks of my lips.

Animation slowly returned to everyone in the room, and self-consciousness replaced my brief show of bravery as I watched each occupant. Donovan poked the fire logs back to life with an iron rod painted in soot. The tart played with her colorful nest of hair as she watched her reflection in a tarnished mirror. A bartender noisily arranged things in the back. Two men bent over a chessboard. One eyed me through wire-rimmed spectacles, and the other fervently plotted his chess move. I looked twice at the man with glasses. My gut tightened as his face shadowed, and I was suddenly grateful not to be alone with him.

The man by the window obscurely tilted his head as he reclined with his ankles crossed. He toyed with an ivory smoking pipe. The confessions of his attire—impeccably trimmed uniform, casual posture, but alert poise—signaled him as a sailor. He seemed near Donovan's age but blessed with Adonis' untarnished, youthful beauty. He was cleanly shaven, and his tawny-colored hair was perfectly coiffed. My chest tightened with longing, and I wondered what kind of woman would be his equal. Briefly, my imagination ran with possibilities of our acquaintance, but he represented a world I could not touch.

Donovan brushed a finger over my elbow. "Where do you belong?"

With you, I thought. But I knew what he meant. "I will be missed at the workhouse on Marysgate if I'm not back before the lamps are lit."

"Too late." The sailor pulled a long puff from his pipe, lipping the end like tasting a drop of tea from a cup. His movements were slow and graceful, purposeful. I could imagine him sitting on the front pews of the Minster with the rest of York's upper class. Body situated at a comely angle and pipe pinched between pink lips, he turned his look toward me again, watching me with eyes the color of highly shined silver reflecting a clear blue sky. His effect arrested me, and my heart fluttered.

Donovan squeezed my arm. "I will return you." Stretching for a woolen cloak strewn on a table, he pulled it over his shoulders and buttoned it high around his neck. He hastily tucked me in the flap, smothering me in the damp wool that smelled of smoke and sea.

We moved to the door, but the sailor interceded. "I can take her if you like." His eyes, now clearly glowing with intrigue, bore into me. If Donovan hadn't gripped me tightly around my ribs, there was a risk I might float right into the other man's arms. Donovan exuded strength and safety, but the sailor's beauty was nearly godlike to me.

"I have this handled," Donovan said, pulling me out the door.

He held me tight as we stepped back onto the cobblestone street. Although I had heard him say he was walking me home, I shook uneasily. My waifish figure was no rivalry for his bulk. Still, his flank was warm and steady, and it felt comforting to cling to his taught stomach. I willed my shivering to stop.

He spoke into the cloak. "Do you always shake so?"

"I'm cold."

It was true. But I was also nervous about his aim and my unknown greeting at the workhouse.

"Not that it matters, but why were you on the street?" There was a softness in his look.

No one had asked me that. "I watch for culls for the older girls."

He frowned, "But not for you?"

The other girls changed from threadbare dresses, redolent of mildew and sweat, into ill-fitted and faded gowns before their evenings romping in cots ridden with mites. I longed for a post as a maid or even a governess. Time with small children brought me joy. I'd always assumed it was why Camilla allowed the Minster priest's *tutelage*. At least, that is what I had hoped.

I answered him with guilty truth. "I don't want to be like them. I want more."

Donovan released a slow sigh. "We all want more."

We walked down High Petergate toward the Bootham Bar and a wooden entrance separating York's central city from Bootham. A knave sheltered us from the steadily falling rain as it rhythmically beat on the guard platform. Donovan concealed me behind his thigh and cleared his throat. "I need through." His voice vibrated in his chest as he responded to a guard's inaudible inquiry ". . . even a street rat can provide pleasure. Let me pass before she melts away, and I lose my chance to taste her."

His comment was alarming. What was worse—the foul workhouse I knew or a stranger's dubious intentions? Still, I held his belt and tucked my head under his arm.

The gate opened, and the rainy wind stung my exposed legs. Donovan pressed on, and we turned a corner, cutting us off from the harsh weather. The world around me quieted again. I bore my own weight to walk beside him. Galvanizing courage reheated my body, and I forced us to a slower pace.

"Are you really going to taste me?"

He pulled the cloak aside, revealing the street behind us lit with oil lamps tightly sealed from the imposing rain. Vagabond makeshift homes in shadowed doorways hid occupants tucked tightly away after begging for alms or picking pockets. He pushed me out of the cloak's shelter with a pop of his hip. The sudden temperature change was shocking.

"I said I was taking you home."

A woman with sores marking her cheeks lurched toward us. Her gaping foul mouth betrayed her disease. She pawed at my shirt and Donovan's chest with cracked fingertips. "Here, dearie, you don't want an old mam to suffer."

I recoiled, but only because I was so terrified of becoming like her. I couldn't articulate it then, but I was observant enough to register how easy it would be for an orphan with no connections to fall into abject squalor. I could never glimpse such a face in those days without imagining it as a specter of my fate. And I always wondered whether all beggars had also begun as butter-faced orphans.

"Off." He shoved her, and she retreated to the shadows.

Shaken by the woman's sudden appearance and Donovan's sharp response to her, my voice quivered as I asked, "Why are you helping me?"

He had a stoic expression. "I'm not sure, other than there's something about you. Maybe just pity. But leaving you to rot in the rain felt wrong."

Before I could ask more, a wailing cry froze us both—the kind telling of pain, fear, and desperation.

We turned in unison toward the sound. I eased back into his awaiting cloak and peered through a small aperture in the cloth. I held him, and he held me. We barely breathed as we waited.

Then came the cry again.

I strained in the direction of the cry, transfixed on a flickering spot in the dark. Shadows and blackness accosted us from the open space. The wind blew a branch to the side, revealing a glint of light.

"What is that?"

"It is the asylum," he said flatly. "It used to be Bootham Hall, home for the sick and insane."

Of course. I knew that. But Camilla had forbidden me from going near. I hadn't seen what lay beyond the trees in all these years. Something always kept me blind to this place.

We listened to a third cry.

It was sickeningly familiar, for I'd heard it nearly every night in my dreams. "I have to see who is making that sound."

"Absurd. Why would you want to?"

"That voice, it is calling to me." I couldn't explain my struggle to know if my nightmares were imagination or a forgotten memory. I clutched his hand and was warmed by his strong presence. "Please."

Donovan shook his head but allowed me to tow him toward the asylum.

A wrought-iron gate barred the long lane, but we squeezed through a gap loosely tied by a chain and padlock. A rectangular building loomed to the right. It was plainly designed with a row of uniform windows and alternating chimney stacks. A thin hiss of smoke floated from the last smokestack. The loud clang of metal-on-metal startled us to a halt. The sound of a second strike and then a cadenced third indicated someone hard at work. Ducking low, we scuttled along the building toward the wooded area that opened to a sizeable lawn. To the far left stood a modestly high but ornately designed brick house attempting to impress the landscape like a castle. To the right was a chapel, narrow and pristine. A ghost of a bell sang lightly in the wind.

THE CURSE OF MAIDEN SCARS

Donovan scowled. "Are you satisfied?"

"Not yet."

His chest expanded in a resigned huff.

My nerves roused me to life and made me forget my wavering health. We quickly moved in unison across the open space to the brick house. We were soon next to a tall window trimmed in white. The sill's bottom was a few feet from the ground, and we crouched in the fecund earth.

"Now what?" Donovan panted.

I had to stand and look, but I felt paralyzed. I wasn't sure I wanted to see what was on the other side of the glass. "What if it is horrible?"

"What do you think you'll see through an asylum window?"

I cautiously lifted my eyes past the sill's edge. My vision met with a sheer curtain muting the outline of a vacant bed and end table. The door to the room was closed, and no one stirred inside. I was ready to go to the next window when a strident cry came from the other side of the wall. I was shot through with alarm and ducked into the covering beside Donovan.

"Let's go." He uttered, face tight. I could hardly breathe. My heart raced. Donovan pressed his lips to my ear. "They do awful things here."

My fear bid me flee, but curiosity kept me frozen. I had to have another look. I stood on my tiptoes and daringly peered through the glass, trying to decipher someone sequestered in the corner, out of sight. The shapes were different on the other side of the room. A dark mound moved. It something out of place in the sterile space. It grew large, to the point of bursting.

A banshee's shriek pierced the air.

Hands and fingers splayed wide. Deformed bare legs stomped with darkened feet toward the window. Dim light shone on breasts that jiggled slightly with the amble. There was a yellow stain down the loosely fitting nightshirt. The creature floated more than walked.

I was spellbound as it crept closer. I fixated on the space where a face would appear. I tried to envision what sort of being could express such anguish.

It ran out of air, and its scream quieted. Then it inhaled deeply. I blocked my ears from the caustic din, sure to follow. A flash of fingers and fists beat at the glass. The wraithlike beast rushed at me, swatting away my intrusion. I rebounded and fell to the ground. The jostle knocked the breath from me, nudging my cough to life. Determined to confront this beast, I detangled my skirt from a thorn bush crushed in my drop.

The creature pressed its forehead against the window, wrinkling a film-thin curtain and creating a worn look. Yet, something about this being, hunched and impish, indicated someone young. It drew a long breath and bawled brightly. It was not a voice worn with time and protestation. Instead, it was frenetic. As the yell quelled, it came to my level and reached for the curtain. Its yellowed nails were chewed and chipped, and there was a long gash down the right index finger.

It pulled aside the vale. I was stunned when not a nightmarish beast but a haunting girl's face mirrored mine. Darkness encircled her eyes. Cracked lips and deep-set lines from a stern expression marked her look. A purple bulging scar marred her right temple. I was petrified, like an ancient garden statue.

Donovan yanked me, and I became aware of the immutable wind. "We have to go."

She must have understood our imminent retreat, for she slapped her palm against the glass. Deep burn scars bubbled over her hand and misshaped her fingers. They looked like the scars on my back. Time slowed as I touched the matching wound on my shoulder, feeling the raised skin through my shift. I didn't know of my scars' origins. I wondered if she knew of hers.

The girl and I statically held each other with our gazes. I placed my hand on the glass to outline her fingers with mine. She was smaller than me and withered, and her natural vitality seemed long drained away. I'd seen pain in the workhouse, but not like this. I'd been told only the forgotten belonged in places like this. Not a girl, not a child who could have been my peer. Looking at her eyes, flooded with pain and agony, I had a whole new sense of fear. There worse things than living in the cotton house or on the street.

"A lamp was lit in the next room." Donovan hauled me back. "We have to go."

THE CURSE OF MAIDEN SCARS

My heartstrings frayed like a cloth torn in two, stretched between the desire to comfort the girl and my desperation to flee. With every retreating step, she smashed her face tighter against the window. She scratched at the glass, and her mouth gaped wide as she wailed. Tears caught in my throat. I was flooded with guilt.

Donovan clasped my hand, and we broke into a full run, like two horses gathering momentum for the home stretch, fleeing the asylum and my shame for leaving the girl. I stumbled as we reached the row of decaying buildings with the clang from the farrier's cottage.

Dazed by the experience, my apprehension of home vanished. I'd never imagined there could be something worse than the perils of poverty. My senses were dulled when we halted at the door and the weather-beaten sign, *Cotton*.

I desperately turned to Donovan. He had not offered anything except a walk back. And now we were bonded by our interloping. He held me in the crook of his arm, his look unfaltering.

"Your eyes are glowing—such an unusual color, something akin to tree moss and the green of a shallow sea." His chin bent toward me.

Despite the evening's events, my pulse quickened, and the heat of my body rose. I closed my eyes, envisioning his face moving closer, his warm mouth hidden behind rough stubble, finding a path to my lips. I imagined how his kiss would vanquish the evil I'd witnessed. I'd read a story of a princess rescued by a knight in shining armor, and the image materialized in my mind. A scruffy seaman differed from a gallant paramour, but I wished to be like that princess and freed from tonight's horror and my hopeless life.

But all he did was wrap on the door.

Gripping me by my shoulders, he forced me away to face Camilla, who stood in the doorway with a queer grin. How could I explain to her what I'd seen and how—I knew it in that very moment—it had forever changed me?

Wounded Child

Light Attributes: Awakens compassion, open to forgiveness
Shadow Attributes: Resists moving on, wary of others

Arriving home with a stranger altered my circumstances. Camilla did not ask me to patrol for culls, and she reduced my cotton load to nearly nothing. I had spent enough nights in the rain and days milling through baskets that I didn't complain. Still, it left me uneasy about what came next. Camilla had talked of legitimate employment, but nothing concrete was decided. A few of the girls stayed at the workhouse past sixteen, but they were often mothers before seventeen, suckling babies at barely formed breasts. After hearing and seeing the burned girl, working as a maid or making it through life hand-to-mouth were not the only choices. A horrific alternative loomed.

I desperately wanted to share my worries with Max. He was Camilla's lame son, and my only friend. I played with a chipped mortar and grooved pestle as I sat on my bed in the far corner of the women's section of the workhouse, going over in my mind all that happened. I struggled to understand my reaction to Donavan's unexpected friendship or the sailor's memorable presence. The asylum girl's desperation still sickened me.

Max tottered around the corner from the kitchen. His oversized shoes scoffed over the stones like a barber's knife on a leather-sharpening strap. He plopped on the end of my bed with a basket of cotton bulbs. He slipped from his shoes and dangled his dirty feet over the edge. A towel hung from his head like the turban of a benevolent leader, signaling his desire to play *Sultan*, a game we'd invented long ago where he was master and I his grateful servant.

The sight of him brought welcome relief.

He pointed to the mortar and pestle. "You love that."

"I do." I brushed the hair out of his face. "And it's mine, thanks to you."

One Sunday afternoon, awaiting our bath rituals, we chased each other around the island cutting block, dizzied by hunger-induced lightheadedness. Max was small for his age and tired quickly, often needing a reprieve from our play. I sensed his fatigue that night and dramatically stubbed my toe on the table leg. I was instantly drawn to the mortar and pestle carved from a dark slate. I had snatched up the cudgel and declared, "I want one."

The mortar and pestle were tucked in my cot when I woke the following morning. Max and I never spoke of the gift, nor did we pay mind to the shouting when it was discovered missing in the kitchen. The house had many visitors. It was not a typical toy a child might fancy. We weren't suspected. But my *toy* allowed me to grind cottonseeds into a paste to moisten our hands before bed each night—one of the many ways we cared for each other.

I scattered a handful of husks over his lap and head like flower petals. "Do you know why I am being treated differently, *Grand Sultan?*"

He straightened his *turban* and shook his head. Max's large brown eyes peered out like an observant owl, and he clutched his stunted left arm to his chest with an invisible force.

He was missing the bottom half of his left arm. He was two years younger than me, though he could pass for four years less. Max's quiet demeanor and tiny form made him easy to overlook, which he often used to his advantage. He collected information in return for continual attention. He was as close to a brother as I knew.

Max ignored my question. He sorted the cotton into piles resembling miniature frost-coated boulders. "Who did you come back with the other night?"

"His name was Donovan." We took turns stacking the cotton. "He was nice."

Max looked up at me. Part of the towel-turban obscured his eye.

"*How* nice?"

I knocked him in the shoulder of his good arm with my knuckle. "He walked me home after warming at the Inn and giving me a glass of whiskey."

Max's eyes widened, "And?"

I glowered, partly because I knew Camilla might ferret out some of my divulged secrets but more because I sensed his skepticism.

Max swept the shells and fluff into the basket. "I heard you are getting a bath."

The prospect left me frozen as if I was still on the walk in the rain. A bath? All to myself? On a Thursday? Baths were kept for Sundays, and I couldn't recall a time when I'd had one alone. "But I thought Camilla sought a place for me. Whom did you hear this from?"

Max tugged the towel from his head and slipped off the bed. "Mother."

I recalled my years of servile obedience, which now seemed to result in no protection. Disheartened, I drew down my skirt and torn linen apron over my legs and decided to share my secret with Max. "Donovan and I passed a place—it was horrible."

"What place?"

"Donovan said it was the asylum." I pulled my blanket over my shoulders and glanced at the stack of newspapers I arranged like a pillow, noting the headline of an old Yorkshire Post: *King George Hospitalized in Lincolnshire for Madness.* Tremors chased down my spine as I thought of the girl from the window.

"Mother has told us not to go near it." Max's complexion blanched. "What did you see?"

"A girl. She looked a bit like me but was more your age."

Her face. Her cry. Her pleading. It was indelibly unsettling. I could not forget the similarities I found in our wounds. No one told me the origin of my scars. Knowing another might bear the same unforgettable disfigurement both sickened and comforted me. I felt pulled to go back, to find her and tell her she was not alone. But I also longed to run, to hide from the horror searing my memory.

"You need to forget her and be grateful that's not us." Max patted me on the leg. "I'll see you later. Mother wants me to get a few things ready." He shuffled back to his side of the workhouse.

A tiny horde of children collided into the edge of my bed as they ran past playing tag. The rumpus in the room left me detached, and I didn't notice Camilla's shadow cast over me.

"You look tatty," Camilla's voice was steady. Her stalwart figure obstructed the candlelight, and shadows cast over her expression. She reached her hand to me.

Capitulating, I took it, and she led me to the washroom. Hanging lengths of cotton layered over a line formed a persistently oozing curtain of sop, smelling of wet animals and lavender. We ordinarily bathed in the kitchen, where the basin could be drained out along the sloped floor. Camilla must have thought I deserved privacy, or maybe she didn't want me interrupting the evening tea.

"Remove your clothes. I need to see your markings." Her soft cheeks and cobalt-colored eyes were impossible to ignore.

Camilla was round but sturdy, at once welcoming and foreboding. She was part of every memory I had, and many weren't pleasant. There had been moments where she'd taken her discontent out on me with the length of the leather belt she kept cinched tightly around her billowing blouse. Her reprimanding lashes stung me to the core and left scars of resentment. Still, she'd been my comfort when I was sick, cooling the outbreak of fever and seeing to my survival with an array of remedies. Camilla would diligently tend to my illnesses, much as she would her own son. But come the clock's strike, twenty-four hours after falling ill, she'd expect a miraculous recovery. Her intimidating regimen succeeded in cultivating an unshakeable faith in her. Indeed, she was my guide and my protector.

"Come now, Renna, I can't have you dilly-dallying. We are on a schedule." Camilla crossed her arms and awaited compliance. "I promise something nice for you after we have you cleaned up a bit," she purred soothingly.

I disrobed and stood in front of a stool. I wasn't sure if Camilla was sincere or if the placating was only to coax. Like any good English woman, she obscured her messages behind flat expressions and emotionless words.

I shyly displayed my back to her. I didn't have to see it now to picture the purple bulbous puckering skin over my right shoulder and spine. I forgot about them mostly, except when the flesh tightened on summer days and felt like a confining jacket. Camilla said the scars were products of oil burns, but I couldn't remember how I'd gotten them. She'd told me some memories are meant to be forgotten.

"They are the same as always. Somehow, I imagined the scars might fade in time, but they seem to glow as you grow." Her expression softened. "Maybe one day you can paint over them and show them as art rather than a stain."

I knew she intended a kindness, but her words stung. I couldn't imagine how the obvious imperfection would become art.

Camilla pointed at a table fixed up with bathing utensils. "Clean where dirt finds a home and makes an odor."

"Have you been to that place across the way, once Bootham Hall, now the asylum?" I huddled to both hear and see her meaning.

She gave me a side glance. "Aye. I don't go near it, and neither shall you."

I played with the cracked edges of my cuticles and considered pressing the point. Camilla could blather irascibly for hours about tightfisted merchants, but if she cared to hold her views in check quietly, she would do so with custodial skill.

She took up a basket of dried yarn. "Why do you ask?"

"The man from the other night, Donovan, he mentioned it."

She patted down the yarn as though dampening the coat of a cat. "All types can end out there. It's rumored the man running it was once a colleague of Francis Willis, the doctor who treated King George in his madness, but that was years ago. I suppose one ought not to listen to rumors. I once had family interned in such a place. . ." Her skin blanched. "Now, about your business." She abandoned me to my chore.

I was interested in her confession, but there was a draft in the drying house. Delaying would make the washing even more miserable. I started with my face. A mirror revealed shadows of tiredness marbling my complexion. I scrubbed off most of the grime, but my cleaning hardly affected the dark circles under my eyes and the hollowness of my cheeks. My lips cracked in the corners—something that never seemed to heal.

My hazel eyes were muddy, and the fleck of gold flickered like a dying ember.

Setting the mirror down, I brushed through my tresses until my dark strands lay flat over my chest. I tamed the greasy pieces into a tight rope. Another look in the mirror showed a comely image. I remembered to pull the damp cloth through my soured armpits and around my bum before tidying the soiled rags.

Camilla returned with a stack of plain clothes and she handed them to me. "Dress. Go wait by the door."

My heart sank. Maybe it was my turn to earn a wage with my body. I did as she said and hustled toward the rearmost door, where the senior girls communed before venturing out at night for their *walk*.

"Where are you headed?" Camilla barked. "Go to the front."

I was breathless with confusion. "Yes, Ma'am." I was outfitted in weathered travel clothes, nothing truly suitable to find my first cull, if that's what she intended. As I stood waiting, I shook in the growing possibility that there was an option.

"You look cold"—Max turned to take in a full view of me— "and scared?" He had on his outdoor coat. His hair was slick with oil and combed nicely to the side. His cheeks were rosy, likely from a pinch between the fingers or from a dash of rouge.

"Why are you here?"

He cocked his head, and his bright brown eyes glowed with excitement. "I get to go with you." He grinned, revealing his mostly straight smile. He pulled his stump into his chest as he wiggled.

"Max, there isn't any place we can both go together, except for maybe another workhouse, or worse." My voice trailed off as I thought of the girl with burns.

He doubtfully scowled. "You know we are supposed to always go together."

I kicked the toes of my leather shoes, feeling sad and frustrated. "That's not how things work for people like us, Max. You're old enough to see what happens to the older ones. We grow up, and we go away, seldom together."

There was a loud knock on the front door.

Max stirred to answer it but stopped. "Mother wanted me to make sure you had this." He struggled to remove a parcel from his pocket. He eventually placed a hastily wrapped brown paper package tied with twine into my hands.

I turned the parcel over and pulled at the covering, noting a faint smell of cinnamon and cottonseed. I didn't have to undo it to know it was my mortar and pestle. "She knew?"

He tugged the door open and said over his shoulder, "Of course. Mum wants you to take everything important to you."

I was overwhelmed by surprises, one after another. Nothing made sense. I was about to shower Max with questions when two massive figures approached him and handed their cloaks to him to shake free of drizzle.

"Don't you clean up fine, little street rat?" A silky voice washed over me. The grey-eyed man in the uniform from the Inn stepped up. Toe-to-toe with his polished boots, I was forced to stare directly at the crisp lapels of his coat. He was close enough for me to take in his scent of tobacco and vanilla.

Donovan moved from the sailor's shadow. "Hello again." His whiskers wriggled with amusement as he smiled. "You do look much improved."

"We are not introduced." The sailor solicited my attention with an extended hand. "I'm Captain Henry Abner Moore."

My body shot through with electricity. "I am Renna."

He brought the back of my hand to his lips. "My pleasure." His eyes never left my face and held me with a look of pursuant intent. "Dark hair and white skin—but your eyes—I imagine they appear differently, depending on the light." He was beautiful when I saw him at the Inn, but now I felt entranced. And yet, my instinct said safety was nearer to Donovan and far away from Henry.

Camilla broke our connection with her arrival. "I see we are introduced. All is prepared, but is there anything specific you want me to collect?" She, too, was dressed in a sturdy outfit, wrapped in a long cloak, with tall boots tightly laced up her ankles, seemingly ready for an evening constitutional. She gave me a quick, telling look.

Donovan answered, "We need to move on now. We can find our way in the dark, but it would be better to use what light we have to our advantage."

"Where are we going?" I dared.

"I've had something arranged," Camilla replied. "Mr. McGuinness and I spoke again after he brought you back. He works with Captain Moore at the West India Company. It's time we all change our fate, I think. Captain Moore has told of a new opportunity."

Donovan faintly winked. "You said you wanted more."

Henry took my hand and turned to Max, who waited with his cloak outstretched. He slid into the garment, never losing contact with me, and glibly remarked, "You will be most grateful for your new arrangements." Speechless, I let him tow me outside.

The wind had picked up, and the rain pelted us from a side angle. Henry would not release my arm. A mix of annoyance and relief left me at his mercy. We shuffled toward the street corner and in the direction of the asylum. My fear mounted. Despite Donovan's and Camilla's obscure explanations, after seeing the girl with scars like mine, I was sure the journey would end with me entering the front of the asylum—as a patient.

Panic made me try to yank free of Henry. "Let me go."

His grip tightened, but he suddenly released me. "What is with you?"

I stumbled backward into Donovan, who opened his cloak and tucked me under his arm, closing the garment to the weather and Henry's exasperated expression. I clung to his belt. His familiar scent was calming. We stepped in time together, but he, too, came to a stop. He maneuvered me to his side, much like he had on the night of our first meeting.

It felt like something ripping when he released me, whispering beneath his collar, "You have to let go." He pushed me up into an awaiting carriage.

Max and Camilla were already on the opposite side. Henry found the space next to me, leaving Donovan to sit catty-corner and as far away from me as the cabin would allow. I tingled with the closeness of his presence. I'd never been in such an intimate space with a handsome aristocrat. He tugged the door shut, and we were awash in quietude, except for a hiss through the window and a blustering wind shaking the carriage.

Henry drew his watch from his pocket. "Time to move." He pounded on the roof.

The carriage jostled to a start. The trapped air from the closed door warmed, and a rocking motion mimicked a boat at night in gentle waters. My eyes grew heavy, and my mind lost focus. Blinking, I first watched Max, who nestled into Camilla's bosom. His eyes closed softly in a deep sleep. Then Camilla, who smiled faintly as we rocked, slowly drifted off herself.

Lastly, Donovan—I caught him looking at me. I watched him, too, with fondness but allowed the sway of the carriage to work with hypnotic effect. I hoped his vigilance meant safety, at least for the remainder of our time.

Samaritan

Light Attributes: Benefactor
Shadow Attributes: Expecting recognition for offered help

My head knocked against the window, jarring me awake from a nightmare of the asylum girl—the image of her gaping mouth and haunting injuries chased after me down a desolate hallway. It took a moment to blink away the vision and understand my reality. A lush blanket partially covered my legs and over Henry. I stretched to adjust it.

"Did you rest well?" He touched my fingers. "We are almost there. I was going to wake you to go over the arrangement, but I figured you could have a few more moments of comfort. Your new home is not bleak like the workhouse, but it is also not luxurious."

Still not freed from my troubling slumber, mad panic shot through me. "I won't go. I won't be trapped like that girl." My snap was lost in the rumble of the wheels.

Henry's face pressed closer to me. "Mind your voice."

I recoiled into the tight carriage quarters. "I won't let you lock me"—I glanced at Max— "us away."

"What are you about?" Henry closed the space between us, and our noses brushed together. His breath puffed over my lips and neck, and his features blurred in the closeness. The tip of his tongue parted his lips, and he traced his mouth like tasting a grain of sugar from an evening treat. "You will go where I send you."

Paralyzed like a freshly bitten animal, I asked, "And where might that be?" I was still sure he would say the asylum, although I knew the travel shouldn't have taken so long.

His breath brushed over my cheek with the lightness of a feather. "Where I can watch," he murmured. Then, startlingly quick, he reposed. "We are headed to Harewood House, an estate needing fresh staff." He stared ahead at Donovan, whose eyes remained closed but whose muscles tightened with alertness. Henry continued. "It is a grand house, constructed in 1770 on the grounds of a ruined castle, several hundreds of years old and long deserted. My father was a trusted investor for the family."

I inquired in a quiet tone. "I can't imagine they would need all of us, including Max."

Checking the time on his pocket watch, he cleaned smudge marks from the glass with a handkerchief before tucking the timepiece into his corduroy vest.

I questioned him with a wide-eyed expression.

"You will all work there. The owner died nearly six months ago, and I oversee transferring the property to the new heir." He rattled off the specifics of his story as though I could track him. "Harewood House is full of modern comforts—custom furniture, interior gardens, and terraces. Of course, as servants, you will not enjoy the property as a guest, but it is safe and will allow you to build a life."

"As a maid?"

I thought he might have something else in mind if he were watching over me. Last year, a workhouse girl found a maid position, but not more than ten months after her departure, I discovered her near the docks, her body misshapen from pregnancy, and a baby crying at her bosom.

"Yes, as a maid." He coolly confirmed. "Tell me a bit about yourself to ensure I'm not vouching for a criminal."

"I don't know what to say. My first memories are of the workhouse. I live there, work there, sleep there." I didn't want to expand on the countless instances of noise and filth, hunger and coldness, sweat and fatigue.

Henry combed his fingers through his hair. "Is there anything special about you besides your unique look?"

I wasn't sure what he meant. I was well-read, and had some carnal knowledge from the priest, but Camilla had been particularly careful to hide me from the outside world. When she'd presented me to the priest at the Minster for my first lessons, she'd said that at least one of her girls needed to be literate. Despite her stern countenance, she'd show me a look of pity at every bath and never demanded I walk the streets.

"I can read and write."

Henry glanced at me before resuming his graceful poise. "I'd already guessed that. Why do you think I picked you?"

Donovan chimed in. "You are not the only one to help barter this arrangement."

Henry ignored the comment.

I looked at the still-sleeping Camilla. "What about the workhouse?"

"I have dealt with that. My father owns the workhouse. He owns many things." Henry's clear and unemotional grey eyes stared me through. "When I return around Christmas, you will have settled into the places you belong." His simple statements carried vague threats. Henry gazed out the window into the dark. "We're here."

We passed through an archway attached to a high wall stretching indefinably to either side. Lanterns and flames fueled by oil canisters lighted the entrance. We rode down a sapling-lined road. There was a chapel huddled in the trees' long shadows. The carriage angled toward Harewood House, standing three stories high and set with wide stairs. I thought we would stop before the grand entrance, but my misconception was short-lived. The carriage continued toward analogously designed stables. We stopped in an open-air enclosure, crowded by another coach and equine riggings. The carriage's final jolt awoke both Camilla and Max, and they stretched like cats from a long nap.

"Are we here?" Camilla chirped with excitement.

Henry disembarked, stood in the middle of the stable courtyard, and straightened his outfit before his gloved fingers reappeared through the door, commanding that I follow. I had to move past Donovan. Our gazes locked in on each other, and I noticed his frustration and a soft longing. Equally conflicting emotions rose in my chest. I wanted both to slap him and beg him to shut the door and whisk us away. I would have given much at that moment to crawl into his lap. And yet, holding Henry's hand and taking in the first scent of our new home, fresh and damp, I was exhilarated by his dominance. He had alluded to his wanting to watch. My growing desire for him made me shiver with excitement. I remembered the Minster priest saying *sometimes surviving was about taking the bold step.*

Gliding down onto the tiled ground, I felt woozy and swooned.

Henry supported me and whispered, "I've got you." He took me to an upended barrel in the middle of the courtyard. His comment felt like a statement with many meanings.

Leaving me to soothe myself, I pulled my shawl tighter around my shoulders and stared at the interlocking bricks making up the floor. Someone put considerable thought into the stables. The walls were unglazed limestone. I'd seen similar material in the Minster. Although Henry had said all was constructed years ago, everything was pristine. Smoke shadows along the walls were the only signs of wear, but even those appeared as part of the design. The courtyard seemed eerily quiet in comparison to the years without solitude in the workhouse. A fine mist collected on my clothes like light grey paint, slightly muting my brown skirt. The shifting weather signaled both the transition in my geography and life-station.

"Good evening," a man's vibrant voice announced from the stable entrance.

Henry abandoned his task of untying trunks at the coach's rear and turned to greet the man formally. "Mr. Popplewell, thank you for coming to meet us."

Mr. Popplewell was an older man and oddly slender. A neatly pressed suit with a modest lapel hung loosely off his square shoulders but was well-tailored to his unique proportions and accentuated a build resembling the spritely fronds of a palm tree from drawings I'd seen in a book on the Spice Islands.

Henry brought Mr. Popplewell to me, and I felt scrutinized under his observation. "This is the maid I mentioned."

Mr. Popplewell eyed me. "I am the Steward of Harewood House and the head of staff."

I was hesitant to meet his gaze. Upon doing so, I found deep brown eyes, hooded in thick lids and lashes, curiously studying me.

"My name is Renna."

Camilla stumbled from the coach and interrupted the introduction. "Serenna, she means. Renna is a nickname. Her proper name is Serenna —*the serene*, peaceful." She said as she reassembled herself, finding her poise and shaping her hair.

Mr. Popplewell seemed not to appreciate the clarification, nor did I. I'd never gone by Serenna. If that was my name, I was a little confused to know it now for the first time. And *peaceful* hardly seemed fitting.

"I apologize for the informality," I said.

"I'm sure your previous employment did not teach the proper behavior, but I imagine you will learn our ways once you assume your tasks." He stood a bit taller, pleased with his summation. "Nothing quite puts us to ourselves like knowing our real place."

Knowing my *real place* was an existence I'd longed for, I doubted Mr. Popplewell and Harewood were necessarily the answer. Still, a maid's position in a grand country estate was a great improvement from the cotton house.

He turned to the rest of the group and retrieved a narrow leather-bound ledger and a blunted pencil from a well-polished satchel sagging across his chest. Thumbing to his desired page, he squinted to read, "I understand the young man will also be joining us. Maxwell?" He nodded to Max.

Camilla interrupted. "Mr. Popplewell, this is my Max." She tugged him forward but concealed his crooked arm behind her hip. "Shake the man's hand."

Max extended his hand.

Mr. Popplewell stepped to the side, towing Max from Camilla's concealment. "I see." He gestured to Max's left arm. "You are properly lame." He noted it in his book. "This will impact your wage, but it can be addressed later."

"Mr. Popplewell, he is skillful, despite the missing hand," Camilla brightly placated as she tried to twist the truth of his visible disfigurement.

Mr. Popplewell ignored her. "I understand you can write."

Max held his chin steady. "Aye, sir. I have excellent handwriting."

Watching his stoic reply made my heart drop, but I was relieved he could find work with his talent.

"I will be sure Father Thaddeus and you are acquainted. He requires an assistant."

"Father Thaddeus Humboldt?" Camilla's voice was pitchy. "I may be familiar with him."

He turned slightly to her but then looked back to Max. "Don't call me, 'Sir.' I am not in the military, nor have I rank or position in polite society. I am simply Mr. Popplewell. As to you," he referenced his ledger and then Camilla, ignoring her inquiry. "You are Camilla Jane. I don't have a surname listed."

Camilla curtsied. "I am Camilla Jane Worthington."

He noted that in his ledger. "Worthington. Does your family hail from Leister?"

She seemed the actress, trying to convince him of her tale with her delivery. "Some do, but I have no connection to them at present. I have been abroad. I believe much of my family moved to the colonies."

I had known her all my life. If she had been *abroad*, it was before my time.

"They are now called the United States of America," he corrected her flatly. "Your post will be downstairs. We do not require another housemaid, and I fear"—Mr. Popplewell penetrated her with a glare—"The work may not be to your ability."

Unshaken by his insinuation, Camilla said, "I have extensive experience, Mr. Popplewell, and am happy to assist wherever you see fit."

He closed the book. "We will settle the rest of the affairs after breakfast. For now, you will find the servants' quarters." Mr. Popplewell looked at Max. "I will take you to the chapel." He gracefully walked to the arched entrance of the stables, assuming an air that all should follow. "Captain Moore, a tea tray set in the gallery. Ann is in attendance."

Camilla and Max were quickly in step behind Mr. Popplewell. Henry sauntered after, seeming to flee the mist collecting into regular rain droplets.

I was frozen with indecision. The changes were more than I could manage. As Henry moved away, I felt a desire to drive after him, cling to his coattails, and await his command.

Donovan reclined, holding with pregnant intention, and made no gesture to shelter me. "You need to follow them. Mr. Popplewell does not seem a man to repeat himself."

"But what about you?" An impending dread rendered me invulnerable to the inclement weather. "Everything is changing so quickly." I stepped toward Donovan, pleading with him. "What about what we saw at the asylum, that girl? I can't forget her. Maybe there is some way we can help"

"You should be glad it is her and not you." Donovan watched me with a kind expression. "I knew when we met that I couldn't just leave you to the cruelties of this world, but I'm not in control. Henry has arranged this, and upsetting him would not go well." He opened his stance and flung open his arms, startling me to obedience. "Go."

Donovan's tone moved me, but I paused under the stable archway. Sheltered from the rain, I took one last look at him, feeling sure he was the place of protection. He shook his head and pointed his chin. I stepped toward the house and into the rain.

Bully

Light Attributes: Confronts inner fears
Shadow Attributes: Conceals deep fears of abuse

Rain pelted the window like stones flung from the sky. A streak of lightning momentarily illuminated the tree outside as it violently slashed about in the wind. Thunder echoed. I cowered in my cot, bracing for the rain to break through the window. The hour was indiscernible, a wee bit into the morning. Little made this room appear an actual bedroom, besides the bed and side dressing table, on which a porcelain bowl and pitcher stood. A smoothly honed cross over the bed opposed a watercolor painting of spring flowers on the far wall. The scant decorations echoed the asylum. The memory tightened my stomach. I was safe here, and the asylum girl was left alone. The battle between my head and my heart was at a standstill. I huddled deeper into my bed, waiting for the storm to settle.

I must have dozed off, for when I opened my eyes the second time, the scene at the window shifted, and pastel light filtered into the room. The tree outside had stilled, and the window remained intact, not shattered by the threatening weather from earlier. The cold nip at the tip of my nose told me the room was as chilly as an icebox cooling evening supper.

A sharp squeal followed by a loud "Get upstairs" got my heart pumping.

I flipped off the blankets, brought my bare feet onto icy floor stones, and hustled to wrap myself in my cloak. It was painful to shove my numb feet into my stiff shoes. I pressed my ear to the hardwood door. My heartbeat battered through the veins in my neck as I listened. Sensing the way was clear, I opened the door to an empty hall with impeccable floors and whitewashed walls. The brightness was a change from the crowded filth in the workhouse, always in want of repair. I went toward a series of shouts. A closed door concealed an audible debate between two shrill voices. I rested my hand on the nob, squeezed, and turned.

"I won't have it!" Standing with fists on hips in determined protestation, a wisp of a girl stared down an elegant but much taller woman. "How can I do my work if I have to train someone new?"

The lankier woman replied, "Ann, these are your instructions."

Her rigid figure slackened as her argument seeped away, and she skulked to an extended bench running the length of an equally long dining table. She thumbed the handle of a practical teacup, seeming to drift off into some imagined distraction.

The taller woman whirled lightly around and came face-to-face with me at the door. "Here you are."

Taking my cue, I tried to curtsy. "My name is Renna."

"Don't do that." The woman's forehead scrunched into a dozen lines. "I am Mrs. Brearcliff, the housekeeper of Harewood." Her expression softened but not quite into a smile. She gave me the once over. "This is Ann." She nodded to the girl on the bench. "She will instruct you on your work and where to find proper attire." Mrs. Brearcliff gestured to a girl slightly older than Ann but with much less fire in her presence. "And this is Allenor. She will also be working with you." Allenor had dark circles under her eyes and looked like a polecat. "You need to become acquainted with several others, specifically Mrs. Connolly. She will oversee the details of your position." She drew a watch from her dress, much as Henry had done in the carriage.

This triggered a recollection of the others. "Do you know about Camilla and Max?"

Mrs. Brearcliff's slender brows narrowed as she studied me. "You mean the other two who arrived with you?"

My mouth felt dry. "There were three, including another man."

"Only two others. We were told to find positions for a capable young female, an experienced older female, and a lame boy." She put the watch back in her dress, neatly knit to her tapered ribcage. "As the others will not be working with you, it is not your concern regarding their whereabouts." She finished with a tilt of her chin before exiting the room.

Mrs. Brearcliff's censure left me bemused, which Ann took as an invitation to probe any latent vulnerability. I felt like a dog being sniffed.

The servant's hall was spacious with the same stone floors as the passageway and lined with freshly whitewashed wainscoting. Massive pillars reminded me of the Minster's lower levels, where columns supported floors for the pious as they championed their cause with the mighty Lord. I was curious about who walked above me now and what aim they sought. The room had two identical tables, each flanked by benches. Dishes were outlaid on a matching sideboard. A narrow desk sat in the corner. Overall, it was clean and very plain. My hunger sprang to life when I caught a waft of toast, and my gut tightened. I reached for the nearest pillar.

Ann gripped me firmly. "You can't be taking ill, for the day has just begun, and you're late already." She poured tea, pushing a cup into my fingers. "Drink this. It's not hot."

Last night I had been ushered straight into my room. Sleep found me after I shed my coat and shoes, exhausted from yesterday's life-altering events. Now, I eyed the loaf of bread, and my stomach responded with an audible grumble.

"Your stomach speaks louder than you." Ann cut me a wedge from the loaf. "Eat. Quick. We need to be moving."

I choked as I tried to eat the dry bread. The tea washed down the crumbs. Ann snatched up the cup before I could ask for more and headed for the door.

She commanded, "Coming?" to both Allenor and me.

Allenor barely blinked. Her gaze was the clarity of a muddy well. Stirring slowly, she ambled down the hall to a narrow flight of stairs and beyond where I could comfortably see her without craning my head. Ann held the door, her wide blue eyes instructing, *let's go*. I walked after Allenor until I came to the same stair, curious about which path to choose.

"Keep going," she snapped. "Do not tell me you will be one of those who needs an invitation for everything." Her nose crinkled like a mouse.

THE CURSE OF MAIDEN SCARS

The toe of her shoe kicked the edge of my skirt. Ann wanted me to know she could make my life uncomfortable if she desired.

We passed doors marked *Baking* and *Still* rooms. A little further on, she flipped her hand to the right. "The Kitchen." She continued to a paned glass door at the end of the hall. I thought we might be heading outside into a steady wet downpour. She turned sharply at the last minute through a final doorway and halted at the top of a stair landing leading into an elongated stone room. "This is the Scullery. You will work here."

There was a measurable temperature difference between the scullery and the hall. The room was even icier than my bedroom. The scullery was on the lower level but also not entirely below ground. Large windows extended to the ceiling, and a table at the back was lined neatly with baskets. A second countertop featured a copper sink and a pump waterspout. I knew cold from the workhouse, but something about Harewood was worse, unwelcoming and frigid.

I turned to Ann with an unspoken, *now what*.

"Not impressed?" She spun on a heel and returned to the room she had gestured as the Still Room. "Come in here. You will need something to wear." She stopped and shook a finger, like a little girl mimicking her mother. "You get one uniform. It will be washed on Sundays and ready for work again on Monday."

I collected the necessary clothing for my duties, and we returned to the servant's dining area. My hunger grew. Unwisely, I questioned, "Can we return to breakfast?"

At her full height, she came to my nose. "Eating is over. There will be food out for lunch and again at evening tea." She swirled about, very much like a dancer's pirouette, and went back toward the bedrooms. She held the knob of my door. "Change."

I nodded, and she allowed me to pass. Before the door closed all the way, she poked her head in. "Two things. Don't think the food is for you because you work near the kitchen. Also, don't," she looked around the room, "get comfortable. You work here. It does not mean you *belong* here." She let the door slap shut for emphasis.

I shed my heavy wool dress and tossed it over the back of the chair, leaving me in my linen shift. Slipping the uniform on, I noticed the warmth, although it was not a weighty material. I ran my hands down the simple dress and fastened the drawstring under my breasts. The dress was a pale cream with dark tan trimming and hung straight on my body. I matched the walls and décor. Perhaps that was intentional, to render the staff invisible. The work costume came with a puckered cap. I secured it around my hair, tucking in stray strands and disguising my dark locks. I was curious about my look, but there wasn't a surface to study my reflection.

Before leaving, I hung my coat and dress on two pegs behind the door. The mortar and pestle were still in my coat pocket. I placed it on a high shelf next to my worn shoes. Ann had also given me simple leather slippers with firm but flat soles. I hoped the shelf height would keep my precious belongings from Ann's curiosity.

It didn't take long to find Ann. Her voice echoed around the lower level. "We are behind. I need to get the carrots and the potatoes peeled. Where is the girl?"

Presuming the 'girl' was me, I went to the kitchen. There were different workstations—cabinets and overflowing baskets, a copper sink, and an iron stove. A massive wooden cutting block was scattered with ceramic bowls, baskets, and trays. The smell of warm, fresh bread made my stomach clench again. This seemed a consoling safe harbor.

A woman by the stove spoke to me. "Come here." I quickly descended the steps and stood before her, offering myself for inspection. She smelled bitterly of onions. "I'm Mrs. Connolly"

"I'm Renna."

"I know." She stirred a pot of boiling milk, able to monitor the temperature without looking. "I understand you have been shown around. Do you know how to wash and clean potatoes and carrots?"

"Of course."

Mrs. Connolly had a slight eyebrow raise. "Good. You will first need to get them."

I nodded. "Are they stored in the scullery?"

"Normally, aye, but we have emptied the lot." She pulled the pot from the heat with a cloth wrapped around the long handle. Dipping in a wooden spoon, she cooled it before tipping it to her tongue. "Nice." She placed the pot on the cutting block and coated a metal spoon in the white sauce. "Here, you try."

I tasted it a little too eagerly and burned my tongue. It was too thick to swallow. I moved the creamy coating around in my gaping mouth, finally gulping it down.

Mrs. Connolly smirked. "Your mouth looks a bit like a fish on a line." She poured water into a ceramic cup. "Drink. Cream sauces don't cool as quickly as others. The texture holds in the heat." She looked at a clock next to the door. "Ann will explain how to go to the gardens. I need you back within the hour. The potatoes must be finished by half-past one."

I wasn't sure why food was my primary worry, but working long without a meal seemed torturous. "What time is lunch, Mrs. Connolly?"

"Your work must be finished before you eat or I'm afraid you must wait until tea."

Rushing from the kitchen, I slammed into Ann as she eavesdropped from the other side of the door, absorbing our conversation. "You have to find the gardens?" She handed me a tarp-like cloak. "Go past the stables until you find the lake and a brick wall."

Fastening the cloak under my chin and draping the bulky hood over my head, I asked. "What do I do when I get there?"

She headed toward the Stillroom. "Samuel will find you."

I stared at the door. It seemed easy, but I couldn't fight the growing sense of dread. Facing the unknown was all part of my life at the workhouse, but the weather, Harewood's strangeness, and Ann's unfriendliness left me spinning. I felt like I was ignorant of a hilarity that everyone else knew.

I wove through the terraced garden, retracing my steps from last night toward the stables and Ann's mentioned lake. Although mist moistened the earth, rendering it slick, I rushed toward the stables with one name in mind—Donovan. I was confident he could explain more about my role at Harewood and how Henry played into my future. The heat from my body chased away the chill for the first time since rising this morning.

I was panting as I crashed into the stable doors, dismayed to find them now closed to me. Clasping the iron handle, I fought with the door, but all was tightly secured. Barely remembering my instruction, I followed the stable walls, pausing to listen for anyone nearby. There were indistinct sounds, like an animal rustling or wind turning leaves. I continued around the back and located a side door, which was also locked.

I saw the lake, and its vastness deflated me. It would take at least twenty minutes to walk the whole of it. I could barely see the wall Ann referenced in the distance, way on the other side. The landscape's beauty was not lost on me. Beyond the walled garden, a forest drained into rolling fields with black sheep, white horses, and hairy orange cows. I was determined to have a closer look. The only cows I'd seen were half slaughtered at the butcher.

A horse's whinny brought back my attention, and I realized the cloak's extra layer was ineffective at keeping out the rain. Seeking shelter, I went to the stables. Maybe Donovan was waiting, ready to correct his mistake of abandoning me to Harewood House's chilly welcome. In my search, I found a cylinder-shaped building with a dome roof made of tightly plastered bricks. An image of the Pantheon from a book about Rome came to me. The priest from the Minster had said the design could withstand time, or at least it predated Christianity. I was curious why a similar building was here in the Yorkshire countryside.

The door of this *pantheon* swung open freely. I was not prepared for the blast of frigid air. The space was small, with stone walls and a dirt floor with a steep drop-off into murky darkness. There was dim light. The gloom and contrasting temperature made the room dizzying. I stumbled. Despite my instincts yelling to stay clear of the edge, I was drawn toward it. Scrambling for something to brace me, I dug my fingers into the brick walls, clinging with desperation. A wave of nausea brought me to my knees. My vision faded, and the asylum girl's shrill shrieks rattled my brain as I lost consciousness.

Servant

Light Attributes: Serving with a loving heart
Shadow Attributes: Resents lack of position

Someone shook me by the shoulder, and my head felt like it would burst. I remembered entering the dark *pantheon* but couldn't recall much else. I couldn't see the doorway from my position. Chill penetrated me deeply, provoking a violent tremor.

"It's all right," a man's voice soothed. "I'm going to wrap you in my coat." He gripped me by both arms, hugging me to his warm body. He pulled a heavy coat over my back, cutting the cold and calming my shivers. "You've had a nasty spill. Lucky I'd come to fetch some ice."

The upright posture aided my throbbing head, and the edges of my vision sharpened. The thought of ice brought attention to my cold legs. I pulled long stalks of grass from beneath my skirt. In the faint light, it felt like yanking on handfuls of horsehair. Brushing my fingers beneath me, I realized hay covered a smooth layer of ice. What if this was a well, and I'd tumbled in?

"We need to get you out of here." Without asking, he deftly hoisted me aloft.

My head hung heavy, needing the gentle support of a guardian's hand —A hand I received.

A second person with smaller fingers collected me as the man lifted the bulk of my weight. Together, they maneuvered me onto the dirt floor, where the light from the door was visible. I must have fallen over the edge after I fainted.

Although the fingers of the girl who assisted me were little, her frame was not. She was several stones heavier than me, with an ample bosom strapped tightly within a jacket. The buttons stressed and threatened to pop. Most noticeable was the color of her skin. She was darker than anyone I'd seen in York. I'd known a few servants with dark skin, typically dressed in some pompous English costume. She did not wear impractical attire. Instead, she dressed in a man's clothes, duly equipped for work. She touched my cheek and gently pressed up my chin to close my mouth.

"I am Diana, but most friends call me Dada." Her voice was light, lyrical, with deep traces of an accent I could not place. Trying to nod, I winced. Dada touched my head. "You have a bad cut, and I think a mark will rise off you soon."

"Mark?" I said.

She dusted off her skirt. "I think the colors of a bruise are a way of us knowing the healing, as the dark sky of a storm fading and revealing the light."

"Looks like we have a new one to show around," boomed a deep heavy voice, perfectly matching the hands from before. "You sure managed to get yourself into a dangerous place, and what, within your first week?"

"Day."

Dada hollered. "You're that new?"

"Let me guess. It was Ann who sent you. She's always making things harder." The man bent low to introduce himself. "I am Samuel, the gardener." Samuel's face was as proportionately big as his hands. His high cheekbones were stained pink with fine red lines, often a sign of someone who kept warm with a bottle of strong spirits. He smiled with a wide-toothed grin, displaying straight teeth, only a few missing. He grabbed me by both arms again and shuffled me to my feet. "Must get you moving."

My head throbbed, and a wave of anxiety grew. "The Scullery?"

"Don't worry. I know what she set you to. Again, a mean trick," replied Dada. "There is no way for you to get to the garden at this hour, collect vegetables, requiring a cart, as hauling the basket back is too heavy, even for me, and then peel them for dinner." She smoothed down

THE CURSE OF MAIDEN SCARS

her jacket, still begging to be unbuttoned. "Tomorrow, I will properly show you around."

I thought of Donovan. "My friend was in the stables last night, an Irishman. Do you know of him?"

Dada and Samuel exchanged a look.

Samuel replied, "A man left on horseback early this morning. I don't know where he went." He tucked the cloak around me and tightened a hat over his ears.

I recalled Henry and had a deep urge to find him. "Captain Moore?"

"He too is gone, but he always comes back," Dada informed. "It's none of my business, but it seems a maid like you don't have any reason to deal with a man like him. Besides, he has his favorite already." Dada glanced out the door to the parting clouds in the sky. "Time to move. Looks like the rain has lifted." She left without goodbyes.

"Don't mind her. She keeps busy to chase off homesickness." Samuel effortlessly aided my weight, and we were back into the light of day—if it could be called that, for the clouds hung low, and the sky threatened to open into a downpour.

"Homesickness?"

"She was born on Master Lascelles' sugar plantation in Barbados. Many of us hail from someplace other than Yorkshire." Although Samuel carried me along without a care, his wheezing breath betrayed the effort. "I'm from Belgium."

"I'm from Yorkshire, I think." I pulled the cloak hood tighter over my head and asked, "Why use hay with the ice?"

He paused. "Seems like an untimely question, especially as you have no idea where you are going, and Dada has left to substitute for you. I figured you would be more concerned about your well-being than how ice is stored."

"I like to learn," I replied truthfully.

He trekked toward the lake, and what I concluded was our destination—the walled garden. "It's for insulation. It keeps the ice and the icehouse much colder. It would be sad if, on a warm day, the ice melted into a pool of unusable water."

The weather prompted us to move faster. We rushed the length of the lake to the opposite shore and walled garden, crowded by a derelict cottage, and tumbled through a rough-honed door marred by years of exposure. I shook the rain from the cloak and saw we were not alone in the room, warmed by a hearth fully ablaze and big enough to stand in.

Sitting at a table by the fireplace, balancing elegantly but precariously on a three-legged stool, was a slender woman with silver hair, several strands hanging loose from a casual bun. She didn't look up at our entry. Instead, she remained fixed on the knitting that pooled around her feet. Her tight stitches replicated a loom's work.

Samuel mumbled. "This is the new girl. New girl, this is Mother."

The dim light obscured the full effect of her, but she had a faint, haunting appearance. Drawn to the fire's warmth, I knelt beside her. She rested her knitting in her lap and looked at me with the brightest eyes, like the blue of a cloudless spring sky.

"And what is your name? I'm sure it's not 'new girl.'" She glanced back at Samuel. "Don't mind him. He doesn't call any of us by our Christian names. It's his way of protecting his heart." Her eyes smiled.

"My name is Renna, short for Serenna. What are you called?"

"My name is Olivia. But Samuel's nickname for me is Mother."

I extended a hand. "Pleased to meet you."

Olivia placed my hand next to the knitting. She turned over my palm and rubbed her thumb on the skin in a rhythmic circle, causing the flesh to pink up. "Don't mind me," she announced before spitting into my palm. She rubbed the spit into the skin, moistening it to my fingertips. She rested my hand in hers and blew a deep breath over it. "It's not good to look at the lines when the skin is dry and cold. I might misread something."

"Are you a seer?" I'd hoped she could tell me why I was here or what happened to the asylum girl.

"Of a kind." She bent my hand to the fire's light, chasing away the shadows.

"What do you see?"

She pressed her thumb hard in the middle of my palm. I winced but didn't pull away.

"You know pain. You have been marked." She looked up at the spot

THE CURSE OF MAIDEN SCARS

on my head. "And not only today. Your skin tells your story."

I sank into my space on the floor. I would have been happy if it had opened and swallowed me whole. "Haven't we all experienced pain?"

She studied my hand again. "You are from a family that knows suffering. It seems you will follow in their ways."

I surged with interest. "You can tell me about my family?"

"Careful what you wish for. It may come true." Olivia leaned back in her chair, freeing me. "I can't tell you anything today. I come here for herbs to make a few curative things."

"And rest," Samuel interjected.

I stretched my still-wet slippers to the fire. "You do not live at Harewood?"

"No," she replied levelly. "I enjoy the ride once a week from a town called Knaresborough. It's a beautiful place on the river with a great mill and an extraordinary cave."

"Mother, we shouldn't fill the new girl's head with ideas of adventure." He presented a plate of crisp carrots and soft bread, along with a jug of beer. "I think you might need refreshment." He poured a clay cup to the brim. "It's a small beer, nothing too strong for the day. I brew it myself. Do you know Belgium?"

Eagerly accepting the tumbler, I drank the whole of it and gave it back.

He filled it again. "You shouldn't have more, but I suppose that knot needs a bit of a painkiller."

"I had a friend from Belgium who often spoke of the culture and the beer." I smiled over the cup's rim, not mentioning that the *friend* was the Minster priest. My stomach settled, and my head no longer throbbed, but I was woozy. I broke off bread and snatched a carrot. "I hear Bruges is quite lovely."

"My family is but a few miles from there. I miss it." He sobered and left us, busying himself in the back of the cottage.

Olivia's skin gently folded around her mouth like a crinkled stretch of paper. "In this place, you either belong or you do not."

There was a warning in her comment. I felt it. I found it suddenly hard to breathe. I heard the asylum girl in my mind, and nausea overtook me. I felt panic rising in me, and I looked desperately at Olivia.

"Samuel," Olivia shouted. "She needs help."

He was quickly by my side, settling me in a chair and pushing my head between my knees. "Breathe."

Olivia pulled my cloak down to my waist. Her fingers were at my neck, fumbling with the tie at the back of my dress. A wet cloth was pressed to my neck, and the sensation calmed my heat. My mouth watered, and spit trickled to the floor. The garment loosened, and the wetness washed down my shoulders. I was too dizzy to withdraw from her intrusive inspection.

Samuel's mud-clogged boots moved out of sight, and he went to the back of the cottage again, leaving me with Olivia.

"Shh, dear, shh," Olivia soothed. "We are your friends. Shh." She came down to the floor. "Dear, dear Renna, can you look at me, dear?"

I opened my eyes to her pleading expression. Her countenance was unnerving. I had not seen such a genuine concern for my well-being, not even from the one person who knew my body best—Camilla.

"Relax, dear. I don't know what you have experienced, but you have been mistreated. A lovely bird like you should not bear such marks." She cooed, "Without judgment, I would hear your story. You do not owe me your tale, but I will listen if you like."

I believed her but could not tell her a truth I didn't know. A vision of the asylum girl's hand flashed in my mind, and my defenses mounted. "Perhaps another time."

Olivia pried no further. Instead, she stretched her feet toward the fire, much as I had, and began to remove her shoes. "Let's stay longer, and then Samuel can take you back." She struggled with her boot.

I came off my seat. "Let me help, please."

Her expression sobered before she hesitantly nodded. I managed the second shoe without much fuss. She gestured for me to remove her socks. A tie at the bottom of her pantaloons held up her stocking. Loosening the knot, I shimmied the hose down her calf, exposing her skin to her ankle. The change in her skin color was revealed as the sock came lower. At first, it was a crisp red—as if it had been smacked, but the hue deepened to dark burgundy and then purple. The edges of her big toe were ashen grey like it had been rubbed in soot. The skin was hard and cracked. I slid the sock down on the opposite foot, showing similar but less discoloration.

"It is worse," Olivia said. "My feet are always cold and often hurt."

Samuel appeared with a ceramic pod. "Here is the ointment."

I took the pod from Samuel. "I can do it."

Olivia supported herself with her hands. "Thank you."

I uncorked the pod and smelled the contents. Whiffs of peppermint and rosemary prickled my nose. "I've smelled this before, but it also had a more mineral scent."

"Sulfur is usually used, but I don't have any now. I mix this with calcium-rich water near my home. The calcium is not as potent as pure sulfur." Her silvery eyebrows raised high. "Is there any chance you know why I use this mixture?"

"No." I took a dab of the ointment and rubbed it into her feet.

"It relieves pain and warms the skin without exposing it to heat, leaving me a few more moments of mobility throughout the day." She squinted. "But something tells me you understand more than you let on."

I massaged her feet, careful not to press too hard. "I was taught many things in case I received a learned position." The priest from the Minster had a similar lotion. I rubbed him with it, and often more than his feet.

A speculative look crossed her face. "It would be in your interest to adjust your story. It rings false." Her comment was more of a warning than a judgment. "You would do best to pick one line of your tale and tell it honestly."

How could I tell her that the reason I could read, write, and speak bits of Italian, French, and German was all from the *kindness* of a curious priest? His favorite pastime was for us to recite poetry while he used my leg as a dinner plate. He'd painstakingly place food along my thigh before devouring each morsel. The Minster priest left my virginity intact. He also gave me books and street smarts.

Samuel joined us. "You can count on our silence and Dada's too, but the rest, no."

Olivia stretched a hand to me. "I believe we all share a bond of survival. But not everyone understands that surviving frightening and often unclean events is a virtue. Rather, they see it as a fungus contaminating the ripe and healthy. You will be seen as such a fungus. Keep your body covered. Don't expose yourself, especially your back. A few in the household will see the marks as signs of evil."

I wondered if the same would be true for Max. He was so visibly maimed.

"There is a reason Olivia comes to me concerning her health. The others, not all of them, but a few, will look for any indication of imperfection." Samuel added.

Olivia clasped my chin and bore into my soul with her expression. "Your body craves one thing, but your mind says another. In the end, our hearts guide the balance."

"Don't forget about Father Thaddeus."

"Father Thaddeus?" The name seemed to stick in my throat.

"He oversees the All Saint's Church. I suggest, until you get your bearings, you stay away. He has a great nose for smelling out untruths." Olivia warned.

It seemed Harewood was full of noses interested in sniffing out my secrets.

WINTER, 1795

Prince

Light Attributes: Romantic charm
Shadow Attributes: Using power for self-promotion

I gazed out the scullery window at an enervated sun peeking weakly through December's morning clouds. The garden was smothered by a thick blanket of still, silent fog. It had taken some time to become accustomed to Harewood—clean, safe, and dry—and relax in the peaceful seasonal changes of the countryside instead of quelling the incessant yowls of the workhouse children. My work at Harewood was not hard compared to the cotton house duties, but the expectations were inconvenient. I was the first to rise every morning, around four-thirty, to ignite fires on the main level and ready the kitchen for Mrs. Connolly. Some mornings I rose even earlier to finish my duties and meander about the house, memorizing its exquisite details.

After awakening the downstairs, I set myself to the library, my favorite room and one I diligently cleaned. I pushed back the shutters, and the sunlight illuminated the brightly colored wallpaper, depicting a foxhunt in autumn. Having restocked the fireplace, making it ready for lighting, I wiped my hands on my apron, careful not to shake soot onto the carpet. Surveying the line of books on tightly packed shelves, running floor to ceiling, I daydreamed of exploring the worlds locked within their ornate covers. There were the authors I knew: Marlowe, Shakespeare, Dekker, Galileo. Then there were histories of Rome, Constantine, and the Hun Dynasty. An entire shelf was devoted to Europe's flora and fauna.

The Anatomy of Melancholy, by Robert Burton, interested me. I wondered what inspired him to explore sadness's nuances. I was tempted to abandon bucket and cloth, snatch up a title or two, and curl up in the window seat for a long afternoon, but I dared only to slide my finger across the line of engraved leather, feeling every wrinkle, bump, and groove.

"Renna," Mrs. Connolly's voice called. "Lass, you're not loitering, are you?" She pushed through the door. "I've needed you downstairs for the last half hour."

I didn't want her to catch me in my reveries. "I'm sorry, but it takes longer to do Ann's job and mine."

Ann had been away from Harewood House these last few weeks. She said she was needed at the church for the Christmas preparations and was "invaluable" to Father Thaddeus. I didn't know exactly what she meant then, but instinct said it was more than Mass arrangements.

Mrs. Connolly peered at me skeptically and returned to the servant's stairs off the main hall. I struggled to control my bucket of soot as I followed her. I paused to take in the hall's decorations for the dinner we would be hosting. Bouquets of white flowers and a freshly cleaned carpet runner leading to the main entrance's large double doors offered an opulent welcome.

She impatiently commanded. "You will not enter the dining hall tonight, but we are short-staffed. You will take up the dishes, set them in the butler's pantry, and wait for Jon."

As one might expect from the cook in a great house, Mrs. Connolly was round and stout. She had hands like Samuel's. Burn scars marked her solid and stubby fingers. She had more energy than three women together. But, when the day had run long or when she transported herself to a distant memory, one fraught with ghosts, her energy waned, and her tone soured. Curiously, her food reflected her emotional well-being. Sadness equaled bitter sauces, and gayety might mean over-sugaring the tea.

I found Mrs. Connolly in the Scullery one afternoon, tearfully scrubbing pans. (Our evening meal ended in cold cuts from the lauder.) Mrs. Connolly told Mrs. Brearcliff, "Today is the anniversary. I don't know how I've made it another year. When will God end my sentence and take me as he has taken my Tom?" The thought of Mrs. Connolly dutifully working—and waiting—gnawed at my heart. From that moment, she had my loyalty, and we struck a silent understanding of friendship.

"What would you like for me to do next?"

"Your favorite," she smiled. "Peel the potatoes. I plan to make dough for dumplings."

This would mean huddling in the icy Scullery for hours, but quiet servitude grew on me. I was safe from York street life—syphilis or convulsive attacks, hunger or being harangued, being with a child, or jealously protecting my meager possessions. For such tranquility, I would scrub bottomless pits of potatoes, pluck dozens of chickens, and empty grossly soiled chamber pots. Moreover, the work mostly kept the asylum girl's images at bay.

"Renna," she called after me. "You can work here, next to the fire."

I scampered to the Scullery and returned with my load, occupied until Mrs. Connolly broke our agreed silence.

"Are you done?"

"Nearly." I doubled my effort. "Mrs. Connolly, do you know who is dining here?" I was curious how Harewood House kept operating minus a Lord Harewood.

"The estate consultant. Captain Moore and his guests will dine in a final party before heading south." Mrs. Connolly puttered around the kitchen. She checked the roasting pig in the oven. The smoky meat's sweet smells of garlic and rosemary wafted around us.

She missed the effect Henry's name had upon me. A choking feeling caught in my throat. I had not seen Henry since our arrival. His gray eyes flashed before me, and my belly tightened in longing. He said he wanted to *watch* me. Maybe this was what he meant.

I shoved the basket aside. "I should clean up if you want me to carry things."

Mrs. Connolly nodded. "Be quick about it."

I hustled to my room to change into a clean uniform I'd filched from the Stillroom, one not speckled with pig's blood. I brushed my hair and watched the rainwater wash down my windowpanes, catching distorted glimpses of my reflection. Grooming complete, I returned to Mrs. Connolly.

"Take up this tray."

The tray spanned twice my width and demanded I move sideways through the doorframe to keep from wrapping my knuckles along the wood edges. I climbed a pokey narrow staircase, only wide enough for two slim bodies, and pushed through a set of disguised doors leading from the hall into a corridor toward the dining room. We servants had our maze of passages to travel the house without encountering guests, creating the illusion that apparitions prepared the evening pork and port.

Once in the Butler's Pantry, I found Jon, the footman. With the house partially staffed, he was the only one in service. He dressed splendidly in a long day coat with tales and impeccable golden buttons fastened tightly around his waist. The entire costume was trimmed in gold brocade. A light sage green coat paired with black trousers gave him the look of a lean tree suited more for the garden than serving the revelers behind the closed door.

Jon's brows, unusually long and unruly for his years, contracted tightly above his nose, and he looked at the tray of appetizers.

"Have the pâté at the top, and the mint sauce at the bottom, much like a ball being hit by a racket," I explained.

He brightened with a wry expression. "Fitting for the energy of the evening. I think someone will be bounced like a ball from player to player." Jon pushed the door open with his boot before I could scoff at his comment.

The door swung wide, giving me a full view of the dinner guests full view of me. The lively visitors were tightly packed around a rectangular table. Three large candelabras sprung up like saplings from the center, each ablaze with a half-dozen long purple tapers. Splotches of wax dotted a white tablecloth.

The guests were all unfamiliar to me, except one. Henry's face was flawless from this angle, as though plucked from a painter's masterpiece. He spoke to a woman with an elegant look. Her hair was pulled high, her lips stained deep violet and matching the candles. She flirted with the man beside her and his female guest but focused on Henry. She teased the men and the woman with a long-stemmed feather, something from a marvelous pale-colored bird. Envy flared in me. I was not born of privilege and could never belong to this group, but the flirting woman filled me with ire.

THE CURSE OF MAIDEN SCARS

My staring drew attention. The voices quieted. I thought that the voyeuristic portal would momentarily stand open and then close. Instead, it stuck wide. Jon tried to shoo me away.

Henry noticed me.

He was not in his uniform but clad in gentlemen's attire with a fitted grey jacket and deep blue ascot—and absolutely the most beautiful man I'd ever seen. He rose from the chair and came toward me. At first, it seemed a dream, for his movement did not dissuade his dinner guests from their conversation. They re-engaged in their evening of cat and mouse.

Henry stopped short of the butler's pantry, looked at me unblinkingly, and pushed the door back.

The door closed inches from my face, shutting me out. I couldn't barge into the dining hall. It might be dangerous since the revelry reached a new pitch. The dinner guests might need satiating with more than mere food. With a heavy heart, I decided to return to the kitchen. As I reached the staircase, slapping footfalls approached through the main foyer.

Henry was going to the library. He closed the door behind him, but not all the way.

The temptation was too great. I tiptoed to the door and listened to him shuffling papers and opening and closing cabinets. He went about the room searching for something. I readied myself with my hand on the doorframe but took too long contemplating my next move.

The door swung open, and Henry barred the way with his arms crossed. "And what do you want?"

"I have questions," I barked at him.

He considered me momentarily, then clasped my upper arms and pulled me to him, his face inches from mine. I wasn't sure I wanted to struggle. Henry's nostrils flared as his face came closer, much like our moment in the carriage to Harewood. His breath was sweet with wine. Suddenly, he forced his lips on me, hard and hot, chewing at me in a deep, ravenous kiss.

I was overtaken by some primal instinct and pulled my arms free of his clasp. Wrapping myself around him, I clung to him as if mounting a tree in a threatening storm.

Henry tore me off him and held me at arms-length. "Well, quite unexpected." He watched me. "Is this what you wanted?"

Wriggling from his grip, I stared at him. "No. I want answers."

Drawing his jacket down at the waist, instantly grooming his look, he made to move around me. "I don't have time for this."

Involuntarily, I touched his hand. This was the most alive I had ever felt, not scared but roaring with command.

He brought his face closer to me, softly brushing my lips. He touched my cheek and coaxed me into a deep kiss that left me dizzied. "Perhaps we should continue in the library."

Henry lifted my weight with ease. He swept us to an oversized velvet settee, big enough for a tall man to rest fitfully for the night. Plopping me down, he secured the door to the main foyer and then checked the door to the adjoining sitting room. I stroked the smooth velvet and waited, feeling my mind spin as though with too much drink. He went to the desk, giving me a full view of him as he removed his jacket and shirt, laying them precisely on the back of the chair. I was frozen in amazement as I watched him unbutton his pants.

He kicked out his shoes and lined them up behind the chair. He placed his pants next to the immaculately folded clothing and turned—showing a full view of his nakedness. I scooted back, holding myself tight to the wainscoted walls.

Henry sat on the settee next to me with no attempt to hide his goaded manhood. He rested his hand on the velvet and leaned in, keeping his distance but close enough to kiss if I dared. "You shrink from me. Why?"

My desire flared, but this was a sudden and an unfamiliar predicament. The Minster priest explored my body, but not all of it. His fondling was always measured, never going too far. I sensed Henry was interested in more than guilty teasing. He wanted the whole experience of unwrapping and devouring me. My mind was reeling. I should have returned downstairs, but my exhilaration kept me still, awaiting his next move.

He crept closer, giving a full view of his interest. "Did you not think I would return for you?"

His comment left me confused. "I don't know what you want from me."

THE CURSE OF MAIDEN SCARS

Reclining a bit, he brushed a lock of hair from his forehead. "I'm hungry for you. I have been for a while. I could lie and say you were alluring at the Inn, but you were quite disgusting then."

I couldn't understand what was more potent in me—the need for safety or the burn for his touch. It was bound to happen at some point. Why not give my unspoiled self to a clean English officer who had some care for my wellbeing?

He reached for my blouse's neckline and unbuttoned the top two buttons. As I didn't withdraw and had no further retreat available, he unbuttoned the rest as he moved toward me on the settee. My hands pressed hard into the velvet. I was passively receptive and noticed how the trepidation faded, and my hunger grew. He caressed my face and kissed me again, deeply. I could feel the heat of his body rise from his skin. I returned his kiss, pushing my tongue into his mouth, tasting the wine he had drunk. He slid his hand down my blouse, massaging one of my breasts, which tightened and rose to his chilled but hungry fingers.

Kissing and touching, breathing and pushing, we melded together. My hands brushed over his manhood. Our kisses stifled my gasp. He repositioned us on the settee, pressing into my chest.

He whispered, "Do you want to disrobe?"

I had forgotten I was still clothed against his nakedness. The heat between my thighs was all the readiness I needed now. I shook my head. I didn't want him to see me. Notice my scars. Remember me as less than perfect.

"I can tell I will be your first." He had an expression of triumph.

If he won, then who lost?

Lifting to his knees, he remarked, "You are lovely, and I've missed your face and those eyes." He kissed his fingers to my lips.

Folding my skirt up to my waist, he clasped the waistband of my pantaloons and shimmied them down, not bothering to remove my shoes. With his gaze locked on mine, he sucked his fingers in his mouth. I was frozen by his advances. He massaged me, mixing his saliva with my wetness. My yearning grew. My back arched, and I longed for him to explore me. He pressed his palm against my hips, forcing me back on the settee, causing me to gasp.

"I want you as ready as I am." I cried out. He clasped his hand over my mouth. "Shh."

An ecstatic ache grew in me. My mouth closed around the thick of his palm, and he coaxed me further into pleasure. He pulled me to a swollen brink.

Suddenly, he pushed my legs apart with his knees. He ignited a wave of intensity I'd never known. I bit his hand harder. He plunged into me. His movement matched my muted groans.

The excitement in me shifted. Desire in me dulled as his seemed to grow. I tried to slow things down, but there was no retreat. He moved against me in a strident rhythm, and with a final cry, he collapsed onto me. Pinning me under his total weight, I listened as his panting slowed. The sudden change from being milled to stillness left me dizzy.

Henry rolled off and went to a pitcher of wine by the desk. He looked at me as he lifted his palm. "I have something to remember our first pleasure—until next time." Deep-purple, angry marks blotted the fat of his palm.

My tongue found a metallic drop of blood on my lip. I closed my legs, numb from his weight, making movement awkward. Trying to lift myself, I couldn't decide whether to pull up my clothes or get off the settee and redress.

Henry gently help me upright and handed me a glass of wine. "Drink."

I sipped at the wine at first and then took it down in long gulps. It burned my throat but stole focus from the growing ache between my legs.

"I will want to do this again."

"What?" I sputtered. "When?"

He casually placed a hand on his stomach above his nest of hair. "Whenever I can. It is rare to find an untouched girl I can enjoy."

I thought for sure that finer women could entertain him. "I'm the maid."

"Why do you think I was interested in getting you this position?" He turned his back to me. His firm thighs narrowed into slender hips, with only a hint of a rounded behind. "Camilla is naïve. I told her I had an opportunity to change things for you. And that is true. Finding a replacement at the workhouse for you and her was easy." He glanced back at me before jerking his shirt over his shoulders. "Donovan has a tender place for you, so I sent him to the docks in Hull. I thought maybe you could be my secret treasure. And what better place to keep you safe than Harewood?"

His comments about Donovan and Camilla worried me. Placing the glass on the table, I scrambled into my pantaloons. "Did you plan all of this?"

He turned fully to me, as neat as when I saw him in the dining room. "Not exactly. I didn't think tonight would be to my advantage. I thought it might take longer, but it is what I had in mind." He clasped my chin. "I am not your enemy." The intensity of his look transfixed me.

He bent low to the bookshelf at the far corner, finding a slender leather-bound book. Unless someone was searching, it would have been overlooked entirely. "I was jealous Donovan recognized your beauty first. I wouldn't have walked you home if I were him. I would have considered many other things—after a bath." He handed me the book. "Since I understand you are learned, try this."

The leather was slick with years of handling. *"Aretino's Dialogues."*

"Lovely little tale. Pietro Aretino was a Venetian courtier who masterfully told of women's lives in Sixteenth-Century Venice. You might enjoy his imagery. I would enjoy it if you picked up a few ideas."

I turned the book over in my hands before slipping it into my apron pocket. I stood and released a shuddering breath. "And now?"

"And now what?" He smirked. "I will watch after you the best I can until I think of something else. Until then, be a good girl and wait for my return." He pecked a soft kiss on my cheek and went to the door. Peering his head through the opening, he said. "All seems clear."

I reluctantly returned to back into the hall. He shielded himself with the door. I eagerly sought his reassuring expression.

"This was lovely." He grinned as though he thanked me for a cup of coffee rather than my first coitus. "If you had some understanding of your origin, I might develop a reason for a more official connection. But for now, goodnight." He closed the door.

Worry flooded me, and I went to the far stairs. I was ready to dash down the steps when I came face to face with Ann.

Looking me over, she blocked my way and then stepped aside, letting me pass without explanation.

I was down the stairs when I heard, "I hope you had a nice evening."

Priest

Light Attributes: Serves spiritual commitments
Shadow Attributes: Seduced by spiritual role

I woke the following day from my recurring nightmare of the asylum girl wandering the halls of Harewood House. She was hunting for me, desperate to tell me something. Since meeting her, I'd thought of her every day, and she'd invaded my sleep every night. But I didn't think of only her. There was now Henry. He'd had me, but I'd had him as well. He'd enchanted me from first sight, representing a world I longed to belong to.

My nightgown clung to my stomach, drenched with sweat. I was sore between my legs. Touching myself, I explored a slick wetness and brought bloodied fingers into sight. At first, I thought it might be signs of my lingering dream chasing me into the waking morning, but then I realized it was the start of my monthly blood.

Work at Harewood House had changed many things—primarily regular meals and consistent rest, which improved my chest sickness, and I had gained a little weight. My bleeding still did not come regularly, like Camilla said it would, like the wax and wane of the moon cycles. I had no way to forecast when I'd next need padded undergarments.

I went to the pitcher and basin and hoisted my nightdress under my armpits. I hovered my bum over the bowl and poured water over my stomach. Pink water splashed onto flawless porcelain. The skin around my privy parts was tender. I longed to bandage myself and crawl back into bed, but that was not an option.

NICOLETTE CROFT

Ann's protesting voice rang clear. "I've lit the fires upstairs."

My time at Harewood House often left me feeling more insecure than when I tromped through the York alleys. Ann's sudden appearance last night added to my disquiet. I sensed she sought an opportunity for confrontation. I needed a place to escape and think of all that had changed, especially regarding Henry. If Ann was under the watchful eye of Mrs. Brearcliff, then it was time to explore the chapel and find Max.

Cleaned and padded, I pulled my cap around my ears, flipped up my wool cloak's collar, and secreted out of the downstairs. I headed opposite the lake and the walled garden toward a wood adjacent to the main house. It was foolhardy to trudge across the grassy field, open to any onlooker. I traced the tree line, crisscrossing my way toward All Saints Church. I skulked through the shadows, fearful of who might discover me: Ann, Henry, or Father Thaddeus. Ann colored my impression of him upon my arrival when she told me the entire house was required to attend Mass on Sunday to "uphold moral standards within the community." I had pictured Father Thaddeus Humboldt as a lithe, stern man, although he was reported as meek and placid.

I found stairs leading to a tunnel under the churchyard wall. Toeing my way down slick moss-lined steps to a dark, brief underpass, I quickly climbed a second set of stairs, halting at a graveyard's edge. I was instantly wary of proceeding between the headstones. I was curious about what kind of people lie in eternal rest before me, but disturbing the dead was always ill-advised.

Opting for a quick turn around the churchyard, I stepped onto a well-groomed path lined in shaved grass. A bent poplar tree, barren of leaves, swayed and creaked in the breeze. I imagined it bore the weight of a century's grief, for it resembled a slumped, haggard woman with an aching back and crutch.

A dozen headstones surrounded the base of the tree, bright and new. One read, *Jane Myer, wife of William Clark Myer, born 4 January 1769, died 2 April 1790*. She would have been twenty-one on her deathbed. She'd be in her late twenties now and already headed into a life I could not imagine. I shuddered, wondering what would become of me as I neared thirty.

I went toward the front wall and the church's main entrance, figuring the older stones might tell of those who previously worked here, and found a gravestone decorated in a rose-carved banner. *Here lies*

THE CURSE OF MAIDEN SCARS

Elisabeth Burrows, aged 50, former loyal and beloved Housekeeper of Harewood House. Elisabeth must have preceded Mrs. Brearcliff in the position. I wondered what Mrs. Brearcliff made of her forerunner dying not more than three years older than she was now. Was it a forecast of Mrs. Brearcliff's life course?

I noticed a neglected but elaborately decorated grave. Unkempt ivy suffocated the bottom and obscured the lettering. I wasn't sure why I was drawn to it. Bending lower to push aside the vines, I read *Cassandra Serenna . . . born 1755, died . . .* I couldn't make out the death date or a surname. The woman's middle name was not lost on me. I'd never heard someone called *Serenna*, yet that was me, and now her.

The back of my neck trickled with sweat. I slumped down on the wet grass, struggling for a reluctant breath. I replayed my first night at Harewood, and Camilla calling me Serenna for the first time. Questions bubbled in my mind. I did not understand how I came to the workhouse or acquired my scars. Not having a family connection was one of my greatest pains. I'd never dreamed of a grand ancestry. Still, I longed to be the daughter of a respectable working-class couple who sewed their family together with Christmas traditions and family dinners.

I ripped away the vines and noted another name. The elements had long faded the lettering, but the date of birth was well-defined. There wasn't a death date. The weather did not wear away the missing information. It was never actually etched in *Amelia, born 1781*. This was a year after I was born. I was sad that the mother and daughter were interned in the decaying earth. Horrific, but at least they had each other.

Neither of these names was familiar, Cassandra nor Amelia. I was eager for answers. Grasping the gravestone, I scrambled to stand. My tingling feet prickled back to life. I scrunched my toes in my shoes and held my weight on one foot and then the other, ungracefully. I didn't hear the approaching company.

"It is sacrilege to dance on the graves of the dead," called a deadpan voice.

I faced my accuser.

A broad smile spread across a calm face with light eyes, free of genuine accusation. The man extended his hand. "I am Father Thaddeus."

I took his hand, which required I move closer to him. Unintentionally, I leaned in. Our gazes met levelly, our faces within inches of each other.

He watched me with a thoughtful expression. "The woman entombed there suffered greatly in her last days. I'd advise we move inside, lest her fate contaminate us all."

The irritation in my feet faded as my wonder memorized his features. He was utterly disarming, and I succumbed to the gravity of the situation.

He looked down. "Something seems wrong with your feet. Are you all right?"

Trying to respond affirmatively, I only managed to exhale, "Ahhh." It sounded a little too much a sigh of pleasure, much like I'd heard from Henry.

"I am Renna, Serenna." I wasn't sure why I gave my full name other than I still had the image of the grave in my mind.

"Let me help you inside. I can feel the rain coming." He dragged me after him toward a wooden door at the side of the church. We hustled under the arched stone covering. "This will give us a moment for a proper introduction."

He removed his wide-brimmed hat, revealing a mound of curly honey-colored hair and a receding hairline. He had freckles on the top of his forehead from too much sun. I couldn't imagine where he would experience sunburn in Yorkshire. He shrugged off his canvas cloak, shook it hard, and then turned into the church, leaving me to follow him.

I repeated his steps and removed my cap and wool cloak, now heavy with dampness. Bunching the garments under my arm, I smoothed the stray hairs escaping my braided bun. With too many to place, I pushed them around my ear.

All Saints Church had the typical trappings of a sanctuary. Stone pillars, wooden pews, and stained-glass windows. It was clean, resembling the rooms in the main house of Harewood but quite different from York churches and bars, which smelled rank with sweat and the ammonia of dried urine. Even deep in the recesses of a church, the sacred spaces might be polluted by sorrow, desperation, or perversion. I could have stayed there for hours and be of no mind to anyone, not even Father Thaddeus. Conjuring the thought of him, I noticed how the corners of my mouth turned up, and a wave of satisfaction washed through me.

He studied me with an unassuming expression. "Tell me what makes you smile."

"I appreciate the quiet."

He gave a look of contentment. "Even during service, I preserve stillness. Sermons are not only to feed the spirit and mind with the Lord's message but also to provide a space for his grace, his tenderness." He bowed his head in a brief prayer. "Of course, I don't mean I provide it. I try to maintain his divine peace." He had an internal dialogue with God and whispered, "Amen," before regarding me. "I hope to see you this Sunday."

Unintentionally, I nodded. The hairs on my neck prickled. Realizing my passivity, I moved to the far wall to study a Station of the Cross. Although rudimentary, it was a better discussion piece than Sunday Mass attendance. It would inevitably lead to a conversation of faith and my experience with God, an exchange I was not interested in having.

Father Thaddeus modestly approached. "These woodcuts were placed here by the Lascelles, who added battlements and other embellishments to the church, bringing life back into the building. Harewood's long history as a castle and seat of governance needed updating. The Lascelles provided a way for the people to move into the future and decreed the church reflect the same effort."

Relieved the conversation turned to a topic I could contribute to, I gave him some attention. I thought it was safe to talk about books. "It is a beautiful building. The ceiling arches remind me of architecture in books from the Veneto region."

"I have such affection for Veneto. I spent a summer there and must credit all of my knowledge for healing to the experience. Sadly, my English skin was not used to the sun." He touched his forehead.

I had a longing to know what he'd seen. "I would love to visit, especially Venice. I hear it is a wonderful city, full of culture and light."

"Venice has a history of merging lives, both heavenly and diseased." Father Thaddeus went to the next station and straightened the block as though tidying a beloved living room. "My experience in Venice, although I deplore the debauchery of the city, was an important time for me. I researched interventions for lunacy at a hospital in San Servolo. It was once a Benedictine monastery."

"Lunatic hospital?"

He glanced at me. "In Venice, they confine the wicked to islands."

My mind flooded with images of the girl in the Yorkshire asylum. I clumsily aimed to change the subject. "It is endearing how you care for your church." He raised an eyebrow. I regretted the compliment. "I do not intend to be rude, Father, but I have chores. I must get back." I shimmied around the last pew and headed for the front door.

My hand rested on the handle to pull it open when the door's weight pushed inward, and I stumbled, dropping my cloak and hat. Scowling at the intruder barring my flight, I found Ann looking back at me. Gaping at her, I collected my things and hastily pushed the cap down my head, not caring how the damp cloth suffocated my brow. Trying to breathe strength into my garments as though they were armor against my adversary, I waited for her insult.

She steadied on flat feet, emphasizing her compactness. Her eyes narrowed for a fight.

"Ladies, we are not here to wash the church in the rain. Ann, please come inside," Father Thaddeus said.

She moved wordlessly past me.

This was my moment to leave.

I was closing the door when Father Thaddeus commanded, "Serenna, I need you to stay."

My heart thudded as it often had when Camilla called me to attention, although Father Thaddeus bore no semblance to her. I stepped between the doors but still left one partially open.

"I need you to close it," he directed with frankness.

Not wanting to seem childish in my stalling, I came inside, leaving a hand to rest on the door for the fastest possible retreat.

"I cannot in good conscience let you both return to the house alone. At least if you go together, there is some safety." His equable expression and light tone seemed genuine. "Now, Ann, what brings you here?"

In a grand show, she gestured to me, "I saw Renna crossing the lawn and assumed she came to confession. I thought she might need comforting." Ann stretched her hand to Father Thaddeus as though to touch him. "Or perhaps you called her to tell of our duties at the hospital?"

"Wonderful thinking Ann, thank you." He looked at me. He adopted a crinkle around his left eye and forehead. Something of Ann's meddling had inspired him. He came to me. "Serenna, as you are new, and I imagine you might enjoy exposure to the grace in our community, will you join us at the hospital? It is styled with Venetian glass and mosaic floors. The visit may be a change from your duties at Harewood House and potentially shocking. I do not wish to offend your sensibilities. The patients suffer from sicknesses of the soul, and we deal with the needs of the unfortunate and bring prayer and practical necessities."

I realized the *hospital* he referred to was the asylum. I wanted to know more about the asylum girl and perhaps help her. But I was also dreadfully afraid of going inside and possibly not getting out.

He took my lack of response as a *yes.* "We usually go after Mass on Sunday, but I have an errand this week. Perhaps you can join us after the new year." He extended a hand. "It has been a pleasure. I am most grateful for your service."

I stared at his fingers, unsure if he meant for me to shake or kiss them.

"My position at All Saints Church, and my affiliation at Bootham Hall, has fortuitously expanded my Venetian practice of healing the sick, the insanely minded. I care for the citizens of Yorkshire now. I believe a sick mind reflects a contaminated soul, and new measures are being implemented." He warmly gripped me. "I support the church and the state to remove the unfit from society, helping to cleanse our community."

I didn't know what to make of his explanation, but every instinct said I needed Harewood House's safety. I curtsied goodbye and swiftly left, ignoring his suggestion that Ann and I walk together. Dashing as quickly as my skirts and the weather would allow, I hustled back to the kitchen. I turned and saw Ann trailing after me, and I raced across the field and was grateful she did not completely close the gap between us before I found my way to the side door.

Scurrying to my post in the Scullery, I hung my things on a peg behind the door. I was tying my apron when I heard Ann's feet stomping off the rain. I hoped she would move on to her duties, but hopes are often as good as preventing flour from escaping through a sieve.

Slightly breathless, she materialized in the doorway. As there was no getaway in the kitchen burrow, I busied myself scrubbing the dirtiest pot in the sink, clanking about to drown out conversation.

Her comment rang clear above the bustling, and her meaning was utterly unmistakable. "You're going to love the hospital. I imagine you will fit right in."

Storyteller

Light Attributes: Expresses life through stories
Shadow Attributes: Exaggerates harmful tales of others

Since that fateful evening in front of the Board Inn, the changes in my world had been dizzying. I'd escaped street life and the cotton house filth for stable employment. I'd found unlikely allies in Olivia and Donovan, although he was nowhere to be found. I'd been embraced by Henry, a man only my dreams could conjure. A new dilemma now lay before me—visiting the asylum. My experience was the theme of most nightmares, but I also had an uncontrollable longing to see the scared girl again. My heart and mind were in turmoil, and I desperately needed guidance. I sought Camilla in the laundry, only to learn she had been sent back to York to deal with unresolved matters at the workhouse. I could no longer postpone church attendance with my presence now fully known to Father Thaddeus. I prayed that appearing at mass would help me find my Max.

A chill fell over my shoulders, and I tried to shield myself from the temperature in the chapel, made frigid by the gaping front door and the gloomy congregants' at All Saint's Church. I hoped my face was hidden under my cap's shadow, angled in the right direction. My anxiety came not from the risk of recognition but from my desire to observe others from my seat at the church's center. Thankfully, the men and women who settled around me did not regard me, not even with the usual morning pleasantries.

Playing with the tips of my gloves, I stiffened as a small body scooted in at my left. Staring hard at my fingers as though they held the power to render me invisible, a hand with dirty nails and cracked knuckles gripped me. I knew the hand well and tucked the familiar fingers in my gloves to warm them. I was grateful to have my companion back.

"Where have you been?"

Max glued himself to my side. "Here, with Father Thaddeus. I was here the day you came to the graveyard. I was going to speak to you, but he found you first."

I was engrossed in the gravestones and taken by surprise at Father Thaddeus' approach that I'd missed Max's presence. The afternoon would have produced a different outcome if I had met with him. I would not have such apprehension for the foretold visit to the lunatic hospital.

The simple act of holding Max was like being anointed with water. He had played the most significant role in my life, more than anyone else. I wondered what part I had played for him. I wanted to share my discovery of the tombstone—and confess to my tryst with Henry. I desperately needed to rekindle my relationship with the one person I trusted with all my heart.

I glanced at him to find his gaze and communicate my longing. Our eyes met as they had hundreds of times before. A knot grew in my throat. Max's color had not returned, and he appeared ashen. I had hoped clean and regular lodging would revive his health, as it had mine. But the dark flat pools of his eyes had lost their zest. He was a murmur of his former self. He squeezed my hand, and growing guilt tightened my head into an ache. I should have come to find him sooner.

He hushed, "I'm all right."

"I have much to share, and I'm saddened we are not alone."

He nodded distractedly. "I don't know if we will ever be quite alone again."

His comment left me feeling we had exchanged our dangerous life for suffocating simplicity. "What do you mean?"

"I don't know about your days, but mine are monitored and planned." He checked for eavesdroppers before continuing. "Didn't you wonder why I had not come to see you? I have not left the church grounds since arriving from the workhouse. I bathe here, for Father Thaddeus expects me to be clean. I eat and sleep here, too."

"How's the bathing going?" I teased. His fingers looked like vanilla biscuits trimmed in thin lines of chocolate.

He pulled his hand out from mine and tucked it inside his coat. "I was in the yard before service and did not have time to wash. I cannot let Father Thaddeus see. He will be quite angry. My fingers are often dirtied by ink, and he demands I'm diligent with washing."

His warning rocked me with a nervous tremor. I was astounded that a mild priest conjured this sort of fearful subservience. I tilted my chin toward the front of the chapel, where Father Thaddeus stood with his back turned to the growing congregation. "He seems friendly."

What little color was left in Max's face drained away, and he looked a perfect camouflage against the grey stone pillars. "Friendly, perhaps, but decisive. Once his instruction has been given, there is no room for negotiation."

I tried to add levity with a nudge and smile. "So, Father Thaddeus won't look kindly if I excuse myself from the outing to the hospital?"

"No, he would not. Hellfire, Renna," Max seethed in a low tone. "How did you bloody 'eck get yourself into that obligation? Do you know how dangerous that place is?"

Thunderstruck by his reprimand, I shook my head. I bit my tongue to keep from sharing more, particularly losing my chastity on the lush furniture in the library. Initially, I was sure Max would hold my confidences, but his reprimand made me wonder if his sickness also represented a change in heart and values.

"You're different. Are you all right?"

"I'm sorry," he acquiesced. "I don't feel well. Father Thaddeus has been giving me tea he says will help *revitalize me to the Lord's work*, but I don't feel better."

My worry mounted. "Can you stop drinking it?"

"No. We all do what Father Thaddeus tells us." He cuddled me closer. "You've opened yourself to his authority. From what I've seen, even if one only intends to visit the hospital, doing charity work, they risk getting stuck there."

"And Father Thaddeus has something to do with it?"

"I don't know, really, but the people in there, the doctors, are on a mission to collect the undesirable of the community and lock them away until they can be rehabilitated. Father Thaddeus leads them, although he's not a doctor. He once lived outside Venice and rid the mind of evil to *free the lunatics of lunacy*. He said he contributed to several books published on the subject." Max's cheeks were pink from his exertion.

Father Thaddeus' language had burned into my memory. "He mentioned living there and feeling *fortunate* to continue his work here in Yorkshire. What would be fortunate about attending to the insane?"

"He's very passionate about his work. He is well-meaning." Max looked to Father Thaddeus as the priest thumbed through his sermon notes. "But I think he may be misguided. I can only imagine what interventions he performed in Venice, but here, he focuses on prayer, cleanliness, herbs—mushroom tinctures and such—aiming to free the body of demonic spirits."

"And you've been with him to the hospital?"

"Aye. And Renna, I've seen her, the girl."

I grew wide-eyed, knowing immediately whom he meant.

"She's really sick. Father said she is the daughter of a murderess—but I can't imagine it." He blanched. His mind seemed to vanish into an elusive dream. "Father Thaddeus said his predecessor was responsible for isolating the girl and her mother many years ago. He said the girl was a product of an *evil union,* and the mother and her extended family were all ill."

I was unsure what to say. "I didn't mean to get tied to going to the hospital. It was Ann, the kitchen maid from the house." My imagination was bursting. "She really must hate me if she intends to find a way to keep me at the hospital."

"She is wicked." He inched closer to me. "Do you remember the little whore who lived around the docks and would pick-pocket her johns and bed them, usually in plain sight?"

"She was a lurking liar, always on guard, yet I had sympathy for her."

I wrinkled my nose thinking of her. She had met her just desserts when she bedded and robbed a Prussian man who caught her trying to shove his rings in secret hiding places. After his entire entourage of men raped her as they saw fit, he suffocated her with his bare hands. The authorities never pursued the offense. One morning, her body was seen floating in the harbor, and she was left to wash out to sea. I had detested her, but her death wasn't something I had wished for. I wasn't sure if I could even wish it on vile little Ann. Still, Max's comparison to the whore was enough to fortify my guard against her.

"Ann typically goes with us to the hospital. She makes fun of the patients and does her best to upset them, causing the orderlies to punish them. She's like a child tormenting caged monkeys." Max pushed his chilled palm back into my glove. "My fingers are cold."

I longed to hug him tightly. "As though you have to explain."

His gaze darted left. "Do you see that woman with the bonnet partially covering her head, ready to fall off?"

I followed the path of his look toward a woman with no remarkable expression, and yet, somehow, something appeared unseemly. Her head covering was askew, as was her posture. She slumped over in the pew like a rag doll. If it weren't for her nose twitching with regularity, I would have sworn she was a stuffed puppet and not a real woman.

"She was the first in here today, as with every Sunday. Her husband brings her down the aisle and positions her on the pew. He adjusts her bonnet and her skirt. Then he stands at the side. She will be the last to leave." His story was rattled off in a monotone fashion. "She causes no fuss unless she needs the privy. Her need is only known when the pew drips with urine."

I gasped, trying not to advertise my horror.

"She can no longer speak. Her husband brings her dutifully to Mass. He hopes she will one day revive, by God's grace." He reverently bowed his head.

"How often do you go to the hospital?"

"Three times a week as part of my position with Father Thaddeus. He attends the insane through prayer and cleansing. Ann comes every Sunday.

The explanation left me chilled. "And what do you do for him?"

"I record his observations when we return in the evenings. He is healing a woman sent to the asylum by her husband. She has bruises and cuts on her arms. Her husband says she paid a witch to rid her body of their ninth child. He said she conjured a demon." His little eyes splayed in excitement. "He says the demon beats at her womb." Max excitedly recounted the woman's story.

I felt sick. The veracity of Max's explanation of the unfit was out of character. "Max, you don't believe that, do you? You've seen as well as I have how some wives are treated by their husbands. Maybe the man did it himself."

He raised an eyebrow. "I don't know, Renna. She's unmanageable. There haven't been any new marks since coming to the asylum. She screams when Father Thaddeus prays over her. She must be possessed if she can't stand the presence of a man of God or the sound of prayer."

"Maybe she doesn't feel safe with men. She has been pregnant how many times?" I was trying to do the calculation.

"According to her husband, she birthed nine children, and five survived. He said she'd been pregnant double that many times. He says a demon haunted her body and killed her babes before they were born."

I couldn't imagine a woman suffering so much grief. "She must be around thirty—with that many pregnancies." I figured one a year from the time of marriage put her at thirty years.

"She's barely past twenty-four, married since thirteen."

We locked eyes, neither of us having to comment.

"I have an idea about the people, but what about the hospital?"

Max looked long into my face. "I cannot explain it. It is nothing you have seen before. Once you see it, it cannot be unseen."

We held each other quietly as the congregants filed in around us. I felt pulled in many directions. Part of me wanted to know more about the asylum and the girl we'd seen the first night and understand what Max had faced these last months. Another part wanted to snatch up Max and flee Harewood altogether.

"Have you seen your mother?"

Max nodded. "I have, but Father Thaddeus has forbidden me to speak to anyone who is not a child—he has prohibited my mother as well."

"Absurd," I hissed. My voice was too sharp, and stern faces stared me down.

THE CURSE OF MAIDEN SCARS

"He said something about knowing my mother and crossing paths in Veneto, but I don't understand." Max sidled closer. "He mentioned meeting you. He said you were *good*. I dared to sit next to you today."

I felt even angrier with myself for not attending church. Max had needed me. His isolation was for his protection, but it was unimaginable that he would need to guard against his own mother. "Does he mistreat you?"

"No. Father Thaddeus says he is safeguarding me." Max shook his head. "But I have learned as much at the asylum or reading his notes as what we saw on the streets."

I couldn't imagine what he meant. Then I remembered my own latest information. "There is much I need to share with you. I found a headstone in the graveyard with my name, but the dates are from long ago." I inched closer to him. "Oh, and a woman I've met, she's extraordinary. She's called Olivia, but Samuel refers to her as *Mother*."

Max became paler. He whispered in my ear, "I know her. If you've met her, then you may be in danger already. Your visit to the asylum will explain things. As for the gravestone, I saw you studying it and know what you're referring to. Did you notice the other name on the stone, born 1781?"

It was amazing that he knew which gravestone I meant.

He sealed the last bit of space between us. "The girl is alive. You've seen her."

"I have?"

"Through the window at the asylum." He stiffened and faced the pulpit, reverently bowing his head. He registered an unspoken signal that resonated throughout the church. The parishioners echoed his posture and focused on Father Thaddeus. Max recited "Hail Mary, full of grace . . ." with his attention engrossed in Father Thaddeus. He had pulled away into his own space on the seat as though we were simple churchgoers sharing the same pew and not longtime companions.

Realizing the rest of the conversation would have to wait, I mouthed the prayer along with the congregation but held my voice in my mind. I observed those around me. Most appeared clean and genteel, with heads covered in lace and linen bonnets. The men had modest top hats. The few children present sat obediently near their parents, with only momentary outbursts of restlessness before being tapped and pulled into submission by their mothers and older sisters.

My eyes settled on the mute woman Max had noted earlier. The sadness of her tale made me feel ill. I continued to assess the parish, coming to an abrupt halt on the smudged face and spry eyes of a boy, maybe six, sitting two rows ahead and fixated on me. He sat at the end of a pew and contorted to face my direction. I found it unnerving. I pulled at my cap and averted my eyes. With a furtive side-glance, I checked for his watchfulness. He held me in an intense gaze, mouth slackened, spittle draining from the corner.

I murmured to Max, gently poking him with my elbow and pointing with a sharp chin jab. "What is *his* game?"

Max didn't look up from the songbook in his lap, seeming to know whom I referred. "Thomas Finch. It's not a game. His body is twisted. You can't see it, but his legs hang over the side aisle. It's best to support him, draping him over the back of the pew."

The parish was signaled to stand and join the chorus. Partially horrified yet sickened with a longing to know, I craned to see if Max's description held sway. I saw two little legs with scuffed shoes dangling to the side, kicking rhythmically as the organ struck its first chords. Thomas's expression softened. I relaxed as the music rose and fell, finding calm in the crowded room. It seemed Father Thaddeus did not shy away from horrifying tragedy. Perhaps he wasn't someone to fear. If the misfortunate could find a home here, maybe those like me—the merely human, flawed, and sinful—were also welcome.

Thief

Light Attributes: Sheds light on potential
Shadow Attributes: Pilfers ideas, money, affection, power

The Harewood staff were busy decorating for Christmas, something I'd only experienced at a distance when I watched York families at Mass or shopping for dinner at the market. This was my first time tasting, touching, smelling, and relishing in creating a Yuletide memory. The downstairs bustle was refreshing compared to the gloomy fog of the mid-winter day. We were told Christmas dinner would cater to Henry and his guests, along with a representative from the new family taking over the house.

This year had been such a time of transition, not only for me but also for the servants. Some grieved the loss of Lord Lascelles, for he was remembered as kind and tolerant. Others were nervous about the security of their positions under the eventual new Master. Mr. Popplewell replied perfunctorily to those concerns. "Our positions are as secure as our service."

This was hardly heartening. I had been here four months, long enough for it to feel comfortable, and I feared losing it all.

I carried a basket of fresh herbs and aubergine I'd gleaned from the garden stores on a quick visit with Samuel and Dada and pushed through the door with a familiar bang of my boot. Shuffling down the scullery ramp, I struggled to disentangle my apron as it caught in the wicker basket. I couldn't fully secure the basket on the counter without pulling half of my clothing with it. I opted to unload the items one at a time, aubergine with the most care, for it was the most precious. With its various shapes and shifting hues of deep purple, and ribbons of lavender and green, the aubergine was rare this time of year.

Samuel said the crop he tried to keep going year-round would usually be subject to a cold snap and killed. This year, he changed strategies and had kept a section of the crop protected and plucked them free of their vines two weeks ago, leaving us the option to offer roasted aubergine with béchamel, topped with a crispy parmesan crust.

I unloaded a bed of tightly wadded rosemary, sage, thyme, and garlic bulbs and was surprised when I saw a small burlap parcel among the herbs. I had packed the basket myself and couldn't remember putting in anything besides the vegetables and herbs.

Unhooking my apron, I stared at the package and considered my options. There was no need for sneakiness, but my heart pounded at the mere thought of opening something not directly addressed to me. There wasn't a name attached to the parcel, and I couldn't imagine how it was mine, but I wanted to know what it was. My imagination made my chores tedious. I decided to save my curiosity for a quieter moment and slipped the burlap into my apron. It weighed down my garment.

After washing the aubergine and sorting the herbs for bugs and dead sections, I checked in with Mrs. Connolly. "I need to relieve myself. I'll be back in a quick moment."

"Hurry!" She shouted after me. "We still have six more loaves to bake."

Breaks were infrequent, even for the toilet. If we needed a wee, Mrs. Connolly preferred we relieve ourselves in the bucket in the kitchen corner, but she continued to show me grace.

I rushed to my room. Fearful my absence might spark curiosity, mainly from Ann, I quietly shut my squeaky door and knelt at my bed. My body blocked the line of sight from the door. With ragged edges and a slight tinge of tobacco, the burlap invited me. I thought of Henry. He had said he would "care" for me. Maybe this was from him.

British West India Company was written on the burlap. Three large pins pinched together layers of canvas, and it took tugging to pull them free. A sweet aroma of whiskey and ocean scented the room as the flaps released. At first, I thought Henry might have sent a token of his affections. His father worked for the India Company. Then Donovan came to mind. My hands started to sweat. If this was from him, then he was close. I wasn't sure if that was what I wanted. My life was finding a rhythm and a purpose. Henry and I were now connected. If Donovan sent a sign of his affection, that complicated things.

Unfolding the parcel revealed a locket with a winged lion engraved in a crest with three sparkling sapphires. Cautiously, I unfastened a delicate latch, anticipating a picture, but found it empty. Velvet backing marked places for two small images. I turned the locket over, admiring the ebony back. I slid my nail around the edge and found a compartment containing a dark and delicate, tightly tied locket of hair. Resealing the hair, I admired the exquisite necklace. It lacked a chain, and I could not wear it nor even dare. But I imagined how it would look with a dark blue dress positioned above the arch of my breasts and the intimate crease of my décolletage.

I tried to make sense of finding the locket. It had to be meant as a Christmas gift, but who from? Maybe it was more than a gift. Turning the locket over again, I looked closer at the compartment. I felt an engraving but could not make it out in the dim light. I went to the oil lamp on my table and turned the toggle to revive the flame. The light grew, revealing the letters C. S. C. My heartbeat pulsed in my ears as I tried to think of the person behind the initials.

I heard footsteps outside my door.

I slipped the locket into the waistline of my skirt. I snatched up the burlap and pins and shoved them into my apron pocket, pricking my finger. Rightening myself, I held my wrist to the lamplight and yanked at the frayed end of my sleeve to enlarge a tear. Blood stained the edge.

The latch lifted, and the door hinges squealed. "What are you?" Ann snapped.

With my wrist and shirt outstretched, I turned around, pretending to signal for help. "I think it's quite torn. I have blood on it. Do you think I have time to mend it?"

Ann took the bait and marched straight toward me. She thumbed the ends of the shirt. "You can't deal with this now."

I played dumb. "Mrs. Brearcliff, won't she be cross?"

"Of course she will. But would you rather be scolded for not attending to your work or damaging your clothes while finishing it?" Ann tried to fold the sleeve together like it would knit itself through again. "If you are lucky, she may not even notice, and we can deal with it after supper."

I was fleetingly moved by her care, both for my clothing and well-being. I softened to her. But the feeling quickly passed.

Her features hardened. "I value you because you make my life easier. I have other things I want to spend time doing. Do you understand how miserable I could make you if that changed?"

There it was—her real intentions.

Ann went toward the door, and I did not miss her scanning appraisal of my room. With a sweep and a flounce, she rendered her judgment in a disapproving "huh."

I, too, studied my space, fretting about leaving a clue exposed. All seemed well. I turned my back to the hall and took one last peek through the gap between the doors when I saw one of the pearl pins. I was sure Ann saw it. I whispered a prayer that she would not return and take it.

The burlap and the locket were my constant preoccupations as I nervously worked with Mrs. Connolly to prepare the Christmas dinner for the guests of Harwood House. On an ordinary occasion, I would have longed to participate in the happenings above the stairs.

We worked for several hours, putting the final additions on potatoes roasted with rosemary and garlic, aubergine, and pickled herring with sweet fig sauce. The baked pies stuffed with savory meats, rich sauces, sautéed vegetables, and creamy toppings smelled heavenly. Mrs. Connolly had over a dozen loaves of freshly baked bread and little pancake cups called Yorkshires. By the time the dinner bell rang, the footmen had carted over twenty trays to the butler's pantry outside the dining hall. The kitchen was left bare.

I was wiping a fine flour coating on the counter when Samuel came in. "Now, Mrs. Connolly, what have you left us for our Christmas tea?"

"Happy Christmas," Dada announced lyrically as she trailed in after Samuel.

Mrs. Brearcliff, with her tightly pulled bun and high-buttoned collar, followed them both. "Samuel, I'm sure you will be pleased to have whatever Mrs. Connolly chooses to serve." She accompanied her reproach with an expectant glance at Mrs. Connolly, who sided with Samuel.

"Here, you two. Don't fret. Do you think I would leave the best foods only for that lot upstairs?" She smiled with misaligned teeth in various shades, from dull eggshell to mild caramel. "I have made a second serving of every dish I sent up. Everything is warming in the oven or on the stove. It seems wrong to serve delicacies and only sample simple turkey and gravy for our meal."

Mrs. Brearcliff looked aghast. "Mrs. Connolly. That is quite out of hand. We are not to partake of what the Master might have. What if we are all found out?"

"By whom?" Mrs. Connolly retorted. "We have yet to have a proper new master at Harewood House. The start of the new year might change things for us, but for today, we can enjoy the fruits of our labors." She winked at Samuel, "Literally, I say."

Mrs. Brearcliff sighed. "I suppose. Shall we sit while the guests dine? This may be the only time we have to enjoy your exquisite food before being summoned again."

We gathered in the servant's hall. The table was packed with platters of food. We passed each dish clockwise from person to person. It took more than five minutes for everyone to have a spoonful from each. With everyone served, we gathered hands for a prayer. Before bowing my head, I considered those in attendance and those not. I was squished between Ann and Dada, and Samuel sat across from me. I'd been told Camilla would stay in York until Boxing Day.

"Where is Father Thaddeus?" I whispered to Ann, also thinking of Max.

"He will sup in his room, preparing for midnight mass." Ann bowed her head, completely unaware of the pain her words caused.

Christmas meant lovely cakes and songs, firesides, lushly decorated trees, and presents, all things I had yet to enjoy. I thought Harewood would mean something new. The only Christmas celebration I'd experienced was the occasional surprise from Max. In our childhood, my favorite gift from him had been a pocketful of stale chestnuts he'd pinched from the local merchant. If there were no Father Thaddeus, then there would be no Max. Again, I had made a discovery, and he wasn't here to share. I squeezed my eyes shut to block the threatening tears. This would mark the first Christmas I could remember without him.

We exchanged small pleasantries and short anecdotes, but no one entirely dominated the conversation, for we all anticipated the signaling from the guests upstairs.

"This might be the finest meal I ever tasted," Dada grinned with a mouth full of food.

"Thank you, Dada," rejoined Mrs. Connolly. "But if I recall, Mr. Lascelles told stories of the many fine meals your family served him on the plantation in Barbados."

Knowing something of Mrs. Connolly's intentions, I knew the comment was meant to strengthen their friendship bonds. But the effort landed poorly.

Dada replied with a sullen, "Aye."

Mrs. Connolly continued to chatter away with Mrs. Brearcliff and Mr. Popplewell.

I whispered to Dada, "What's wrong?"

She looked at me. Her dark eyes showed anger. "As though that family knew finery. Mr. Lascelles was all right himself, but baddies always surround them." She gulped down a spoonful of potatoes, and her heavy chest shuddered. "I am a product of my Mam and one of the foremen-bosses. I am guessing if Mam ain't died trying to bring me into the world, I would still be on the island, better and worse."

The conversation with Olivia rang with me—we either belong or don't. I learned Dada hailed from the Caribbean, the island of Barbados. I'd done some reading about the area but knew little except the slaves toiled for twenty hours a day and were considered as expendable as feathers off a chicken. I wondered how Dada had managed life at Harewood House without ill befalling her.

The large bell in the hall rang, heralding the guests needing attention. Mrs. Connolly looked at Ann. "You check, as you take forever to eat."

With a resentful sigh, Ann pulled away from her cramped position.

Mrs. Brearcliff stared me down mid-bite. "I think you should be helpful." She tipped another perfectly rounded Yorkshire pudding onto her plate, ladling it with a generous spoon full of gravy over turkey.

Still chewing as I stepped from the table, I followed Ann. It was uncharacteristic of her to be diligently compliant. But once I stepped through the door into the hall, I was surprised to find her already gone. I made my way up the servant's stairs to the main floor, unsure where the guests might be. I went toward the dining room, but a loud crash drew me to the library. Crowing laughter sang along with a "Hurrah."

I recalled what transpired the last time I'd been there with Henry. As I still had the locket tucked into my waistband and more than half my Christmas dinner awaiting me, I was not interested in ending up on a settee, at least not tonight. Pushing the door open enough to know the mood in the room, I froze when I saw Henry on the far side. His shirt was half-tucked, and he had a long pipe in one hand and a full glass of whiskey in the other. He danced, half circling around a girl stretched out on a couch.

I heard him snicker, "This isn't the maid I'd thought I'd summoned, but you will certainly do."

He moved aside, and I saw Ann casually seated before him, no expression of apprehension. She reached for his belt and welcomed him closer. "And since when am I second to anyone?"

My heart sank as I spied on them. I couldn't believe what I was witnessing. Ann invited his vulgarity. What was her game? Mixed with disgust and jealousy, I nudged the door open more.

The other revelers showed little care for Henry and Ann's interaction. They engaged in various forms of their amusement, from misplaying the flute, to kissing and laughing and arguing around a card table. The scene reeked of jeopardy.

If Ann wanted to spend her Christmas night as something Henry and his guests unwrapped for their enjoyment, I would leave her to it.

Advocate

Light Attributes: Inspires action
Shadow Attributes: Pursues causes for personal gain

The year ended in isolation. Agitated impatience stirred in me as if my mind wasn't my own. I heard that Henry had left on Boxing Day. At the time, I was devastated. He'd taken my virginity—or perhaps I gave it as the only gift I thought he'd want. He'd confused me and elated me. I wanted him. I wanted to be part of the world he walked in. His book was a prized gift and a bitter reminder. The image of Henry enticing Ann soured my memories, and I questioned my affection. Subtle inquiry revealed he might return in the late spring, but that was months away. He'd abandoned me without a goodbye and with only the memory of our interlude to trouble my days, even as the asylum girl haunted my nights.

I was at breakfast on a quiet Wednesday when Ann came tripping in, gay and light. "Good morning, Renna. Isn't it pleasant today?"

I didn't share what I thought—it was one of my most miserable mornings yet.

She danced to the sideboard to pour tea and scooped up a soft-boiled egg. "I think Father Thaddeus will be here soon."

Utterly confused, I snapped at her. "What for?"

My defensiveness didn't seem to dampen her mood. "The hospital, of course."

I lost the taste for my breakfast. "I thought that was next Sunday."

"He said today was better. The hospital is full of patients." She finished her tea and flew to the door, holding it open with expectation. "I think you will appreciate Father Thaddeus's knowledge. I know I want to learn from an expert who can discern evil in others."

I assembled myself and waited with Ann at the back entrance for Father Thaddeus to bring around his open-top wagon. The prospect of Max accompanying us bolstered my mood. He sat up front with a straight posture. Seeing Max huddled in the back with rounded, burlap-covered baskets made me wiggle joyfully.

Ann sat alongside Father Thaddeus on the front bench as we went to the hospital. and Max and I bounced together in the back with fresh vegetables from Samuel's garden and prayer pamphlets Father Thaddeus insisted aided the healing of the souls and minds of the patients.

Max occasionally murmured, "That house there, that's one too."

"One what?"

He wore a guilty expression as he pointed out the sights on our half-hour ride. "Another place where the mad are isolated. Some are completely forgotten."

When we turned down the lane toward the asylum, I was carried back to the discovery of the burned girl. We drove around the front of a brick building of balanced design, columns framing wooden double doors. An even number of windows stretched side-to-side, indicating two floors above ground. The horses stopped, and the noise of our turbulent travels quieted. With few trees to shield us from the wind, the breeze was penetrating.

I held to a basket filled with fresh lavender and verbena. Ideas of discovering the asylum girl's identity played through my mind. I pieced together Max's reference about her and the gravestone. My throat turned dry as I mapped out the course to find her in my mind.

Ann took up a basket and stared me down, lips firm, eyes with a flaming expression. "She's not going to be much help if she remains there all afternoon."

Father Thaddeus offered his hand. His look was tranquil and without spite—as usual. I took his hand and jumped off the end of the cart, a little too near Ann, causing her to stumble backward. She lost her balance, and her cap flipped free. Her blond hair flapped in the wind like unpinned laundry. In her attempt to regain both her hat and composure, she dropped her basket of apples.

I stifled a snicker but was stunned when a sudden bark of laughter boomed from Father Thaddeus. He stood with both hands on his hips. His face turned toward the sky. I took this as permission to release my gayety, and my laughter poured forth until my cheeks burned and the muscle in my forehead pulsed with energy. Still in the cart, Max restrained his pleasure, but color returned to his complexion, and his eyes brightened as though the clouds parted for the sun. But quickly, they shadowed over again.

Ann's face raged with humiliation. "You uncouth oaf."

Father Thaddeus was between us. "Ann, we do not attack our friends. Serenna has shown herself to be one of us. She is a daughter of faith, like you." He rested a hand on her shoulder. "I apologize for laughing. It must have been distressing. But I thank you for lightening the mood, even if inadvertently."

Her words whistled like the sound of a steaming teapot. "It wasn't my intention."

"You are always a picture of grace." His face was all sincerity. "Rather, you and Serenna may have been brought together at this moment by God's doing, allowing a moment of levity. Some days I need extra effort to perform my duties with gratitude. The bleakness in the sky often drains my spirit."

Ann swept up her hair under her cap, now well tangled by the breeze, and gave each apple she collected a wipe in her apron before placing it in the basket. I bent for an apple and held it to her as a peace offering. "I'm sorry to have been clumsy."

Ann shifted her look to me, exposing her eyes' whites, strangely with a faint yellow hue. "I think we can arrange a lesson for you about being aware of your space." Ann could suck the air out of an interaction with only a phrase. Whatever niceties she had, they would not be spent on my behalf.

Father Thaddeus ushered us into the hospital foyer. Max closed the doors behind us, shutting out the fresh air. If silence seemed heavy before, now it was suffocating. I dared not shuffle my shoes about the mosaic floor. Holding still, a newfound skill in my time at Harewood House, I waited as Max came alongside me. We turned to Father

THE CURSE OF MAIDEN SCARS

Thaddeus.

He took to explaining the day. "We will attend the women's ward. Max, you will oversee the pamphlets. I expect you know what is best and how close to get to each patient."

With a flat expression, Max replied, "Each is to have one placed either on their lap or on a table. I will recite the Lord's Prayer and wish a fast recovery that they may resist their slothfulness and bear fruit in suitable work and increase in the knowledge of God, to accept their inferior circumstances humbly, with sacrifice, without complaining, lest their souls are tempted to the deeds they have already committed by their evil and rebellious natures."

I never heard him recite such cruel pronouncements, utterly devoid of feeling. I worried had he become cold to the conditions of the less fortunate.

Father Thaddeus patted Max. "You are a blessing. I pray for many years of service together." He glowed as he gave his compliments. He moved toward Ann, shadowing her features from light shown through a window high in the ceiling. "As you have been here before, check on the direst patients. You seem to know which have the most afflicted minds, for they speak loudly to you. I marvel at the courage it takes to bear witness to the wretched souls." He touched her shoulder. "Many blessings to you."

Ann looked at me. "And what of her?"

"Serenna will follow me today to get acquainted with our mission. I learned techniques in Veneto to rid the body of evil spirits. While plying the insane with tonics or mixtures, one can rapidly return the inferior to a modestly cured state." Father Thaddeus removed his hat with a composed expression, adding to his docile image. He focused on a chime clock opposite the door. "It is half past twelve. Shall we all meet back here at three to make our journey home in time for tea?"

"Yes, Father," Both Max and Ann replied.

Father Thaddeus stepped down a corridor. "Serenna, please bring the basket of flowers and follow me."

I stared speechless at Max, waiting for him to signal escape somehow. He turned mechanically toward the opposite hall, the heels of his shoes snapping on the tiles with rhythmic percussion. Ann looked at me with a queer smile, clasped her basket in both hands and swayed after Max. Their departure left me alone in the foyer. A growing panic swelled deep in my belly. I felt powerless by a raging conflict between obedience and escape. Sadly, my flight seeped away.

Closing my eyes, I allowed my hearing to discern the world I could not yet see. I heard wood-on-wood slapping together and the sound of a door closing. The foyer was stale. I knew I would gain little by staying here, so I stepped into the hall's long shadows. As I continued into dimmer areas, my heart raced. I felt that the darker the world became, the closer danger crept. With a sudden sense of being watched, I rushed to an empty, sunlit room. My heart thudded faster, like a fist on my chest. I focused on the next area of light, where the hall bent into another corridor.

There was a quick and short squeal and an eerily slow rhythmic squeaking, something I couldn't place. Then the wood-on-wood sound again. An acidic smell crept around the corridor in an invisible fog, permeating the hall's tiles and crevice, stifling the fresh air. I coughed and rubbed my nose, and the smell vanished as though it never existed.

"Serenna." Father Thaddeus was in a room lined with windows with slanted skylights. It was a tranquil dayroom with people around the edges, lounging in wooden rocking chairs. All appeared ordinary, yet I was dizzied.

A nurse with a white kerchief hat, silver tray in hand, floating from patient to patient, caught my attention. Father Thaddeus shot me an eye of authority, bidding me tend to those he had not yet seen. I headed into a corner illuminated with rare winter sunshine. A fern grew in the sunbeam, and I was glad for a touch of nature.

The first woman I met absently stared out the window. She did not acknowledge my approach. She did not look at me, but her posture indicated awareness. Dried spittle caked the corners of her mouth, and snot dripped from the tip of her nose. Chapped lips and messy hair showed neglect. When I placed a bundle of tied lavender on her lap, she did not stir. I took a handkerchief from my apron and touched the corner of her mouth.

I shuddered with a new queasiness and scuttled onto the next woman. This one looked right enough, with a face as broad as it was long. She smiled. I smiled back. She smiled again and then again, pulling her lips wider with each grin. Her smiles became fervent, the edges of her mouth twitched, and her lips quivered. I shoved flowers in her lap.

Her eyes darted from them and back to me. Her expression filled with panic. Wide eyes exposed whites streaked with red veins. Her mouth opened and closed like a guppy struggling for oxygen. I pressed myself against the window behind me. The welcoming warmth of the sunlight on the pane protected me from the haunting woman. She released a hair curdling scream. Although I stood frozen with shock, I knew she was trying to communicate something, but it was lost.

Barely noting the clatter of a metal tray on the floor, hard heals and a growing yell bounded toward me. "Move. Move! MOVE!"

Despite the nurse's demand, I was unable to move.

The nurse separated me from the howling woman. She threw the flowers from her lap, hitting me. Placing both hands on the woman's face, she said steadily, "Timmy, Timmy, good girl Timmy."

The screaming patient slowly calmed, which released me from my paralysis. I inched away from the windows and waited as the nurse soothed Timmy and patted down her hair. Scuttling into a quiet corner, I focused on the room's design. Father Thaddeus had been correct—It was pretty. The intricate inlay of mosaic greens, blues, and golds traced a pattern around the floor. I saw a woman beside me, silent and still. Her feet were soaking in a large copper tub. Her legs were bare to her knees, patched with slough and prickled with black hairs, much like cactus thorns I'd seen in books of desert flora.

"It's a nightmare, is it not?" She spoke in an even tone, knowing and coherent.

The voice was instantly familiar, and I sought the woman's face. "Olivia. What are you doing in this awful place?" I stretched for her hand, which was covered by a blanket. I was surprised when she did not reach back.

She sat squarely on a wooden chair and was positioned like a sentry in the corner. "My dear." Her eyes were wide, but her voice was level. "You need to step back. Move completely to the other side of the room if you can."

Her rejection was harsh, especially since I needed a friend. "But you're here. How can I help you?" I groped at her further, feeling a large strap over her forearm. "What is this?"

I uncovered her arms and found them bound to the chair with a belt. The leather cut into her skin, turning her fingers blue. The buckle dented the flesh atop her forearm. She was molded to a straight oak chair, stiff and squared-off. I bent to unfasten the clasp and caught a pungent stench beneath her skirts.

"Stop." She insisted. "You must go back."

"I can help. This is absurd." I tried the buckle, but releasing her meant pulling it tighter and bruising the wounded arm. "Olivia. This is barbaric. Why are you here? How do I free you?" I asked her questions as I tried to pry up the buckle toggle.

She sucked in a hiss of pain between her teeth. "Please stop. If not for yourself, then for me. If you are found here, and if I am released, things will worsen for me."

"Worse? You do not belong here." I wanted to rebel but stopped because of her pleading and the assaulting smell. I pulled back the edge of her skirt, "It is as though a rat . . ."

". . . Died." She finished for me. A bedpan full of golden-brown urine and feces droplets was beneath the chair. The pungency was tinged slightly sweet. "There is a hole cut in the bottom of the seat. It allows me to stay positioned for hours." Her faint voice trailed off again. "And I can still relieve myself."

I was outraged. "How long have you been tied here?" I tugged again at the buckle.

"Renna!" She demanded. "Step back."

Her final command was enough to make me drop her skirt and the blanket.

"I see you have found *Mother Shipton*." Father Thaddeus came up from behind. "This is an extremely sick woman, Serenna. I warn you to keep your distance. She is known to bewitch without remorse." He stood before her with his hands clasped before him as though he would break into prayer.

"And how is this woman bewitching, Father? I am unfamiliar with such things."

His glare hardened. "Olivia believes she is *Mother Shipton*, a witch residing near Knaresborough. There is a tale of a scandalous woman, a

THE CURSE OF MAIDEN SCARS

few centuries back, who could make wishes come true. Every few decades, a new woman takes up the burden and tells fortunes, stealing from others and diverting them from God's path."

I looked at Olivia. This explained why Samuel had referred to her as *Mother* and why Olivia was in search of healing remedies, but it did not explain why she was strapped to this torturous chair, filth gelling in a stagnant pool beneath her. "Thank you for the warning, Father. But why is she here?"

He pulled his chin higher as though summoning God's will. "Her feet are left in frigid water to chill the hellfire burning within her. We drain her of her filth and her evil. She will be released when her urine clears, and we know God has cleansed her."

I nodded for a moment, unsure of what to do. "Is there any way I may help, Father?" I took in a breath of courage and feigned sympathy. "I see you fight to win the souls teetering on damnation. I am awed by your faith, Father. How may I serve as you do?"

Father Thaddeus gave a delighted expression. "Perhaps your presence will bring the blessing of your name, Serenna the *Calm*. She needs the waters. Make her drink." He pointed to a jug and glass on an adjacent table.

I found a stool and took a position near Olivia. This would give us time to share secrets, ones I now believed only *Mother Shipton* might be able to understand. "Thank you, Father."

Father Thaddeus stepped back. "You may read the material from the pamphlet but discuss nothing more."

I opened the page and started with the Lord's Prayer. "Our Father, who art in Heaven."

Olivia joined in with me, "Hallowed be thy name."

Father Thaddeus left us. Waiting until he was out of earshot, I whispered, "Why are you compliant?"

"It allows me time to heal. I truly am a sick woman, but not as he thinks."

We discussed what the *waters* did for her. Her filtering organs, her kidneys, and her liver were failing. She told me she subsisted on a diet of ale and potatoes and needed to be cleansed. I was shocked she would consent to be tied to the chair, but she reported the purging would make her violently ill, and she often saw apparitions and fought with her mind for what was real. When I asked her why she did not stop consuming alcohol, Olivia said she desperately wanted to, but the drinking helped stifle the nightmares of her past that she'd survived but still plagued her.

Sensing I could not fully understand the torn identity Olivia described, I dared to ask about the asylum girl. "Olivia, a girl is here in the hospital. I've seen her once through her window. Her name is on a grave in All Saint's Graveyard, but not her full name. It said *Amelia*. Do you know her? Do you know how she came here?"

Olivia held me with an unwavering stare. "Her first name is Felicity, but it's such an unfair name, for it means good fortune. She is one of the forsaken—an undesirable."

"We are connected." I pulled at the neck of my dress to reference my scars.

She scooted backward in her chair and became tremendously agitated. "*There once were three sisters, and now only two . . . of two, there are three.*" Her eyes fluttered, and white foam crusted around the edges of her mouth.

I shook her arm. "Olivia. Olivia!"

She held my gaze with clarity for a moment and seemed ready to speak. But then her eyes rolled back, and she shook violently. Before I could get more from her, Father Thaddeus and Ann were beside us.

"She's shifting," Ann declared.

Father Thaddeus dragged me toward the door. "It is time to go. I don't want Serenna and Max to see this. It may contaminate them."

I craned to watch her. I was frantic to know the connection between Felicity and me.

If she was now Olivia or *Mother Shipton*, I did not know. But she certainly was beyond helping herself, and I felt terrible guilt for leaving her there.

I could not rid my mind of her baffling riddle. . . *three sisters, and now only two . . . of two, there are three.*

SPRING, 1796

Companion

Light Attributes: Loyal, tenacious, unselfish
Shadow Attributes: Misuses confidences

Some experiences are unforgettable, no matter the effort to erase them from the mind. I nightly dreamt of Olivia—strapped to the chair, her feet in the ice bath, the festering defecation beneath her. Her riddle tormented me— *three sisters, and now only two . . . of two, there are three*. I moved mechanically about my day, bracing myself for when my mind would float back to the asylum and hold me prisoner to the lingering unknown. My daily wakefulness focused on answering the growing questions around me, including Felicity's well-being and Father Thaddeus's uncharacteristic cruelty. He'd inquired whether I might revisit the hospital, but thankfully, chores kept me restricted to the house.

Besides my curiosity for Felicity, Father Thaddeus, and Olivia—*Mother Shipton*—I longed to know what Harewood meant. Henry was never far from my mind, and although I would never admit it to anyone, including Max, I fantasized about his return and him somehow being the answer to all my questions and perhaps a path to the life I wanted—a secure home, and a sense of purpose beyond the scullery. Once I would have been happy with a service job for life, but my encounters with Henry had made me long for more.

March brought surprisingly mild weather as the sun dwelled longer in the sky. If it rained, it sprinkled shortly in the mid-afternoon, and the sun returned to warm the walkway, leaving a fresh smell to greet the evening. We opened the windows to circulate fresh air and rushed to ready the house for the new owner, which helped keep my haunting images at bay.

Mrs. Connolly reserved the day for canning and pickling. It needed collecting ice for chilling. I sought the icehouse's dark sanctuary and took my time to fill baskets with ice.

A crescendo of clamoring pans echoed from the kitchen windows as I closed the door to the icehouse. While inside, Samuel had bolted up the walk. "Come help!"

I debated whether to lug my load or abandon it. At first, the commotion seemed a typical encore of Mrs. Connolly's kitchen mishaps, but Samuel's reaction signaled something worse. Flinging my basket of ice chips aside, I dashed up the path.

My chest was tight when I arrived at the back door. Two maids blocked my view of someone's groaning from within. I rushed down the stairs into the kitchen and struggled to see around a huddle of people kneeling over Mrs. Connolly. I scooted someone away. "Let me see."

It was Camilla. Her presence brought relief, for she could fix anything, but it also raised the alarm in me. She looked at me. "Serenna. Do you remember when Lou burned her hand a few years back?"

I immediately understood her reference. An ill-tempered suitor followed Lou, one of the older girls, home after a night of soliciting. Trying to capitalize on his investment when he felt unfairly short-changed, he surprised her from the kitchen shadows. During the struggle, he bumped an oil lamp, lit several dishrags on fire, and set his sleeve aflame. Camilla and I happened on the commotion in time to keep the kitchen from going fully ablaze, doused his minor arson, and smothered his sleeve in a heavy tablecloth. The event permanently wounded him. A cold compress could not ebb the fire's fury upon his skin. The memory of the man's inflamed and blistered hide turned my stomach.

My eyes welled at the idea of Mrs. Connolly being injured similarly. "Is she burned?"

"Aye, but not by a straight fire. It's metal, worse in a way," Camilla commented. "Do you remember what we need?"

The irony made me feel sick. We needed ice. I tore back to the icehouse, praying my work from earlier had not melted in the sun. I was relieved as a white mound came into sight. A little dirtied and resting in a shallow puddle, the ice melded together solidly enough to place the ice chips back into the basket in one gesture. I stumbled over my skirt as I waddled back to the kitchen.

Camilla supported Mrs. Connolly on a stool as Ann tripped cool water over her hand. Knowing my role, I tipped the ice in and watched it bob in its suspension. Realizing it would take too long to melt, I snatched a butcher's knife from the center cutting block and assaulted the hunk with sharp, successive blows.

Mrs. Connolly shrieked. "What are you doing?"

"The water cools faster if the ice is in pieces, or she can put her hand between the bits." I assumed I was right but had never actually tested the idea. After more slices at the block, the ice floated in a slushy shell.

Camilla gingerly unwrapped a dishcloth from Mrs. Connolly's hand, revealing a darkly scalded mark. Mrs. Connolly endured Camilla submerging her hand. The tightness around her mouth relaxed, and she slouched over the edge of the sink. We took a collective breath of relief as the height of the crisis fell, but we exchanged questioning looks.

"Olivia can give real healing," proffered Samuel.

Ann's scowl shot accusations of shame through us, much as I had stabbed at the ice block. "You mean your little *Mother Shipton*? How can Father Thaddeus allow her presence here? She is evil, and it is sinful to seek her help." She retreated to the stove, careful not to touch anything. "I refuse to allow you to taint our Mrs. Connolly. If you do, I will tell Father Thaddeus, and you will all be out of work and locked away for your thoughtless suggestions."

I watched Ann with perturbed curiosity. Despite being the least trustworthy, her pious approach was ill-timed and too hasty, ringing false.

I was astounded that Olivia could have been strapped in the asylum months ago and now be back to her everyday life. "She's at your cottage now?"

"Of course. It is her weekly visit to Harewood," Samuel replied plainly.

I watched each of their faces, searching for understanding.

"They let her go when she's no longer mad," Ann said.

Camilla tenderly placed a hand on her shoulder. "Ann, you are right about us not wanting to entertain the healing practices of a renowned witch . . ."

"Hardly renowned."

"Olivia has ointment that would ease Mrs. Connolly's pain." Camilla paused in anticipation of our acquiescence. "Besides, as you told Serenna, she's no longer insane or would not have been released. She is of no danger to Mrs. Connolly."

Ann held a hesitant posture. "Father Thaddeus would need to bless whatever touches our dear Mrs. Connolly, especially to ensure her speedy recovery." There was a twinkle in Ann's eye. Her suggestion had advantages. The basest was a reason for her to seem the heroine.

"I couldn't agree with you more," Camilla said. "I don't suppose it is too much to ask that you fetch him, or would you rather I have Serenna run the errand so that you don't exert yourself?"

She took the bait. "Renna has done much already."

Samuel retreated to the door. "Let's get more ice, and we can go to my cottage. Olivia is there now. We should give her time to prepare."

We each dealt with our jobs and were reunited at the stables. Samuel and Allenor balanced Mrs. Connolly between their shoulders. She grimaced in her pain. Her skin was sallow, and her lips were dry and cracked as if she'd been hours in the sun. I huddled close with a hay-lined basket brimming with ice and wrapped a chunk in a cloth. I pressed it to Mrs. Connolly's hand. Although not as soothing as the ice bath, it was better than allowing the flesh to continue cooking.

Father Thaddeus and Ann, both winded, arrived at a hurried pace.

Father Thaddeus' face contracted tightly with tenderness. "Here, let me take Mrs. Connolly." He shouldered her weight as he and Samuel singularly progressed around the arch of the lake toward the garden.

As we followed in step, I wondered about Max. I had not seen him since the hospital visit. Whenever I attempted to locate him at the church, he was unavailable. "Father, is Max not joining us?"

"No." Ann snapped. "He must earn his place."

I wanted to whack her.

Father Thaddeus tilted his head but didn't take his look from me. "Ann, what example do I set if we are all away and Max remains behind?" He extended his hand to her as though presenting a communion wafer. "May I ask a great favor of you? Will you please fetch Max? He is in my study copying my sermon for this week."

She said nothing as she nodded compliantly.

Humor played dangerously at the corners of my mouth, and I concealed my delight with a cough into my apron. Ann glared back and forth between Father Thaddeus and me before hurrying toward the church again.

Camilla gave an amused look. "I think we must keep going for Mrs. Connolly's sake."

We maintained a steady pace, which was still slow, given Mrs. Connolly's condition. We were midway around the lake when Ann and Max appeared.

Father Thaddeus greeted him. "I thought you could use some time in the sun. Today has brought us an unexpected outing."

Max had dark circles under his eyes and deep creases around his mouth. From this vantage, his expression vacillated in the midday light, mixing with the shadows of waving tree leaves. I felt sickened that my time at Harewood House had improved my station, health, and access to knowledge, while Max seemed aged and withered, wrecked, and mistrusting.

Max eased close to me but did not take my hand. I wanted to spirit him off into the forest. "Thank you, Father. I have completed your sermon, and it is on your desk. Can I carry anything?"

Father Thaddeus guided us toward Samuel's cottage. "No, we will manage." We were silent as we finished the rest of our trek.

Songbirds, a bubbling brook, and our scuffling shoes sounded our arrival. Father Thaddeus and Samuel coped sufficiently, but something about the journey left Camilla spent.

She mouthed breathlessly, "Find Olivia."

I rushed to the cottage door, and Olivia surprised me when she swung it wide before I knocked. "We need help."

She stared at me blankly. "I could sense that."

I reached for her, hoping to use the moment to ask what had plagued me these last months. "Olivia, may we speak?"

She scuttled beyond me and down a small path to the lake, disregarding me as though I were no more than a breeze moving through the trees. Part of me wanted to snatch her up and demand that she explain her riddle from the hospital and what she knew of Felicity. But the other part of me needed to be away from it all, to be free of the growing pressure.

After glancing at the group, Olivia directed them to follow her back to the cottage, leaving Max and me alone with Ann. Seeing my opportunity to distance us, I headed for the lake's edge, presuming Max would follow. He did. Thankfully, a backwards glance showed Ann going toward the cottage.

Max and I strolled along the lakeshore toward the shade of a weeping willow. Although the spring weather was warm and the reemergence of sunshine welcomed, I didn't think Max could manage the direct daylight for too long. He had a ghostly effect, and I feared he might evaporate.

Finding a niche in the lakeshore, I sat down on a dry boulder and signaled for Max to join me. A shallow stream babbled into the lake, singing a tune for our respite. I playfully removed my socks and shoes and plunged my toes into the water, letting out a squeal of shock at the chill.

A smile scratched the corner of Max's lips.

"Something funny?" I flicked water at him with my foot, splashing him more than I intended.

At first, frozen in a wide-mouthed expression, he quickly transformed into rueful friskiness. "You'll get yours." He kicked his shoes onto the riverbank and strode into the lake, socks and all. Tugging off his shirt and plunging it deep into the water, he flung it at me, smacking me in the face. It stuck to my hair like al dente pasta glued against the kitchen tile wall.

Wrenching his shirt from my head, I was warmed by his laughter. Waist deep in the water, head turned high with hilarity, his coloring faintly improved. He morphed back into my little brother. Clutching my chest with mirth, I fought to maintain my balance on the rock and landed bum-first in the lake, right next to him, water cascading over him. When I sputtered to the surface, the newly baptized Max was hooting and pointing at me in amusement.

"You are a mess," he playfully scolded.

My cap hung low over my brow. Branches and damp leaves clung to my tangles. Although thankful for the momentary joy, the frigid water chilled me, and I sought the sunshine warming the dry riverbank. Trudging my way out and marking the sand with deep footprints, I collected my shoes and huddled on the shore.

"Where are you going?" he shouted.

I removed the outer layer of my dressing and was clad in my shift. I stretched the dress over a warm boulder, hoping it would dry faster from the heat beneath and the sun above. Nestling into the earth, I began the daunting task of combing my hair through with my fingers. Max scooted alongside me and stripped off his outer jacket and trousers, leaving him in thin shirt and knee-length pantaloons.

I glanced at him, and he at me. His familiar smile made me feel we might look every bit our age and, for a flash, had roused the children we once were.

Max knelt behind me and began working on the tangles, starting at the top where I could not reach. I echoed the efforts at the end. Eventually, we would meet in the middle. I rubbed stretches of slick green slime from my hair. I stifled a gag as I thought of its sickening texture.

Max lingered at the collar of my shift, drawing it low to the middle of my back. I stiffened, knowing what he studied. He tenderly traced the length of the scars. "It's very purple at the top," he said, fingering a bump near the meat between my neck and shoulder. "This must have been the hottest part." He touched lower, tickling me slightly as he progressed toward my spine. "It gets lighter as it goes down. If I didn't know it was a burn, I would imagine the claw of a lion tore you diagonally from shoulder to waist."

I enjoyed his image. Surviving a lion attack made me a warrior.

His warm cheek brushed over my shoulder. Tenderly, he breathed down the length of my back to the end of the scar. He pressed his chin against me and bruised me as he neared my neck again. He collapsed onto me in an awkward embrace, his mouth closed in on my skin, much like I imagined a tired child would resign itself to a mother. I scooted away, although I felt the instinct to hold him.

He protectively tucked his left arm in his lap. He appeared to be a fully intact, non-maimed boy from most angles, including my current vantage. We locked eyes, his functioning hand still resting on my shoulder. He slowly revealed the stump of the other arm. I had forgotten how shocking his raw appearance was—a petite boy with a blunted left arm stunted below the elbow joint.

"Max, why are you so pale?" I reached for him, but he balled up.

"I don't know. I eat, and I sleep. My job is to watch and write, but I'm always tired." He shriveled as he spoke.

Ire welled up in me. "There's something wrong. What does Father Thaddeus feed you? Maybe you're not supposed to see what he exposes you to."

Max glanced at me with a look of shame. "Renna. I have learned about the asylum girl, Felicity. She had a whole family. She had a mother."

"The grave—I know—Cassandra."

"And she had a father too. From what I can tell, he is, or was, French." Max folded in on himself, striving to conceal the rest of his speculations.

"Do you think she might have other kin? Brothers or sisters?"

Max looked long at me. "I have something I have to show you."

"And what would that be, my dear?" Camilla appeared from a tree's shadow, a short distance from where we sat. She shouldered Mrs. Connolly, aided again by Samuel. Her intrusion halted us both.

Mrs. Connolly donned a heedless expression and an unfixed stare. A soft-footed Olivia was in tow, her eyes keenly trained on us. She curiously no longer limped or used her cane.

Max stood and faced his mother. "Nothing."

I struggled to maneuver my shirt over my exposed shoulders. Watching Camilla's expression, I missed what Samuel or Mrs. Connolly might have seen.

Camilla considered us both before commanding the group. "Samuel, how about you and I get Mrs. Connolly back to her room?" Camilla speedily hustled her girth down the path and away from us. I wanted to inquire about her neglect of Max all these months.

Olivia came behind me. "You are baring your mark?"

THE CURSE OF MAIDEN SCARS

"It's not a problem." I rebuffed her as I dressed.

"Dearie, this is a dangerous scar. You know that?" Olivia touched the top where Max said it angrily flared purple. "You must keep this covered. Your scars tell stories."

Her rising concern diverted the conversation, robbing Max of his opportunity to share his news and souring our play.

Max inquired. "Who?"

Olivia's tone was dramatic, but it achieved her desired effect. "I had already discussed this with her when we first met," she said. "Only the unfit would be scarred as she is." She motioned to Max. "It won't take long for someone to draw their conclusions about how you were both malformed."

I touched her hand, still resting on my back. "Thank you, Olivia. We will be careful."

The snap of a branch and the clumsy plodding of Ann through the bush interrupted us. We held still. "Isn't this a peculiar picture?" She paused with a cunning smile, she retreated into the shadow of the trail along the river.

Despite Olivia's warning, protecting myself from suspicious inquisitors appeared impossible.

Warrior

Light Attributes: Toughness of will
Shadow Attributes: Trading principles for victory

In the days following the lake incident, I was jittery and tried to avoid Ann at some moments and seek her out at others. We had come to an unspoken truce in the last few months, but her uncanny timing—the church, the library, the locket, and then at the lake with Max—left me worried she sought to cause trouble. I had met her type before and knew I should not dismiss my instincts. She'd perceived something, and I had to know what it meant to her.

The mild weather that allowed our day at the lake had passed, and rain now daily drenched the ground, leaving the earth soggy but very green. It was weeks until Easter, and life at Harewood had become dull and draining. As it was Sunday again, and I was expected at church, my feeling of foreboding was enough to keep me in my room and prevent me from venturing out. Still, the opportunity to see Max, learn what he'd found, and mull over recent events motivated me to explore All Saints Church. I hoped to be alone with him before the service. I might have an advantage if I entered through the graveyard and avoided attendees filing through the front door.

I found the tunnel for the churchyard and cautiously plodded up the damp stone steps into the open lawn. The sky's grey matched the greyer tombs, and I felt sad as I eased through the plaques and the dew-licked grass. Before I could go further, my skirt snagged. My hand brushed across a cluster of wilted thornapple to free it. The thorns scalded like a lit match against my skin. I kissed the mark to will away the burn as I

THE CURSE OF MAIDEN SCARS

peered across the yard for onlookers.

Reaching into my bodice, I clasped the locket hanging by a length of leather I found in the laundry. I dared to wear it on the days when my mood soured. It nestled low on my breast, concealed behind my shift, shirt, jacket, and cloak. I was sure the gift was from Henry—but it could be Donovan. I loved the necklace but I secretly hoped it was Henry. I kept the burlap tucked in the waist of my pantaloons for fear of its discovery during a room search. I had yet to decide if it had a more significant meaning. The *British West India Company* somehow seemed more relevant to Donovan.

I settled squarely into the damp earth, weaving around the tombstones towards Cassandra's grave, hoping a more concentrated study would help me understand her history. A large oak branch partially shielded me from the slow drizzle. Shrugging my cloak from my head for a better look, I read the name: *Cassandra Serenna*.

I ran my fingers over the engraving at the top. It was like the lion's crest on the locket with the same initials. I tugged on the leather thong and reached into my blouse for the locket. The low light allowed me to see the lion and the jeweled inlays where bright sapphires glistened. Turning the locket over, I found the ebony compartment again and fingered open the flap. I thumbed the wad of tied hair in the slot, longing to know its owner. Although I couldn't prove it, I knew the locket, the grave, and I were linked.

Cassandra's tombstone lacked a birthdate, listing the date of death: *Died, 9 October 1782*. A tremor ran through me as I connected the pieces of her story. Her little Felicity Amelia would have been a year old at her mother's death. I drew in a troubled breath and considered the haunting fact that Felicity was a forgone conclusion, destined for this plot of soil, and squeezed the locket as though it would solve the mystery.

A shadow passed into my periphery, and Max nestled with me into the damp earth. "I'm glad I found you. I have something to show you. Come while Father Thaddeus is busy." He looked down at the necklace. "I can't believe you're wearing that."

He was right. It was utterly ridiculous to wear the necklace, but it had become my talisman for channeling my past and perhaps my future.

Tucking it furtively in my dress, I followed Max around the church's rear to the side door covered in ivy, dropwort, and moss. He inched open the door just enough to squeeze through a gap and softly closed it behind us. Once shut, my senses adjusted to the darkness. The congregation's sounds crept under the door gap between the main church and the antechamber. If I could hear them clearly, they might also listen to us. My hunch must have been correct, for Max silently waved me up a narrow flight of stairs.

We ascended to an office space built into the rafters, stacked high with piles of parchment, scrolls and books, candle nubs, and ink quills. Particles of dust swirled in the light from the window. I squeezed to the side, as the space was designed for only one person, and given how packed it was, one only as small as Max.

"Is this where you have been all this time?" I was saddened by his isolation and better understood why he never seemed healthy. The cramped space, dank with no direct light, was blanketed in grime. Rodent feces dotted papers on the desk. The smell of mold was penetrating. "This is an unfit place for you to work."

He looked at me with a tired expression. "I'd give much to go back to the life we had. But I suppose once we know something, it can't be unknown." He busied himself, searching for something in the room's far corner.

Allowing him a moment to find what he needed, I fingered the rim of a teacup with tea leaves stuck to the bottom. Tasting the residue left a bitter flavor, faintly smelling of celery. I ran through the catalog of my memory, struggling to remember the specific combination of characteristics. I couldn't recall the name, but my instinct screamed it was poisonous. "Is this the tea from Father Thaddeus? I'm certain it's toxic."

Max shrugged. "It's not like I can say no." He returned to rummaging.

I was disgusted that my friend was only made worse in a role meant to shelter and protect him. Trying to distract myself from a growing wave of rage, I looked at a mass of papers near me and focused on names and dates listed on long wooden sticks protruding from the pile stacked to the ceiling: *Bradford, 1763. Bolton, 1772. Keswick, 1751.*

Curiosity spurred me on, and I stole a page from the top of the nearest pile.

THE CURSE OF MAIDEN SCARS

Name: Cecily Appleton

Admitted: 7 September 1791

Age: Thirty-four.

Age of first attack: Thirty

Married, single, or widowed: Married

Occupation: Milkmaid

Religious persuasion: Church of England

Previous place of abode: Leister

Nearest known relative: James Appleton (husband), Leister

Attack: Third

Insane: Three months

Supposed cause: Alcohol, cowpox, death of two infant children, possible evil possession

Facts observed by Father T. Humboldt: Interest in household affairs nearly nil; paces incessantly, claiming need to return to work and to feed her children, blisters on palms and fingers that spread when she touches other parts of her body, memory impaired, unable to tend to personal daily needs like washing and eating.

Mental State: Third visit to the asylum. First two admissions were brief (one week) cured with isolation and restraint. Current stay admission exacerbated by alcohol. Patient walks halls at night, screaming for her children, and inflicts harm on herself. Husband reported she is unfit to care for the family and a danger to them and herself.

"Max. What are these?" I placed the page back on the pile.

He defensively retorted. "I told you. Father Thaddeus visits houses of the insane where people are locked away, sometimes for nothing more than fighting an abusive husband, other times for being mute from birth or otherwise undesirable."

I nodded, uneasy about where the conversation might go.

"Do you remember the woman I showed you in the church when we saw each other after arriving at Harewood House, the one whose husband settles her in the pew before the congregation assembles?" He shuffled through a stack to his left and retrieved a half sheet of paper. "Read this."

> *Name:* Janelle Minny Ashton
> *Admitted:* 31 October 1790
> *Age:* Twenty-seven
> *Age on first attack:* Twenty-six
> *Married, single, or widowed:* Married
> *Occupation:* Miller's wife
> *Religious persuasion:* Lutheran
> *Previous place of abode:* Leeds
> *Nearest known relative:* Miles Ashton (husband)
> *Attack:* First
> *Insane:* Thirteen months
> *Supposed cause:* Brain impediment
> *Epileptic:* Yes
> *Suicidal:* No
> *Dangerous to others:* No

> *Facts observed by T. Humboldt:* Reported history of consistent mood and moderate levels of intelligence before accident. Told she fell from the barn loft onto the grinding stone. Hit head and crushed left arm. Although able to return to duties, with no apparent residual injuries, unable to respond to verbal or written directions. Was literate before accident. Husband reported unwilling to seclude her to asylum. Patient was released to his care.

"Unbelievable." As I handed back the page, a shudder raced up my back. "I suppose her husband should take care of her."

Max replaced the page and went to work on a different stack. "It might be better than leaving her in the asylum. But he still considers her a *dutiful* wife."

His suggestion sickened me. Did the woman even know what

happened to her? I watched Max struggle with the pages and was dismayed that my sweet friend worked so hard, despite his handicap. I imagined how much more difficult it made his endeavors. He clutched a single sheet to his chest and tentatively tipped it in my direction.

I noticed the page but was more irritated about Max's passivity. "How can you help him? Especially if he is hurting people?" I wanted to whisk us away from the growing danger of our seemingly privileged opportunity more than ever.

"He's not bad. He sincerely believes the devil pollutes the insane. He tries to counsel and heal, but his superstition still influences his methods."

I snatched the page Max held away before he could secure it. "What is this?"

"Wait," he shouted as he scratched at me, and I moved the page from his reach.

Name: Cassandra Serenna Covert

Admitted: 4 February 1782

Age: Twenty-three

Age on first attack: Twenty-three

Married, single, or widowed: Married

Occupation: Housewife

Religious persuasion: Catholic

Previous place of abode: York

Nearest known relative: Desmond Covert (husband) unable to locate. Two sisters, also unable to identify. Two children—girls, ages nearly one year and three years.

Attack: First

Insane: Nine months until death 9 October 1782

Supposed cause: Not known

Epileptic: No

Suicidal: Yes

Dangerous to others: Yes

Facts observed by J. Pullman: Immobile most days with little responsiveness to stimulation. Burn scars on hands and face. Confined to bed. When verbal, she screams indiscernibly. Thought to . . .

I turned the page over, looking for the missing information, finding nothing more. My frenzy grew, and I pushed Max back and held the page to the light, searching for any writing that might have been rubbed out. "Covert?"

He seized it and slid it under a pile on the desk. "You now know what I know."

"Why did you take it?" I clamored for the page. There had to be more. "I want to read it."

"There isn't more to read. What is important . . ." He touched my arm gently. "What is important is your relation to her." His fingers closed over my skin. "Can you guess?"

I knew the answer deep in my heart but needed visual proof. "This is the mother, the asylum girl's mother."

"And?"

"Cassandra Serenna Covert. This is *my* mother. That means the asylum girl, Felicity, and I are sisters." I touched the locket again, thinking of the engraving C. S. C. "And this belonged to her."

"Exactly." He clasped my hand in chilled fingers. "And if Felicity is in the asylum, and your mother is dead," he nodded toward the window. "You might get hurt if someone discovers you're her daughter too."

"I don't understand why. I've done nothing . . . all this time." Admitting I had a sister, one interned in the asylum, and a mother, who now had a name, buried in the grave warmed and frightened me deeply. "I have a family."

He squeezed my hand. "You've always had a family. I don't know the full tale and can barely piece it together myself but being connected to her . . ."

"Felicity. Felicity. Felicity!" I was filled with panic and excitement. "I have to see her. I have to share what I know. I have to comfort her."

Max eyed me soberly. "She is in there for a reason."

I gasped and held myself from striking him. It was unfathomable that a child could deserve such inhumane confinement. I studied Max's flat expression, searching for evidence of compassion. My mind bounced from thought to thought: *He's been poisoned. He's repeating what he was told. He's involved in a ruse.*

"Max, Cassandra had sisters. Who are they? Where are they? Maybe they can tell me why all this happened. And there's a husband—my father?"

The stair below us creaked, and we froze. I glanced around the room, but there wasn't space to hide.

Sweat collected on Max's upper lip. "This will be bad." Admirably, he pushed his little body before me, pinning me against the desk.

An angling form stepped from the stair's shadow and absorbed the office's remaining space. Dim light highlighted Father Thaddeus' tight brow as he came in, leaving no area to maneuver. "Do tell me why you might be up here." He grimaced. He lacked the warmth from previous encounters.

I tried pushing Max aside. "Max was showing me some of his work."

"Max." Father Thaddeus said in a drawn-out tone, his eyes darkening with anger. "You know better than to share what you discover."

"She's a friend. She's good." Max tenderly fought me for a position closest to Father Thaddeus. "I think she can be helpful, Father. She is learned."

Father Thaddeus held stock still, utterly impervious to our reasoning.

"I wouldn't tell anyone." I adopted a more confident pose. "I don't know anything anyway. I wanted to see where my friend has been working."

"You are a bad liar. I am on God's mission to rid our community of the unclean, and you reek of sin and mistrust. Mrs. Connolly has explained that you might be of issue to Harewood House and me. I understand you're marked." Father Thaddeus cocked his head to the side as though he could see right through my dress to my burns.

"I'm maimed too. What about me?" Max spat at him.

Father Thaddeus' expression calmed. "Dear boy, you are harmless. I have ensured that. I appreciate your skill, and your lame arm means you'll never find a better position than I offer."

I clutched Max's hand, knowing that we had to leave with every fiber of my being, and soon.

"You are intelligent." He glared at me. "And well-read. A learned girl is surely malevolent."

I stared, amazed at him. "You always treated me kindly."

"Things have changed." His shoulders slackened, and his presence deflated, slightly less sinister. "Mrs. Connolly and I have discussed the health of Harewood House and how to continue my work of cleansing the community. She has a friendship with Olivia and believes Olivia might be cured of her affliction if you were also treated. I do not comprehend the association, but she says Olivia has been much ailed since your arrival. And, I also realize you have family already confined in the asylum." Father Thaddeus blandly explained his reasoning as though giving direction in a sermon. He looked at Max. "If it weren't for your discovery, I would never have pieced them together."

Max tried to defend me, leaning in closer, bringing us into a tight huddle in the room, and forcing our faces to look up. "She's innocent, Father."

I thought confessing my newfound knowledge would provide reprieve. "I don't know how I'm connected to Felicity."

"You're lying." Father Thaddeus grabbed the neck of my dress, and his fingers wrapped around the hanging length of leather. Pulling tightly, the leather dug into my skin, strangling me. I slapped Father Thaddeus's hand to shake him off as I felt the blood in my neck pulse around the tightening band.

Max yelled. "You're choking her."

Father Thaddeus pulled hard on the leather. "What is this?" He brought the freed strand and locket, raising it high for inspection. "I know this." He glared at me like I'd stolen the piece from a sacred shrine. "It's been many years, but it is enough evidence to bring your presence into question." He stepped into the shadow, and the energy in the room settled, signaling an opportunity to escape.

Father Thaddeus reemerged, holding a round mallet by his shoulder. "That necklace belongs to an important family. I've seen it travel from

England to Venice, exchanging hands with ill-fated women whose blood and souls are surely contaminated with the same sins." Father Thaddeus's expression was cold and unfeeling.

At that moment, I was terrified of him.

"My experience demands I deal with you myself."

He brought the butt of the mallet down on me. That was the last I recalled.

Exorcist

Light Attributes: Freeing from devastation
Shadow Attributes: Fear of facing demons

My face ached, and my neck felt like it might snap as I struggled to lift my chin off my chest and fought to open my eyes. My right eye was glued shut. The sight through the left was like peering through a grimy window. I couldn't move either arm. Thick leather bit my skin and bruised my wrists, strapping me to a rough, splintered chair. I strained to discern my surroundings. At first, there was little to hear, an occasional door squeak or heels clapping down the hall, but otherwise, the air was thick, stale, and silent.

I was in the asylum, but this was not the sitting room where I'd found Olivia. A slight breeze provided the tranquil illusion of being outdoors. Olivia's room had been crowded, full of other convalescents. Here, I was very alone. I was sure of it. Chill coated my skin. I wasn't wearing my outer dress, clothed only in a thin sleeveless shift and no pantaloons. Panic made parts of my face numb, or it could have been the growing bruising.

I awkwardly tried to stand and move out of the moldy hospital corner. Thankfully, my feet were not in an ice bath, but my ankles were strapped to the legs of the chair. My heels hurt as I squirmed. My mind raced to recall what Father Thaddeus said. The memories evaporated like whiffs of smoke. Pressure around my eye throbbed, and I longed to explore my wound with my fingertips. If I couldn't see what befell me, my fingers could read the damage. I bent my head lower, but a confining strap across my chest held me upright. I flung my head about, which only advanced the headache.

A loud voice announced, "She is having a fit."

I stopped struggling and turned toward the voice.

"Oh, how sickening. What happened to her?" The same pitchy voice questioned.

"This happened when she was detained." Father Thaddeus's silken tone rose in my ears.

Although he'd been soothing in our past encounters, his image with the mallet was forever seared into my memory. I now felt a wave of horror as I was trapped and utterly helpless to his whims. I wondered how he'd hurt me next.

"I suppose if the devil entrances her, we should not be surprised that she fights. Give her the rye mixture. We will then know why she is here or if she intends to lead our good congregation astray." An icy fingertip touched the top of my shoulder. "Ann, I cannot believe you all had not noticed her markings for all these months. These are obvious signs of sin."

Ann placated. "Father, if we had known, we would have brought her to you."

"You are naïve. I am beginning to doubt your skill and strength to serve the Lord. If it had not been for Mrs. Connolly, Renna would still be a poison to our souls. Give her the rye," he barked, entirely out of character from the man I'd known. "I will do my rounds and then return. This mixture has worked in the past. I cured my first patient in Venice with this rye, and she was able to return to society. Sadly, she ultimately chose a sinful life."

"Do you think her other companions know of her danger?"

She asked the same thing I was thinking.

"Perhaps the woman, Camilla, but not Max. I have checked him myself for markings of evil. Although he bears that stump, he is with me daily, and I know his soul to be pure. He drinks my tea and never falls away from his duties. He is no danger to us and truly serves me in my study." Father Thaddeus's voice trailed off, and I heard his shoes click away.

I was relieved, and my breath returned as I heard him walk away.

That was quickly replaced with seething anger when I realized I was alone with Ann. "You bitch. You said something to Mrs. Connolly. She could not have seen my back that day by the river."

"No." Her voice softened, and she moved closer.

I turned my face toward her, hoping my grotesque features would keep her at bay. "Don't touch me."

Her delicate touch found my arm and tightened on me. "Please, Renna. I know we are not friends, but I want to help." She pulled on the leather strap. "I promise. I want to help."

I recalled our first meeting and her treatment since. "But you have been so cruel."

"I am sorry. But if I had known you were like me, someone trying to redefine your life's role, I would think I would have treated you better." She released a long breath. "They fastened you in tight. Can you move your fingers?"

I stretched out my hand. Although my forearm ached—and I was sure the buckle left a deep gouge—everything seemed to work.

"You came to us mysteriously. When I saw your wounds by the river, the burn, I knew your body was misused." She took an audible breath. "But there was something about how you handled yourself over the last few months that made me wonder if we might be friends." Although I couldn't see her, I felt her grinning. "I stay close to Father Thaddeus. How else am I to keep *my* secrets hidden? Keep enemies close and all."

Her words began to sink in. "I'm not a prostitute."

"But the book I found in your room, *Aretino's Dialogue*. And then Captain Moore, he wants you—or he's had you."

"The book was a gift. And I didn't pursue Henry."

"You are definitely unclean, whatever you protest."

I conceded that she was trying to position me as a buffer rather than a foe. "But what about Mrs. Connolly?"

She pried at the other strap, and the buckle bruised me. "This one is tighter. We must free you, or I think your purple fingertips might turn permanently blue." The band released. "She saves Olivia from being consumed by this asylum. Mrs. Connolly and Samuel keep alive her persona as *Mother Shipton*, something advantageous to everyone. Mrs.

THE CURSE OF MAIDEN SCARS

Connolly needs *Mother Shipton* to stay tied to her Tom, to talk to him during her séances."

Motivations were aligning, but I couldn't piece it all together. "The day by the river, you were angry about Olivia taking part. Why do you have sympathy for her now?"

"She really *can* tell the future and the past. Although she is mostly Olivia when she comes to Samuel's cottage, we risk her being *Mother Shipton* before Father Thaddeus. He'd put her in the asylum if he saw her that way and never let her out again. We all do our part in keeping the real dangers at bay. We all need her intuition, even me."

I wiggled the circulation back into my hands. This made sense. Mrs. Connolly needed to stay connected to her Tom, and the Harewood House staff loved their fortuneteller. I had known survivors my whole life. None could ever really be trusted. "And me?"

"There is a rumor you may be more than an orphan turned maid."

I winced as I explored the spongy flesh around my swollen-shut eye. I wondered if my cheekbone was broken. My scar-free face was one of my only gifts. I worried I'd never look normal again or if I'd be lovable with a disfigured face. My right eye seemed fine, but it was obstructed. "Why can't I see?"

There was the sound of water trickling into a bowl, and Ann dabbed my face with a cloth. "Blood is coating one eye, and the other is swollen. You must have hit your face Father Thaddeus confronted you." The compress was soothing. I pulled at the lids, and a splash of light came through. I blinked my surroundings into clarity. Ann's face was ashen and sorrowful. "I wouldn't have wanted this for you. I wouldn't want this for any girl. We women give up too much and are forced to take too many risks because the future is not secure."

I touched her hand as she cleaned me. "Thank you, but now what?"

She placed the rag in my hand. "I'm torn on what to do next." She found a flask in her apron. "Father Thaddeus wants me to give you this rye he makes. It's not exactly whiskey or true liquor, but it will put you out of your senses."

I looked up at her. "I don't understand."

She presented the bottle. "Father Thaddeus swears it forces a *possessed* soul to speak the truth, to reveal the evil within."

"And what if I don't take it?" I was inclined to hurl the bottle at the wall, shattering it and any chance of Father Thaddeus's plans playing out.

Ann slipped the bottle back into her apron pocket. "He will have more. If it is up to him, he will have you take the rye, and then I will be of no help to you."

I stared at her, puzzled. "Then why are you putting it away?"

Her face darkened. "Renna, despite our relationship, you would have to do something beyond repair for me even to consider giving this to you. It is rotten rye mixed with mushroom fungus. It will make you mad and wish you were dead in the same breath." Her voice softened. "I've seen one woman take it. She spoke in insane riddles and then slammed her head against the wall until she broke her skull." Ann's skin blanched. "She is in one of the isolation rooms down the hall and is left to mumbling and drooling, completely void of choice or power." She returned her cold stare to me.

My stomach clenched at the thought. "As it seems obvious you want to stay in Father Thaddeus' good graces, what are you proposing?"

Ann stared at me in earnest. "I must ask you to trust me as though we were sisters."

I dreaded my vulnerable state, putting me at her mercy, but I wasn't sure what my options were, even if I were freed entirely. "I don't want the details. Instruct me."

Ann found a different flask in her apron. It was round and ceramic, with a cork stopper. "This is also rye-based, very alcoholic. It will taste like whiskey, but it produces a different effect, one of euphoria. In the first moments after consuming it, you will lose consciousness. I want Father Thaddeus to think I gave you too much of his mixture, so he will wait to question you. It might give us a window of opportunity."

I took the bottle and watched Ann's face. "Why do you look as if the vapors will take you over at any moment?"

"This only works provided Father Thaddeus leaves after he sees you asleep. Then, I must find some way for you to escape. If he chooses to wait until you wake up, the medicine's effects will take hold, and you will answer his questions."

I gripped the edge of the chair until my fingers dug into the wood. My first choice might make me mad, and my second left me entirely in

Ann's power. Still, it was an obvious decision. Thumbing the cork top, I popped open the bottle and downed the contents. It burned the same as the first sip of whiskey. Having imbibed every drop, I stared her down desperately. "Get me out of here."

*****

My head was swimming, and I still couldn't see from my left eye when I came around. Ann supported my weight, but her body was too small to do much good. She smelled vividly of sweat and rose oil as she lugged me through the hall toward the front door.

I stopped us, pleading, "I have to see her."

"I know who you mean. Mother Shipton told me." Ann's expression sobered. "No."

I braced my hand against the cool tile wall. "She's my sister."

She pressed me toward the front door, but my weight left her effort inept. "As you wish, but don't chastise me after." Ann gripped my elbow as we went toward the back of the asylum and away from escape.

We occasionally paused to listen for passersby, but the path was clear. We finally came to a freshly painted door with an eye-level, square window. A chill ran through me, and regret tightened my heart.

Her blue eyes darkened like the last hues of a twilight sky. "Cover your mouth so you don't scream. The lamps are lit, and you can see her through the observation window."

I balled up my night shift and bit down on the gag. The bed was under the window, where Felicity and I had first seen each other. Heavy curtains were closed tight. Four oil lamps at the corners of the room enhanced the shadows.

Felicity lay supine on the bed, her ankles and wrists strapped to the sides with leather restraints. Clothed in a thin gown, her form was robbed of modesty, and her chilled nipples pushed high, the shapes discernable. Gauntly thin, her clavicle and hips protruded like small hills in a white field. The room must have been cold, for her blue-tinged skin left her seeming to lurk on the edge of eternity. I was horrified at the dark mound of pubic hair pressing against her gown and fought my urge to burst into the room and shield her. Her face was turned toward me. Grey and gaunt, her skin tightened around her jaw, so taut it seemed like it might tear. Her gaping mouth showed yellow-stained teeth. A deep purple gash arched over her forehead from temple to temple.

I snatched myself from the window, knowing what I saw was forever unforgettable. I retched, spitting out the hem of my skirt.

Ann wiped my mouth. "I told you, you wouldn't want to see her. Father Thaddeus said Felicity would stop hurting herself if she had a procedure." I slid down the wall to the floor. Ann yanked on my shirt and clasped my wrist, bruising where the buckle dented me. "We can't stay here, not after I told Father Thaddeus you had too much rye. Get up. If not for you, then for Felicity and me."

My head swam nauseously with anguish as we went to the front door, stumbled into the courtyard, and crossed the dirt drive. My legs would not comply with my need to run. I kept tripping over my toes.

It was twilight, and the shadows created pockets of darkness and played with my imagination. Feeling a sudden wave of bliss, I couldn't tell if the trees we passed were swaying in the breeze or dancing to some unheard tune. The gravel beneath our feet kicked up and settled back in dust puffs. It felt like we walked through a layer of powdered sugar covering a large confectioner cake.

"I feel so strange."

Ann prodded me. "You have to keep going. The drink has dulled your senses."

We made it out of the gate, the one once barring Donovan and me on that fateful day of discovering Felicity. I wished we had heeded the chain and lock, forgoing our previous trespass.

We silently walked toward the river, and I sobered in the cooling air. Wanting to vanquish the images of Felicity from my mind, I returned to the conversation we had while I was still strapped to the chair and asked, "Are you a whore?"

Ann adopted a crooked smile. "I was." I pulled away from her, and she burst into laughter. "And, I think you're like me, especially after seeing you leaving Henry in the library."

"You know that?"

"Of course." She led me down the lane like sisters on an outing. "I was once at the top of the Covent Garden's list. I was particularly good at my job."

"I don't know what that means."

"It is a London list that describes whores and details of their specialties." She smoothed the length of her bodice. "I am well known for my *exotic* tastes."

"So you're a maid now but a whore before. Are we alike, and you were once an orphan, too? Seems unbelievable." She had to be part of the effects of the alcohol. I reached toward her cheek and pinched the satin-smooth skin. "Are you real?"

"As real as you." She pushed my hand away. "But no, I'm not an orphan. I have a well-to-do family, but they banished me. Let's say my maid position is penance, in a way."

I saw her in a new light. She no longer hid bitterness and malice. Instead, she was a petite bird protecting her delicate gifts, open only to those who would appreciate her beauty. The word *exotic* conjured a different fantasy, and I wondered what she meant by it.

"I've given away my virginity. Now I am a whore too, I suppose." My words slurred.

"Bedding Henry does not make you a whore, unless he paid you."

"He did give me a book, *Aretino*." I'd work up in my mind that he loved me. It was precious, written more than two centuries prior. It had to be a sign of his love, his affection.

"That's a payment of sorts." She nestled into me for warmth.

It felt exciting to confess to her, but I was downcast at her insinuation. "Why are you at Harewood if you're good at your trade?"

A shadow passed over Ann's expression. "Let's say I suffered the fate most women do if we are not careful."

"A baby?"

"No," she barked, resuming some of her previous hostility. "I stopped using my head. I have a watchful brother, and he found me at Covent Garden. He said he wanted me someplace safe until he could sort things through."

"I'm very lost."

She gave me an irritated look. "My family is wealthy, but I made a mistake a woman of class can never make. I fell in love with a man beneath my station. Upper-class men can marry—and bed—whomever they like. But a girl must marry her equal or better. Why do you think so many women are alone? Their fathers refuse to be disgraced by an unfit union that will result in offspring belonging to men of an unfit class. Rich women marry men with titles. She moves up in society. He gets her money." Her eyes flooded with tears.

"But you get safety, too, right?"

"Damn your ignorance." Ann's expression railed against my unintended insult. "I broke with my family after they made my lover disappear. To spite them, I took my talents to Covent Garden. My brother found me not long after and brought me to Yorkshire. He's lovely but insufferable."

I wished I'd known she wasn't such an uptight twit. These last few months would have progressed differently if I had a confidant.

We walked silently as the sky faded from deep purple to an opaque sapphire. The trees created long shadows and an impending sense of dread. I clung to Ann for comfort. If someone asked me yesterday if I trusted Ann, I'd have answered *never*. Now, she was my lifeline to the next safe place. "Where are we going?"

"Knaresborough."

"Olivia . . . *Mother Shipton*. But I thought you said she's dangerous."

"*Mother Shipton* has spent her life supporting forlorn women."

This was the first time I'd noticed the difference in intonation when Ann spoke of them as two different women. The name *Mother Shipton* was said with deference. "Why do you separate the two?"

"You will see."

We approached Knaresborough from the opposite side of the river, giving us a full view of the picturesque town beneath a ruined castle. Mill-wheel paddles rhythmically splashed in a slow-moving river current and dim candlelight illuminated stone houses. We proceeded up a steep embankment. Perhaps it was the medication and my throbbing head, but the climb was unimaginably difficult. I fought waves of faintness.

I leaned into a tree to gather my bearing. "Please slow down. I'm afraid I'll tumble down the hill."

A sudden rustling of leaves startled me, and I stopped myself from crying out. For a moment, I saw Henry in my mind. Had he come to save me, to rectify his abandonment? I was surprised when Donovan stepped from the shadow and wrapped an arm around my waist.

He enveloped me in his arms, and his sweet breath brushed my cheek. "I've got you."

"Where have you been?" I melted into his embrace, and my sadness flooded from me in deep sobs. The tension and confusion from the last few months utterly vanished. Although I'd given my heart and body to Henry, Donovan brought balance to my world. I couldn't say it then, but part of me knew that if Donovan had stayed at Harewood, nothing for the last few months would have transpired—both good and bad.

He cradled me as he climbed the hill. "I'm here now." Nestling against his coarse, unshaven cheek, I listened to his draw and release of a long, slow breath. He stopped under a rock outcropping. "You have to let go." His voice cooed. He brushed his lips over my forehead. "The rock ceiling is too low, and you must walk alone."

I opened my eyes and stepped away from him on a sandy path. My vision strained in the pitch dark, but I didn't have to see to find courage in Donovan's presence. Knowing he was with me made my night's horror evaporate.

Mystic

Light Attributes: Reveals union with the divine
Shadow Attributes: Delusional understanding of divine

Bracing myself on Donovan's forearm, we passed a tumbling waterfall and followed voices resounding on the cave walls. The voices grew louder. Candlelight illuminated a lushly decorated room with thick carpets on the floor. Some were affixed to the walls. A pit in the middle hosted a roaring fire. Smoke funneled into the night air through a slanted roof.

Two women crouched together at a table by the far wall, and I immediately recognized one of them as Ann. Although the same size and general appearance as Olivia, the second woman left a different impression—wild, wind-spun hair, a grimy face, and torn clothes revealed parts of her body Olivia would have kept concealed. Barefooted and hunched in her chair with her feet on the edge like a sullen child, she rocked as Ann talked.

I eyed for clues about what to do and thought of my belongings. "Where is the locket?"

Ann's eyes narrowed, revealing her knowledge and a bit of bitterness. Reaching into her pocket, she pulled on the leather thong attached to the locket. "It took a bit of doing to steal this away. I figured it must be precious." She set the locket on the table and removed my *Aretino* book, pestle, and mortar. "I believe these are your things."

Before I could gather them, Olivia placed her hand over the locket. Her head snapped high, and she emitted a piercing, prolonged scream.

THE CURSE OF MAIDEN SCARS

Her howl continued, and we all covered our ears. As she calmed, I marveled at the length of her breath. She inhaled again and let out another long wail. Ann jumped from her seat this time and came to my side with Donovan. The three of us made a barrier at the cave entrance as Olivia screamed at the smoke. A third time her voice cried out with the howls of unfathomable anguish. She sounded like Felicity on the first night I saw her. Olivia bowed her head to her chest with energy spent. Ann and I held hands and turned to Donovan, pleading silently for understanding.

"Wait." He answered me without looking. "*Mother Shipton* is not done. The first part is her realizing what is important. The second part will be your commitment to the knowledge. And the third part will explain."

"Why is she now, *Mother Shipton*?" Olivia looked different, but how could she *be* different? Confused, I clung to Ann.

She shook me off. "Don't be daft. Can't you see she's a different woman now?"

Mother Shipton raised her head and pointed toward me. "You will make a promise."

I rattled in my boots, but I quickly agreed. "I promise."

Rising and speaking simultaneously, she moved toward me, seeming to float.

"You will need to go with her, and we cannot come," came Donovan's ominous command in a low, clear tone. "Whatever you say to her, or whatever she reveals to you, do not speak of it. Do you understand?"

This all felt unnecessary, shrouded in lore and the ridiculous. I chided myself for my judgment, but this was beyond any hallucination I could fathom.

Mother Shipton drifted up slick stone steps and waved for me to follow. I was careful not to lose my balance as the waterfall splattered onto the walk. Calcified objects around the stoneface projected from the water. The forms had conventional shapes of a cylinder and a wheel. A closer look revealed them as regular items. A boot still strung with laces and encased in a white, callused stone dangled from the ceiling. The Minster priest and I discussed the power of minerals. He had said water with a strong, sour taste often acted like hard water or stone. I outstretched my hand into the stream, tasting the droplets on my fingers, and noticed the sulfuric bitterness. *Quicklime.*

It took a moment to recognize a rhythmic clapping of *Mother Shipton* signaling me. She stood in a ledge's shadow. I moved away from the waterfall and toward the dark hollow. The pounding water from above quieted. She extended her hand. "Your promise." She grabbed my arm and instructed, "You will dip your hand into the water three times. The first is for your *mind*, the second is for your *body*, and the third is for your *heart*. Make your wishes carefully, for you will be bound to each."

The confined space, her voice, and the pungent stench of her greasy hair brought on a wave of nausea, and I couldn't focus on a balancing point.

She snatched up my hand. "Breathe. You will feel better."

It seemed unlikely. A bath in a thousand liters of rose and lavender-infused water could never rid my memory of her stench. Still, I did as I was told.

Mother Shipton's voice was even and commanding. "After you wet your hand and make your promise, I will tell you a fact. One promise for one fact."

I nodded.

"Most importantly, besides not sharing your promises and my facts, you must completely let your hand dry in the air. If you wipe away any of the water, you will wipe away the promise and information that goes with it."

I nodded again in the dark and waited.

Mother Shipton submerged my palm into a pool of water. The sharp cold washed over my left hand, and I tried to retrieve it, but she held me firm.

"Now, promise your *mind*."

My *mind*. What was there to say? I had experienced such confusion and been deceived. I scarcely thought myself capable of keeping a promise.

"Promise!" she commanded.

Silently, I vowed, *to my mind—I promise to make choices with even measure, clear of lust or craving, and as protected from fear as I may.* This at least seemed what my mind needed.

"Now . . ."

"Wait . . ." I added that *I promise not to make a permanent decision when my mind is clouded.*

"Yes, that is a better way of saying it." Mother cooed. "I approve of you starting with, *to my mind.*"

I gasped. "Can you hear me? Did I speak aloud?"

"No words came from your lips, but I can still hear you." She giggled a little, echoing the Olivia I'd experienced. "Now, your fact. *Your mind is your source of power. It is tied to your heritage and will lead you to your future, but it is also your master of fear. When you are clouded, you will fall.*"

I whined. "Isn't a clouded mind anyone's *source of fall*?"

She did not soften. "Now, promise your *body.*"

I sighed with exacerbation. "Very well." I closed my eyes and felt her dip my hand into the water again. *"To my body—I promise I will keep you protected, either by my will or someone else's."*

"Again, this is good. Now your fact. *Your body is your house of fear; only when the mind and heart work together will you conquer your fear.*"

I repeated her words in my head. She was right. My choices to this point, including lusting for Henry, were all body and little mind.

"And to your *heart* . . ."

Right, what did I want to promise to my heart? *"To my heart—I promise to know and love myself before loving another."* The words came without forcing them. It seemed selfish, but it was utterly genuine.

"And your last fact. *Your heart is for love but is also for power. Only the heart can truly know the difference in your motivation—love, fear, or power.*" She released my hand and stepped from the cove. The light of the moon shone on her. "Remember not to wipe your hand." *Mother Shipton* turned and slid away, leaving me to the cove.

Holding my hand high, I recalled what she had said. Her monkish statements irritated me. She said my mind was connected to my heritage, but I knew I would have to discover the complete tale of the necklace, Felicity and Cassandra, on my own. She said my body was my source of fear, and my mind and heart had to work together to protect me. I wasn't sure how that would happen. Lastly, the fact my heart would know my motivation seemed odd. Inspiration comes from the mind, something I was more willing to trust than my heart or body. I recounted my promises and her facts until they burned into my memory. Hoping my hand was dry, I tested the edge of my finger with my cheek.

I returned to the cave and found Ann, Donovan, and *Olivia* sitting around the table by the wall. Olivia's transformation was remarkable. Her hair was tamed, and her clothes were restored. She even donned boots laced halfway up her calves. She spun the locket between her fingers and lifted it to the light for observation. Donovan hummed something as he sipped a glass of whiskey. Ann played with the tips of her hair, sorting through its broken strands. The scene was uncannily ordinary, considering what occurred earlier.

Hysteria rose in my chest. "What are you all playing at?"

Ann came to embrace me, but I stepped back. "Renna, after *Mother Shipton* left, Olivia returned to us and said you were in the alcove and to wait."

"Olivia?" I studied the old woman. There were a few echoes of *Mother Shipton*, but this was undoubtedly my friend. She hobbled to me, far from the deftly balanced, barefooted *Mother Shipton* who had glided around the cave.

"Dear, please come sit." She seated me by the fire. "The glint of gold in your eye shines bright. I want you to have some whiskey. We must develop a plan. You cannot stay here."

The cup tasted like the mineral waterfall from the outside. On closer inspection, I realized it was coated in the hard water. I wondered if the water had an ill effect, which would explain the link between *Mother Shipton* and Olivia. The whiskey burned boldness into me. "Have you seen what they have done to my sister?"

Coming to my level, she placed a hand on my thigh. "You must leave and find your answers where the source of this originates."

I glanced from Olivia to Donovan and back. "But to where? And alone?"

Ann piped. "I can't go back to Harewood after helping you."

Donovan stood before us and breathed heavily like he'd run a race. "We will go to Venice. I have business there and will sail within the next fortnight."

Ann gleefully turned about to an unheard tune. "Venice is ideal."

Donovan averted his eyes. "Camilla has said she has acquaintances there."

I raised my glass to Olivia, Ann, and Donovan. The three met my cup mid-air in a solid clink of stone and glass. I hiccupped. "But what about the locket?"

Olivia interjected. "The locket is quite important."

"I know it was Cassandra's, my mother's."

She nodded. "It was gifted to her. But now, you are the rightful owner."

I snapped. "You must tell me more,"

"Renna." She placed her hand on mine. "In truth, I know not of the tale."

Her refusal was infuriating. "Unbelievable! You are *Mother Shipton,* for Lord's sake. How can you not know?"

Ann, Donovan, and Olivia all reeled back. Olivia slumped down against an inverted crate. I searched their faces for answers. It was bewildering that Olivia did not recognize her alter ego, the hag who had moments ago led me to the well to make my wishes.

"You, too, have been told of *Mother Shipton* and how I resemble such a woman. But I assure you"— she cleared her throat—"I am simply an old widow, one never given the blessing of a living child."

"My apologies. I shouldn't insist on what I do not understand." That seemed as honest a retraction as I could muster. I tied the locket around my neck, which familiarly weighed on my chest. Looking at Donovan, I asked, "Now what?"

Donovan pushed himself into a heavy woolen coat. He handed a smaller one to Ann. "We will leave for the docks at daybreak. It will take me a few days to ready the ship. We will make several stops on the way to Venice, and the journey will take over a month."

Olivia approached me with an oversized cobalt cloak. It brushed the ground as she placed it around me. She fastened the garment around my throat and helped me slip into my arms. A damp smell emanated from the elegantly decorated wool. Although pristine, the cloak was dated.

She finished her ministrations and whispered, "Travel safely, and remember to keep your promises to your *mind, body, and heart*."

Architect

Light Attributes: Designs resolutions
Shadow Attributes: Solutions disregard emotional consequences

The soothing warmth of the fading afternoon sun gently woke me from a deep dream wherein I searched the asylum halls for Felicity, with Ann and Olivia at my heels, only to find her in the arms of *Mother Shipton*. Then came the image of Henry, his grey eyes, wavy hair, and svelte form. He smiled at me, but I was confused, unsure if I was what he smiled at. And Donovan, he was ever the presence of strength. I was comforted by him. I knew he wanted me, but he did not captivate me like Henry. I felt torn. I'd thought at the time I'd wished someone—one of them—would save me. *Mother Shipton's* messages haunted me. I was beginning to think any saving I'd have would come by my hand and choices.

I tried to blink away the images in my mind and welcome the light of reality, but my left eye would not open. I strained to draw myself into the sunlight, but the movement shot through my skull with excruciating pain. I let out a groan.

Camilla came to me. I couldn't see her clearly, but her warm scent of vanilla and soap pacified me. "Let me help." she put a cup to my lips. "Drink."

My right eye was now just a small aperture. I recognized a pewter cup as she pressed it to me. I drank water, but it did not quench the burning thirst in my throat. I tried to take in more liquid but spit it up in a cough.

"Shh. You need to try to quiet yourself. The men on board won't appreciate a woman's cries as they prepare to get underway."

"Where are we?"

Camilla continued, "Hull, but will be leaving soon. Donovan has stayed the departure for a day more until we can ensure you are stable for the trip. Your condition has wavered. Father Thaddeus's concoction was mixed into the bottle Ann gave you. I can't begin to know what has poisoned you." She touched my face with cool fingers. "It will be a long journey to your next home." She sounded weak. "Drink, darling." She stroked my head.

In all my time at Harewood House, I saw Camilla only briefly. "Where have you been?"

"I was sent back to York." She settled beside me on the boat's deck and gingerly laid my head in her lap. "But now it is time to leave England."

"Donovan said it is for Venice."

"I have resources there. And Max, he was born there."

My aching head interfered with my senses, leaving her message confusing. I hadn't known Max was born abroad. "Why would you leave Venice?" I asked. I felt sickened by her expression as I watched her. "There's more, isn't there?"

She nodded. "I moved to Venice long ago to watch after my sister. She did something that changed our family. We had to leave England. Our father sent us to Venice, for he was an investor in the British East India Company. The rest of my family moved to Massachusetts." She paused and gazed down at me to see if I was listening. "I wouldn't go back if I had a choice, but I can't think of another place right now where we can start over, and where someone will help us. I wish we could stay here, but Father Thaddeus will find you." She stopped petting.

"Why am I such a threat to him?"

"Max told me you saw the note about your mother, her confinement years ago, and how you've met your sister. Father Thaddeus's predecessor was responsible for secluding your mother. Father Thaddeus oversees Felicity. From his training in treatment for the insane in Venice, he believes that lunacy is hereditary and contagious. He thinks if one person in a family is insane, they all are—that if a demon has possessed one family member, it will infect a whole community. I can't allow him to lock you up. He deeply believes in his endeavors, however ill-guided they may be."

The image of Felicity strapped to the bed burned into my mind's eye. "But she's a child."

"Felicity has endured treatments Father Thaddeus learned abroad, using heavy metals and tinctures. His treatments serve more as poisons than cures. As her health declined, he resorted to more extreme methods. The local doctors are more prone to surgical approaches than prayer and medicine."

I recalled my time in the asylum. "I didn't witness much prayer when I was there."

"I suppose not. We are fortunate that Ann freed you." Camilla stiffened.

I mistrusted her role in my adventures. "Why would she help me?"

"Olivia, or *Mother Shipton*. Ann believes her prophecies."

I recalled *Mother Shipton's* predictions at the well, the cave, the asylum, and Samuel's cottage. "She keeps referencing my family but never shares much. When I first saw her in the asylum, she mentioned something about three sisters, but it didn't make sense."

Camilla looked at me as if a chill had passed through her. "I can't tell you what she meant. I'm afraid the mystery of Olivia or *Mother Shipton's* mind will have to await discovery on another day." She slowly rocked me. "Little love, I need you to sleep. We have to ensure you are well before we depart."

*****

Her soothing efforts must have worked, for I woke again to the sound of waves lapping against the side of the ship. Feeling like we were floating away, my stomach turned and panic set in. Although I didn't recall dreaming, the image of the asylum, Felicity, Olivia, and Cassandra's grave, was as clear to me now as ever. If we had left already, I could not learn of Felicity's fate, comfort, or mourn her.

The sun had not fully set, leaving a rim of sapphire blue along the horizon. The water slapping at the hull drummed with stretches of sail dancing in the wind. The water in the bay, dark and turbulent, forewarned an impending storm. A few straggling men tied down the cargo and secured the sail fixings. The ship was large, highlighted by three vast masts and a deck half the Harewood courtyard's length. The vessel was made new for our voyage, with clean floors and freshly painted trimmings.

I had full vantage of the dock and shore. We were not sailing yet. We were securely bound to pylons in the bay and swimming distance from the most outstretched dock. I didn't know much about ships, but this beast needed its space. My instinct to find my way back to shore and to Felicity evaporated as I acknowledged I couldn't swim. Weary again, I closed my eye to the water's vastness and focused on the breeze. For a moment, I was transported to a calm place, where everything from the last few weeks seemed a detached nightmare.

Settling into the ship's motion, I strained to recall my promises to *Mother Shipton*: *Mind—choices in measure. Body—stay protected. Heart —love me first.*

Darting off to find Felicity, particularly in my condition, did not respect my mind's promise or keep my body protected. As for love, although guilty and pity played with my motivation to seek out my sister, holding my place and sailing with my friends answered *Mother Shipton's* call for self-preservation.

"Enjoying the evening air?" I blinked open my eye to find Ann crouching in front of me. "Can I get you anything?" She inquired.

I reached for her. At first, she did not move, looking me over but finally taking my hand in a gentle clasp. I squeezed her fingers. "What happened?"

"We need to get you inside before we talk. Also, I want you to have some medicine." Without asking, she pulled a slender vial from the waist of her skirt and tipped it to my lips.

"Are you keeping me sick?" I recoiled at its metallic bitterness. It tasted like what Ann had given me in the asylum.

"Good God, no." She sternly stared me down. "Father Thaddeus poisoned the liquor I gave you, and then the alcohol at *Mother Shipton's* cave worsened things. You have been in such a state, saying the most absurd things about love, fire, and graves."

Even if I pieced together the timeline, from Father Thaddeus' office, Max, and the archives to the asylum and *Mother Shipton's* cave, I couldn't remember it all.

"Have a sip, enough to dull the sickness." Several drops touched the tip of my tongue, and she tucked the vial back into her apron. It took some effort, but she had me on my feet, urging me into a room under the main deck.

Candlelight highlighted a narrow vase of fresh flowers on a table next to a big bed, topped with plush bedding and a portrait of an attractive woman. The woman looked like the female from Henry's first dinner party, the one with the feather. Ann romped around the bed, arranging pillows before easing me down to nestle between them. The pressure in my neck was much relieved.

"You must be weak from the asylum mixture, but your head has something wrong. Your eye is still swollen. Lie on your stomach with your good eye on the pillow. This will hopefully help the swelling." She spoke with strict authority.

I shuddered as my body cooled in the enclosed room. Lifting my right arm, as the left one felt deeply bruised, I explored my hair and found it neatly tied high.

"If you are going to check yourself, it is better to see your reflection and not inadvertently poke something tender." She came to sit beside me. Holding up a mirror, she asked, "Ready?" before tipping it to me.

My mouth watered with anticipation. The first look made me gasp. My hand went to my eye, but the movement was too quick, and I felt a sharp stab in my back. The left eye was completely swollen shut, and the bone, from eyebrow to cheek, was raised to the width of a walnut and stained dark. I stared back at myself, finding my glint of gold in the right eye faintly glowing and seeing my face was unscathed except for the bruising.

"From what we can tell, the bones are not broken. We cannot know for sure, but Camilla said keeping you steady for the next two weeks will be imperative. No severe sneezing."

The mention of Camilla made me think of Max. "Is Max all right?"

"He is fine. He is improving since being away from Father Thaddeus's office," she reported calmly. Setting the mirror down, she brought me a cup of water. Palming it in her hand, she continued. "Camilla says your head seems rattled. I told her you came to the asylum like this. Do you remember how it happened?"

Her question was straightforward, but I couldn't recall the memory. Closing my eyes, I focused on the pain in my head and remembered Father Thaddeus' office with Max. So many things happened at once. Our interloping laid the foundation for a shocking revelation. My mother was buried in the churchyard. My sister was in Bootham Hall. Then I saw Father Thaddeus' stunned and betrayed expression. He was angry, but he was also scared.

"Father Thaddeus, he hit me on the cheek with a mallet." I sipped the water as fatigue tempered my thoughts. "I'm tired."

"You might as well rest. I've been told Camilla has a job for you when you get to Venice." Her face tightened with a saddened look, but I didn't trust my observations. "I am resourceful and expect to find a place in no time."

Bile surged in my throat and garbled my words. "What does that mean for Max?"

She stood and replaced the stool. "A gimp will be of little use where we are going, but Camilla said she has something. We will sail, hopefully within the day."

"We're leaving? You've changed everything," I rasped.

She cast an angry expression. "I thought you'd be grateful I rescued you. And you have your Max and Camilla." She went to the dresser, retrieved a leather-bound book, and tossed it into my lap. "Here's your precious book."

I didn't have to read the title to know it was *Aretino's Dialogues*, the book Henry gave me after our time together. "Have you read this?"

Her face held a peculiar expression. "No, but I want to."

Before I could ask more, the door opened, and daylight chased away the shadows, causing the candle flames to dance. Donovan's massive physique blocked the doorway. He walked into the room. "This is not your cabin, either of you."

"Let me help Renna." Ann was by me, snatching up my arm and the book in the same motion, tucking it into her apron near where she'd produced the vile. "I think I might take it off you now, as I suspect I have already experienced what the pages describe, and you seem in no condition to read." She hoisted me up, and we hobbled toward Donovan.

He held open the door, careful neither to touch me nor formally regard Ann. "Both of you will sleep downstairs. Be careful not to disturb the men." He met my gaze directly. "I can't protect you from them all." His eyes, cold and unyielding, were changed dramatically from our first encounter at the Board Inn and from what I remembered at *Mother Shipton*'s cave.

"Are you angry with me?"

He cast me a disgusted look and moved away. "It seems you have made new friends while I've been away." He glanced briefly at Ann and looked back at me. His look penetrated me deeply as his brow furrowed, taut with both ire and despondency.

I cringed when he said *friends*, for I knew he meant Henry. I pushed out of the room, glancing back to see Donovan glaring at me from the shadows.

Ann hauled me down a narrow stair and into the hull's darkness.

"What did you tell him?" I said.

She returned my stare. "Nothing. Now that you and Henry are acquainted, perhaps a life in Venice is what you're made for." She retrieved the book from her apron again. "The tales here, of nuns and wives and whores, will give you an idea of how life goes there."

"Why do you talk in riddles?" I huddled into a ball.

Max joined us. "I told you she was hateful."

It was hard to see Max in the dark, but there was spirit behind his words, like nothing I'd heard from him at Harewood. I inched my fingers up his shoulder and pulled him into an embrace. "You're here. It would've been impossible to go the next step without you."

"I told you we are always meant to go together." He pecked me on the cheek. "Come. I'll show you our room."

We staggered to a narrow cabin door. Rosy light illuminated the room through a window lined with delicate curtains. A low-slung hammock swayed on one side, and a bunk bed was tucked into the opposite wall. Max helped me onto the lowest cot.

"Who gets the hammock?" I asked

"That's mine." He played with his untamed hair. "You get the top bunk once you can get up alone."

Ann barked. "And what about me?"

Max stood at his full height. Although slender, with his clavicle holding up his loose-hanging shirt like his shoulders were a hanger, he had an air of authority. "You can stay here, but I think you won't find it difficult to slither into someone else's bed."

She lifted her arms like an actress at the end of a performance. "But what if I'm feeling out of sorts?" She nestled next to me on the bed. "We can share, right?"

Max's face was bright with mirth. "You will sleep on the floor." He snatched a blanket off the hammock and threw it on the boards for effect. Dust billowed like whirling clouds.

I watched my friend. "Max. You seem so much better."

"I am. I don't know what Father Thaddeus put in my tea every morning, but I've improved since leaving. Whatever Father Thaddeus's motivation, I don't care now. I'm so pleased we are leaving England." Max twisted a blade of grass between his teeth.

Hot tears welled in my eyes, and I despondently cuddled in, inflamed with fever and exhaustion. "Max, it might be easy for you to run away, but I can't forget what I've seen.

"Looking back serves nothing." Ann tapped my shoulder with the edge of the book. "How about I distract us with some of *Aretino's* experiences. She opened the book to a marked page. "*Speak plainly and say, 'fuck,' 'prick,' 'cunt', and 'ass'. . .*"

"How can someone talk so?"

"You're an orphan. You know people speak rapidly and to the point. Let me finish, '*If you want anyone except the scholars at the university in Rome to understand you. You with your 'rope in the ring,' your 'obelisk in the Colosseum,' . . . your 'key in the lock', 'your bolt in the door,' your 'pestle in the mortar'. . .*"

Max burst into laughter. "Renna loves her *pestle and mortar.*"

"Max!" I felt outnumbered.

THE CURSE OF MAIDEN SCARS

"Come now, Renna. As you told me when we left the workhouse, *you know how things go for children like us*. And I do know." His words burned with judgment.

"Get used to it. The lifestyle in Venice is more refined than the London alleys, but the lusts and acts are the same." Ann demurely stroked her hair. "I think I might find someone to try *key in the lock*. Perhaps Donovan is willing." She bowed and swiftly left us.

My stomach tightened as I imagined Ann finding Donovan and climbing him as I had Henry, dominating him as Henry had me. Nausea rose again, and I wanted to perish.

Max patted me. "She'll make her way around, and the men will be sick of her." He pulled back to look me over. "Why do you care about Donovan?"

Tears overwhelmed me. "I don't know, but I feel very alone now."

"I'm with you. I'll always be with you."

The reassuring pressure from his little hand was enough to relax me into a deep sleep. My last thoughts were: *English to Venetian, orphan to daughter, virgin to soiled, maid to . . .*

VENICE, SERENISIMA REPUBLICA VÈNETA

AUTUMN, 1796

Explorer

Light Attributes: Passion for experience
Shadow Attributes: Compulsive need to keep moving

Our sailing from Hull to Venice took a month and blurred with the past year's events. Memories of the workhouse, the scullery, and the asylum plagued me like a festering illness. Although physically healed, my mind was a battlefield of confusion. The childhood I'd never understood was more confounded by a family history I'd barely begun to know. I had a living sister and knew the fate of my late mother, but there had to be others, more family to discover. I'd never dared to dream of having a real connection to *my* people, to be the orphan no longer, but leaving England meant leaving that all behind.

In the moments when my mind quieted, I thought of Henry. He was my illusion, my princely knight, who had intervened in my life. If Mother Shipton's prophecy had merit, I'd have to learn to love myself before relishing the love of another. But, oh, how the thoughts of him chased away my sadness, if only for a moment. In the rare minutes when I was not ruled by fear or fantasy, my sober mind reminded me that girls like me don't get happy finales.

Only in the last days of our sailing did I realize Venice might give opportunity for my other secret desire, freedom and power. Venice meant a new beginning, but what kind was still unknown. I'd hoped the next turn of fate meant genuinely finding my place in this world and perhaps discovering real love and a connection to a community all my own.

The bell atop our ship's mast steadily clanged in tune with the waves' crest and fall. Lulled by the motion, I set *Aretino's Dialogue* in my lap and closed my eyes to the titillating images in my mind. Thankfully, his descriptions often distracted me from my haunting dreams.

Knowing I had to prepare to disembark, I opened my eyes to the surprise of a great bird swooping low and landing on a nearby guideline. The miraculous beauty of a petite owl perched before me. Its talons clamped tightly around a squirming rat.

Ann stepped from a cabin beneath the ship's helm. "You have a naughty expression."

She played with the lace edges of a deeply plunging neckline to a bright orange dress made from wool and satin. She had piled her hair high at her crown in a mound of curls. Elevated shoes made her look as tall as an average man. She had transformed from a tiny hellcat to a reveling socialite, and I studied her jealously.

In our crossing, Ann had captivated Donovan at every port. His comforting protection slipped away from me. Watching him succumb to Ann's lusty solicitation during our sailing sickened me. She represented so many things I could not be.

I didn't realize I was staring when she quipped, "You might want to wipe the corner of your mouth. Slovenliness is not in fashion." She gave a gentle twirl for me to survey her efforts. "What do you think?"

I couldn't lie. "You look exquisitely beautiful." She'd blossomed into a princess of the night. All this time, she played the part of a bitter maid, but I could see now how she was bread with class and grace. "You will be the center of attention."

Upon landing in Venice, Ann's vaguely outlined scheme included integrating into the Venetian social elite. We both listened diligently when the status of the region's political turmoil was recounted at every port from Hull to Venice. Locals spoke of Napoleon Bonaparte's trek through Europe, conquering one city after another. It was not politics that made me wary. I had a mind for strategy and appreciated his lack of compunction. Rather, I was concerned about the role I would assume. Ann was a given. She would entice the nobles with feminine gifts, but what about me? Camilla said her sister lived in Venice. I assumed we would head to her home.

Camilla joined us. "We must get on our way. I don't want to be late." She'd been the most excited of us to get off the boat, and now she held a haunting expression as if a demon was riding her back. She gave me a disgusted look. "Are you still reading that?"

I raised the cover to her. "Is this true? About the daughters of Venice?"

She turned her back to me. "I've already told you, yes. Daughters of wealthy families whose fathers are reluctant to pay prospective bridegrooms a suitable dowry end up in convents. Annual donations prove lesser sums than funding valuable marriages."

She *had* told me. But I was still confused about her certainty. It was like she knew first-hand what *Aretino* reported 200 years ago. "It says nuns might have sex lives as varied as whores. That these women indulge in worldly, wild activities, but with sisterhood secrecy."

"Catholic convent laws from other Christendoms do not apply to Venice nunneries," Camilla calmly explained. "Some Nuns become pregnant. If so, they leave the newborn child on the church doorstep and pretend it is an abandoned infant, and thus raise their *foundlings* within the convent refuge, all funded by their fathers' *dotal alms*. Too bad they wouldn't let their daughters marry in the first place, giving the bastard children a name and a station in life."

Knowing women of all occupations—the poor in Yorkshire and the noble in Venice—might be locked away without cause made me question if my new city was merely an exchange of one confinement for another.

Chilled at the thought, I tucked the book into my dress pocket and watched the owl. The rat's tail weakly battered at the owl as its claws dug into the flesh. Its slowing movements became fatefully still. In one final dramatic effort, the rat lifted its head before relaxing into the maw of death. I hoped neither example, *Aretino's* nuns, nor the rat, was my fate.

Donovan appeared from below deck and stepped behind Ann. He gave her a once-over. "You look very pleasant." He'd been clear about not staying with us once we landed in Venice. Despite the emotional distance between us, knowing I would lose him left me deflated.

Ann slipped an arm through his. My stomach clenched at the gesture. "I need you to balance me down the plank." She teetered some, I thought, for show. "I must stay pristine." She kissed him on the cheek. Donavan stiffened against her affection.

Max's hard-soled boots thudded on the deck. "I've checked the lodgings as you requested." He looked at Donovan. "Everything is quiet.

I tried to cross the canal to the Ghetto as a shortcut back, but the gates are closed."

Donovan pulled a long leather glove from the back of his belted waistband and slid it on his arm. "Yes, every night at dusk. You'll be aware of that in the future. The Jews are not keen on Gentiles being in their quarters after dark. But, more importantly, there are dire consequences for the Jews if found on the other side of the gates after they are shut." Stretching his arm out, he clicked his tongue. The owl took one flap of its wings, released its kill, and hopped from the guideline to his forearm.

Ann recoiled. "Is it yours?"

Donovan stepped carefully towards me. His green eyes brightened as he watched me. "I hope some of your reading covered birds of prey."

Exhilaration quickly replaced my envy. I stretched to touch the owl. "It's beautiful."

Donovan's mouth relaxed. "There's another glove on my belt. Get it slowly." He waited for me to glove my hand. "Now, hold your arm firm. He doesn't like to perch at an angle." With my left arm outstretched, I held my breath. Donavan clucked his tongue again, and the owl stepped over to my forearm.

I realized I couldn't maintain the angle of its perch for long. "It's heavy."

Donovan drew a length of leather from under his belt. "Francese can seem a burden if you're not used to him." Donovan pushed the leather over my shoulder, securing it under my arm and back. "This will protect your skin, but you will still feel the pressure of his talons, perhaps to the point of bruising." He encouraged the owl to reposition on my shoulder.

I nervously thought of the owl's talons digging into my skin. The same talons that clutched the dying rat moments ago. I winced but settled into the pressure of its firm grip and awkwardly turned my head to spy on my new companion. I realized it would take only a moment for the owl, if it chose, to pluck out my eyes.

"I found him in the market. He's small for his size. Hunting birds are easy to train, as long as you have courage and are gentle." Donovan touched my arm. "And you are both."

"Thank you." I could not count my affection for Donovan as strict friendship, for his low steady voice with a lyrical Irish accent, brought the urge to curl into his lap and purr. Our bond was stretched these last months, but his words gave me hope, and his gift was healing.

He tipped my nose with his finger in a familiar gesture. "Your expression and sparkling gold in your eye tell all the thanks I could ask for. I hope you will know you're protected every time you see Francese."

I stroked Francese's breast and repeated his name. "Why is he called that?"

"It means *French*. It will offer a clever talking point with the current political climate."

Ann's manner altered from affably self-possessed to teeming resentment. "Are you ready? You're supposed to take me to the Casino."

Donovan turned from her. "I will help Renna down the ramp. Max, aid Ann. We don't want her stumbling." Donovan's steady hands gripped me. "Your hard shoes are not useful on the wet wood."

Although his care was comforting, his authority was irritating. I snapped. "I know that."

He held my weight with a single hand and anchored himself to the rope railing. We shuffled down the plank to land on the dock. He released me to a throng of people—the stench of fish and dirt—sweat and sadness—wafted from each passerby.

"*Attenzione!*" A girl glared up at me. I guessed her around twelve. She was of average size, with warm sun-kissed skin, the color of browned butter. "Don't raise 'ur fancy' brow at me." She bumped against me and made a bit of an ordeal about jostling around me. " 'ur in my way!" She struggled with a basket strapped to her shoulder.

Others paused to gawk at my owl, but none commented as they shuffled sacks, baskets, buckets, and rods from one end of the dock to the other. Vexed by the rudeness and a welling wave of nausea, partially from being on solid ground but more from the stifling crowd, I was suspicious when a stranger stood beside me. His immaculate garb, marked by a large yellow letter "O," caught my attention. He seemed a year or two older than me, but he held poised and knowing.

"It is time we make our way."

I uneasily readjusted Francese. "I'm not going with a stranger."

Camilla stepped between us. "No need for suspicion. This is Alistair. He will help us."

"And me too." A girl with dark wavy hair and delightful brown eyes peered from behind the willowy Alistair. I was relieved to see someone my age, although she was quite petite. "I'm here to help."

"This is Asha. She lives near me and insists on meeting our new visitors." Alistair eyed Francese. "That's a unique pet."

Asha stroked Francese's breast. "Owls are good luck. They mean you're guarded by wisdom." Her bright smile was infectious.

Alistair walked toward the main dock. I watched him with different appreciation, noting his cleanliness and directness. He was ordinary in every way except for wire spectacles atop a flat, blunted nose, which seemed smashed on his slender face.

I hurriedly followed in his path, noting Donovan on my heels. Camilla now had a firm grip on Max, leaving a solitary Ann to toddle behind. Donovan rolled his eyes and halted for Ann to catch up, letting her balance by the crook of his elbow.

We were at the end of the mix of people and mounted a short stair to a cobblestone alley. I looked back at our ship and the dock. From this distance, the people appeared like ants scrambling over food scraps. The vessel swayed next to it all, neither amazing nor foreboding. Even from the space we gained by crossing the dock length, it seemed the time aboard the ship would be nothing more than a memory.

Alistair cleared his throat. "We need to hurry. I will be in trouble if I'm caught out here."

I concentrated on the empty alley ahead of us. "Why?"

He pointed to the yellow 'O'. "I am a Jew and belong in the Ghetto," Alistair said plainly. "*Ghetto* is derived from this city, as it sits next to the copper foundry. The gates that keep the city's *filth* from mingling with the *God-fearing* citizens of Venice close at dusk. They are a form of punishment rather than protection."

I was confused by his influx of information. I couldn't muster a comment and stared at him dumbfounded. He grinned and pulled me after him. We filed one after another, winding through unmarked alleys and over bridges of assorted designs. So turned about was I that it seemed impossible to return to the docks.

Donovan shouted from behind, bringing us all to a halt. "This is as far as we go."

Careful of my balance for Francese's sake, I glanced back to Donovan and Ann, who clung to him as her triumphant captor. The look of them said it might be a long time before we crossed paths again, leaving me to venture into the next stage without them. I wondered if this was why Donovan gifted Francese, knowing he was leaving me, much like at Harewood House.

Donovan held my gaze in a heated and stern look before clasping Ann by the elbow and leading her down a side alley.

Max turned a curious expression to me. "That's it?"

I confirmed with a shrug of my free shoulder. I had to look away from Max's knowing eyes for fear of revealing my disbelieving tears.

Alistair placed an arm around me. Francese's steadiness and Alistair's clean scent, peppered with notes of clove, were comforting. "This is a small city. It may seem confusing now, turning this way and that, but it is impossible to avoid anyone or not find someone." He familiarly took my hand. "We need to keep moving."

We wove through a maze of villas, some barred by doors crawling with mold and rotting through, others freshly painted and open to bustling shops. Up and over bridge after bridge, we emerged into a courtyard with welcoming vastness. A cylindrical steal-capped water well marked the middle. Children danced about as their mothers chatted, ever watchful over them. The scene was safe and loving.

I inquired, "Are there many courtyards like this throughout the city?"

"We call them *campos*. This is where Venice's real-life plays out, not on the boats floating through canals and lagoons." He pointed to the façade over the open church doors. "This is the entrance to Santa Caterina, a convent for forlorn women, or at least women whose families have abandoned them to the church."

"That happens?" I was astounded that my new friend confirmed *Aretino's* account. "Do you know what they are like? Their lives?"

THE CURSE OF MAIDEN SCARS

Asha appeared. "Look for yourself. There is one."

She pointed to a strikingly dressed woman, donning high shoes and a long, sheer vale that draped over her shoulders. Her dress was a waist-synching bodice clasped around a shirt that opened dangerously low. Oversized billowing sleeves made her look like a floating bird rather than a sister of the cloth. An ornate gold cross emphasized her breast line. The woman looked nothing like the unadorned stern Christian women of Yorkshire.

I was entirely amazed. "That can't possibly be a nun."

"She certainly is," Asha said.

Alistair prodded us forward. "We need to keep going."

I observed the others in the campo. "How would anyone know you're a Jew?" Alistair and Asha looked much like the other young men and women around us.

He pointed to the 'O' on his shirt and the one on Asha's dress. "We are marked. We all wear yellow badges. Currently, 'O' is required. It stands for the *ostracismo*, or the ostracized. Only doctors, like Asha's father, can go unmarked. He can even wear a proper black hat." A facetious expression pulled at the corners of his eyes. "Come now. You will like the lady in your new home. If you're interested in convent life, she can share details with you, for she once lived at Santa Caterina."

After several turns around a maze of buildings, Alistair halted, exclaiming, "We are here. Please move back so Mother may see you." Alistair rapped his knuckles along the bowed and splintered door.

Another Mother? I wondered if this was an omen of hope. Francese's weight, although significant, quickly became a reassuring comfort.

Max shuffled his shoes. Camilla yanked him by the sleeve. "Be still." She paid odd deference to the forthcoming stranger.

The door opened achingly. Holding my breath, I anticipated a bent and derelict hag that would match the door to an equally old building—someone more like Olivia, *Mother Shipton*. Instead, well-manicured delicate fingers pulled at the door's edge, and it scraped across holed and dented tiles. With another tug, the door swung wide, and candlelight lit the foyer, revealing plush carpets and massive tapestries hanging from the far wall.

Poised before us was a sensuous and regaled woman. Her dark hair, streaked with thin silver lines, was tied intricately to her crown. Clad in a snuggly fitting velvet and silk dress dyed a dark purple harkening to the aubergine from Samuel's garden, the woman seemed to breathe vitality and exhale prosperity. I fought the urge to touch her. She tilted her chin as she surveyed our party. Her glance danced from Alistair to Max and Asha, pausing briefly on me, particularly my locket. But she fixed a deadlocked expression on Camilla.

Camilla dropped her gaze, garbling a greeting, "*Buonasera.*"

The woman purred. "It has been a very long time, Camilla."

I looked between them, considering the differences between Camilla's modest stoutness and the woman's slender confidence. Camilla suddenly appeared aged in a way I'd never known of her. This woman was everything Camilla was not.

She pulled Max in front of her. "Max, please greet Danielle, your aunt."

Danielle clasped Max's good hand. "You will call me Mother, as everyone else does." She leaned in to kiss Camilla's cheek but hovered over her, breathing, "Sister, welcome back."

Camilla's gaze seemed to burrow holes into the walkway.

"Please forgive our tardiness," Alistair interjected.

Danielle's expression softened. "It's fine, but how will we get little Asha back to her home?" A muscle down the center of her forehead tightened as she looked longingly at Asha.

Asha curtsied. "I know how to get through. It helps to be small."

Danielle touched Asha's hair. "Off you go then. Don't want your father worrying."

With a quick smile and a round of goodbyes, mainly to me, Asha did as Danielle bid and hurried down the alley. Her waist-length hair waved in her wake.

Danielle—Mother—eased intimately close to me and brushed her cheek over mine. She repeated the gesture on the other side and again on the first cheek, paying no mind to the owl still fixed on my shoulder. "You, my dear, are welcome as well. *Parli Italiano?*"

"*Si. Certo, le basi.*" It was true. I knew basic Italian from the Minster priest. The meaning of such heated moments was impossible to forget and poured spice onto the foreign tongue.

"*Eccellente.*" She pulled back into the foyer and waved a hand for us to follow. "*Per favore, mia casa è la tua casa.*"

Trickster

Light Attributes: Transcends convention
Shadow Attributes: Manipulates others

Mother escorted us through the foyer, pausing at a nude painting of a woman, gifting fruit to a heavenly being. "This was done by a local artist and loyal admirer, who thought it resembled me. What do you think?" She held herself in a gesture similar to that of the woman.

"You are far more stunning," Alistair cooed. I could've imagined him licking her hand and nosing under her skirts if he were a dog.

"It's lovely," I said. Mother was indeed splendid, but there was approachability about the woman in the painting that made me want to put my head on her lap. At least at the first meeting, Mother did not inspire the same reaction.

She spoke to Camilla. "Take the owl and find your rooms. I want to get acquainted with this one before we have dinner. I will explain the expectations of my house. You'll love the menu. Cici has made tripe."

Camilla's brows wrinkled. "Cici is a wonderful cook. Glad to know you still have her."

"I take care of my devoted companions," Mother's voice soured, and she pushed on large doors to an adjoining room, revealing a vast window outlined with books. "This way."

I was astonished by the vastness of Mother's library. I handed Francese to Camilla, barely mindful of giving her the length of leather on my shoulder, and hustled behind Mother. Relief rushed over me, for it was the first time I was free of the sea's salty suffocation in a month.

This library was different from those at Harewood House and the Minster, inspired as one might hope by the passion for a comprehensive private collection. At Harewood House, the library was not for a dedicated reader. It was an assortment meant to intimidate the nonreader—recognizable titles in pristine condition but with little coherence in theme—A dabbler's knowledge buffet. The Minster library was unprecedented, renowned, but inaccessible to the ordinary reader. Men created Harewood House and The Minster. A woman made this room. I excitedly cataloged a theme of titles ranging from medicine to curative herbalism, western and eastern history. And philosophical discussions, particularly about those sick of mind and body.

Alistair closed the doors behind us, making the space silent.

I was too amazed by the volumes of books, both on shelves and stacked about on tables. The room was fitted with a plush settee, large enough to function as a bed, donned with feather pillows and a fur throw. It took a moment to notice I was enclosed with two strangers in an inescapable space.

Mother rounded the desk, messily organized with stacks of papers and books, wine glasses, and candles. She gracefully lifted a lengthy sheet full to the edges with writing. "Please sit down," she nodded toward the settee.

Gratefully, I sank into the down-filled couch, soft enough to lull me to sleep if I let it. I was careful not to touch the purple silk with my soiled fingers. I craned my neck to take in the room. In York, books, knowledge, and learning meant a way out of an inescapable world.

Mother had titles I thought would never be displayed on the Harewood House shelves: *Les Liaisons Dangereuses*, *A Vindication of the Rights of Woman*, *Critique of Pure Reason*, and *Justine ou Les Malheurs de la Vertu*. *Justine* seemed familiar, but I couldn't place it. I noticed a book's bold lettering on the table next to me, *Current Remedies for the Insane*. This had to be a coincidence.

Instantly, I recalled the vivid images of the wooden chair in the asylum, Olivia sitting over her putrid bowl, and dear Felicity strapped to her bed. I thumbed the healed abrasion above my eye, evidence of Father Thaddeus' cruelty.

Mother reviewed her page, never looking up as she poured two glasses of wine. She retrieved a tall crystal beaker, half full of greenish liquid, tipped a few drops into the second glass, and swished it about before presenting it to me. "This will help with any discomfort."

I took the glass. "What did you put in it?" I sniffed the wine cautiously and smelled nothing but alcohol and perhaps a dash of vanilla. No matter, I decided, for I was thirsty.

"Laudanum. It won't hurt you in this amount but will allow you to relax." She escorted me back to the settee. "Please, let us talk together." Still poised and elegant, Mother exuded power. I submitted to Mother's authority. We settled on the couch, and I sipped the drink while she referenced her page. "I see here that you like to read and are quite independent." She touched the length of my hair.

I sipped the wine. "A priest in York taught me. He was thorough in my learning."

"A certain kind of education is not valued—for women. It is a rarity that we are afforded the opportunity. I was learned at an early age, taught by a proper governess in my father's home." She watched me, scrutinizing my every feature. "You are lovely. I appreciate the uniqueness of your eyes, particularly the glint of gold. She kissed my cheek as she leaned in to inspect me.

Her touch was off-putting, but I didn't feel the urge to protest.

"Do you know of your family?"

Enamored with my wine, I spoke into the glass. "I have a sister locked in an asylum, and my mother is buried at All Saint's Church at Harewood House." I looked at her face. An obscure vigor strengthened her eyes and complexion. "One is unfit, the other is dead."

Her gaze narrowed, and she moved back, cooling the space between us.

A ceramic doll on the table next to me—supine, naked, and detailing a man's form—captivated me. I collected it, awkwardly balancing it with the glass in my hands.

"Careful. It will fall to pieces if mishandled," Mother warned. She seized my glass and set down her page, scooping up the doll in both hands and showing it to me. "Here, you have to hold the base, and then you can take it apart."

THE CURSE OF MAIDEN SCARS

She rested the sculpture on my lap. Mother was right—I could lift the arm, and underneath were carved lengths connected to the abdomen. It took a moment to understand what I held. I touched the enticingly rounded surface. The image of the doll's manhood was as equally detailed as his face. I was tempted into stroking the thighs of the figure, wondering if she would think me uncouth to see what was beneath the portion of the packaged manhood.

She broke the tension with a light laugh. "You can look. It's not remarkably interesting."

Sliding a nail under a section of the marble covering detailing the doll's belly and sex, the stomach came free, showing mounds of organs and a serpentine intestine. "Do you know how it all connects?"

"Not entirely. I am fascinated by anatomy. As it is quite forbidden for us to study the inside of a body and is impossible while a person is still alive. We learn what we can from the local doctors and what has been written over the years. I am interested in the nervous system, which seems to connect intimately to the sensations." Mother watched the doll and appeared lost in her thoughts. "I was once interested in curative medicines."

"How do you know so much? The only people I have met who would ever consider such things are men, and they have dedicated their lives to learning—or locking people in asylums." I fought my instinct to touch and know Mother with my hands. She was the most attractive woman I'd seen. And for her to possess both knowledge and beauty seemed unfair. She was the house's mistress and true ruler.

"That conversation is not for tonight. I will leave it like this—an unwitting exposure to knowledge of mind, body, and heart has taught me to fend for myself." She gave me a long look. "I came to Venice, not of my own choice. I was granted redemption at the Santa Caterina convent and freed to find my way in life. At that time, the only avenue was as a courtesan."

She was, as Aretino's said, both nun and whore. Had she also been a wife?

"I understand you have experienced hardship." She nodded toward the page.

As I tried to put the doll-man-puzzle back together, her look eluded me, but I caught something in her tone and glanced up to find her deep brown eyes intently examining me. "You are speaking about the asylum."

"I am delighted to know you are not closed up in such a place." She took the doll and gave back the wine glass. "Some patients never get out." Her words sent a chill through me. "Try drinking more."

I sipped as she gestured to Alistair. "I think she will enjoy a bit of lemon, don't you?"

Alistair removed his jacket. He moved to complete her puzzling request out of sight.

Mother's voice leveled, and her tone sharpened. Her eyes and the muscles around her mouth mimicked the change. I thought the wine played tricks on my perception momentarily, but a check of her restrained posture confirmed my instincts.

"You will find that Venice has many dangers, including asylums, convents . . ."

"And the Ghetto," Alistair added.

She glanced at him. "We are careful who we make as both friends and enemies."

I drank the rest of the wine. Unsure of where she was going with her conversation, I took the opportunity to ask about Camilla. "When was the last time you saw your sister?"

"I see you don't have much guard of your thoughts." Mother's expression gave the impression of annoyance. "How old is Max?"

"He's two years younger than me, and I'm sixteen."

"Then, about fourteen years, Camilla gave birth before leaving Venice." Mother turned all her attention to me. "What do you know about them?"

A wave of drowsiness washed over me, and I found it harder to focus, but I was curious about how they allied. "I can't remember a time of not knowing them. I'm an orphan that Camilla shielded."

With a downcast gaze, Mother continued. "Camilla returned to England after bedding an unavailable man. She would not take my advice of terminating her pregnancy and finding meaningful work in Venice." Mother gestured around the room with a graceful bend of her wrist. "This place has prospects that don't exist elsewhere, especially for women."

My heart thumped a bit faster, and I longed to hug Max. The thought of him not being part of my story seemed impossible. Yet, I could tell how Camilla's life would have had more freedom if she'd stayed out of England. "York is dreadful, particularly in the winter. Do you know why she went back? Was it to flee Max's father?"

"He would not have married her but would have cared for them." Mother rose from the couch. "No, she left to address a tragedy at home. I told her it was none of her business and she should steer clear, but she did not heed my warning."

The answer was perplexing, and I wasn't sure if I now had the mind to understand the message Mother was telling and hiding, given the wine and laudanum. "Without Camilla, I don't know what my life would be like."

Mother laid her page and glass on the desk. "Very well. This may seem abrupt, but I need you to undress." She commanded me without compunction, leaving no room for argument.

"Pardon?" My thoughts were sluggish.

"I need to see what you are about." She took the glass. "I will help. I don't bite. At least I won't bite you."

My balance wavered, and I was again transfixed by her face, as white as the doll from moments before. My need for comfort was akin to what I had felt with Donovan, but she possessed the same commanding presence as Henry. I chastised myself for my sudden faintness. "Is it appropriate for you to ask that of me?"

"Perhaps yes, perhaps no."

"You like that word." Irritation pinched my throat. Henry liked *perhaps*, also.

"I want to inspect you. You'll live in my house, and I will know your condition."

"Am I a fish you're examining at the market?" I imagined myself nestled into a bed of ice, readied for scrutiny and consumption. "Your laudanum has an odd effect."

Mother reached around to untie my skirt at the back and was quickly at my neck, unbuttoning the blouse. Swiftly, she had my clothes in a pile around my shoes, and I didn't seem to mind. She stroked the outside of my arms as she held me in her intense expression, her mouth pleasantly tame. Her fingers brushed over my hair.

She eased me away from the settee. "I will keep your hair for another day, for that will take a careful inspection for lice and all. I understand that you have marks. That's of no real concern. We can use them to your advantage, but I want to see how they have grown." She pushed at my shoulders, and I faced away. "Very dark at the top." She touched the length of my scar. "It is an odd shape. I'm not sure exactly what it resembles." My back cooled as she moved away. "Alistair, what do you think?"

"Yes, very dark." His voice was shockingly close. "If petals were added, we could conceal the scar as the stem of a flower. It's fitting imagery."

"Lovely idea, but necessary only until she is known, then the rest won't care. It can be her signature mark if she does well—flawed but beautiful. As she tires of some, we can show the bloom off the rose." Mother chuckled. "Alistair, would you please look more closely, so we can understand what others will see?"

I held myself, waiting for him to touch the scar as she had. But that's not where he touched. His breath was close to my shoulder, and I felt pressure low behind my bum. He clasped me by my upper arms where Mother had soothed me. "I won't hurt you, but you will feel me. Don't struggle. This is not a fight."

I had trouble formulating my thoughts. I couldn't sense if there were danger. Under other circumstances, I would have fought against Alister's advances, but the laudanum in Mother's wine made everything feel acceptable. For the first time in years, I was absent of worry. Mother's library was my dream room, and a beautiful new friend now adored me.

He pushed in on me, and he found the space between my thighs, stretching to the tip of my budding sex. A wave of embarrassment washed through me when I realized Mother was still close by. I stiffened.

"It's all right. Forget about her and focus on me." Alister moved on me, comfortable and warm. His manhood rubbed against my womanhood but never entered me. I had a floating feeling as I relished his touch and smell, rich with lemon and lavender. I didn't know if my growing pleasure was due to Mother's potion or that I'd only been touched by the Minster priest and then Henry.

THE CURSE OF MAIDEN SCARS

Mother's voice was calm and sounded like a song on the wind. "Please turn her around."

Alistair turned me. I had to tilt my head to see his face. Without his glasses, he seemed young, certainly near my age. "You are beautiful. Your hazel eyes are a mirage of colors—a fleck of gold." He stroked the side of my cheek. "Maybe if things go our way, I can keep you mostly for myself." His message seemed remarkably loving for our short acquaintance.

Mother came to the edge of the settee. "Her expression is priceless. But now I want to see her look while in the act. Lay her down. If there is any fear, this will take too long."

Alistair pressured my arms but did not shove, asking permission for me to submit to him. By the expression on his face, he wanted me to want him. That was different from Henry. Amazingly feeling no angst, I sat on the settee, putting me at eye level with Alistair's manhood.

"It's so clean."

"Circumcision. You won't find that with all your men. It is a blessing to prevent disease and for sheer beauty," Mother said. She took a sip of her wine. "Do you want to taste him?"

"No!"

"Fine. We will leave that for a later time. Please lie back." Mother stroked the top of my head and eased me down onto the settee. My feet were still clad in my shoes, but I was naked and open to observation. "She is nice, is she not? That hair, both high and low, will have to be dealt with, but overall, she is in wonderful condition."

Alistair licked his lips. "Beautiful and fresh."

"Let's see how she manages you." Mother continued to stroke my hair.

Alistair came down on me. He parted my legs and eased the length of his body on mine. I could feel him, his chest pressing hard to my breasts, the rough hair of his thighs brushing over mine. "Are you ready?" He whispered next to my cheek. "The laudanum will make this nice."

He entered me. Although his body pushed me to the settee, I felt free and lost in the sensation of our skin. He moved against me, and I against him. I waited for the moment when the energy would shift like it had with Henry, but that moment did not come. We stirred together, dancing in each other's exhilaration. I focused on the ceiling fresco painted brightly with birds, and the image of the morning sky created a sense of buoyancy. I closed my eyes to the scene, and the lush garden penetrated my vision. I imagined us rocking together on the floor of an open field, free of worry, lost to each other's yearning.

"Very good." Mother's voice was not an intrusion. "You will do very well. Your complexion, dark and light, punctuated with glowing eyes, like gems polished by the sea, will be memorable." She combed her fingers through my hair as Alistair continued to ride me, his rhythm gaining momentum.

Wet warmth sealed our bodies. I nestled into Alistair's neck, kissing him, crushing my lips hard into his skin. He tasted as fresh as he smelled. My teeth closed around his flesh, much like Henry's palm, but I was careful not to wound him. Alistair was like a sweetened lemon, and he balanced on me in all the right places, neither hurting nor pulling away and leaving me longing for closeness. I felt united, held, and pleasured, yet pleasing.

Alistair's breath quickened, and then he exhaled deeply. It was neither a cry nor a groan. He steadily exhaled his satisfaction. My heartbeat slowed in time with his deep breaths. He gradually pulled me to the side and freed me from his pressure. I turned to him and found us nose to nose, leaving his expression distorted by my myopia.

He hugged me tightly. "I want to keep her."

Mother's voice echoed behind me, "It would be a shame to keep such a treasure to ourselves."

Temptress

> Light Attributes: Erotic feminine energy
> Shadow Attributes: Inappropriate use of sexuality,
> attachment to money and power

My life rapidly shifted over the next six weeks, leaving little space to remember my time in York. After Mother revealed her agenda, outlining my worth as sellable goods and the primary breadwinner in the household, I was introduced to various men. Culls ranging from young to old, foreign to Italian-born, were all interested in tasting the *English Bird* with the fair skin. At first, I was devastated that the whoring life I'd sought to escape in York eventually caught me in Venice. When I said *I wanted more*, being a high-class whore was not what I meant. I had wished for the freedom to choose my life, not live under the blows of a devious madame.

My first few nights of whoring left me ashamed unless dulled. After each encounter, Mother demanded I drink a concoction she swore staved off pregnancy. It left me feeling ill, but nothing like my childhood ailments. As my resentment grew, so did my consumption of laudanum and wine. It wasn't until I met a common street whore at the local bordello, riddled with pocks and barking sputum from consumptive fits —only four months younger than me—that I reluctantly warmed to Mother's tutelage. If I couldn't govern my desires at the time, I could at least learn about the world around me.

Alistair was a regular companion. Occasionally, Mother allowed me to *practice* on him. He ran a print shop in the Ghetto and regularly gifted works of history, fiction, and sex. He was the Minster priest's counterpart in every way, although he knew me carnally in a way the priest only dreamt. I thought the Minster priest would have progressed quite well in Venice. For in a brief time there, I learned how lust exposed itself behind every curtain, including liturgical ones.

Tucked in the protective cocoon of my canopied bed, illuminated by a single candle's light, my novel enraptured me—the story of an English country girl becoming a maid and eventually a courtesan—John Cleland's *Memoirs of a Woman of Pleasure*. I compared the allegory to my adventures and hoped my life wasn't a foregone conclusion like this tale by a licentious male author.

"Serenna." I heard my name called from the kitchen below. Although Mother said I needed my rest, she had limits and would not tolerate perceived laziness. Besides, it was my birthday, and I hoped I'd have something special from my friends.

Snatching aside the linen curtains that muted the midday sun, a stream of light shined onto my satin pillow. I squeezed my eyes against it but reveled in the sun's energy. The Venice light made sunbeams glow like a *God's Light* from a Tintoretto fresco. A breeze ruffled Francese's feathers as he rested in his cage. Dust particles swirled together, and the room was dappled by lavender and coral hews. The sun warmed the floor stones, intensified the floral scents, and refreshed the crisp bed linens' aroma. The temperature change did the trick to awaken my senses. Retrieving a silk dressing gown draped over the foot of my bed, I drew it around me like a cape and stepped into the hall's cold shadow. Scuffling barefoot down to the kitchen, the noises of my friends scurrying around about their duties accosted me.

There were seven of us in our part of the house: Mother, Cici, Camilla, Max, two maids, and me. We had the first two levels of what was once a massive villa. The owner, Signore Pietro di Domino Basso, *Peter of Domino the Short*, lived in a tiny apartment on the third floor of the four-story villa. Like many Venetians, he had gambled away most of his fortune. He chose to divide up his birthright, bit by bit, striving to maintain the thinnest grasp on his legacy. Venetian pride is boundless, and the idea of forgetting one's entire inheritance to become nothing was tantamount to choosing eternity in Limbo.

Max kicked open the kitchen door as he carted in baskets of herbs and fruit. Sweat beads collected on his lip from the effort. Camilla was equally strained as she demanded the exact placement of each item. Cici had her back to me as she worked at the stove. Wiry and robust, she swiftly addressed tasks and appeared to understand our needs even before we did. Her friendly ways instantly bound us together.

"*Buongiorno Uccellino. Buon Compleanno.*" Cici hugged me and kissed both cheeks before presenting me with a long peacock feather. "A gift for the *Little Bird* on her birthday." She insisted I was her *Uccellino*, and I found the affectionate sign endearing.

"Good morning," I responded. "Everything smells heavenly."

Cici and Mother had been together since Mother left Santa Caterina. She occasionally spoke of Mother's courtesan lifestyle but minimized any factual details. She did tell of Mother's first suitor—an aged priest enraptured by Mother's raven locks, who favored her above all other postulants. Father Giuseppe, Venetian-born and a nobleman's son, taught Mother how to integrate into society without dowry or connection.

Even then, I had to reluctantly acknowledge the advantages of a courtesan's life beyond the learning. We were gifted every luxury—food, wine, pets, parties, dresses, and powerful connections. If Mother had found a new way to live, I could too. It was a modern time, with oil lamps, the printing press, and hot air balloons. We could light the way around the world, documenting our travels. If I couldn't be with my family, or have a family of my own, that was what I dreamt of doing.

Camilla whirled to me with a smile. "Morning, my lovely." Her English accent, slightly halting, played like a song. She placed a stool at the head of the cutting block. "A birthday breakfast, fit for the princess of the house."

Cici presented a plate full of melon and sliced prosciutto, crumbled Pecorino over tomatoes topped with herbs, and a single soft-boiled egg perched in a silver eggcup. I thumbed a basket of fresh croissants, muffins stained with cuttlefish ink—a new favorite—and delicate cinnamon twists. The last plate had salty garnishes. Pickled artichokes and gherkins, sliced beets, and crisp carrots. I finished my special meal with one last bite of cuttlefish muffin slathered with butter and washed it down with Riesling from a dutiful Hapsburg patron.

The skin on my back prickled to the screech of the copper tub Cici slid into the middle of the room. Bath time. We had a full bathroom in residence, but the kitchen's light was more favorable through the window well once used for canal deliveries. Cici had the opening stoned-shut after they moved in. She said the canal door made the villa less secure.

The stone wall and window retained light without intrusion from an unwanted visitor.

My friends filled the tub with buckets of heated water from the copper-boiling bladder. The bladder held ten suitable buckets of steaming water. The sound of the splashing stopped, and I knew what was next. Max shyly departed, and Cici moved into the scullery to deal with the morning cooking pans.

I rose from my stool and shrugged off my robe. Camilla commenced her inspection with a pregnant pause, averting her eyes as my shift fell to the floor. I knew she took in every detail of my body from the peripheral vision of her downcast gaze.

I stepped into the tub. "I think the bruises on my thighs are gone, but the abrasion on my back is still red." Water washed over my knees as I squatted in the cask. The partial submersion left me a mix of hot and cold.

Camilla crouched to the floor and dipped a rag into the hot water she had scented with lemon rinds, lavender, and rosemary sprigs. She pulled my hair into a knot on top of my head. It was not my best feature, indeed very average. Still, I had learned to tie the waist-length mass of brown locks into fashionable but functional styles. Current trends at the time dictated that the hair start high on the head but tumble down its length with little more than the release of a few pins. This alluring trick usually sparked immediate arousal.

I closed my eyes to her firm, soothing touch. Her hands pressed over my cheekbones and around my jaw. She palpated the nodules that tended to wane in size, depending on my health. "Your neck feels good. You are past what left you poorly last week."

I opened my eyes to catch her inspecting my face. "My nose is still difficult to clear, and I wake with a dry mouth, but I feel much better."

She slid her hands around my shoulders and down my arms as I rested them on the tub. Turning over my palms, she checked my nails. "I'll trim these once you're dressed." I winced as she found the bruise on my left shoulder blade. "Still tender? There isn't any discoloring, but we'll send for Benyamin if it's still sore in the coming days."

Benyamin was Asha's father—the girl I met with Alistair at the docks the first night—and a physician. Although I hadn't seen either of them lately, the duo frequented our house for both libations and to maintain my health. They lived minutes from us in the Ghetto.

Camilla wiped her hands in her apron, signaling it was time for me to rise. I crossed my arms over my breasts against the cold. Camilla continued examining the rounds of both buttocks, pausing at the graze at the base of my spine. "I'll treat it with the almond butter paste I bought from the market." I shook my head. "Would you prefer spending the day uncomfortable, the clothes rubbing against you?"

"It is not that. But almond is an enticing smell. It brings even more attention to the area."

Camilla chuckled. "My lovely, that is one of the best areas of your body, designed in a Master painter's dream long ago. I doubt it's the almond that attracts your patrons. But I'll see if there is a butter with a less sweet scent. Bend forward." Staying low, she spied the back of my nest between my thighs before continuing to the bruises. "There is very little discoloring." She touched the softness of my legs. "Tender?" I flinched but held my place. "Perhaps you choose someone tonight with different tastes."

I had little say about whom I bedded and what they desired. Even the most predictable patrons could be surprising. Some nights my endeavors were strung between boredom and debauchery, and little was left to my design. Still, I was learning. My job was to give them what they wanted and what they never knew they needed.

Not wanting to dwell on impossible choices, I focused on Camilla's life years ago with a domineering older sister and then a new baby, deformed and fatherless. "Why did you and Max leave Venice? I am not proud of the life I have crafted here—at Mother's behest—but Venice is full of opportunities, a chance to become something new. Why would you take Max from this place? You see how improved he is by the sun. Why return to the dank dreariness of Yorkshire when you could have had Veneto all this time?" My questions teetered on unfairness.

Her face was within inches of mine. "It was not all my decision. Our family sent Danielle here. She'd done something wicked, so wrong I can't even speak it now. Being her younger sister, my father sent me too."

"Were you in the convent with her?" It seemed remarkable that Camilla would leave that detail out.

"Danielle was not first sent to the convent. She was sick when we arrived and placed in a hospital." Camilla's face shadowed, concealing a secret. "I was given work as a laundress for a Venetian dye master specializing in scarlet."

Interestingly, she'd traveled halfway around the world to learn her trade but never bragged about her experience. "Why didn't you tell people that? I can't imagine many cloth makers in Yorkshire have such skill."

"I learned much in Venice. The dyeing process includes Kermes. There are strict rules to make *Venetian Scarlet* a generic name for anything red from Venice, but I wasn't interested in being noticed. Notoriety has its drawbacks." She wiped at her moist brow before continuing her inspection. "It was a terrible choice, torn between two worlds, two . . ."

"Two what?"

"Sisters. Danielle and I had another sister, a middle sister, a year older than me and a year younger than Danielle." Something happened to her and her family, and I had to go back to retrieve parts of her lost life." She abruptly stopped her story. "I don't want to share this now. We have work to do, and you know the consequences if Danielle finds us lollygagging."

I flushed with irritation at her withholding. But yes, I did know the penalties for displeasing Mother. Although I was free of the asylum and its tortures, Mother's exacting temperament could rival any treatment there. She might give me to someone undesirable.

Brushing my arms away, Camilla cupped both breasts and pressed her fingertips toward my armpits as her thumbs rounded my nipples. Her hands were warm and firm—bigger than most women of her small stature—but capable and tender, much like her spirit. She traced my ribs to the waistline. "Now for the rest." She lowered to the floor again.

I watched the chipped ceiling as she pressed her fingers into my nest of brown hair. I kept it cut short but not wholly shorn. French fashion stripped pubic hair bare and left the region as clean as a child virgin, but that taste had yet to reach Venice, or my patrons were old enough to like a bit of color still. The sheering was less for their visual pleasure than for smell and sweat. Like the hair on my head, oil and fluid collected, and I even caught myself sometimes remarking on the strength of my odor. Not my favorite confession, but one every woman knows. It is a constant preoccupation to stay clean and dry in the Venice humidity.

Mother's entrance sucked the air from the room. "My, how often do I find you in that position?" Her voice was crisp as a whip snap.

Camilla wobbled as she stood. She readjusted her skirt and apron, offering her girth as a moment of shelter from Mother's scrutiny.

A trail of dust brushed through the sunlight as Mother crossed to the basin. "Move aside."

I lowered my arms and met Mother's gaze. "Good morning. Did you rest well?"

She stared at me before looking at the water in the tub. "Holy hell, your filth is astounding. Do you go to bed this dirty?" Her rapidly firing comments were most cutting.

I did not answer her. The floating particles were residue from the copper bladder and present in every kitchen bath I took, which was not an answer she wanted.

Mother tucked a lock of hair behind her ear and turned around the basin, missing the nuanced tell-alls that Camilla had thoroughly addressed. She dressed in a perfectly tailored cinnamon-hued gown. Her pepper-minted breath prickled along my cheek. "I assume she is in good condition for tonight?"

Mother pinched the top of my right buttock close to my graze. She withdrew to the threshold as quickly as she had emerged and spoke to us from the doorway. "You had better be prepared. Tonight will be long. I have booked you at the Arsenal. A new regiment of soldiers has arrived from Pest and Vienna." She looked directly at Camilla. "Be sure her dress is to their liking, but do not stoop so low as to make it something *their* women might wear." Her gaze was affixed on the canal outside as she commanded me. "I expect your best. The men will be in the city for at least a fortnight. Win many tonight, and we will be paid handsomely." She gave a snap glance at me. "No squeamishness, regardless of what is requested."

I held her stare. Instead of leaving, she leaned against the doorframe. She casually inspected her fingers, forcing me to either stand in the rapidly chilling water, open to her scrutiny, or leave without her permission.

Her brows furrowed. "Do you understand how lucky you are? When

I came to Venice, I was not given such tutoring on a courtesan's life. Rather, I was told what I could *not* be and slowly watched my life opportunities seep away, like the sun consenting to the passing season."

My teeth chattered. "I have not had the privilege of knowing your tale."

She flipped her fingers like shooing away a fly. "I doubt you could understand the sacrifice I've experienced to the benefit of many—rarely for myself." She looked to Camilla, who seemed to cower into an even lesser version. "I'm not interested in your *curiosity*. My story is mine and will remain so." Again, a look of warning. "Your job is to bring in money. The day you cease doing so and start making mistakes is the day you leave. *Capisci?*"

Prostitute

Light Attributes: Surviving without changing spirit
Shadow Attributes: Values security over self-empowerment

Mother's account of my worth had soured my mood, and I longed to rip off my dress, lock my door, and wait for tomorrow. I stayed on my settee, rhythmically kicking my feet over the marble floor, listening intently for the signal to leave. I combed through Francese's feathers to subdue my rising stubbornness. "We don't need her. Do we, Francese?" His golden-hued irises, like my own reflective fleck, answered back. "You're right. I have to make the most of the life I have now. I could be locked up with my sister."

The image of the purple scar cresting Felicity's forehead flashed in my mind. I had escaped the asylum. She was confined, and robbed of choice and dignity. Although, it occurred to me that I might have exchanged one form of detention for another. How easily we could have traded places. Shaking off the memory, I aimed to focus on the life before me, assuming my role as the *learned* whore—for what other choice in life did I have now?

Engaging with clients ranging from sea captains to church clergy took little effort. As it turned out, the priest from the Minster had inadvertently groomed me for a courtesan's life. Conflict raged in the Mediterranean between the revolutionary French and austere Austrians, but Venice held unbiased. The outbreak of revolution across Europe left a palpable strain in the air that positively impacted my trade. Anxious men craved the company of women like me.

Knuckles wrapped at the door. "Renna, are you ready?" mumbled

NICOLETTE CROFT

Max.

Shooing Francese back into his cage and fastening the latch, I memorized my look in the mirror. I needed to know exactly what effect I might have. My hair was high and tight, with soft ringlets pinned at the crown. The bodice of a royal blue dress strangled my ribs and flirtatiously curved around my breasts. Loose silk hung over my shoulders and hips. Capped sleeves and a sturdy skirt cage created hourglass symmetry. The frock's hue contrasted nicely with my complexion, for I ran the risk of being washed out in a fairer tone. The design was all Camilla's making. She said I deserved something uniquely mine for my birthday. Next to Francese and my locket, the dress was the best gift I'd been given.

I touched the locket barely concealed inside my gown's lip, a talisman of luck for the night, and garnered my energy. Wiggling my feet into flat slippers, I grabbed the skirt's hem and held tight to my platform clogs. I threw a cloak over my shoulders and lifted the door latch.

Max smiled wide. "Very lovely."

I could have worn the bedsheets, and his response would have been the same. I thanked him with a kiss and swished down the hall. He trailed closely behind, as he would for most of the evening. We made it through the house and out into the alley without a word from Mother. This was a relief but unusual. She rarely missed a departure, saying her scrutiny was to *ensure my quality.*

Once in the alley, Max led us through narrow pathways over several bridges, from Santa Caterina to the *Canale delle Misericondira*, the *Channel of Mercy*—aptly named. I moved quickly in casual flat slippers instead of my four-inch raised clogs. If the weather were worse, I would need the elevation of my artfully designed shoes to avoid the filth-drenched streets. Tonight, the dusty alleys, sans sewage, aided my expediency.

Mother said arriving on foot at the Arsenal was unseemly, but the grand show of a gilded gondola made a statement, though costly. She was a calculating businesswoman and favored utility up to the final moment. She instructed me to ride the gondola for the last part of the journey, forcing us to walk most of the way.

We found our hired gondola tied a few blocks from the Arsenal side entrance. Silvio, the gondolier, waited in the shadows along a small inlet.

He was of a grandfather's age and had been my guide on many nights. Our arrangement was the same every time: He waited. I boarded. We left. We arrived. I departed. Once at the Arsenal, Max would stay with Silvio.

Silvio outstretched a hand to pass me into his boat. "*Buonasera signorina. Guarda i tuoi passi. I gradini bui sono lisci e ti invieranno a nuotare.*" I heeded his warning to watch myself, as the *dark steps were slick and could send me for a swim*. He gave the same advice every evening I met him.

Firmly seated in the gondola with Max opposite me at the bow, I noticed we were not alone. Mother was hidden in the shadows of the gondola's cabin. I couldn't see her, but I knew her smell, a combination of peppermint, lilies, and wine. "Glad to see you understand punctuality."

Silvio slipped the pole into the water without a ripple, noiselessly moving us through the canal. Seawater tickled against smooth moss-lined walls, where the water festered in tight confines. I focused on a candle flame flickering from a third-story villa window. There was a soft cry of a violin and the lilt of a woman singing. Remnants of light from a recently set sun tinted the curves of the villa's Turkish embellishments. The fading light muted the pastel walls around us, concealing chipped plaster and worn wood, much like the ladies attending the night's event would veil their flaws in shifting candlelight and layers of paint, striving to recall their youth and hiding the truth of their fading beauty.

"Do you see that door that leads straight into the lagoon?" Mother waved her hand to the moldering building to her right. "This was once my home, Santa Caterina."

The haunting canal-side entrance differed from the welcoming campo I passed on the way to the fish market. If this was what greeted future postulants as their families abandoned them to the beckoning church's lustful bosom, no wonder so many turned from Christian values to heathen ways.

Mother retreated under the shadow of the gondola covering. "Look at the girl leaning out the window. We will pass her soon. I want you to notice her clothes, her face."

The girl's skin was flawless. Her complexion rivaled my own. Then there was her dress, a deep red, signature Venetian scarlet. Her neckline plunged deeply, revealing the bottom of each budding breast. Something about the image recalled the street trollops from York—the same nakedness. But this girl's dignity betrayed their shame.

I was envious of her costume. "She looks like she could join us tonight." I wondered if my dark color did me justice in comparison.

Mother tilted her head in unspoken longing, seeming to return to a younger day. "She need not attend the Arsenal to find a suitor. Her suitor has already chosen her, or she would not dress so. Sadly, although well attended, she is only as desirable as her newness. Once other girls arrive at the convent, she will be set aside, and her lovely dresses will eventually be replaced by one drab habit after another, unless . . ."

"Unless?" Camilla said these girls were born to proper birthrights, which I was not. I felt desperate to know the girl had another option, although she would rival me or any other girl in my trade. But I still did not wish her ill.

"Unless she is willing to do what she must, defy her family and marry anyone—but run the risk of losing her heritage entirely. Or step out on her own, much like I did. She'd still lose her family connection but have freedom." Mother closed herself in the gondola's shadow and left me to watch the convent girl and thus leave her to view me. "You've read *Aretino*—nun, wife, or whore. That is an excellent example of a woman's fate."

Mother's explanation made me think of Ann. She spoke of a "new way." She said she'd disregarded her family—found someone to love who was unacceptable, and then, I supposed, did as Mother and made her mark in the world. What choices did that leave someone like me? I was not born to a reputable family.

Silvio turned the corner onto a broader canal connected with the *Grand Canale*. My heart raced as we inched closer to the revelry of the night. I felt sucked toward the Arsenal entrance like a fish falling from a net onto a boat deck. The gondola eased in front of the long dock, lit with lanterns at each pylon. Max disembarked and pulled the gondola lip to the edge.

"Shall I go first?" I asked Mother without looking for her.

"You shall. I will find you inside." Her voice had a comforting and cautionary tone I'll remember for the rest of my days. "You are here to earn. You may have been saved from the street, but I can return you there or any place else I see fit if I find you displeasing."

Her warning left me shaking, and I desperately stretched a hand to Max. He helped me stand on the wooden planks. I couldn't flee Mother fast enough, but I had to assemble my attire. Using Max's shoulder to balance, I slipped from my flats into my platforms. He secured each shoe by a length of ribbon that coiled around my ankles. He smoothed the bottom of my skirt and helped to adjust the cloak around my shoulders.

Max reassured me with a tight smile. "Ready?" Max would see me to the door and wait for me to exit later, conquest in tow.

I strode the dock length to the Arsenal entrance, chin held high, feigning confidence. I smiled at a stout, clean-shaven youth to my right and moved past him into the entrance hall. "Good evening."

Merely crossing the threshold emboldened me. I continued my descent through a foyer that opened into the vast room of the main hall. The lobby's marble floor felt slick under my platforms, and I wobbled nervously. Luckily, a servant in a gold-embroidered waistcoat with a tray of champagne flutes glided past. I gripped a glass stem tightly with my silk-gloved fingers.

Before I could drink, a woman in yellow dashed toward me. "Renna." Her voice was loud but drowned by the din of laughing revelers and shouting soldiers.

I greeted her with the customary double kiss. "Ann."

I couldn't say I was glad she was my first acquaintance for the night. We had not interacted much since our arrival in Venice—I'd seen her at this party or that. She said Donovan had returned to his work with the British West India Company and left her to make her way. She had no problem establishing herself with the Venetian elite and was already told to be one of the city's best courtesans. I was jealous. She always seemed one step ahead of me. Still, I welcomed the familiar face.

"You will not believe the number of new men here tonight. Most are staying for at least two weeks, possibly a month." She reminded me of a curious kitten bounding after the newest oddity. "I think I've found one that will absolutely love you. He's English." There was an odd twinkle in her expression.

Apprehension tightened my chest. I preferred picking my own conquest. It gave me a sense of choice that I was not wholly subject to someone else's desires. I watched the room, looking for who Ann might mean. There were a few women with partial masks concealing their eyes.

I assumed they were known companions, and thus it was allowed. Face covering was usually prohibited. The women were energetic, each flirting as though their lives depended on it. Half were already intoxicated. Men responded with groping and grinning, comely glances, and unseemly laughter. In my experience, drunkards tended to share their dalliances or *strum* with an audience. That was not my taste.

I calmed myself with the champagne's aroma and admired the golden buttons of a double-breasted officer's uniform. The thoughtful detail in the embroidered satin waistcoat was visible from my distance. A saber hung from his narrow hips. I admired how his pants billowed instead of pulling tight around his thighs as they would have on a stockier man. My gaze moved to his face and a cleanly shaven chin and jaw, one seared in my memory—Henry.

His eyes were upon me.

Ann pinched my arm. "I thought you'd be pleased."

Finishing my champagne in one gulp, I handed the glass to Ann and took another from the nearby footman. The direct path to Henry was through the gambling tables and men huddling over their hands of cards, crowded by women in low-cut dresses playing with the edges of their wigs. My heart raced as I weighed my choices. It was a *work* night. But how could I pass up the opportunity to speak to Henry?

I stepped around a couch with three girls teasing at a man's collar nape. Many hands disappeared into his lap. When I intruded on their space, the girls glared at me like hungry animals. They protectively guarded their shared conquest for the night. From the man's look, he was too drunk to manage one of them, let alone three. Desperate whores and younger courtesans often worked together. Little did they realize that working as a group made them far more forgettable. After a while, a mix of skin and lips, hips and hair, teeth and tits were all the same.

I stepped toward a group of foreign soldiers huddled together. The tone of their accents said they were neither French nor English. Although I had other intentions, making new acquaintances was never bad.

"Excuse me, sirs, I have a matter only the most delicate palate can settle." I nodded in the direction of Ann. "My sister and I were told this is Venetian prosecco, but I believe this is champagne." I twirled my glass stem.

The men looked at each other puzzlingly and then back to me.

THE CURSE OF MAIDEN SCARS

One responded. "Prosecco."

I sipped, allowing my lips to linger on the rim in the shape of a kiss. "I'm not sure." I handed the glass to the second man as the first watched. "What do you think?"

He shyly smelled it before handing it to the third. "I don't drink." A sober man was an unconventional romance. It was typically more about the mind than the body.

The third man downed the glass. "No, champagne."

I tilted my chin again to Ann, who had taken in the interaction. "Thank you. I dearly despise losing a bet. Now my little sister owes me. Perhaps one of you would like to collect that debt." On cue, she sashayed to us.

Her smile broadened, and her girlishness subtly faded. She morphed into a wickedly wise nettle. The third man pulled his lapels tighter and patted his unruly wig into place, to little avail. The first readied to join his friend in meeting my *sister*. The second man shrank back, knowing his companions were lost to him.

He removed a bright, red-foiled candy from his coat pocket and offered it to me. "It comes from my country and is called Szaloncukor, or *solon sugar.*"

I unwrapped a dark chocolate bonbon, noticed the strong smell of marzipan, and took a nibble. The aromatic flavor melted across my tongue. I quickly ate the rest and lifted my gaze to find the man's much-pleased expression. He inhaled his chocolate and tucked the wrapper into his coat pocket.

Extending his hand with a partial mouthful, he spat, "I am Sandor, and my family is from Pest." He was stout, with round cheeks and brilliant blue eyes.

I gave him a slow shake, noting the points of his seduction—nationality, pride, and food. "*Köszönöm.* Hungary? That must make you, Magyar?"

Sandor's face brightened like a lamp turned high. "You know us?"

"I am very well-read."

The cacophony in the room increased, and I remembered my aim. Despite the extra height of my platforms, I felt tiny next to the taller foreigners. I couldn't see Henry. But my survey did find a familiar face —Mother, center, and still. She stood with one hand on her hip and held a long pipe in the other—a thin line of smoke trailing from the end. The subtle lift of her brow was a silent command: *Get to work.* I searched again for Henry without avail. I was ready to start over with the Hungarian when a full glass of wine appeared.

"*Prosecco.*" Henry's voice was smooth. His grey eyes transfixed me.

My hand shook, and wine bubbles ignited like fireworks. "You're a long way from home." I took in his jaw's straightness that narrowed to a slight chin point.

He touched my elbow with his index finger. "As are you."

I was trying to think of something witty to say, but I could only envision kissing the crescent indentation at the base of his neck, created by the firm muscles of his chest visible under his open collar. He had a casual air about him. This might mean I would not be his first romp of the night. I breathed deeply to compose myself. He smelled as clean as he looked. His shirt was spotless and lacked the typical yellow tarnish.

He tightened his grip on my elbow and nudged me toward the window. "Perhaps we should have a conversation where I can have your complete attention."

The movement brought me back to myself. "I'd like to go home." My words conveyed finality and lacked the flirtation I had intended.

"As you wish." He stood stock-still, eyes fixed upon me, waiting.

I clasped his hand and led him toward the entrance. We washed through the throng of drunken soldiers and courtesans. The people before me scattered like dry, fallen leaves blowing apart and whirling back together once we passed. We bustled into the foyer. The change in sound and temperature slowed my thoughts, and I turned around. Excitement danced through me. It was my birthday, and I had picked my present.

Mother's smooth voice broke through my fantasy. "You can't venture out into the night air without some guard against the weather, my dear." She presented my cloak.

"Thank you." I wrapped in the garment, left the fastening unsecured, turned on a heel, and pushed past the guards to the dock. Henry trailed after.

Max was waiting with Silvio by the farthest pylon, barely visible in the lantern light. I pulled my cloak tight to shield myself from the wind.

Henry placed both hands around my neck, tilting my head high, forcing me to meet his energetic eyes. He caressed my face with his thumb and brought his mouth down on mine. He moved his mouth over me. A flick of his tongue on my lip made my knees weaken. I felt myself grow limp as I kissed him back, melting into his heat. I wobbled when Henry released me.

Max cleared his throat and bridged the gap between the dock and the gondola, offering a hand to board. I gladly steadied myself in Max's firm grip. "All right?" Max asked.

My eyes said *yes*.

Of course, Max recognized Henry and Henry him.

Seated on the bench, I looked back to the Arsenal and Mother at the threshold, hawkishly eyeing our departure. Without pomp, Henry sat next to me. Silvio pushed away from the dock, and his voice carried us toward our home on the notes of a melodic song.

Lover

Light Attributes: Passion and attentiveness
Shadow Attributes: Obsession, self-destructive devotion

I led Henry up the stairs to my still-locked room. My heart was racing in anticipation of being alone with him again. Much had changed since our night in the Harewood library. Tonight, we would reacquaint ourselves in *my* space. Pulling on the chain around my neck, I found my room key. The locket trailed out as I lifted the key out of my bodice.

Henry thumbed the necklace, remarking, "Lovely."

Curiosity gave me pause. I couldn't tell if he saw my necklace with familiarity or newness. Shrugging off my worry, I unlocked the door and brought him in.

Candles were burning, highlighting the central elements of the evening. A table with a silver-serving tray decorated with juicy fruit and a crystal decanter of red wine was on my desk. My bed was freshly made with laundered sheets pulled back as if inviting its guest to enter. Moonlight lit the settee by the window, and a burning candle reflected the golden sheen of Francese's cage.

I was more nervous than usual. My palms were sweating. I dismissed this as excitement because of my birthday, but I knew better, and lying to myself was the surest way of losing control. I wanted him. I wanted those soft lips on my skin. Thinking of him tracing my body with his mouth, discovering what I knew would come alive under his touch, made me ache between my legs. Excitement at tempting him with my new skills made me squirm with satisfaction.

THE CURSE OF MAIDEN SCARS

I poured wine into two glasses to ease the tension and handed him one as a welcoming gesture. It was not a cheap vintage, and he savored the aroma. The wine left a stain on the corner of his mouth. I memorized the shape of his lips.

He met my gaze. "Is there an issue?"

"A drop on the corner of your lips."

He moved to wipe it with the back of his hand.

I clasped his wrist. "That's my job." I gently licked his mouth.

He hesitated, but he did not return the kiss.

Sensing he wasn't ready, I moved to the settee by the window where Francese rested motionless, his eyes wide and knowing, and enjoyed my wine. If Henry were not interested in my company, he would not have come home with me.

He stayed by the door, giving me an undisrupted view of his form. His pants hung lightly from his hips. He was about average height, but his hands and feet belonged to a man closer to six feet. His upper back was slightly curved, like someone carrying a heavy worry. And something was peculiar about his appearance, with sizeable eyes like Francese. He set the glass on the desk near the door. With deliberation, he unbuttoned his jacket and folded it, laying it on the desktop. He slipped his pant stays off his shoulders and pulled the shirt free—his cream-colored skin showed like moonlight on water. Still not looking at me, he dropped his trousers from his narrow hips and draped them over the chair with the remainder of his attire.

"You have settled into a new life," he gestured toward the bed.

I sensed his displeasure and felt ashamed. "This was more thrust upon me than chosen."

He looked closer at Francese, leaving the angle of his body protecting his manhood, hiding any evidence of arousal. "Is that so?"

Anger tightened my throat. "It's been a long time since I've seen you. You cannot know what I've been through or what I've learned."

I thought about him nearly every day since he had claimed my virginity, but hearing Mother's story, her salvation from the priest in the convent, sparked the idea that someone might rescue me from my courtesan life. *Might Henry be that someone?*

He held a model's pose and sipped his wine like I were the artist blessed by his inspirational presence. "I know a great deal about your situation. I am sorry you have such a deformed sister locked in the asylum. A tarnished family dampens your appeal."

My hope and desire drained from me, and I sank into my seat. This was not how I'd imagined our meeting. "Why would you care what my family is and be so cruel about my sister?" The words came sharply. Our first encounter left me with the misconception that he'd equally want me if we met again, not to pepper me with judgment.

His expression narrowed, "Perhaps yes, perhaps no."

That sounded like Mother. I felt edgy, and the wine loosened my tongue. "I will happily spend time with you tonight. It turns out I am good at my new vocation. And my years of tutelage, along with the book you gifted, have given me knowledge of sex."

Henry bridged the space between us in smooth strides. His manhood shone in full view. It swelled before me, and a thick vein pulsed the length of his cock. I longed to touch him as he grew excited, but he was out of reach. Henry was unlike Alistair, but I did not mind his uncut prick. I'd seen enough of them by now, but I would have preferred to wash him first.

He sipped his wine. "Again, perhaps. For now, I am interested in your cleaning regime. Your appeal before had much to do with being untainted."

I finished my wine and placed the glass on the windowsill. I readied to offer the same careful undressing, but Henry gestured for me to stay. "Don't you want to inspect me for any *tainting*?" My tone settled into tempting teasing, but my mind was bubbling with irritation.

He stepped closer. "I will assume that all is well. Your room is clean, and your skin does not show signs of sickness other than your thinness."

He pulled out the pins and ties that kept my hair high, releasing my tresses with expert hands. They fell over my shoulders. He bent low and removed my shoes, placing them at the foot of the settee the way he'd laid his own. He fixed on my skirts with a determined expression and lifted them to my knees. His hands disappeared under my hem and up to the garter and neck of the stockings. He guided the socks down my legs and draped them over the couch. He looked at me long, his countenance unreadable, even as he removed my knickers. My heart was burning with his orderly advance.

He'd promised to look after me at Harewood House, but surely my hasty departure hindered his plans. I watched his eyes. The energy behind them rolled like the sea, yet they were inviting. Doubt played at the edge of my enthusiasm, but I fought it back, searching for proof of his interest. He gently kissed my lips and returned to his observant posture.

I anticipated what Henry would remove next. I wished he would untie my bodice and release me from my gown's tightness. I was disappointed when he stopped. I'd dreamt of our reunion so many nights. He bent forward, and his hands found my nest, wet and warm. He looked long into my face as he explored, his expression slightly unnerving. I wanted to lean in, kiss him, and participate in our growing desire.

Henry scooted me to the edge of the settee, perching me upon the threshold. He kneeled and slowly pushed into me. My nest closed around him like a fist. He pressed his hands atop my thighs, pinning me to the couch. He found a rhythm, and I was forced to cling to him as he moved with satisfaction. He panted. I pressed my mouth to him, taking in the heat of his breath. He inched deeper into me in a rapid, frenzied dance. He cried out a low moan and plunged in me hard, igniting sparks of excitement. Henry's chest rose and fell as he steadied himself and his skin cooled. I wasn't sure what would happen next. It all went so fast.

Henry bent his face inches from mine, recalling our interaction in the carriage on the way to Harwood. He snatched a handful of hair and smothered me in a deep kiss, accosting my mouth with his tongue and taste. Then he released me. "Perfect. Absolutely compliant." He kissed me again as he slipped away.

Deftly rising to his feet, his knees red from supporting himself in his dominating position, Henry stepped back to the desk. In precisely reverse order, he redressed. When every button was in place, he went to the wine decanter and filled our glasses. He handed me a glass, clinking it against his own. "*Saluti e Grazie.*" He fished through his jacket, finding two large bills. "I'm sorry, but I only have Pounds." He set the money next to the decanter and asked for my hand.

I reached for him, dazed as though in a dream. "Did you come for me?"

He kissed the top of my fingers and freed me, much as he'd released himself from me moments ago. "Not quite. You were a lovely surprise tonight, but I'm in Venice on an errand for my family. I must bring a family member home—someone present at the Arsenal tonight. But seeing you was irresistible, and I thought my family duty could wait another day."

None of this played out as I romanticized. Henry was treating our interaction with the same coldness as our first encounter. And worse, giving cash now instead of a book.

He lifted the door handle. "May I see you again?"

I mustered a nod. Henry moved to leave, and I was on my feet. I rushed to him and clutched his arm. "Is that it? Are you going to treat me like that? I thought I meant more." Even as the words came from me, I was surprised by my neediness. I snatched at him, pulled down on his necktie, and pushed my lips to him hard. "You have to stay. You promised to look after me."

He drew away and touched the edge of my cheek, still holding gentle decorum.

I was desperate as he slipped through my fingers and clamored to hold his coat tightly. I tried to kiss him again.

With a sudden force, he slapped me, the heel of his palm connecting with my jaw. "Enough. I will not be pawed at." I retreated in shame. Like a fish fleeing from a net, he swam back to the door, re-straightening his ruffled clothing.

I held myself in check, chagrinned by my hysteria.

Clothing righted, he cautiously edged in my direction, perhaps out of pity, but remained out of reach. "I would be lying to say you are a simple distraction. You are special, and I would love to keep you to myself. But you have changed that again. At first, you were an orphan that I could rescue. Then you were a maid that I could favor. Now, you are a . . . courtesan."

I was glad he chose that term. I couldn't bear the thought of him calling me a whore.

"I'm sure we can arrange something, but I can't imagine what that might look like. I'm expected to marry soon. Of course, I can have consorts or a companion, but how would it seem if I settled for one used by anyone in the Adriatic? Still, I want to see you again." His look

THE CURSE OF MAIDEN SCARS

traveled to the open neckline of my bodice. He gently tugged the key and locket from my dress. "And this piece is exciting. Do you know to whom it belongs?"

Feeling protective as he spied on my treasure and me, I seethed. "It's mine. It was once my mother's, my real mother."

He gave a surprised look. "Well, that might be interesting." Henry stepped through the door, leaving me to my humiliation and loneliness.

Energy drained from me as though I'd been walking for days. I couldn't understand his intent. I downed my wine and set the glass next to his on the windowsill.

I struggled to walk on unsteady legs to the bed, crawling to the top. I buried my face in the feather pillows, and a low, painful sob filled my throat. I bit down on the pillow for fear of being overheard and let out a wail of anguish rivaling my abject sister. He had left me baffled and despondent.

I hollered, soaking the cloth in tears and snot, suffocating in my desperation. I made one misstep after another in my intent to survive and make sense of my world—and I missed vital details. He'd said he could have liberated me as an orphan or dominated me as a servant. Now I was sullied and disposable, the very thing Danielle warned me not to be. Courtesans don't marry. They don't get happy endings.

My promise to *Mother Shipton* from months ago came to me. *To my heart: I promise to know and love myself before I love another.* If I were to keep that promise, this would be the last time I'd give my heart to another before I *loved myself*.

My sobbing ebbed away, and I was completely drained. At least I knew tonight I would sleep. At least Henry left me that.

WINTER, 1796

Don Juan

Light Attributes: Seductive qualities
Shadow Attributes: Romantic attraction with private agendas

We had been in Venice for six months, and I felt like I knew no other life. Somehow, I managed to endure a barrage of suitors who needed rubbing, kissing, cuddling, fawning, and fucking. Stubbly faces, wafts of sour-smelling cologne, brandy-tinged breath, tickles, and grunts invaded my waking mind. At the same time, haunting images of Felicity's marred form, the heartbreak over Henry, and a growing fear of Mother's sinister agenda suffocated my sleep. Venice had replaced one limitation with another. There were days I would have traded it all to recede into the routine of pulling cotton or procuring worldly knowledge within the Minster priest's bedchamber. But I now had a reputation, relative freedom, and money. All of it made the heartache of Henry's absence more tolerable. Until it didn't.

Not long after my night with him, Mother produced a note:

Departed on business and will return in the Spring.

Captain Henry Moore

I had turned the page over so often that the edges wrinkled from perspiration and tears. As I did not know his hand, I could not confirm if he had sent the note. Mother said he was one of many suitors, and I made a mistake thinking our connection was more than professional. Her words seared my heart, and I found rising from bed each day more arduous.

THE CURSE OF MAIDEN SCARS

Last night I had consumed more wine than food. I reluctantly slipped from the bed and clutched my gurgling stomach as my head swooned. Tapping Francese on the beak, I dramatically thundered, like many of the Dukes I had serviced, "It's time to make my presence known." If only I had the same power as them.

I met Camilla and Mother in the kitchen huddled over a fresh pot of tea. Little provisions were laid out—cold cuts and day-old bread. The kitchen fire was not lit, nor was the bladder boiling. This meant any bathing would happen with the quick wipes of a cold cloth.

Something was amiss, and I sensed Mother's mood reflected in the chilled kitchen. She glanced at me and then stared at Camilla.

Camilla took her unspoken cue and swiftly left us, avoiding me as though shifting around a pile of soiled filth. I longed to know what resulted from their exchange, but this last season had disconnected us. Any familiarity from the workhouse and Harewood was now replaced with stony indifference, one only an Englishwoman could manifest.

Mother's command rang clear. "Come here." She glanced at me and then turned to the far cutting block for a mortar and pestle—*my* mortar and pestle. Grinding the baton in the bowl, rhythmically crushing a red pigment against the sides, she took roost on a stool. "You will douche all the necessary parts for servicing in your room before you go. We need to leave within the hour."

"We?"

"You must think me a fool to let you go to another gathering like the Arsenal and allow you to miss several grantors in one night. Tonight, we are going to the Casino. There are numerous businessmen in town, not like the pitiable soldiers from before. I will ensure you are acquainted with the right few, leaving you engaged for the remainder of the Yuletide. Do as instructed, and perhaps the balance of January will equal a break for learning." She rattled off her observations, still ever attending to her concoction. Mother drew at the tie of my nightshift, sending the gown cascading around my feet. "Hold still." Mother's breath mixed with peppermint and the acid of wine. "I want you to wear a dress that will display this, understand?"

I knew what she wanted. She had designed several dresses for me with low plunging backs that offered a full view of paintings blending my scars. Mother's artistry should have hung from a villa's walls, for she had a steady stroke and knack for blending color. Some nights a flower wrapped around my shoulders. Other times the plume of a great bird danced over me, brightly colored and vibrant, projecting the health and vitality that garnered a hearty sum. The nights she painted my back were always the most profitable and often the most adventurous.

Her hand hovered over my shoulder, and she applied the first coat of paint to my skin. "Tonight is the start of the Christmas festival, and husbands will entertain each other as their wives are away settling details for the holiday festivities."

I didn't focus on her words and let curiosity govern my thoughts. "Cici said you wore paint as a courtesan as well. How did you learn to create such art?"

She continued adding color to my back. "My sisters and I had the blessed benefit of the finest teachers in England—music, painting, dancing, languages. Even though I was trained as a wife and a lady, my skills enabled a lucrative courtesan's life."

"Did you hope to marry at one point?" The question was bold, but I wanted some comfort, knowing I was not the only one lost and confused.

She answered directly. "Yes." The expression lines around her eyes softened. "I was once engaged. He was not English. I met him while I was traveling abroad. He came from a good family, and I was proud to be his fiancé." She became breathlessly still, and her features hardened like stone. "But then he met another woman after returning to England with me. Several weeks before our wedding, I was jilted, and he took the woman back to his family, declaring *she* would be his wife." She took her paints and brushes to the sink.

"That is heartbreaking."

She continued with her posture utterly straight, as though her spine was made of a metal rod instead of bone. "It is a horrible pain to love someone and have them revoke that love." She took a long breath and released it slowly. "I gave myself to him before we were married and thus was spoiled to any other suitor. My family sent me here. My father often traveled to Venice on business."

That verified Camilla's account, but it still seemed unfair that Mother was sent to a convent and not have another marriage arranged to someone ignorant of her past.

THE CURSE OF MAIDEN SCARS

"You were told at your arrival that this city has many hazards, not unlike York. I have made my way, avoided such things, or escaped them. I learned to survive. You will do the same. I don't keep you here out of the goodness of my heart but rather because you bring value." She readjusted her hair instinctually, like preparing for a new lover. "Tonight, I will help you find someone who will bring a fair price, perhaps for the season. I can't have you bungling your opportunities with an unfeasible paramour. I don't want you bringing anyone back here. As their houses will be primed for Christmas, you will not be invited to their beds either."

Mother's little speech had deep meaning. Either I find someone without a family and thus an empty house, or I'd be forced to entertain my suitors in some scandalous corner, opening me to observation and indiscretion, bringing me closer to the definition of a street whore.

She surveyed her work. "I've given you a cluster of grapes. I want someone to crave your fruitfulness." She pinched me on the back of my arm. The assault chillingly vibrated through me.

*****

We went to the canal and the awaiting Silvio and boarded the gondola without regard. My heart thumped in time with the oar as it cut steadily through the quiet canal when Mother intruded upon my thoughts. "I will escort you in. It is the festive season, and proper that I make an appearance. But I will not tarry. I have a few acquaintances to make and a bet and a bit of a drink, but you will be left to find your way home tonight. Once I return with Silvio, he will no longer be at your disposal."

I felt as though she was setting me up for some unavoidable disaster. But to what end, I couldn't imagine. I shrunk in my seat, oblivious to our arrival at the opulently lit dock in front of the Casino.

Mother clasped my wrist and lugged me onto the dock. She hurriedly marched toward the Casino, forcing me to cling nervously to her arm. Once inside, she removed my cloak and handed it to a butler. The noise of the over-packed room was disorienting.

Mother's grace and beauty rendered me invisible, and she conjured feelings of my tattered orphan past. She parted the crowd, filed straight to the craps table, collected a goblet of wine from a passing waiter, and flipped him a coin. She pushed me between two men and gave me the wine. Both men turned to me with angry expressions, quickly fading into hungry smiles. The darker color of my emerald-green dress distinguished me from the ladies in gold and pastels. I finished the wine for added courage.

Mother wrapped an arm around my waist. "*Signore Parvicini.*" She bowed to the right. "*Signore Nicolo.*" A reflective bow to the left. "May I introduce Renna?"

Nicolo turned to me, forgoing his game of betting on numbers. I remembered the power of unwavering eye contact. "Good evening," I cooed.

Nicolo bowed low and tipped my nails to his lips in a graceful gesture of familiarity. Although his attire was immaculate, all topped with an embroidered velvet coat and silk necktie, something was amiss. A dusty smell wafted from his powdered wig. The texture of his chaffed hand enveloping my fingers left me bemused. I couldn't explain my apprehension and dismissed it as anxious confusion.

My bodice stitching made it impossible to breathe. My skin pushed against the binding wire and wool. The design, forcing my breasts high, painfully chafed at me. Blinking away my discomfort, I sought what Signore Nicolo wanted but would never explicitly state. Wasn't that what Mother said? *Find what they crave and make them think you were made only for them.*

I took the dice from his outstretched fingers and offered a wink. "*Pardone me*, Signore. I can bring you some luck." It must have been the wine, for I felt soft and pliant. I kissed the dice and flung my wrist over the table. I didn't know the game's aim but knew it was about chance and numbers. I could play fate with a bit of luck and charm. "I hope I rolled what you long for."

Something good happened. The dice settled amongst hushed breaths and quieted whispers. I watched Nicolo with romantic longing, or at least it was what I hoped to project. At that moment, my feigned confidence manifested into power. The dice turned corner-over-corner, and Nicolo faced me with queer delight. I understood how bravery could turn chance into triumph. I had won my man without degrading blandishment. Pleased, I observed the other men shaking their heads in disappointment.

That's when I was caught by him, by his wide grey eyes. His expression was like a raging sea. Henry stood not even ten feet away at the card table, arm around the waist of a thin blond in a gold dress. I sensed his disgust. He didn't watch Nicolo like the rest of the crowd. He said he'd return in the spring. How was I to anticipate him here? This was my way of surviving, and some of me blamed him for it.

I eyed Mother, who nodded slightly, her lashes closing in a wink. She did not look at Henry, but instinct said she'd known all along that he would be here tonight. Here I was forced to engage in an affair with another man while Henry watched with seething resentment.

I heard Mother's voice in my mind. *I couldn't do my job if I was pining for another.* Painfully, I took my attention away from Henry, although his look burned into my heart. I returned all my energy to the man I'd won, my patron for the night, and passively submitted myself to his domination. He clearly wanted to win, to win all night long.

Nicolo considered the painting on my back. "I appreciate your decoration, my dear. Are you as artful under your dress?"

I helped myself to his wine before answering, hoping the libation would banish Henry from my concern. Distractions might mean a mistake. "I am artful everywhere, *signore*."

He slid cold fingers into the back of my dress, clinging to me with expectation. "I imagine so. My luck has peaked tonight, and I should relish my kitties privately."

Nicolo led me toward the Casino's back entrance, and I craned to catch a look at Mother, who was engaged in a lively conversation with several men. Feeling frantic verve rise in my throat, I thought it impossible to depart without some assurance from Henry. But how could his blessing at this point do me anything but harm? I scanned the room for his face, his form. The dancing frenzy of strangers wavered like an ominous ocean, with no beacon of his affection to anchor me.

Nicolo asked. "Do you need something, my dear?"

Remembering myself, I covertly slid my hand around his waist, allowing it to hover over his pants, before whispering a kiss on his cheek. "No. The liveliness of the Casino is distracting."

Sadness threatened to overwhelm me. We were retreating like plebeians through the unremarkable rear, not the opulent entryway facing the Grand Canal. This would speak against my dignity and growing prestige. Before we could step from the noise into an uncertain evening, Nicolo bumped into someone redressing in a coat.

"Pardon me," a deep voice rumbled.

Nicolo bowed. "No, excuse me."

We met head-on with Henry, wafting of clean-smelling soap. I shrunk in shame.

Nicolo noticed my shivering. "We must get you to a warm place." He stirred to pass Henry. "Excuse me, *signore*."

Henry's words struck me like the blunt end of a leather belt. "Please forgive my interference. I would hate to disrupt an opportunity with this exquisite creature."

I couldn't bear to look at Henry. Thankfully, Nicolo pulled me into the courtyard and the adjoining alley. At this point, I would submit to whatever he asked, even if it meant public disgrace.

We walked arm-in-arm briefly before he pushed me into an alcove and kissed me roughly. Henry's face flashed in my mind, and I felt weak. I was resigned to bedding Nicolo here if he wanted. Pushing Henry's image aside, I returned Nicolo's kisses with the same force, making him cry as I bit his lip. His kiss tasted metallic and smelled like stagnant water at the bottom of a well. Although his scent was pleasant, there was a core of sickness I couldn't name. My instinct told me that bedding this man might be a mistake, but it was one I was committed to making if I were to get paid. Assessing his lip with his tongue, he frowned and pulled me through a winding path of alleys.

My feet ached, and my bare shoulders were chilled when we finally halted in front of an obscure building. Nicolo fumbled with a large key ring, and the door's bolt squealed as it released under his force. He pushed through a dank foyer devoid of light and kicked the door shut before dragging me upstairs, three flights, to a top-floor apartment in the villa.

Forcing a new key into another rusted lock, the door swung open to reveal a well-lit room. Sturdy candelabras dripped wax onto iron plates, all situated on a velvet table runner on a massive credenza at the far wall. Reds, blues, and purples of the most intense pigments covered pillows, couches, and drapes. The colors alone spoke of Nicolo's position, and I was thankful not to be asked into a bed covered in animal dander. He was a man of some means, even if he couldn't heat and furnish his entire villa.

He spoke with simple gestures, snapped his fingers, and pointed for me to drop my dress. It appeared that nakedness would not come from soft kisses and lingering touches. I looked down at my bodice to undo the laces, which lined the front, or I would have needed help.

Nicolo snapped his fingers again, "Look at me as you do that."

I'd grown accustomed to being ordered around and tugged my dress off my shoulders, remaining in my corset. I secretly thought of Henry without revealing where the yearning expression in my eyes came from. I removed my garter and stockings, leaving them wadded on the floor, out of the way of any advance he might make.

Nicolo drifted closer to me, his direct stare never wavering. He undid his coat and pulled his tunic over his head, standing even closer in wool pants, stretched tightly in the front and secured with leather laces. If he was aroused, I couldn't tell. He nodded to his pants.

Taking my cue, I pulled at the leather cord, which wouldn't untie. I studied how to undo Nicolo's pants, but he lifted my chin. I fumbled, and anxiety built as I pulled harder on the leather strips. He stopped my hands and undid his pants.

I glanced down but was met with a sharp, "No! Stay looking at my face."

Nicolo removed my pantaloons, leaving my corset in place. He held me with intense eye contact and pushed me back on the bed. He chased me as I scooted across the velvet comforter. Hovering over me, he positioned his manhood between my legs.

I glanced down, and that's when I noticed two things—both of which could result in severe punishment if mentioned. First, the flabby skin of Nicolo's member was as thick as his fat thumb. Second, a row of deep purple pocks spread from hipbone to hipbone.

He massaged himself. Exaggerated gyrations and an intense expression kept me compliant and amenable. But I was mortified. His sweat collected on his upper lip, and he struggled to pleasure himself as he fixated on some private fantasy. I panicked at the thought of the rash rubbing against my belly. Nicolo's face contorted, and I could tell he moved toward anger rather than pleasure. I didn't want him to take out his rising wrath on me.

I eased from under him, eyes still locked in our wordless conversation, rolled him onto his back, and sat astride him as I manipulated him. The tension in his face eased, and blood filled his member. I rode my hips on his thighs. His excitement grew, but his expression was pained. He fervently gripped a breast now protruding from my corset. He still could not reach a climax, and I realized another method was necessary.

I cupped his ass in my hand, massaging him. This excited him. His hands clasped my waist, and his claw-like nails dug into my skin. The more firmly I held him, the slower and deeper he scratched my back.

A whimper escaped me.

His gasping turned into a cry, and Nicolo released himself over our bellies, squeezing his eyes shut. Nicolo freed me from his clutches, and I dismounted, tugging the covers over his chest. He cuddled the length of fabric, and I had a hint of sadness thinking about the grape-colored velvet now coated with his disease.

I cleaned my hands and stomach with a cold cloth from the washbasin by the window and redressed, careful not to move too quickly to seem like I was fleeing.

"Thank you." Nicolo's look was soft. "I did not think I could do that again. He nodded to the table next to the bed. "Please take 20 coins from the bag. I am most grateful."

I did as I was told and slipped the money into a deep pocket in my dress. Although I appreciated Nicolo's payment, I felt queasy and needed to be away from him—with haste. I feigned a smile.

He closed his eyes, and I took my leave.

I made it down the flight of stairs and onto an alley. As I stepped out the door, I saw someone standing partially in the moon's light. Max entered the light, revealing his pale skin and cold blue lips.

"Max," I shouted in a whisper. "Come here." I quickly enveloped him under the length of my skirt. "Have you been waiting out here the whole time?"

He shivered next to me, clambering at my body for warmth. "I couldn't let you go home alone." He held me, and we walked in unison. "Are you ok?"

I tried to keep my voice steady but was ready to cry. "I'm ok, but I'll need a bath."

He nodded. "I'll tell Camilla when we get back."

Despite my resentment, I did not want Camilla to see me. Mother was the one who might know what Nicolo had. "No. It will have to be Mother."

Queen

Light Attributes: Regal, benevolent
Shadow Attributes: Romantic attraction with private agendas

I crouched into the copper tub and curled my shoulders to guard my breasts. Mother poured a pail of steaming water over the crown of my head. The water ran through my hair and down my back, burning as it cleansed the scratches left by Nicolo. Mother's touch was unusually gentle as she gathered my hair and knotted it high, pinning it atop my head. Gliding her fingers over my back, reading my skin's stories, she regarded the scratch marks from Nicolo's nails.

"These will scar." Her stale breath blew over my face. "The shape, it's interesting." She collected a hand mirror. "Here, stand up. I'll show you."

I was careful not to splash water onto the marble floor. She turned my back to the dressing table and then gave the mirror to me.

My entire body length reflected in the mirror behind me, but the tub rim concealed my feet and calves. The skin on my legs was pink from the heat. Still thin, too thin, I thought. My legs didn't touch as they eased into my buttocks, gently arching into my back. No great sweeping curves like Mother, but my skin was still firm. Then I saw them. Deep and angry like the seething gashes of a pawing, snarling animal.

I had not complained much when Nicolo scratched me. "Why would he do that?"

"He may not have understood his roughness." Mother traced the edges of the scratch. "Look at the shape. It's like your flower-stem burn marks are growing roots." The muscles around her mouth were soft. She noticed me watching her, snapped to composure, and ripped the mirror from my hands. "Turn around. I want to see where his disease coated you." I faced her and closed my eyes as she scrutinized my lower stomach, hovering and examining but never touching. The skin on my thighs prickled in the draftiness of the kitchen. She penetrated me with an accusatory glare. "How could you let this happen?"

I clasped my stomach above my nest of hair. "What was I to do? He was already on me. But his skin didn't touch me."

Eyes wide with anger, she reached around me to the shelf above the sink, found a sea sponge, and then moved to a cabinet under the mucky stained-glass window. I couldn't tell at first what she unearthed in the cupboard, but she returned to me with the left corner of her mouth cocked. She placed what she retrieved on the shelf behind me before grasping my shoulders and commanding, "Don't move." Lowering to her knees, she plunged the sponge into the water once, twice, three times, until she soaked it through.

She wrapped a hand around my back and brought the sponge to my stomach. Her movements were slow, starting in measured circles. At first, the sponge only tickled the soft flesh, like the way whiskers burn a cheek when kissed too hard. Her rhythm gathered momentum. Faster and faster, firmer, and firmer. She chafed at my skin, digging deeper into my flesh as though she intended to root out the source of my sin in a kind of exorcism.

I cried out and pushed her hands away. I eyed my stomach, mortified at the scratch on my skin. It burned like she'd held a candle to it for hours. "Why would you do that to me?"

"When I came to Venice, I was first at a hospital on the island of San Servolo. I wasn't there long but learned that cleanliness leads to recovery." She dropped the sponge on the shelf and palmed a purple jar topped with a cork stopper. It took some prying, but she removed the top to reveal a creamy, putrid-smelling substance. She tugged at the stick, forming the backbone of her hair stacked high on her head, suddenly causing her locks to fall. The framing of her face revealed her to be years younger, despite the threads of silver weaving from scalp to end. "The remedies we can make from controlling the purest ingredients can do wonders. Some might alter our minds and the way we see the world. Others reduce pain or may unforgettably mark our memories."

I shook because of the cold, her dominance, and my raging fear.

With an expression too gleeful for the task, she dipped the stick in the jar. "Don't move."

At first, a cooling, wet sensation spread over me, soothing the abrasions from Mother's scrubbing. The heat subsided. She rearranged her hair and re-corked the jar. Unsure I could move, dry my feet, and wrap in my nightgown, I held myself.

Then it came, a light tingle to begin, but pain climbed out of my core, one throbbing pinprick at a time. I thought I could bear it, that the pain would reach a zenith and diminish, the way the tide swells to a pitch and retreats. But it kept growing. Throbs and stings assaulted me. I shivered, fighting the instinct to scratch off the paste. Wiping it away would only result in her repeating the process. Blood jumped through the veins in my neck and rose through my head like lava. Clenching my teeth, trying not to cry out, I failingly fought against giving her the satisfaction of my agony.

"Mother, please. Make it stop. Please," I screeched.

Taking her time to dry her hands, she slowly walked to me. Eyes narrowing cat-like, she waited as though eyeing a cornered mouse before dinner.

I refused to surrender the last of my dignity to feverish panic and held her gaze, allowing the pain to carve memory deep into my spirit, hardening me to her healing, forever eradicating my need for her shelter. She was no Mother, and certainly not mine.

I wasn't prepared as she plunged me into the bath. My knees buckled underneath me, and I flopped down. The welcome chill on my stomach was instant relief. Desperately, I splashed the water over me and gently felt my skin, pressing my fingers into the caked paste. It gradually dissolved like plaster. I sat in the murky milk water, fatigued, drained of any energy or will to fight. I could have fallen asleep sitting bolt upright.

She pulled up her dress sleeve, revealing a deep red scar shaped like a heart. Pressing her thumb into the mark, it momentarily whitened before the crimson raged back. "I know the sensation, for it was a treatment I endured at San Servolo. A young priest concocted great tinctures, and as I was one of the first females at the hospital, he thought it right to try them on me instead of the sailors. I'm sorry you will be discolored on your stomach, but you are clean." She tossed a long cloth over me and commanded, "Get up."

Balancing on weak legs, I pulled the dry cloth over my shoulders, exposing my lower body. Although my skin no longer hurt, the thought of something touching me there—ever again—was unfathomable. Knowing the white skin, tight as a stretched drum top, would forever bear a reminder of this night, and Mother's orchestration of it made me want to retch.

She held my chin and forced eye contact. "I hope you appreciate the damage your recklessness could have caused." She released me. "I expect my remedy will keep you clean, but now you have two areas of your body to conceal creatively."

My spoiled figure made me less valuable and one step closer to a common whore's life than a renowned courtesan. Something stirred deep in my belly, and I reignited my argument. "You put him to me. You made this arrangement. You allowed me to bed Nicolo. You were the one to orchestrate all of this, so you can prove what?"

She only grinned at my accusation.

I was ready to rush toward her and demand we have it out. "Why do you hate me?"

We held each other in a standoff.

She cast down her gaze, guarding her next thought. "Liking or hating you is unimportant. I do not regard you except for adding monetary value to my life."

The door to the kitchen squeaked open, and Camilla's full frame blocked the morning light. My breath caught in my throat at the sight of her, bearing a look of both pity and shock. At least for the moment, I would not have to fight this battle alone. Benyamin and Asha trailed closely behind. Max must have informed Camilla of my night, and she must have summoned the doctor and his daughter.

Studied at Padua, Benyamin was one of few Jews with formal medical training in Venice. This alone should have granted longevity in a world of walking sickness, but Venetians like tradition, and he was not of the city. Also, his cure required sacrifice, the kind most Venetians disdained. He believed cleansing and debriding the body came before tonics and herbal remedies. Asha was his assistant and was named after their profession—Asha, the "healer."

Both went directly to the basin by the window and washed before turning to us. Mother's countenance wholly changed, and she stepped to them, touching Benyamin on the arm and gathering Asha into an embrace. It was shocking how tenderly she held the girl, a gentle acceptance I had yet—and never expected—to receive.

Awkward silence made my skin bristle as severely as the angry balm Mother basted over me moments ago. I shivered in the dried suds of the copper basin and glared at Benyamin as he approached, warding him off with an outstretched hand. His trained gaze studied my stomach.

Asha barely looked at me. Her eyes darted from my face to my sex and back.

Mother attempted to shoo Asha from the room. "Come, dear," she cooed. "I think this is too much for you to see."

Benyamin inched closer. "I should have a look at you."

"Mother cleaned me. No more." My teeth uncontrollably chattering, I bit my tongue, washing my mouth with an acid flavor. "Tell me what to do, but don't touch me."

Mother shouted. "Enough!" Her fingers stung my face in an instinctive slap.

Benyamin stayed Mother's second blow. "I can deal with this, Danielle. If you washed her, I'm sure she's clean." He helped me from the tub. "I need to see you in the light." He led me to a bench by the window. Sunlight flooded through the room in flickers as the clouds parted and closed. "Tell me of the man that bedded you." His directness was shocking.

"I saw him at the casino. I invited him, and he accepted." I didn't think blaming Mother for the introduction would help. "He had fine clothes. I did not expect him to be sick. He was nice. It wasn't until he undressed that I became acquainted with his form and function."

Mother didn't try to hide her amusement.

Benyamin's beard splayed like plumed goose feathers, curving in a draft from the window as he breathed steadily. "Tell me more."

I pulled into the shadow, fearing the sun would highlight my humiliation. "He barely touched me as though purposefully trying to guard me against his disease. There were marks on his stomach, but he didn't get close, except for the end, when his fluid washed over me."

"Did his stomach touch your skin?"

"No."

"What *did?*"

My cheeks were hot. "The usual things produced during the final moment of satisfaction, and his hands."

"Anything else?"

I shook my head.

"Think."

"I was careful. I told Mother about the marks because his skin was angry. He was white. The marks stood out." Coarse fibers chafed against my breasts as I pulled the towel tight. My face burned with shame. "He may not have touched me much, but I touched him. It was better than him trying to force himself into me."

"I need to see." He said in a drawn-out way, much like a long whistle. Benyamin gathered himself, blocking the light and casting a long, foreboding shadow. He went to his bag and removed a glass vial. "Hold out your hands."

I lost my grip on the towel, revealing my breasts and back.

Asha gasped, "What are those?"

With wide eyes quickly narrowing into a knowing gaze, Benyamin turned to me for a better look. He pulled my head into his chest and smothered me in his scent of tobacco and cinnamon. My skin prickled as he traced the noticeable scratch.

Slowly freeing me, he raised my hands and shook a few drops of amber-colored oil onto them. "Rub." I was trepidatious after suffering the pain of Mother's balm. He returned to his bag and found another pod with a corked lid like the purple one Mother retrieved from under the sink. My stomach gurgled, and I remembered Benyamin might have kinder cleansing methods.

He set the pod on the bench. "This is for the marks, including your back. It is a jelly ground from the aloe vera plant. It promotes healing and will diminish scarring." He shuffled back to Mother and Camilla. I heard him seethe, "Very poorly done, both of you." Without turning to me again, he left.

Despite the expected decorum, Asha did not follow him. Instead, she sat beside me, tenderly tugging the cloth around my shoulders. I gripped the pod Benyamin gave me and stared into her eyes, glistening from tears.

"Can I help you to your room?"

Relief overtook me. This was the first time I'd experienced someone my age—that wasn't Max—who bestowed such a great show of empathy upon me.

I bit my lip, weighed down by despondency. "Aren't you afraid you'll catch something?"

"No. Besides, you still deserve someone to care for you," Asha replied.

Mother stepped in front of Asha as she supported me over her shoulder. "Asha, your father will worry. You should go home."

She eased past Mother toward the stairs. "He will understand."

As we turned the corner, Mother said, "One more mistake, and you're out."

Asha carried my weight as we went. I breathed deeply, wincing with each rise of my belly. I could sleep uncovered on my back but craved cuddling with my pillows. I crawled into bed, broken and humiliated, with tears in my eyes, weeping despondently into the sheets.

I heard Mother's voice in my mind—*you're out*. She had found the one thing I thought I had hidden, the one weakness I refused to reveal—the fear of exile and belonging nowhere and to no one. She divined my worries, and her threat suffocated my spirit. I would now become as she wished, cowed and compliant.

Healer

Light Attributes: Passion to serve and repair
Shadow Attributes: Taking advantage of those who need help

I faintly heard someone calling my name and struggled to wake myself. My neck ached like my head was as heavy as a bushel of apples. My skin was utterly on fire.

"Renna, wake up." Camilla shook me from a nightmare. "She's been asleep for two days, passing in and out. My remedies are not working."

Max asked. "Do I need to get help?"

"It's Christmas, and Danielle will expect her back to work." Camilla's voice rang with distress. "We need to roll her over. The fever is climbing, and the heat must be pulled from her core." She gripped me with a firm hand and tugged me around.

My head was swimming. I tried to sit upright, but nausea overtook me. My head felt like it would explode, and my mouth flooded with metallic bitterness. I relieved myself in great heaves. When the vomiting subsided, I sank back into my bed.

Camilla's voice was steady, as though she soothed me like when I was a child. "Get Benyamin and Asha. Make sure Benyamin brings his bag." Her girth weighted down the edge of my bed as she dried my cheek with her apron. She spoke louder as the door opened. "Be back before dark. If the gates close and you're inside, there will be trouble."

The fever raged through me with a perpetual shudder, which left my muscles aching like a day's long labor. It was erratic, one moment causing a deep chill like I was back in the Harewood icehouse, then rising again and leaving my legs afire like I had spent all day in the sun. Still, the lavender-scented sheets and the soothing touch of Camilla's washcloth were refreshing.

*****

Camilla had me propped with a stack of pillows and spooned me soup when Max, Benyamin, and Asha returned. She set the bowl on the side table and scurried to Max and our guests. Her tone was sharp. "Why so long?"

Benyamin unabashedly entered. Styled in his typical embroidered yarmulke, with his beard neatly combed, he greeted Camilla with a kiss on each cheek. It seemed too familiar for the English maid and the Jewish physician to embrace each other in such a way. He smiled with dry, pursed lips. "I was delivering a child and simply could not tell the mother to wait."

Camilla relaxed, and she hugged Benyamin again. "Of course. But you take too many risks." She touched Asha's cheek, much as she always did mine. "The gates will shut soon."

"Would you rather I return tomorrow after following the city rules?" Benyamin took a long look at me. "I think the Counsel of Ten forgot that creating a barrier to keep your gentry away for their safety also meant limiting their access to our services. Or maybe they enjoy watching good Catholic girls die from fever." He spoke plainly and set his satchel at my feet.

Mother's bath had brought Benyamin and me to a new level of intimacy. Before Venice, Camilla was the only one to know my scars, but my recent work required new skills. Benyamin kept a record of the changes in my condition. He didn't judge me—morally—but his trained physician's eye scrutinized me like the butcher inspecting a flank steak.

He rubbed his hands together. "I don't want to hurt you with the temperature difference. I think any touch now will be very unpleasant, but I must examine you." He ran his fingers around the nodules in my neck and then brought his palms to my belly, slowly massaging each section. "Does this hurt?" I trembled with fever.

He pressed the narrow part of my wrist, feeling where the blood ran closest to the surface, and removed a watch from the inside of his waistband. "Quiet a moment, please, everyone. Renna, breathe normally while I listen to how fast your heart beats." He studied the watch, the second hand audibly ticking for a long minute. "Well, my dear," he tucked the watch away, "Your little heart is racing at one hundred fifty-three times a minute. Even if you were being chased down the alley, I don't think it would go so quickly."

Camilla stood with Benyamin. Their heads were close as though they could communicate clairvoyantly. They stared at my chest, watching the rise and fall of my breath.

Then Benyamin faced the window and the fading purple and greys of dusk as he spoke. "You don't usually send for me, and you have done so twice this week. I will assume something in the fever is outside of your scope." He wiped his hands on a cloth next to the basin. "You think it is about the other day?"

Camilla gathered my sweaty hand. "I was examining her yesterday morning and felt something was off, more than lying in bed with the chills." She looked at me. "I checked her pee. It had a strong brown tinge. I hoped it was just the light."

"Has it hurt to urinate?"

Camilla answered for me. "She has not complained."

"The Egyptians said, 'sending heat from the bladder' would feel like fire when urinating. With no such complaints, other things must be considered—the kidneys. Unlike the Egyptians, we do not believe the organs are the seat of moral judgment because there are two." He laughed.

His joke was lost on me. "Kidney?"

"Yes, young one." Benyamin looked at me with a tender expression, devoid of the lust I encountered with paying customers. He slid his hand over my belly and around the lower part of my back, letting my body rest on his palm as he spoke. His fingers tapped on me, like keeping time to a marching tune.

I squirmed away from his touch. "That hurts."

"As I thought." He explained himself. "You have two orbs that connect to your bladder. The orbs are called kidneys. They clean the body of pollutants. The rest is deposited into the bladder and eventually urinated out. The kidneys are like a sponge, but if your body fills with poison, your insides become infected. This is what Camilla suspects."

Her nose wrinkled. "The urine, it was strong and bitter."

"It's ammonia. The urine is fermenting. It is why Renna has a fever." He ran his fingers through his beard as he addressed me. "Your body is fighting to kill off what is poisoning you."

The pain increased. "How long will this last?"

"It is hard to tell. The few people I have seen with such sickness eventually died. I learned of this disease through a postmortem examination of their bodies. Don't worry. I will be with you until the end, either when you meet your Lord or rise from this bed." He looked at me long with a pleasant expression. His countenance was amiable, as though he told a tale of sweets and sunrises instead of what might kill me.

The calm description of my healing—or my death—sickened me. Was this how it would end for me?

He removed a bottle labeled *opium* from his bag. "Camilla, a glass of water." She gave him the glass, and Benyamin stirred in a few drops. "You will drink this and sleep."

"I'm not thirsty."

He commanded me with his typical aplomb. "It does not matter. We must cleanse the kidneys like washing a dirty cloth. The more water you drink, the more you urinate, and the more we know. The opium will let you sleep."

Liquid washed over my throat, and a hollow feeling overtook me. I relaxed into the cradle of my bed and envisioned myself rocking in a bassinet as an infant. I did not drift entirely into sleep but was blissfully separated from the fever's heat and my aching muscles.

Benyamin pointed to the bed. "Asha, you will remain with her."

Asha hugged me, and I could do nothing but close my eyes. She crawled up the far side and laid her hand on my chest. A faint smell of chestnuts and garlic wafted from her fingers. "I will take care of you."

*****

THE CURSE OF MAIDEN SCARS

The full effects of Benyamin's tincture wore off, and I woke in a drenching sweat. The heat from Asha's body felt like I sat near a hearth, fully ablaze. I moaned and pushed at her. Her sweet face appeared, and she wiped at her sleepy eyes.

Asha retrieved a wet cloth and began cleaning my cheeks. "You've been sleeping all day. Father said I should get you up and make you walk around the room." Her tone was playful, but she spoke with Benyamin's certainty. She gazed at me tenderly—much like Camilla.

Camilla whisked into the room and set a tray on the table by my settee as though on command. Max and Benyamin followed behind, closing the door—mostly.

Benyamin looked at Camilla. Like a well-practiced team, he hoisted me to my feet, and Camilla stripped me of the blankets. The crisp air hit me, and I limply slipped to the floor tiles like ice. My shift clung to my damp skin. Benyamin averted his eyes. Camilla wrapped me in a blanket from the bed and guided me to the chamber pot near Francese's cage. He stared at me with cold docility as I squatted over the porcelain bowl. At first, nothing came out, nothing but a trickle.

My legs quivered. "Nothing is happening," I reported through chattering teeth.

Benyamin asked. "Does it burn?"

"Not really."

He and Camilla shared a similar expression. "That's not good."

His response disturbed me.

"You need to bathe her. Make her drink and try again." Benyamin turned to Asha and Max. "Bring the water up here so she does not have to go to the kitchen. Be quick."

I was at the mercy of my physician and my overseer. No two people were more capable of my care, but neither were there two people I could control less—except Mother.

Camilla situated me on the settee and gave me a cup of tea before stripping the bedsheets. I fixated on Francese as he groomed himself and wished my recovery were as simple as his shedding of fading feathers. I weakly unlatched his cage to allow him the freedom to fly. The haze of the fading sun indicated it was evening again, and I'd lost yet another day.

Camilla finished the bed as Asha and Max returned, each struggling with a jug and bowl mounded with fresh cloths. Cici quickly followed with the kitchen's copper basin, managing the girth like carting a load of laundry.

Cici's forehead wrinkled with concern, which gave rise to my fears. She placed the bathing tub near my settee. "Dear, I pray for your speedy recovery." With a look of angst, she eyed Camilla and Benyamin. "Heal her quickly. You have to know what it will mean if Mother intervenes." Cici clasped her skirts and fled the room, chased by a foretold terror.

Camilla assumed the practiced reassuring expression I'd seen many times, particularly when she attempted to coax the workhouse children into a dinnerless slumber. "Pay no mind to that. We will have you washed and ready before long."

I scooted to the end of the settee and caught a waft of my stench. Sourness oozed from my sweat like I'd eaten onions for a week. I asked Benyamin, "Why do I smell so bad?"

"It's the poison. I don't know many treatments, but I will do my best." He laid several bottles from his bag on my windowsill.

"I know exactly how to treat her," Mother hissed as she entered the room. Her presence filled the space like noxious smoke. "You are wasting your time. It might help wash out the alcohol she guzzles. But you know as well as I there is only *one* way to clean the blood."

Benyamin growled. "I don't adhere to medieval practices."

"Perhaps you don't." She paused, monitoring her comments, hiding detail of her past. "I was an experiment for *cleaning* and am well aware of what works and does not. San Servolo still uses several tinctures that were first applied to me." Mother lifted her chin in a proud posture, highlighting the elegant sway of her neck.

Benyamin turned his back to her. "There has been good success with triple the measure of fluids, keeping the patients moving, and administering tinctures of cranberry, vinegar, garlic, and *Cordyceps Sinensis*."

"And what is cord . . . issps . . . sinens?" I asked.

Benyamin grinned more to himself than to me. "It is a Chinese remedy. A special caterpillar high in the Annapurna Mountains melds with a mushroom that grows on the mountainside. The insect and the fungus unite, and the union produces a potent medicine."

"How do you know about such things? You're a Jew." Mother snapped. "And you are in *my* house. When did you get here? If you were here the whole time, I could have you arrested," she hissed. We clung to her words with a frightening vision of the consequences of her threats.

"No, mistress," Benyamin's posture cowered. "I only now arrived."

Max stopped abruptly in the bath preparations and sloshed water on the floor by Mother's feet.

"You clumsy little cretin," she spat, shaking the droplets from her skirt. Her expression clouded as she eased back to the door.

"*Pardon*, Mother. We are trying to hurry," Max shyly explained.

Asha poured in the last of the water. She came to me, delicately taking my hand. "Let me help. You might want to stay wrapped in your blanket."

I followed her instructions but caught Mother's look as I lifted my shift and slipped into the shallow bath. "We do not make money while you lie in that bed. What Benyamin proposes could take weeks, or you could die." Mother shot daggers at Benyamin, although he had yet to face her again. "You will give her nothing unless I say. Wash her. I'll give her what I *know* works." Her broad shoulders made her appear as though she'd already won. And my heart sank.

Asha kneeled beside me. With my bottom warmed in the water and my shoulders wrapped in the blanket, I was comfortable for the first time in days.

I admired the complexity of Asha's look. Her light skin was offset by dark hair, several shades darker than mine but still remarkably similar. Her eyes were a different kind of hazel. I'd always thought they were brown, but flecks of glinted green highlighted the edges from this angle.

She glanced at me as she added lemon juice to the bathwater. "You're staring."

Max handed down a cloth. "At this moment, you look alike, like you could be sisters."

"That is ridiculous," Mother barked. "They are nothing alike."

Camilla sucked in a breath through her teeth and seemed jolted into action. "Girls, this is not playtime. We need Renna cleaned and back in bed."

"Camilla."

She froze as if she had been struck cold by Medusa's stare.

Mother glared at her. "I expect that you will not let Renna's disease contaminate others. Max and Asha do not deserve to sink into disgrace. Asha is my ward."

Camilla was filled with the breath of a protective mother. "And Max is my son."

Mother was unflustered. "This is business. Familiarity is inappropriate."

Benyamin moderated the moment. "Danielle, have a heart."

"Get her dressed," Mother commanded.

My companions had me in a fresh shift within moments, and I was folded back under the blankets. All my energy had drained, and I thought I might sleep peacefully for the first time in days.

Asha curled next to me. "I want to stay with her."

Mother coaxed her sweetly. "Did you not hear me?"

My fever played tricks on me, for it seemed like Mother spoke to Asha as I would a stray kitten, luring it to safety.

Asha's voice reverberated against my back. "I can help by staying."

Mother's energy deflated. "Fine. The rest of you, out." She came around the bed with a golden vial. She filled a goblet with water and uncorked the bottle with the edge of her thumb. The top dropped to the bedcovers. She tipped in yellow tincture and swirled it in the water until it shone brightly. She handed the glass to Asha. "Have her drink it, all of it."

Asha lifted the glass to the light, examining the glowing liquid. "What is it?"

"Something that was given to me at San Servolo. The priest made a mixture of mushrooms and rye." Mother brushed a lock of hair from Asha's cheek. "Consumed in pure form, one will swell with lunacy. But, diluted, the mixture lets one sleep and heal." With a quick whirl, Mother moved to the door. "Summon me when she falls asleep. You can leave then."

"Might as well get this over with." At first sip, I recalled the rye mixture Ann gave me in the asylum. I tried to spit it out, but it was too late. The liquid choked my throat.

Asha tucked the blankets around me again. "I've always wanted a sister. Maybe we can at least be the best of friends."

I settled into my bed, and my senses became foggy. "That would be nice."

Asha went to my desk. "As friends, shouldn't we share what we love? What do you like to read?" She ran her fingers over my books. "Of course, you would have things about history." She pulled out a narrow title. "*The Family Herbal—The Cure of All Disorders Incident to Mankind*. What is it?"

I struggled to stay focused on her. "Something from Mother's collection."

She returned the pamphlet. My heart raced as she went for the one book I didn't want her to see. Asha found *Aretino* and held the spine in her hand, allowing the book to open to the center. She read, "*Whores are not real women. They are whores.*" She gasped.

I clung to the last threads of my senses, which were enough to propel me into deep shame. "Please. It's not proper."

"I can tell it is not, but if you've read it," she turned the page, "maybe it will help me understand."

"I don't think you should."

I didn't hear all she read, but I was sickened by her chosen passage. "*They give her the loveliest names . . . Laura, Cassandra . . . and for every girl who has a real mother . . . thousands have been gotten from the hospitals . . . Who is the father of those children . . . they are the daughters of noblemen and great monsignors.*"

Before my eyes fluttered closed, I caught Mother's sharp glare through the partially open door. Her expression said that she might skin me alive if we were alone.

Saboteur

Light Attributes: Fear of self-empowerment
Shadow Attributes: Self-destruction, undermining others

Sun blazed through the open shutters, bidding me to join the morning songbirds in celebrating a new day. Instead of rising to someone's rousting or my fever's heat, I awoke naturally, more refreshed than any morning since my birthday. I was dressed in a clean shift devoid of rank sweat stains. A breeze chased away the staleness.

Francese ruffled his feathers, announcing I was not alone. I was far from myself but felt infinitely better. It pained me to think that Mother's remedies might have worked. I hoped it was all Benyamin's doing.

I didn't know how many days I had been in bed and how many nights Mother would require me to make up for her losses. I recoiled at the thought of sex. The idea of Nicolo's pocks, Mother's remedies, and my resulting fever made me rail more than ever against a courtesan's life. No matter the cost, even if it meant I spent my last days cleaning privies, this would be the end of my life as a whore.

Inching my way up my pillows to a seated position, I sought a goblet of water at my bedside table. Two syringes, neither tipped with a needle, sat center on the table. Lifting one for inspection, I caught a faint acidic smell. An errant drop revealed it as vinegar. A silvery substance clung to the glass edges of the second syringe. As I turned the device in my hand, liquid metal raced around the glass. It never fully hardened.

A wave of pain suddenly hit me. My back ached similarly to my kidney infection. Fearing Nicolo's illness might still affect me, I instinctively clasped my hands over myself. Sharp twinges shot across my belly. Listening to my body's clues, I fixated on several painful places on my stomach and between my legs.

Tentatively, I slid my fingers under the covers and tugged at my nightgown. As I moved my hips, I felt pokes along my back. I touched something slick and pulsating. That's when I found them. There were several bumps over my stomach and one on my inner thigh. I lifted my nightgown and counted the slippery bodies before opening my eyes to verify the horror. Six engorged leeches, grey with wavering green hues, swelled as they drank their dinner from my skin. I did not need to see the rest to know what sucked on my leg.

Panic set in, and I grasped the leech closest to my navel and tried to pull it free of my flesh, but it dug deeper. I had to be rid of them. Braving the pain, I wrapped all my fingers around the leech. It oozed and was slick and hard to grasp. With a firm twist and pull in one motion, I was freed of its jaws. My skin was discolored where it had feasted. A small hole with a drop of blood marked me. The spongy creature turned in on itself as I inspected it, like a worm trying to maneuver to freedom or reattach and feed again.

Francese ruffled his feathers. I sought a place to dispose of it and searched for my chamber pot, but it was missing. Waddling to his cage, I tossed the leech on the straw at the bottom and waited to see if he would eat, but he did not. Instead, he stared at me. I focused on his steady, amber-colored gaze and worked on the remaining leeches, swiftly removing them and piling them with the first. I again waited for Francese to eat—nothing. His stillness signaled the difficulty the last leech would pose—the one clinging between my legs.

I couldn't yank, twist, and pull as I had with the ones on my stomach, but I refused to ask for help. I clasped the leech, but the barest movement shot pain through my core. I had to examine how it was attached, stripped off my shift, and found my hand mirror on my dressing table. Typically, I used the mirror to see how I looked from behind, a critical vantage point for my work. Today I would inspect the parts my patrons paid much to appreciate. A vivid sunbeam lighted my view, and I squatted over the mirror. My legs trembled. The leech sucked in the crease high on my thigh. The dark, throbbing creature morbidly fascinated me. The crisp morning light illuminated the subtle green underneath the mud-brown of its skin.

Camilla ambled in with a tray of tea and placed it on my desk before standing behind me, touching my shoulder. "Why are you out of bed?"

I talked down to the mirror as I watched the leech. "I have something attached." I couldn't tell her what it was. It was one thing to understand in my mind but to say it aloud made it a reality I wasn't willing to face.

Camilla knelt next to me. I heard her suck in her breath when she saw the mirror's reflection. My cheeks became hot, and my feet were sweating. Although I trusted her, my compromised position made me feel like Mother caught me, not my longtime guardian. Camilla straightened her skirt as though she had done nothing more than arrange the fire for lighting.

"Let me help you back to the bed."

I rose but kept my legs wide, walking like astride a horse. Scuttling to the bed and crawling on, rear-end high in the air, I hesitated to lie back, resisting the passive position that had allowed such a violation.

Her warm hand rested on my hip. "We have two choices. You can wait for the leech to have its fill and then drop free, or I can pull it off now. If we move it, we run the risk that it will leave a remnant of itself where it touches you, opening a wound that may struggle to heal and bleed. But if it stays on, we wait until *it* decides when it's time. This leech is large and not yet full. It may be a while."

We were approaching Carnival season, and I had to be in my best health as soon as possible. "What will allow me to work the soonest?"— That would be Mother's question. Although I was committed to abandoning this life and trade, I still needed to bide my time and develop a plan. Carnival might be it.

"If I remove it, you should be up today. If it does not go well, you can still walk, but you may feel weak as it feeds on you, perhaps not more than your monthly bleeding."

Disgusted, I commanded, "Remove it."

"Fine. Hold as you are. I have a good vantage."

She kept a hand at the base of my back. I did not cry out, but my swollen, tender skin threatened to tear as she tugged. Instantly there was a release. She nudged me, and I fell face long into my pillow, completely drained. Camilla curiously stayed unmoving.

Craning my head, I was dismayed by her pale expression. "Now, what's wrong?"

She glanced from the leech to my bare bottom and back. "There should only be blood, but you are stained. The leech doesn't look the same."

I touched between my legs and brought my fingers up to study the shimmery grey liquid coating them. Showing Camilla, I asked, "Do you know what this is?"

"I've seen something like that before, but how did it get on you?" Camilla came around the bed. "I think it may be quicksilver."

Shock subsided, and anger quickly took its place. I pulled myself into a seated position, carefully tucking my shift between my legs. I glanced at Camilla's open palm and was horrified by the size of the leech she held. It was by far the largest of them all.

"What do you remember?"

"I remember a drink Mother prepared, and then I remember waking this morning, feeling relieved, although having prickles of pain all over." I grabbed the leech. "I know now what caused the discomfort." I gagged at the thought of someone covering me with these succubi. Bitter bile coated my lips with an acrid taste.

"You don't remember me tending to you, Benyamin's medicine, or Asha singing to you? It's been many days." Camilla looked deflated. "I left you for only a few hours."

I stretched to her, and the syringes on the bed clanged together. "I found these on my nightstand this morning."

Camilla snatched up the vials. "She must have stolen them from Benyamin's satchel. Or worse, she administers this cure to herself. That would explain her paranoid mind. It's thought that heavy metals cleanse disease, things like quicksilver and lead. I think it is wrong to place something so unnatural in our bodies. I can understand vinegar." She brought the clear syringe to her nose. "That's this. But quicksilver! It is a devil's prescription."

"A small amount won't hurt me, right?"

Camilla's eyes shadowed as her mind took her to a distant memory. "I don't know about that. We can go mad with the simplest intervention."

I breathed heavily as I recalled the heart-shaped stain on Mother's forearm. "Mother—Danielle—has mentioned San Servolo a few times. You said she was hospitalized when she arrived in Venice. What was she treated for? I've heard of Povelglia, the island where plague victims quarantine for forty days. But this San Servolo, what is it?"

Camilla mindlessly played with her apron. "She was meant to join the dye merchant's house where I worked, but Danielle was not stable before we sailed from England and was overtaken by hysteria upon arriving in Venice." Camilla's expression said Mother's crossing from England was indeed grave.

I struggled to reconcile Mother as a discombobulated woman needing medical treatment. "But she was cured? Why would she go to the convent and not the dye merchant?"

Camilla sat on the settee next to Francese, resigned to share her weighty details. "They wouldn't have her. The dye master said she was far too dangerous. I learned to love my life in Venice." She glanced at me fondly. "It makes me incredibly happy to see you appreciate the city as I do. And to answer your question from months back, I wouldn't have left if the circumstances in England weren't dire."

"And San Servolo?"

Camilla's hefty bosom heaved in a despondent breath. "I can't begin to explain. You will have to see it for yourself someday. Like every island in Venice, it has a flavor all its own. It's not like Polvelgia. Nor is it anything like Mirano, but Danielle was healed by the experience. She rediscovered her passions." She nervously readjusted her blonde and silver bun.

I felt like she was hiding something and perspired with irritation. "You are hiding your meaning behind obscurities. Can't you speak more directly?"

She readjusted herself. "I've said all I can. It's not my story to tell."

I let it go. Even if Camilla explained Mother's past, my fatigue prevented me from comprehending it. "But what about this cure that is Mother's doing? I don't know much about metals. Is it something we should discuss with Benyamin?"

She was instantly animated. "Benyamin will be enraged." She

collected the syringes, tucked them in her apron pocket, and accepted the leech balled in my open palm. "What do you want me to do with it?"

This would be the last time I would be subjected to someone else's *medicine*. "Throw it in Francese's cage." Francese still did not feast. Instead, he stood on his perch, unwavering. I appreciated that he was not going to eat. "I don't understand why she treats me so cruelly. We should ask Benyamin about the quicksilver. Maybe it will explain Mother's mind."

Camilla tucked her chin down. Her posture projected disgust.

I lifted my arms and turned around like a performer to my audience. "Am I revolting to you now?"

She opened her arms to me. "No, dear, never."

If not for the tear tracing her cheek and a hiccup restraining her sadness, I might have lashed out at her with all my fury building toward Mother. I collapsed into her welcoming embrace and allowed her to shelter my nakedness.

Her chest heaved in throbbing sobs. "I am never revolted, only at myself, for I have failed you."

I sought her face. "What do you mean?" I tapped away her tears. "You have been my protector, more of a mother than anyone I've known."

She allowed herself a moment to cry. "Please don't say that. I have tried to mother you, in a way, but every time I have aimed to improve your life, to give you an opportunity, the kind I imagine your mother . . . What any mother would wish for a child, I have only further exposed you to harm. All after your start in this world proved most unfair."

My hands clenched. "I thought you didn't know where I came from."

She wrapped me again in a second, awkward embrace. "My dear, when you came to me, I knew you'd been mishandled." She kissed the tip of my nose. "Anyone with a right mind, after noticing your scars, would understand you deserved sympathy."

I touched the scratches on my stomach and recalled the nightmares plaguing me each night and the continual confusion about my identity. I never expected anything but a hard life. But somehow, the years had given me clues that I could have more—governess, maid, sister, daughter. Were they all false dreams?

Despite my need to belong, one thing was true—no one would protect me but me. This would be the last time I'd allow fear to control me. Mother offered no guard, only danger. And my keepers to this point continued to fail me. I would find a way to align my mind and heart with safeguarding myself.

I heard my promise with Mother Shipton: *To my body: I will keep you protected by my will or someone else's.*

Scribe

> Light Attributes: Preserves knowledge
> Shadow Attributes: Alters facts, plagarizes

Camilla came to me the following day with a report. "Danielle has left to meet her new business partner. If we are to learn what she has done to you, now is the opportunity." She searched my armoire for a modest brown skirt, an appropriately matching cream blouse, and a russet jacket. She slung the clothes over her arm like the practiced laundress she was, slid a clean, linen shift over my now flushed body, letting it fall to my thighs, and handed me the blouse and skirt.

I was confused that I didn't add my petticoat or corset first. I pulled the clothes on and waited in my place as Camilla went for a pair of long woolen stockings. She handed them to me. "What about knickers?"

She gave me the jacket. "You will have little need for those. You will leave this house as a normal woman. Not a courtesan. And a normal woman has no need for knickers."

This was a funny idea. Knickers at least kept the nether regions of a woman's body covered. It was curious how courtesans and whores kept that privilege while *normal* women were as naked under their skirts as babies after a bath.

I went to the mirror to see how I presented. My hair hung down, unbrushed, and unpinned. My face was white, more than after a harsh English winter. My eyes were sunken, and I could see that the tinged whites had a light tea stain color. My muted gold fleck was still evident but faded. Dressed in everyday brown garb, with no underpinnings to accentuate my form, I was a clean version of my Yorkshire days.

Camilla twisted my hair in a plain bun, then collected a dollop of palm oil from a jar on my desk and smoothed it over my lips and under my eyes. Gently, she pinched my cheeks to bring up the color. "That is all the fussing you will need." She gave me a grey shawl. "Take this for your shoulders and your head later."

Camilla fluttered around the room, tidying papers on my desk and restacking books in their place on the shelves. She touched *Aretino's Dialogues*. "You still have this."

The comment didn't seem more than a casual observation but nevertheless raised a pang of guilt. I nodded. "Asha read some of it."

Camilla raised her brow in a look I knew very well. She was counting, as she told me was her practice, to keep herself calm and push away her first urge to yell. "Why?"

I hissed. "I was sick and powerless to stop her. Besides, is it wrong to want someone to understand my life, someone not already a whore?"

"I let you keep that book. I knew you would eventually be exposed to the life you live now—somehow. You have been conditioned to tolerate shock. Now you can exist in the world of men and courtesans. This is *your* knowledge." She paused and swallowed. "It is not for you to share. It is like eating from the Tree of Knowledge of Good and Evil. Once tasted, unknowing is impossible. Asha is not like you. Please do not unlock curiosity in her." She paused. "It is not that she is better." Camilla looked at me, gently touching my cheek. "She has others who look out for her, have other plans for her."

"Like Benyamin and Mother?"

Why hadn't there been someone to do the same for me?

*****

We snuck out of the villa shortly after lunch and navigated around crates and laundry bags, rushing through the alley toward the Ghetto. It seemed ages since I'd left the house. I pattered down the cobblestone walk in flat shoes with soft leather bottoms, nothing like my usual platforms. Counting the stones and making amusement by dancing around water puddles, I felt like a child chasing after her nanny.

We crossed the canal over a lesser bridge and stopped next to large, weather-worn wooden gates that closed off the Ghetto each night. They were reopened in the morning by a Venetian soldier. Benyamin noted the precaution's absurdity, but I envied the Ghetto's shelter. *How would my path have been different if Camilla had led me to Benyamin's door instead of Danielle's?*

Max appeared, slightly breathless and panting, struggling with an unwieldy basket. "Rene and Gustavo were arguing about how much to charge me for the salt and flour. It would be half the price if they didn't know I was taking it into the Ghetto. Seems unfair."

Camilla took the basket and nodded toward the alley. "We are late."

We passed through oak gates attached to massive iron hinges. Deep grooves told of the countless times the gates were sealed shut at dusk and reopened at dawn, aimed to confine those relegated to the *Ghetto*. The light was scarce. Many passages rarely saw the sun, as the buildings rose high to accommodate the growing population. The air was fresh, and the noise was low. We walked around austere corners and shopping windows with modest displays of merchandise. For such a robust financial contributor to the Venetian culture, the Ghetto seemed like a humble, unacknowledged orphan—like me. Despite this little burrow's bustling business and industry, crammed with 5,000 residents, here was a place of peace and calmness.

We turned down an alley toward a darkened dead-end where a tattered sign appeared: *La Stampante*. My body wavered in time with the hypnotic rhythm of the swinging wooden plaque. "I thought we were to see Benyamin. Why are we at Alistair's shop?"

The polished door on the lower level opened, and we were met by "Shhh." Asha whispered, "Father is working on something and will be down soon. He said a noisy entrance would only delay him." She tilted her chin high. "The window is open."

Max stared at her hair that hung in loose waves down her back. I smiled as his hand seemed to want to stroke the strands.

Benyamin had tanned skin, a narrow, knowing gaze, and a prominent nose. An unruly silver and black beard framed his face, emerald eyes at the center. Asha had his eyes and nose, but her skin was a different shade, more like a thin coat of honey. Her hair lacked the tight natural curl made untamable by oppressive humidity. It was silken and waved like a gently folded ribbon. I had yet to ask if she took after her mother. It was something we shared—being motherless—but I felt the inquiry would be impertinent. *I knew little of my mother. Why would I assume she knew hers?*

We made ourselves slight, like mice slipping around a room undetected. Once beyond the threshold, Asha closed the door behind us. It took a moment to adjust to the faint illumination of a five-stem candelabrum on the far wall.

"Father is in a foul mood," Asha whispered. "The elders lectured him about his *indiscreet profession*. They threaten to have us removed. We have been here for years. Where would we go?" She lifted her hem to keep from tripping down a dark hallway. The swish of her oversized dress invited us to follow. I envisioned her as a child dancing with a ribbon wroth around a piazza. I couldn't remember a time when I wore such innocence.

We entered a room packed with shelves, books, and bottles, and I suddenly remembered the asylum. I noted an odd smell. The more I concentrated on the scent, the worse I felt. I reached behind me for balance and to brace against a shelf. The shelf gave away. I stumbled back, landing on my backside. The thud reverberated through my head, and everything became dark. I fought to adjust my skirt bunched high around my bare thighs. I tried to hide my whiteness, recalling that I was not dressed for elegance.

"Renna, can you see me?" Alastair pulled me to my feet. "Are you hurt?"

The thud of the impact dulled, and my vision sharpened. "I'm well."

Max rushed to rearrange my mess, and Alastair guided me to a seat near a spitting fire.

"What is that commotion?" Benyamin entered, grinding something with a pestle and mortar. The sound took me back to England, and I felt ever fainter.

Camilla hovered over him as he worked his concoction at a splintered table. "Benyamin, I need something to help Renna. She's improving, but she is not herself."

"I have given you what I can. There is not much else to do but wait for time to heal her. Have you been taking Renna outside?" His cadence matched his metrical grinding.

"I have her out today. As Carnival approaches, Danielle is insistent that we have her ready." Camilla released an exasperated gasp. "Why are you working here?"

"I was taking notes on the medicine I gave Renna. I wanted Alistair's help locating the region where I'd been told the fungus is found." Benyamin stopped his stirring. "I would think you would want her to *rest*. Why do Danielle's commands bear such weight?"

Camilla's back tightened. "Danielle gave her something else." She bowed her head. "My debt has been called. That's why I don't fight her."

I had always known that Benyamin and Camilla shared some secret, for their intimacy exceeded friendship.

Benyamin returned to his grinding. "Absurd. That was years ago. Besides, your *loyalty,*" He glanced at me, registering that I was listening. " . . . has been unwavering. And what good will come from *that* information now?"

"Danielle's on a rampage. It's as though all of the anger from years before is driving her." She stepped toward him, but I still heard her say, "There was quicksilver and leeches."

He slammed his fist on the table, bouncing the mortar bowl. "That is barbaric!"

Camilla glanced toward me. "Renna and Asha are becoming friends. I don't think Danielle likes it."

Alistair gravely turned toward me. "You should come with me. You must know what could happen if you've been given quicksilver."

I felt dizzyingly weak and struggled to follow him. I tripped over the edge of the doorframe. My feet stomped into a pile of dust, releasing black particles high into the air, accosting my nose, and burning my eyes. As it settled, the sweat from my hands turned from glistening translucent perspiration to soot-grey mire. Thick dust from dried ink covered everything, yet the room was orderly and serene.

He struggled to conceal his enthusiasm. "If you want to know something, this is the place to learn it."

I traced a finger along the wooden table and held it high for him to see. "Aren't those rooms called libraries, and aren't they much cleaner?"

He grinned. "Documenting history is a dirty business." Alastair's energy bubbled. "These are not part of my weekly news printings." He beckoned me with outstretched fingers to look at pages drying on lines around the room. "Can you read these?"

It took a moment to understand the text written in Latin. "*Me permittente caecus et leprosus, et sanasti* . . . You healed the blind and the leper with My permission."

"Your Latin is good."

I released Alastair's hand. "Is it from the Bible?"

"No. The Quran."

"For Muslims? Why are you printing it in the Jewish quarter of a Christian city?"

"The Quran has been published in Venice for over 200 years. This is for a Prussian nobleman interested in the commonalities between the Bible, the Torah, and the Quran." Alastair gestured to leather-bound manuscripts stacked together. "The books and reproductions are fine, especially as it brings in regular money, but I have my own work. Come into the next room." Alistair showed me a page with a woman's face on one side and a scrolling poem down the other.

I still felt dazed. "I can't read it."

He kissed my forehead. "It's all right. It's about you. You already know what it says. I've told you many times when we've loved one another."

My cheeks felt hot at his reference. "That's lovely. Is it what you wanted to show me?"

Alistair's expression sobered, and he shook his head, reluctantly leading me into a darker room. With the deftness of a bat on a moonless night, he scratched a match and revived a tired candle. Things brightened. The light chased away shadows. Paper hanging from the line glowed, and deep impressions made an indiscernible but beautiful pattern. He gave me a book from an overcrowded shelf.

I turned the title over in my hands. *Current Remedies for the Insane.* "I saw this in Mother's library."

He took the book back. "I want to read you something: *Quicksilver, known as hydrargyrum or mercury, derived first by the Egyptians from cinnabar, used in cosmetics and medical cures, specifically for syphilis, constipation, melancholia, and toothaches. May cause irritable mood, memory concerns, tremors, headaches, nausea, vomiting, difficulty breathing, and an inability to feel hands and feet. May have long-term effects on memory, coordination, and reproduction.*" Every word made me jump.

"She gave that to me?" I wondered if it had already taken effect, and that was why I struggled to focus now.

He pressed his glasses up his nose in a nervous expression. "I don't know what she did. I just wanted to show you, so you can know what it might be."

"Why do you have this?" I again thought the text was better suited for a library.

"This copy was printed here in Venice. If you turn to the first page, you'll see the printing signature." Alistair said.

I opened the front flap, *Printed 1790, Venetia*. I was ready to run back to the house, prepared to brain Mother for her poisoning when a list of names caught my attention: *Father T. Humboldt*. It had to be Father *Thaddeus* Humboldt.

"Look." I pointed to the page. "Do you know who this is?"

Alistair craned his head to see what I referenced. "Not personally. But it was said he worked at San Servolo. Mother said Father Humboldt was the reason she knew about medicine. He was her consultant."

"Unbelievable! He was why I ended up in the Yorkshire asylum." It seemed impossible to escape Father Thaddeus. "If Mother put quicksilver in me, what do I do?"

He clasped my hand to his chest. "I don't know. I've met others who have had quicksilver treatment, and they were fine. But some"—he hesitated—"some were not. But I will protect you." His voice quieted to a hush. "I promise."

Bursting into tears, I jerked free. "How can you promise that?" I retreated to the press by the door. My mind was racing. Yet again, I faced something that might cause my demise. How could I escape the asylum, sail across an ocean, only to be poisoned?

He stomped toward me. "Please, my dear friend. Don't cry. I can't stand the sight of your pain." He caressed my shoulders.

The last of my energy abandoned me. His affection was surprisingly refreshing, and I melted into his hug. A man had not touched me in weeks, and no one held me as tenderly as Alistair. He was my first real lover and a devoted friend, but he'd also just given me news of what might be my death. Although I let him rock me in a soothing embrace, I knew finding sanctuary in the men in my life was the wrong path. No one was coming to rescue me. I would have to save myself—somehow.

1797

Knight

Light Attributes: Loyalty, romance, chivalry
Shadow Attributes: Romantic delusions

Mother flung open my door without knocking, startling me from a restless slumber. I had nightmares of writhing in pain from burns on my skin and the quicksilver doing its evil work. As my vision cleared, I noticed the look on Mother's face, which only solidified my decision to find a way out of this life, away from her tyranny.

Mother clapped the door to my room closed, sucking air from the window and fluffing Francese's feathers, confining us. "Get up. You have an invitation to *La Fenice*." She threw a sealed envelope onto my bed.

My full name, Serenna Covert, was written in careful letters. Thick with many layers, it felt like a present begging to be unwrapped—gilded lettering of La Fenice shown through the wrapping's surface. I turned the correspondence over, running my finger over a wax impression of the letter "R," pressing the lip of the outer paper closed.

Courtesans frequented *La Fenice*, but I had yet to go. I clutched the note to my chest, leaving it unopened, and crept from my bed. "Who is it from?"

She held poised, ready for a debate, a brawl, or a burial. The invitation did not seem auspicious enough for her blackened demeanor. "By the wax initial on the back, I assume my new business companion, Carmine Royston, has invited you. You have not met him, but he requests your acquaintance."

Tearing open the invitation, I read formal scrolling, stating:

Signorina Covert, your presence is requested tonight at La Fenice. This was the first time I'd received an actual invitation. I was excited not to feel the *puttana* for one night.

"I have taken you in, treated you as my protégé, watched over you." Mother eyed me with her dark expression, although patient now. "We have had our differences, but that could be behind us tonight. Captain Royston and I are opening a new trade avenue. Many changes are on the horizon, and it seems opportune to capitalize on them." She relaxed into a calm smile.

Although her little speech left me skeptical, I wouldn't waste the prospect of a real Society experience. I stepped past Mother to the armoire—the doors open and contents surveyed—and fingered a bold-colored dress. I chose a fustet orange gown dyed bright from strips of sumac bark. "Shall I dress the part?"

"Bright is a good thought, and you must be large. A wig is also necessary, especially if you will be noticed from a private box. I will fetch it. I have one that will bring the ensemble together." She shuffled from the room like an obedient maid and returned before I could predict what was expected next. "Please, sit." She gestured toward my dressing table with regal bidding.

Taking the seat and tapping Francese's cage, awakening him, I perched at my dressing table and bore Mother's attention. I hoped her assistance meant she felt regret for her treatment of me. Of course, I could never trust or forgive her, for I was no longer naïve to her machinations. She spoke little as she arranged the wig, tightly securing it with pins to a bun of my hair. She positioned me where I could not take in my likeness, covertly completing her task. I caught a whiff of the tresses as they brushed against my nose. The smell reminded me of the asylum.

"How did you learn about social expectations?" I was genuinely interested.

"Venice was not always my life. I had a family and was raised as a lady."

I craned to see her face in the mirror, but she stood too far in the periphery. "Camilla said you came from a good family, and there were once three of you. Neither of you ever name your other sister. What happened?"

"She died." Mother pushed me toward the mirror. "Tell me what you think."

My questions vanished from me as I admired her work. I couldn't believe it was me—skin white, flawless like new porcelain. Charcoal outlined my hazel eyes and accentuated the gold fleck. The bright rouge on my cheeks left a healthy complexion. All was topped with the silkily plated wig as if it had been gilded.

I looked at her with astonishment, "Is this me?"

She appeared satisfied. Her fingers brushed the base of my neck. "You are stunning" Her coloring changed, cheeks reddening as the light in her eyes faded as if she had let something slip.

I took the reaction as regret for an inadvertent compliment. Watching myself in the mirror, I needlessly fixed my hair at the side of the wig and elegantly positioned my head. "I don't know what my mother resembled, but at this moment, I'm glad to embody myself." Haughty, indeed, but she had made me beautiful, unbelievably so.

*****

Silvio escorted me to an outlet nearest *Campo San Fantin* and the grand pillars of *La Fenice*. Open only a few years, the opera house was already renowned in Europe for its acoustics and opulence. With my cloak widely draped over my shoulders, leaving my décolleté exposed, I felt bolstered by the locket hanging over the arch of my breasts. I'd chosen to wear it tonight, for this was the first time in a long while that I didn't feel I was peddling. I was an invited guest, although my escort chose not to meet me at the entrance. It wasn't long before I passed through the pink marble foyer and ascended the ornate staircase, lighted by a massive chandelier, to the third floor and located the assigned box. Pushing back the heavy velvet curtain, I found my host peering over the edge into the orchestra pit, watching the patrons below file into their seats. I cleared my throat. An immense man turned around, and I was too astonished to greet him with the recognition he deserved.

It was Donovan.

He was immaculately dressed in a trimly cut suit, waistcoat buttoned from clavicle to hips, hugging his chest like a knight's breastplate. With little frill or embellishment, the quality of his attire made him statelier than any gentleman I'd seen.

Offering me his hand, he said, "You are exquisite."

I took his grip, and my gloved hands concealed the heat of my rising anxiety. I allowed him to pull me into the space by his chest that was familiar to me as any home. "Good evening," I whispered into his neck. "I can't believe it's you."

He held at a polite distance, but I was close enough to smell vanilla and tobacco. I caught the gleam of a woman's gaze from the next box as she leaned into her friend and whispered, gesturing toward us. Perhaps this was the reason for Donovan's formality.

Stepping back, I desperately studied his stoic expression. "Mother said Carmine Royston invited me. Why are you here instead?"

His eyes stared right through me. "He is here too, in the box across the way. He's watching us."

I knew better than to seek out the man he referenced and continued our civilities, unable to divine the purpose in the ruse. "We are to play the part of acquaintances then?" I peered over the edge of the third-level balcony into the orchestra pit—the rainbow arrangement of musicians milled together to form a body breathing as a singular organism.

He focused on the orchestra, giving the appearance that we discussed the musicians. "We are not even that as far as he is concerned, nor Danielle. As far as they know, we've never met."

"And why is that?" I rested my gloved hands on the railing of our box suspended to the right of the stage. I could clearly see the musicians down to their tightly knotted bowties and brightly shined shoes. Glimpses of the singers, as they darted around the stage behind the side curtains, played in the periphery.

"Carmine was at the Board Inn the first night we met." His voice trailed off in an unlikely nervous fashion. "I work for him. It was his ship we sailed on from Hull."

It took all I had to not stare shockingly at Donovan.

Instead, I watched the growing crowd in the opera. The venue appeared the pinnacle of possibility—the attendees dressed in their best, poised, and dignified in their interactions. The opera's history was like any other respectable Venetian patron, one of passion, artistry, conflict, destruction, and resurrection. If I occupied seats with the Venetian elite, could it mean I might find life beyond a lowly orphan or a dissembling courtesan? La Fenice made my ideal fishing pond if I weren't here on Mother's bidding. The instruments found their harmony. I savored the explosion of colors and sounds, all for my taking. I imagined what it would be like to hear the story's first notes.

"You look happy."

I turned to Donovan. "I feel like royalty."

"The opera hasn't even started." His words cut me as quickly as one might slice an apple, though his expression was unchanged. An amused look crossed his eyes, but his chin and jaw seemed carved of marble.

"This is my first time to La Fenice." Gathering myself, remembering this was a *work* night, I pressed my hand into Donovan's thigh, higher than any wife would dare. I could feel my palm's heat connect with his body's warmth.

He rested a hand on top of mine, and his mouth relaxed. "It is spectacular."

I tried to show both my pleasure and genuine longing as the weight of his hand grew stronger. "I promise to thank you later properly."

Donovan straightened his posture. I wasn't sure if this was a cue for me to be more decorous, but I followed suit, slightly resenting minding my countenance. All I wanted was to curl up and lose myself in the shadows, appreciating the moment as though made only for me.

"You didn't say what opera we are seeing."

His energy was warm. "Do you know Mozart?"

I reminisced on a group of Austrians I had entertained who espoused the considerable talents of their *maestro*. "I've had the good fortune of a private recital of parts of *Le Nozze di Figaro*, but not in such a venue." I omitted the detail that the recital was held in the secluded quarters of a very drunk Duke's home as several courtesans distracted more than a dozen nobles, all serenaded by three naked violinists.

The furrow of his brow signaled tension creeping back into his thoughts. "*Figaro* is a mere prelude to tonight's show. I saw this début in Vienna—*Don Giovanni*." He stretched out the name for dramatic effect, but it lacked the typical Italian power.

Leaning into his massive physique, I asked. "Why is *Figaro* a poor 'prelude'?"

"Mozart modeled *Don Giovanni* after Don Juan, but truly it is a cautionary tale for the legendary Jacopo Casanova." His gaze was intense.

It seemed odd to have the juxtaposition of the rough, Irish rogue entranced in the gossip and underpinnings of high society music and entertainment. "So, how does this story differ besides recounting the life of a libertine like Casanova?"

He smiled fully this time, pleased by my attentiveness to his passion. "I cannot share without ruining the ending. But let's say that Mozart and Marlow drank from the same inspirational well."

Arranging like a doll in a shop window, I contemplated how my night might develop and pretended momentarily that I belonged there just as much as the city's royal ladies. I slyly sought the man who secretly watched me. "You didn't say why you're here with me instead of Carmine. Mother said I was invited by him, not you."

"Carmine was skeptical about meeting Danielle's *daughter* protégé. That woman is quite cunning. And when I realized the connection between my employer and her, I thought I could intervene on your behalf. Carmine is ruthless." His energetic green eyes, contrasting with his neatly groomed beard, brows, and hair, brought a sense of peace.

"As is Mother."

His expression hardened. "You are in more danger than ever. Do you know who she is?"

"She's Camilla's sister. She was once a courtesan, and I believe she might have been a patient at San Servolo." I shuddered as I said all the associations aloud.

"Do you know why Danielle was at San Servolo?"

Before I could reply, the red velvet curtains on the main stage parted harmoniously with the orchestra's thunderous opening notes of the overture. A descending chandelier flooded the scene. The explosion of sound and light and the smell of dust and candles quickly hushed the audience and drew our focus to a youthful man standing under a streetlamp near an open tavern window. The image harkened me back to The Board Inn at York, and I almost felt like an orphan again.

A singer hypnotized me as his song grew in speed and pitch. The tale of Leporello, *Don Giovanni's* servant, cheerfully ignited. I was entranced. The brightly colored costumes and dramatic gesturing brought to life the story of the *Libertine*, who wooed and wore out his welcome with woman after woman. Artistic lighting from the stage wings perfectly paired with the orchestra's expertly timed crescendos and subtle nuances. The closing curtains nipped at Don Giovanni's heels as he escaped his pursuers at the end of the first act, leaving me breathless and astonished.

Donovan turned to me with a child's delight. "It's even better than the first time. The acoustics in *La Fenice* is commendable. The production and sets made all the difference. Did you notice how the voices rang clear as the actors moved up and down the stairs?"

"It's nice to see you appreciate high culture." A crystal glass brimming with deep red wine was presented to me. "You look as though you could use refreshing," said a low, raspy voice in a playful cadence.

Donovan stood, bowing to our uninvited guest. "This is Captain Carmine Royston."

Carmine offered his hand to me. I clasped the callused knuckles, tried to put power into my grip, and smiled. I focused on Carmine's right cheek, giving the appearance of eye contact. "It is a pleasure."

Carmine crushed my fingers against his cracked lips and mustache. His forcefulness and lingering grip gave me a sense that he might not care if I were a whore or courtesan. Either way, in his possession, I might be devoured. "I admire your companion, Donovan. Although she seems a bit weary." Carmine studied me and left an impression I was failing his inspection.

The light on his rimmed glasses transported me back to my first night meeting Donovan, Henry, and this man. He'd been there too, playing chess. Although Carmine did not touch me as he took the chair behind me, my skin crawled as if it had brushed against the back of an eel. "So, you are Danielle's daughter. What a treat."

The box closed in on me, and I felt conveyed back to the asylum like my overseers knew a fate I'd yet to discover. I caught Donovan's look before the stage curtains parted and the chandelier lowered to signal the second act. His face was electrified like daylight shooting through passing clouds. We watched the remainder of the opera, occasionally turning to share a reaction. Don Giovanni's story was perplexing but not lost to me. And it gave me pause. I, too, trafficked in seduction. As a woman, my trespasses were considered far worse than any man's. I shuddered at the thought of being dragged into Don Giovanni's hell, either passively or defiantly. That's not how I wanted my story to end. At the final notes of the opera, the house applauded in a standing ovation. The chandelier lowered, and the building brightened once again.

I sipped the last of my wine. A frozen courtesan wasn't worth much. Carmine was assessing me for something, and a dumb doll of a woman wasn't particularly impressive. I feigned energetic curiosity. "I understand that you and Mother are business partners. What type of work interests you?"

Carmine lit a slender cigar and reclined in his chair. His position made it awkward for me to address him formally, yet he could openly observe me. "I work for the British West India Trading Company and specialize in procuring exotic items. There is a market for anything foreign. I can find all kinds of goods in Venice. At this point, I am interested in delicate things and antique collectibles. We have a fast and sturdy ship carrying items that perish over a long land journey. Given our expediency, our items fetch a high price, provided they are in good condition."

My skin crawled.

Donovan rose from his seat and extended a hand. "I think I should make sure Renna returns to Danielle."

Carmine touched the edge of my dress. "But we are only now becoming acquainted." His expression and slurred words revealed his intoxication.

Donovan pulled me closer. "The invitation was for the opera, Carmine."

Carmine stood equal to the height of Donovan but not as broad. He looked at me over his glasses, his gaze shifting from my eyes to my neckline. "Do permit me." Carmine fingered my necklace. "That is a very particular design, my dear."

I flushed. "I was told it is from my family."

"Lucky girl." Carmine bowed. "I look forward to our future acquaintance."

Donovan pulled me after him into the hall, and we rushed out of the opera house. We stammered back toward my home near the Ghetto, but I kept losing balance on my platforms.

Donovan drew me into an elbow-shaped alley and gently pushed me against the wall. "This night did not go as I'd hoped." He kissed the top of my forehead and breathed in deeply. "I can't bring you back with me, for I'm lodging on Carmine's ship."

I nuzzled into his warmth. "That man is disgusting. How can you do business with him?"

"He's a necessary associate." He created space for me to take in his expression, one of melancholy and foreboding. "He is not to be trifled with, and now he and your Mother have crafted a plan."

"She's not my mother." I played with the locket. "You should know that."

He glanced at it. "That doesn't matter to Carmine." Donovan tucked my cloak around my shoulders to shield me from the cold before burrowing me under his arm in our usual posture. He walked us toward the end of an alley that opened to dark steps leading into the green depth of a canal and let out a long whistle. "You'll need to go back. Do as you're told and keep your head down. Try not to entertain anyone privately until I send word for you."

My head was swooning, and I wanted him to sweep me up and carry me away anywhere he liked. "When will that be?"

A fisherman's boat cut through the silent waterway toward us. Not the traditional gondola decked in splendor, but a functional transport craft appeared at the watery steps.

"Soon. I want to show you something. You need to know exactly the kind of woman Danielle is and why she was sent to Venice." Donovan handed me over to the boatman. "Please, take her back."

Before I could protest, he settled me into the boat and released my hand. The boat swiftly glided under a low bridge, cutting Donovan from sight.

Shape-Shifter

> Light Attributes: Ability to see potential
> Shadow Attributes: Mercurial persona serves personal agenda

Donovan was as good as his word and came for me a few nights later. He led me to an awaiting boat and tucked me under a thick tarp. The trapped air in Donavan's dinghy suffocated but concealed me from onlookers. I held open a flap at the bow. The full February moon lit the waters around me, and I watched the city pass by as Donovan steered away from the Ghetto, along the back of the Arsenal, and circumnavigated the perimeter of the Castello.

The boat glided away from the main island's refuge and into the lagoon's blackness. Donovan steadily dipped the oars into the water. I listened to them splashdown, followed by the wood-on-wood of the oar and boat-side achingly grinding together. Donovan breathed slowly, all sounds playing in time with the chilled water lapping at the side of our watercraft. Noticing a flicker of light, like a harkening beacon guiding a wayward ship, I lifted the tarp edge higher, straining to make out images revealed as we gradually progressed.

I loudly whispered under the tarp. "Where are we headed?"

Donovan's voice trailed through the silent night air as if he stood beside me. "San Servolo."

I'd never been in this portion of the lagoon and knew San Servolo by reputation only. I had no idea of its location. It was once home to a Benedictine monks' order, and now it was a hospital. My mind conjured images of haunting patients sluggishly roving the halls in search of something. *What if they were in search of me?*

Donovan called. "Get back under the tarp. I plan to land us where no one can watch us disembark. I don't want to risk your being seen." He showed little evidence of his rowing effort, but his words were tinged with a note of anxiety.

A blazing torch, not the typical greased-end staff with an angry orange flame, but a large bowl of rolling blue fire, like the ancient lights in books on Roman Caesars, was the last I saw of the long dock as I pulled the cover over my head. I played with the idea that our trip transported us back in time. For a moment, it was romantic.

The boat bottom knocked against something hard, and Donovan dropped an oar over the top of my covering. Assuming his sounds and jostling were an effort to affix the boat, I focused on steadying myself. The rocking made me acutely aware of the heat in my smothering space. Acidic spittle pinched my cheeks, and I was ready to retch, mixing my sickness with the smell of fish and sea.

Donovan whipped back the covers and washed me in welcome freshness. The night sky was a bright blanket of glowing stars. The moon, hidden until now behind a thick cloud, highlighted the whole of the lagoon. He handed me to an outcropping of boulders, jutting from a long stone-speckled beach, and went to fully secure the boat, tucking the oars under the tarp and assuring our ride home would not wash away in the rising tide.

I turned to see our backdrop. The top of Basilica di San Marco and the dome of Giorgio Maggiore was clear from my position. Everything glistened with ethereal beauty. Between the city's ever-burning torches and the night sky's illumination, Venice earned her nickname as the *jewel* of the Mediterranean.

"Come now, it is a stunning vantage, one I'm sure you've never witnessed, but we are on a schedule. I want to return home before dawn." Donovan directed me away from the lustrous sight to face a dark path lined with cypress trees. "Hold me as we go. We must step carefully. I don't want to actually need tending by these doctors."

I anxiously clasped him as he walked us wordlessly down the path. The tall trees over-shadowed us, shielding us from the starry illumination and encasing us in blind darkness. "Why are we coming now?" Infiltrating at night made me anxious.

We stepped into a moonbeam, and I made out his features. Although still calm, his brow tightened in concern. "There are fewer patients up at this hour. The orderlies are half-staffed, and most dangerous types are closed in their rooms." Before I could question him, he bent down to the dirt path and rubbed his palms in the damp soil. "You look too clean." He brushed his fingers over my cheeks and clasped my hands in his, dirtying them. "And simply too pretty. I need you to be forgettable, not exquisite, even in your dowdy dress."

If we were in a lighted room, I'm sure my cheeks would have revealed his comment's power.

Donovan dusted his hands on his leather pants and extended his elbow again. "If we meet anyone, don't look at them directly in the face. Your eyes are radiant, especially that fleck of gold. It is entrancing, and we don't need to be stopped."

Beams of moonlight showed through the treetops, and I watched the wavering effect on his features as we walked. I'd always found him attractive, although he was Henry's antithesis. Donovan—his name meant strength and fortitude—was dark, somber, and formidable. And I willingly followed him wherever he led.

His efforts might be in vain. "I know you said I have to know who Mother is, but couldn't you have told me? Coming here seems risky."

He paused at the edge of the trees and gestured to the three-story white stucco building. "This hospital is for the mentally sick, the crazies. Danielle is dangerous because of *why* she ended up here. I want you to see her record for yourself and the drawings from her room."

I observed the building and could understand how it might have been a monastery long ago. Every inch was unadorned and ordinary, except for the vegetation. Even in the nighttime light, the garden's unkempt beauty clashed against the building's prison-like exterior. Four-by-four-inch square metal bars guarded the windows.

"I can't believe this is an asylum. It doesn't resemble Bootham Hall in the least. Why bars on the upper windows?" My heart raced as I recalled seeing the York asylum for the first time and heard Felicity's blood-curdling cries in my mind.

"The higher the window, the more certain the death if someone jumps."

Donovan moved into the building shadow and skulked around the side, pulling me behind him. If someone approached him face on, his girth would entirely conceal me. He found the back door entrance and tried the handle. It released from the latch and noiselessly swung open. A long hall, like the downstairs at Harewood House, had stone tiles and whitewashed walls.

"That seemed easy. For an asylum, this place is not very secure." Our entrance was nothing like what I'd experienced in York.

"The doctors are worried about the patients killing themselves or someone else, not of escaping. Besides, where would they go?" He whispered his rebuttal in my ear and shuffled us hastily down the hall to a flight of stairs. "We need to be quick. I paid the night guard to leave the door open, but he will be around to lock it again at midnight."

Scurrying up two flights of stairs, Donovan turned several corners and found another hall lined by doors. Each entry had a similar square-viewing window to the York Asylum. I shook with flashbacks of last seeing Felicity in her room. Donovan stepped lightly, avoiding the sound of his boot heels on the wooden floors. I was grateful for my soft-soled shoes. He moved too quickly for me to peek into the windows. We were near the end of the hall when I saw glowing light from the last room on the right. Curiosity reigning, I released his grip.

He mouthed, "What are you doing?"

Shooing him away, I raised up on my tiptoes to spy inside. It was a tiled bathroom, triple the size of any standard room. A long bath was at the far side, by the single window laced in iron bars. A man whose hair was shaved in patches was submerged in what looked like a small lake of ice, like the slush I'd made for Mrs. Connolly after she burned her hand.

The entirety of the man was immersed in the water. He vacillated from quiet moments of shivering to bouts of screaming. With each protest, two men in white tunics and matching pants grasped the patient by his shoulders and plunged him into the water, releasing him to sputter to the surface for air. After he regained his breath, a new bucket of ice was poured into the bath, and the process was revisited.

I clung to the door, peering through the window as I sought an answer from Donovan.

"They treat sailors returned from war. I can only imagine what they have seen." Donovan touched me on the arm. "Please come away. I need you calm enough to read what I will show you."

I gestured to the other side of the room where another man as broad-shouldered as Donovan sat in a high-backed chair like Olivia's in the asylum. "Wait."

This man was not strapped to the chair in the same way as she and I had been. He wore a peculiar jacket that bound his arms to his body. His feet were secured to the chair legs like mine had been. His head was held to the chair back with a leather band across his forehead.

Donovan looked through the window. "It's called a straight-jacket. It's tough to get the patient into it. Usually, they are given opium or laudanum to make them more compliant. That man, I would assume by his look, is extremely dangerous. He will stay like that until it is assured he won't hurt anyone."

I looked at Donovan in astonishment. "How can that be assured?"

"Please come away. We don't have much time for me to show you the pages." Donovan pulled me after him to the last door in the hall, one without a window.

He pushed the door open and revealed an unremarkable modest office except for its cleanliness and order. Donovan turned the nob on two lamps situated at a long desk. The fuel smell overtook the space as he secured the door. The experience echoed my time with Max in Father Thaddeus' office, although I was confident Donovan would protect me from whoever might intrude.

He moved to a high cabinet with alphabetically labeled drawers. Kneeling at the bottom, he opened the drawer for the letters *W to Z*. Thumbing through the first ten pages, he turned to me, "Can you bring me the lamp, please?"

Doing as he asked, I cautiously hovered the lamp over his shoulder to brighten the space but not blind him with the direct light. Donovan plucked six pages from the stack and closed the drawer with his boot's heel. Moving us back to the desk, he laid the pages out side-by-side.

There were angrily scratched images of faces screaming, teeth, fire, knives, and the words in English *death, betrayal, burn.* Fearful I might lose my grip on the lamp, I set it next to the pages and braced myself against a shelf. It was apparent what Donovan was trying to show me. Mother created these drawings.

THE CURSE OF MAIDEN SCARS

"This place is horrifying, in some ways worse than the York Asylum, although I can't say exactly why." I shuddered, thinking that the York Asylum appeared peaceful compared to San Servolo. "Why did you feel I needed to see it all? And how did you even learn about this in the first place?"

Donovan brought me a different sheet with Italian writing. "Please read this."

<u>Name:</u> Danielle Worthington

<u>Admitted:</u> 14 January 1781

<u>Age:</u> Twenty-four

<u>Age of first attack:</u> Twenty-four

<u>Married, single or widowed:</u> Single

<u>Occupation:</u> None

<u>Religious persuasion:</u> Catholic

<u>Previous place of abode:</u> York

<u>Nearest known relative:</u> Parents: Maxwell Worthington, Annabel Worthington; Sisters: Camilla Worthington, alive. Second sister—name unknown, as the patient refuses to say it—told to be deceased.

<u>Attack:</u> Presumed second

<u>Insane:</u> Two months at San Servolo. Previous incidents and length of insanity unknown.

<u>Supposed cause</u>: Evil possession due to disturbing events

<u>Facts observed by Father T. Humboldt:</u> Frantically draws images of 'ghosts' she claims haunt her dreams. Has described being unable to control impulses to burn things. Have found the treatment of rye hallucinogenic, and necessary procedures like leeching, bleeding, and bathing reduces fits of rage.

<u>Mental State:</u> Two months of regular therapy have relieved the patient of harm to self or others. She is compliant and deemed ready to return to the world. Parents have entrusted the patient's wellbeing to Santa Caterina, along with a generous endowment for her care.

"Father T. Humboldt?" I stared at the words on the page. I looked back at her family's names: Maxwell Worthington, Annabel Worthington; Sisters: Camilla Worthington, alive. "And the second sister is deceased." I ruminated on the information aloud.

"Aye. Father Thaddeus treated her. That's why we had to get you out of York. Camilla knew what kind of man he was because of treating Danielle." His great shoulders shuddered in a sigh. "But are you also understanding, although it is not explicitly said, that Danielle killed their other sister." Donovan huddled next to me. "Renna, she is dangerous. She was treated here at the hospital. You are living with a murderer."

"Do you think Camilla knows?"

"I would think she must."

I was suddenly shot through with energy. "Father Thaddeus, I remember him saying he trained in Veneto. It is baffling they all knew each other." I shoved the page back into Donovan's hands. "Take it away." The images of Danielle's drawings were forever seared in my mind. "You didn't say how you knew to come here to look for Mother's hospital record."

Donovan hastily collected the pages and returned them to their drawer. "Carmine. Yorkshire is a small place, if you haven't figured it out yet. Everyone knows everyone. He knew of Danielle and Camilla's family and insisted I search out the details of Danielle's past, as they are going into business together. He wanted to know exactly what kind of lunatic she is."

I shuddered, thinking of Carmine's impressions on me, the sickening danger he exuded. "That all makes sense. But it seems that the same investigation should also be done for Carmine. I'm sure he's his own version of madness."

Donovan breathed in deeply. "Very true. Now, we'd best leave before someone finds us and tries to assess *our* sanity." He had me up and tucked under his arm in our posture, reassuringly protective and directive. We hurried down the hall and were back out the door as an orderly came into view. A ring of clanging keys signaled his arrival.

"Cutting it a bit close there, Donovan." The man with a monkish-styled haircut smiled with a mouth full of teeth like a pond of crowded pebbles. "You owe me for this. I expect to have two of the best girls when I'm in San Marco next week."

THE CURSE OF MAIDEN SCARS

Donovan nodded but kept us moving. He spoke over his shoulder, "You'll have them." When we were out of earshot, he whispered to me, "*You* won't be one of them."

Donovan let me nestle next to him as we rowed back across the lagoon. Once reaching the narrow canals, where his strokes slowed to a quiet, gentle pace, I questioned him. "I understand why you showed me, I think. You want me to know what she's really like. But I don't understand why you feel I needed to know this now?"

Donovan moored us at a pylon within walking distance of my home. He gazed at me with his vivid eyes. "Is Danielle at home?"

I shook my head.

"Is there any chance you might invite me inside?"

My cheeks felt aflame with unexpected delight. "We've been sneaking behind closed doors all night. Why stop now?" I extended a hand to him. "I don't want to be alone anyway." We walked back together to the villa.

I found my way to my room without interruption like any other night. Candles were lit, and the wine decanter was displayed on my desk with a fruit bowl. I went to the washbasin to clean myself of the soot while Donovan closed the door.

He slowly faced me. "You asked why I showed you Danielle's history. She and Carmine are planning a new trade business."

I shed my shawl and braided my tangled hair in a rope down my back, much as I would have in my younger years. I kept my back to Donovan as I cleaned my face, mumbling, "Carmine mentioned it when we met at the opera."

"Haven't you figured out what they plan to trade?" Pressing his head against the door as he watched me, Donovan stiffened for a moment, and then he quickly stepped to me, snatching up my wrist. "You. They plan to sell you or use you in more ways than you've already been used. What little freedom you have gained will vanish utterly. They plan to take the best courtesans and whores and sell them to the highest bidders, anywhere in the world. Look at me." There was barely enough light from the open window, with only a single candle burning to see his expression. Once postured passively, he now loomed over me. His mood darkened, and it made me want to flee.

My stomach tightened. "Are you angry?"

He cupped a hand over my mouth and brought his lips to my ear. "That doesn't matter."

I mumbled into his palm, "It does matter. Why are you angry now if you're trying to protect me?" I nibbled on his palm, and he shuddered. I kissed up his wrist and felt his grip relax. "If you know their plan, can't you take me away now?"

He clutched me tightly, hugging at first and then releasing me. "He would hunt us down if I betrayed him. If I take you now, what do you think will happen to your friends?"

My energy waned as I thought of them. Mother's anger would quickly transfer to them if I were gone. Donovan was right.

He traced the outside of my arms, gently gliding his fingers to the top of my collarbone. "You're thin, almost like when we first met."

The night's energy utterly confounded me, and my legs buckled. "I've been ill."

Donovan swooped me up in his bearlike massiveness. I cuddled into his chest as if he were still rescuing me from that drizzly Yorkshire street. He sat securely on the bed's edge with me on his lap. The neck of my dress exposed my shoulders. "You must be tired." He kneaded my flesh like dough. His breath warmed my skin, and his lips kissed my neck. "I may not be able to take you away tonight, but I will devise a plan."

I looked at his face, his expression both distressed and captivated me. "What is it?"

"You have to know how much I want you." He brushed his beard along my cheek, the feel of it more like a cat's coat than stubbly prickles. "But I don't want to be second, not to anyone, and especially not to Henry."

My heart betrayed me at the mention of his name. Henry's displeasure came flooding back to me, and I recalled last seeing him in the Casino before leaving with Nicolo. I denied Donovan's assumption, squirming some but not abandoning the warmth of his embrace. "He's gone now. He doesn't want me."

Donovan eased back with a long, penetrating look. "That doesn't assuage my concerns. And you are very wrong on both accounts."

Donovan brought his face down in a sudden kiss, tasting and teasing me with his tongue. He left me breathless when he pulled away. "I suppose I can't blame you for your attachment to him. He has overpowered you at each turn." He breathed into my cheek, sending chills over my skin. "You haven't been loved by me yet."

He was right. We'd never actually had each other. Always close but intercepted by someone—Ann or Henry. I chewed my bottom lip as I fixated on Donovan's mouth. I remembered staring at it the first night outside the Cotton Workhouse, wishing he'd smother me in his lips and beard.

Donovan gently kissed my forehead and then my cheeks. He moved to my neck, his lips kneading my collarbone, and his hands tenderly found both breasts. His touch became more fervent, more desperate. I tried to kiss back to match his intensity, but his approach left me dizzied and malleable.

It happened in a frenzy. Donovan smelled me, licked me, bit me. I cried out as his teeth touched me for the first time. He grinned at my cries and bit me again on the round of my shoulder, then below my collarbone. His hands did their work, and my dress was down around my knees as he snatched at me with firm hands and calmed his bites to a nibble. Slowly, he turned me around again and sucked on my flesh delicately. I was somewhere between ecstasy and pain. He pushed me down on the bed, undressing me, and exploring me with his hands and lips. Facedown, I was engulfed in the sensation of him discovering me until he stopped. Donovan brushed his fingertips over my skin. Starting at the base of my hair, he traced down my back, touching each place I'd been wounded, finding each violation.

He rolled me over and gazed at me intensely. "How can you have been so pained?" He caressed my face. "Those eyes. They are stunning. You seem to burn with an all-consuming fire. How I should have taken you, taken care of you." His longing appeared silhouetted by shame.

Donovan's waning lust softened the moment, and I realized he was still clothed. I felt vulnerable in my nakedness and stiffened, attempting to scoot toward the safety of the headboard. He crawled to me, pressing my legs apart, his hands finding my nest.

"I'm not finished. You know how to please when you deserve to be pleasured."

An image of Henry flashed to me, and I readied for what he'd done our first time, expecting Donovan to similarly undo his pants and take me from his elevated position. But he didn't. Donovan bent low as though sipping from a well and kissed down my stomach. He caressed my leg with his lips and moved down further. I could no longer distinguish his lips from his fingers. His breath heated my skin as he played and explored. Clutching to the bedsheets, I stayed myself for his advances and allowed him to indulge—kissing, sucking, touching, licking.

I was anxious to play my part, but he held me to the bed, continuing to kiss my nether lips, playing with me until I released myself to the sensation and let out a long cry. The room blurred as if I'd plunged deep into a warm pool. I wanted to move, to righten myself, but my limbs were heavy and the softness of the bed inviting.

Donovan unwound from me and tenderly closed my legs. "That's what you should have every time." He slipped off the bed and pulled the covers over me.

That night had been the most tempestuous experience. I was exhausted and energized at the exact moment. I stretched a hand to Donovan. "Are you leaving me now? After bringing me to the brink of every emotion?"

"I must go. I will start working on a plan. Carmine and Danielle don't intend anything for you until Carnival."

Sweat collected on my upper lip; I wasn't sure if it was from my ecstasy or the growing doom I felt. "I don't know why she hates me so, but after my sickness, the leaches, and learning about the quicksilver, every bone in me screams the impending danger she brings. I have to get out of here."

"You can't manage that alone—I will help you. Carnival night will be a good diversion." He kissed my forehead, as was now his custom. "Stay safe until then, my dear one."

Avenger

Light Attributes: Balances the scales of justice
Shadow Attributes: Resorting to violence

Silvio jockeyed for position amongst other boats near the steps to San Marco. The gondola rocked on choppy waves, like a mother's desperate attempts to soothe her infant to sleep only to heighten its consternation. Water lapped against the side of the boat, threatening to overtake the edge and drench my feet. I held tight, concentrating on staying centered on my seat and maintaining a grip on my mask and headpiece.

It had taken all I had to face Mother in the weeks after San Servolo. Although I knew we had to wait for the right time for an escape, I desperately wanted to forget my commitment and flee for a life of my own—anywhere. Donovan had said Carnival would serve as the best cover for a getaway. But Mother commanded I find Carmine tonight and share my talents. Donovan said he would meet me here but left no other details. I was worried about whom I might encounter first.

The boat knocked against a stone step, and a waiting servant held the helm, deftly fastening a rope around the neck of the gondola and swinging it parallel to the stairs. Two footmen with outstretched hands summoned my hasty departure in unison. "Prego."

I clasped a hand, praying a wave wouldn't pull the footman into the boat or the water before I ever reached the dry piazza. He held steadfast, immobilized against the boat's movement. I hoisted myself to the marble tiles of Piazza San Marco, and he cleared his throat, indicating I release his hand. I straightened to my entire height, maximizing the advantage of my elevated clogs. My belly tightened in hunger and anxiety.

I caught a glimpse of a dark cloak approaching hurriedly, especially given the crowd's thickness and rain misting the tiles. The figure was too petite to be Donovan or Carmine. The cloak twisted around elegantly dressed patrons like a ribbon threading between sewing spools. The figure materialized into my dear Asha with Max in tow. I felt choked by the sight of them. I had anticipated my little friends staying locked away with Alistair and Benyamin in the Ghetto. It was one reason that persuaded me to leave tonight.

Asha's effervescence outshone the painted faces of celebrants, hugging, dancing, laughing, and fanning away whispers of rendezvous yet to come. "Are you surprised to see us? We've been watching for you for half an hour." She expectantly stood before me, her chest pressed high in a tightly bound bodice. "How do I look?"

Seeing my sweet friend's tiny frame crammed into a gown better suited for a night at the Casino than proper attire for an innocent girl caused embarrassment. I was glad for the mask concealing my reaction. "I am amazed."

Asha contemplated the crowd, taking in the costumes, all portraying a story of importance. She was my sister in spirit, and I wanted to shield her, as her small mask made of soft black lace could not. I also didn't want to ruin this moment for her.

My lack of greeting caught Max's attention, and he grabbed my arm. "What is wrong?" he loudly barked, but it was barely audible in the dense crowd.

I lifted my leather mask artfully painted with the sun's dawning. "I am well. It's been some time since I've been with this many people." How could I tell him that tonight might mark the end of my life in Venice? "What do you have planned for the night?"

We had never directly spoken about his attachment to Asha, although he'd been her shadow since my sickness. He shook a crimson cloak free of raindrops. It settled around his canary-colored waistcoat. "We will wait for the opening, and then maybe visit a chocolate shop. I promised Benyamin to have her back safely before the gates close."

"How did you get him to let her out for tonight?" I looked at Asha's barely formed bosom pushed up like a warm bun rising from a tin, not entirely baked through, "And dressed, so lovely?"

Asha hugged my waist tightly as I towered over her in my shoes. "I told him it would keep me from wanting to be part of this world."

The sound of the crowd grew louder, making it challenging to explore the topic. We huddled closer together as bodies jostled us. Someone clasped my elbow. I knew it wasn't Donovan, for the fingers were gloved and too small.

I turned to see Ann, grinning wide and dressed in a radiant white dress. Her complete ensemble had an ethereal effect. I was stunned by her presence, as we had seen little of each other since the Arsenal. I'd inquired about her but was told she'd left the city. She'd crossed my thoughts many times since then. I was perplexed by how she could float through life unscathed.

Ann held her head high, peering through the crowd. "I'm glad I found you. I wouldn't miss Carnival for the world, and I'm afraid this may be my last chance for a long while." She looked at me with an endearing expression. "I wish we'd stayed connected all these months. Much has changed for me, and I have longed to share it with you, my friend. I'm leaving tonight, and I couldn't stand the idea of not saying goodbye."

Her declaration set me back. We'd found an alliance since leaving Harewood, but I had not thought she considered me such a close companion. "Where are you going?"

"I was told the surprise is in the center of the square." She pulled at me, regarding neither Max nor Asha. "Let's move in while there's still space."

I dragged Asha and Max after me, creating a human snake through the crowd. Glancing over my shoulder, I was warmed by Asha's beams of excitement. Although anxiousness prevented me from indulging in their fun, I appreciated the laugh of my playfellows. Catching the surprise seemed precisely the kind of thing a girl like me should do— if I were still a girl.

We reached a barred section of the square. Thick rope suspended from timber stands encircled a sizeable wooden box ten feet wide, high, and long. It was brightly painted with an array of Carnival images— masks, flowers, boats, ladies' decorated faces, men's wigged heads, all with pleading grins. Lanterns positioned at the corners cast dramatic shadows. Light reflected off the gilding. Ann seized me tight on one side while Asha held my other hand. Max pressed behind us.

The crowd responded to a hidden clue and quieted. A dozen men dressed in blue pantaloons and tunics, hoods, and black masks, rushed toward the box—three at each side, crouched at the bottom, heads bent low—and waited. A line of violinists, instruments balanced between chin and shoulder, sauntered around the display. Each took a stance beside the box, turned to the crowd, and waited. Without announcement, the men in blue went to work on latches at the bottom, finding a secret flap and lifting it high so one could disappear inside. In that instant, the musicians struck a harmonious note. Their song penetrated the air and echoed against the surrounding marble facades. Volume and momentum increased, drawing on the still hushed anticipation of the crowd. The sides of the box crashed onto the piazza floor. A length of red cloth undulated in an unfelt breeze, inflating into the sky, taking on an inner glow.

The billowing fabric solidified into a firm balloon tied to a basket, fit for two persons. The crowd took a collective breath and murmured. We watched the balloon rise, ready to lift off the ground. A centerfire lamp with a slightly odd smell made it ascend magically.

Ann turned to me, "I've seen this before. The air beneath is heated and will lift into the sky." Her face was as bright as Asha's had been earlier. "In France, people who ride in balloons like this are called aeronauts. I'll be my own kind of *aeronaut*." She elbowed me. "I am rising up in the world. I am hoping you will accompany me."

There was something about her intensity that reminded me of Mother. I took her meaning but cooled to her idea. I smiled lightly and strained not to recoil from her embrace.

I secretly wished the same thing for myself.

Two men in blue bounded toward the balloon as the basket lifted off the piazza floor, making it bounce and summon a gasp from onlookers. We swayed in excitement near spectators wearing amusing masks, harkening back to the plague era when doctors fruitlessly donned elongated beaks stuffed with herbs and potent-smelling flowers to ward off disease. Couples complemented each other in various masculine and feminine images—sun and moon, bull and cow, wizard and witch. Then there was my least favorite, the Faustian embodiment of the Devil coming to rob. Those in a Lucifer-style tended to wear crimson and were part of the highest social classes. By their attire, I could easily target them as a prospect for the evening if that were my aim tonight.

In surveying the crowd, my gaze fell on Donovan, unmasked and displeased, standing stock still in the swaying spectators' excitement. His stone-like features announced that his plan was in motion.

Ann snatched at my arm, breaking my link with him. "You're going to miss it." She lifted my chin, forcing my gaze skyward. "Look."

I fixed my attention on the balloon. The basket and men were doll-sized from this distance as they floated five stories above the square. One of them upheld a long rod. He touched the rod to a flame and sparked it to life, showering a fiery green rain onto the crowd. I cowered, needlessly trying to avoid the descending embers. The sparks instantly burnt out. The men took turns lighting and showering us in fireworks: red, blue, orange, and yellow. The faster they worked, the higher the balloon floated. The sparks resembled sputtering kindling, and the demonstration slowed. I thought the show was over, but a sharp whistle accompanied by a loud bang and simultaneous explosions of light shot over the Doge's Palace.

We were united in our awe, but I became reluctantly aware of Donovan inching closer and turned to signal to Ann that we were about to have company when I noticed Henry paces away from her. I was washed in a mix of thrill and panic.

Here were most of the figures that had made up my story for the last few years. My heart longed to be with Asha and Max, to be young and playful, and still have my life ahead of me. But my worldly knowledge aligned with Ann's. We knew ourselves in a way I'd hoped Max and Asha never would. Then there were the two men my heart had waged a battle over. I still struggled with who deserved my affection and loyalty. Of course, Donovan seemed the right choice, for he offered me a feeling of protection and a direct plan for my safety and wellbeing. But Henry, a glimpse of him, sent my body into turmoil.

Spying each other, Henry and Donovan hastened their pace, and the men fell on us, much like two barbarians aiming to plunder sacred treasure. The hem of my dress brushed over Donovan's boots, and we were close enough to dance. My eyes took in his unspoken meaning—*It was time*. I dropped my look in a developing shame. How could I leave all my friends here and disappear?

Henry spoke first. "Good evening, ladies. How do you like the show?"

"Spectacular. Even better than the fireworks off Marseille, don't you think?" Without missing a beat, Ann prattled away in her excitement.

I was wary of her familiar comment. Pulling my arm free of Ann, I faced her and Henry with a polite inquiry. "Have you been traveling? Together?"

"Well . . ." Ann began.

Henry silenced her with a touch on her arm. He said, "We will watch for a few moments, and then I will return Ann to her host family outside the city. She is to depart for Naples tomorrow. Tension is growing, and you should return to London immediately."

This news hit Ann with the same revelation as it did me, for she stood agape. "Of course." Her composure closed. "How absent-minded of me."

Donovan interrupted. "You're leaving?"

"I have found what I came for and need to return to England immediately," Henry said as he watched the fireworks. "I have to finish my obligations before I can address my own desires."

I couldn't see if there was another meaning to his plainly spoken declaration.

With a cooled expression, Ann quickly kissed both my cheeks. "I have enjoyed our acquaintance, Renna. If we meet again, I hope we share a new adventure." She glanced at my neck and locket. "And you'll have to tell where you got that necklace. It is of a very particular design." She concentrated on Henry. "I'm ready when you see fit."

Henry gathered my free hand and kissed the tips of my gloved fingers. "May I echo the sentiments," he whispered. "I, too, hope for further adventures." His gaze shifted from my eyes to my chest. "And as for the locket, we need to discuss its maker. It may mean a prosperous path for you." He pressed Ann's elbow, and the throng of the crowd swallowed them.

I gawked after them, dumbfounded that he would leave again and with her. Jealousy and anger washed through me, and I was transported back to Christmas at Harewood House, where I'd spied their intimacy. Had all my imagining of him, his pursuit of me, only been a fantasy? Was he loyal to Ann, and I'd always been a conciliation prize? I had to be missing something important. The chattering of the onlookers, like chirping morning birds, hushed around me.

Donovan assumed Ann's position. He firmly gripped my hands, shaking me a little. "It's time to go." He continued with a blackening expression, "You need to leave them here." He gestured to Max and Asha.

Tears burned my eyes and brought me back to the moment. "I can't do that."

Fireworks exploded overhead, brightening his face and showing his bloodshot eyes. He removed my mask and gazed longingly at me. If we were alone, I thought he might lean in for his familiar kiss on my forehead, begging my compliance with affection. "Fine. Try to send them away as we walk." He lugged me toward the edge of the piazza. I clung to Asha and Max like dinghies to a barge.

We reached a covered walkway devoid of reveler, and our passage became clear. We progressed along the slippery stone pathways beyond closed doors, some splintered and begging for repair, others barred shut. I was thinking of a way to get Asha and Max to go home. Sensing we were a few blocks from the Ghetto, I stopped abruptly. "You both need to leave now."

Asha released me and huddled closer to Max, reacting like being whipped.

Max seemed to take my meaning immediately. He tucked her in with his good arm, nodding, "Of course."

"No. We have to stay together." Asha's expression was fiery and fearful in the same instant. "If you care for us, stay with us."

I wanted to rage. By *leaving, I am protecting you.* But my retort would remain a mere thought.

"What is this? I thought I heard a kerfuffle." Carmine's hefty frame turned the corner, swiftly closing the space between us in long strides, and landed between Asha and me, glancing back and forth before finally addressing Donovan. "Well done. Not one delectable tonight," he winked. "I get two tarts."

His presumption sickened me.

Donovan could not hide his surprise. "I was bringing these two back as a courtesy to Danielle. This is her nephew, and the girl works for her house."

Carmine watched Asha with a salivating expression. "Does she?"

"Not like Renna." Donovan stepped back, creating distance between Asha and me.

"No one will be quite like Renna," Carmine glowered. "I came to find you, thinking maybe you might get lost on your way back." Carmine peered over his glasses at Donovan, his expression telling the game was up. He deftly clasped Asha's wrist, "Perhaps it is time for Renna to educate another in her skills, much as Danielle has trained her."

Max tried to steer the conversation. "We must return home. The gates will close soon."

Without loosening his grip on Asha, Carmine belted Max hard on his left ear and again on his deformed arm. Max crumbled to the ground.

Asha and I cried out.

Carmine glowered down at Max, who looked much like a limp sack of vegetables. He brought his leg up, pounded his heel down on Max's arm again, and then similarly assaulted his back. "Twisted vermin," he seethed. "How dare you interrupt."

Max slumped to the damp stones. Donovan restrained me.

Carmine kept Asha from soothing Max, pulling her under his shoulder. He turned to Donovan. "This disruption has both heightened my appetite and reduced my patience." He stared me down hard and barked, "Come now." He rushed past us with Asha, managing the alley's length toward the canal, and was out of sight before we could protest.

Desperate to help my friends, I huddled beside Max and combed my fingers over his hair, hushing his whimpering. "It's ok. He's gone."

Donovan's leg pressed against my back as he inspected Max. "We must go. You know what will happen to her if you don't appear." This was not a request.

I kissed Max's cheek, crusted with tear-drenched hair. "I love you."

Gathering myself, I readied to pursue Asha and Carmine, but Donovan stopped me, holding my attention with a pained expression. "I don't know if I can stop this. I don't know if I can help her." He became his stony self.

"What do you mean?" I yanked free from his grip on my shoulder.

"Carmine has plans for you. I think he will include Asha in them now." Donovan knelt to Max and, with tenderness, tried to righten him. He brushed the hair away from his eyes and settled him against the wall. "Are you listening?"

Max nodded.

"You have to push this down. Do you hear me?"

He nodded again.

Sweat pearled on Donovan's forehead. "I know you are hurting, but you need to push past the hurt, for there is a much greater danger before us. You need to get help. Bring anyone who can help to the wharf. Understand?"

Donovan clasped my hand and started down the alley after Carmine and Asha, not waiting for an answer. I craned my neck and watched Max struggle to stand. He moved in the opposite direction, back toward home.

We made up some time as we ran over bridges to the Cannaregio neighborhood from one alley to the next. We approached a line of bobbing ships in time to see Carmine drag Asha up a plank to a boat moored at the end of the dock.

"What are we going to do?'

Donovan shook his head. "I can't believe I am taking you here, but I am indebted."

"What does he have to do with this? Why are you obligated?"

"Carmine has been my employer all these years. I have nothing but am valuable to him for acquiring the goods he wants. Until the end of last year, goods meant things like sugar, chocolate, and ivory. But when we arrived in Venice, he said he was turning his mind to something more prized that had taken hold in the American Colonies. Slavery. Little did I realize he meant sex slavery." Donovan spoke with a woeful countenance. "I overheard him talk about bartering an arrangement with a former courtesan to take a *girl* off her hands. That's why I came to find you at *La Fenice*. I knew you would need proof, so I showed you San Servelo. I have made big sacrifices to help you."

"I'm not leaving Asha with him, even if it means I'm sold or killed."

I was desperate to save my friend. Staying in Venice now, knowing everything, was not an option. If suffering had gotten me this far, then I had better be stronger.

"I know. If Carmine didn't have Asha, we would run." He kissed me hard on my lips. "I won't abandon you to his plan. I swear."

"I'm depending on it."

Rescuer

Light Attributes: Provides strength in crisis
Shadow Attributes: Keeps the rescued needy

High-stacked barrels and crates labeled *textiles*, *pelts*, *oil,* and *wine* crowded the deck of the trading vessel that Donovan and I boarded. A mixed smell of wet wood, mildew, and charred scent like the piazza's fireworks permeated the air. Carmine and Asha stood center on the deck, with his arm wrapped around her throat. His hand clasped her breast. Her face was tight with terror, mouth open in a noiseless rejection of the assault. Carmine held his prize and confronted us confidently, daring us to start a fight or bend to his will. Watching him made me ill. He buried his bearded face in Asha's neck, causing her to twist and holler. Surfacing, he traced his tongue along her cheek and into her hair. He audibly smelled her.

"Young, but spicy." He looked at me, "She needs a little refining. And what a spectacular dish she'll make."

I clutched Donovan's arm to keep steady, restraining myself from rushing at them and stealing away my friend.

Carmine spotted this as well. "Who is in charge of whom?" He glared. "Now, you can leave, Donovan. You will be of little help."

Donovan did not follow through with the dictate. Instead, his knees bent slightly, and his weight shifted forward, readying to be rushed. The muscles in his cheek ground rhythmically. His face looked like a dog sizing up an opponent.

Passivity would not serve. I pushed Donovan free and stepped toward Carmine. "Did you ever think that I wouldn't be in charge?" My haughty approach worked, for Carmine's grip on Asha loosened. "I was surprised that I wouldn't be enough for you." I slowed to a swishing saunter, carefully closing the gap, hoping not to spook him with my growing desperation. I tipped my chin demurely. "Aren't we all to be in business together."

He raised an eyebrow and narrowed his scrutiny. Carmine's fingers dug into Asha's breast, causing her to cry out.

Endeavoring to salvage the moment, I played with the lace around my collarbone, gingerly fingering it lower to reveal a glimpse of my breast. "Of course, my part has nothing to do with your agreement with Mother, but I wonder if she knows your plans for Asha. She has always favored her." I stopped and undid the top tie of my bodice. Placing my hands on my hips, a deep breath pulled apart the neckline and exposed my décolleté and locket.

He nearly released Asha.

Once I had his attention again, I continued my pursuit and closed the space between us. "How can I be of service?" I stepped near enough for him to smell me.

A courtesan friend told me once that men crave our ability to bring them to the height of their pleasure. It is not actually for the desire itself. It is for the moment after when they experience a small death. Ecstasy shuts down the senses, nearing a collision of rapture and hunger, only to be revived, rebirthed—a godlike experience. I sensed Carmine longed for such a resurrection.

I thought I should kiss him straight and take him to the quarters under the helm. Or he might enjoy an exhibition right here, and I should continue to undress. The second choice would leave the most flexibility, for I would neither be in his clutches nor in a confined space. I untied my bodice and slipped the sleeves over my shoulders, allowing my chest to rise and fall for his entertainment.

I resisted the temptation to search for Donovan. My escalating insecurity craved reassurance. I listened for him and heard nothing. Carmine remained stoically firm. Donovan must have left. Carmine would have spoken to him if he were still here. It was up to me to stay one step ahead.

Unexpectedly, Asha squirmed from Carmine's hands and came to me for a kiss. He gasped. We both heard it. She held my face, kissed me deeply, and embraced me warmly. It took a moment to understand Asha's idea. We women could not engage in an altercation like men. We must use the tools at our disposal, and two women loving one another with abandonment were among the most enticing spectacles to witness. I knew firsthand, for the same sight had aroused me many moments.

I wrapped my arms around Asha and cuddled her close, thankful for the hug and wishing it enough to whisk her away. Rubbing my lips against hers, soft and warm, I couldn't help but kiss the tip of her nose. I slowed our intimacy to discern the effect it had on our watcher. With foreheads pressed together, I saw relief in her smile. Such a friend—so brave.

I watched Carmine over the top of Asha's head, unsure how long we could keep up our ruse until help arrived or we could devise an escape. I cooed, "I guess you were not the only one with a taste for ménage e Trois."

Asha stepped around my side, her arm wrapped firmly around my waist, and she rested her head on my breast. My dress now opened down to my nipples. She nestled her hair against me but kept her gaze on Carmine.

He let out a laugh. "The coquette and her companion. You must have been grooming her before I thought of the idea. Well done."

Asha and I swayed together, satisfyingly humming, attempting to signal arousal. Her warm body bolstered me. The security would work to our advantage for a moment more, but this situation was bound to escalate. If this night continued as Carmine envisioned, I would be intimately united with my friend within the hour. Although her touch awakened me, she was a virgin and had been sheltered from the sordid affairs I knew. Taking away her innocence in my presence or by my own body made me sick. I swallowed hard and was ready to submit fully to Carmine, feasibly giving her a moment to run if she would take it.

But again, Asha was thinking ahead of me. "I feel a chill. Is it possible to move to a more secluded place?" Her head still nestled into my breast.

Carmine raised his hands in approving appraisal. "But of course."

Asha led me to the cabin under the helm. She reached the shuttered doors and turned the latch. The door swung wide, and she tugged me into a gloomy space. This time, I was clutching her, both possessively and apprehensively. My eyes struggled to adjust. There was no other exit.

I whispered, "Now what?"

She murmured with sibilant breath, "Wait."

Carmine stood at the threshold, viewing the room from outside light before plunging into the darkness. I heard the rattle of a belt buckle. There was leather scratching across his pants. A quick fizz of a wick and the light of a candle brightened the space in front of us. "Well, ladies, it does not do to cower in the corner." His tone was playful.

"We need the light to pour wine." Asha stepped to the ledge under the window and an awaiting decanter and glasses. She turned gracefully to Carmine. "Unless, of course, you prefer to drink from another vessel."

Her comments bowled me over. How could my innocent friend have skill and poise that took me months—no years—to learn, well after my virginity was left on the lush covers of a Harewood settee?

Carmine let out a long chuckle. "How lucky am I on this night? I thought my agreement with Danielle would be for Renna, but now we have you, my sweet. Do tell me your name." He took a drink of the wine.

"I am Asha," she said with a bit of dance that made her skirt float around her.

"Renna and Asha, or Asha and Renna." He tried the combination. "I think this will be a lucrative time."

I tried for the same assertiveness as my petite friend. "Lucrative? I believe I know what you'd like from us tonight, but it sounds as though you have ideas that go beyond the hour." She handed me a glass, which I took gratefully.

"Of course." He finished his wine, reached for a lock of hair escaping my chignon, and wrapped it around his fingers, reeling me in. "I've had a plan for you since we met. But now that we have your little friend, I'll have to better the agreement with Danielle."

"Umm. Do tell." I swallowed the wine, mixing with acid on my tongue.

Asha brought the pitcher to Carmine.

"I like you very much." He snapped her close and bruised her lips with his whiskers, causing the wine to splash over his vest. She didn't fight him. Surfacing with a gratified expression, he continued. "Danielle has wisely guessed business in Venice will not favor her much longer. Bonaparte's campaign has already impacted life. Venice may not be the best city for flesh-bargaining."

I was flooded with the awareness that Mother had been devising this for some time. "Where are there better prospects?"

"That has not been entirely decided." He politely looked at Asha as though he pondered her sensitivities. "I have considered going east into the Ottoman lands. There we can use you for breeding lighter-skinned children, although," he stroked Asha's hair, "I'm not sure you will fetch as much, for your hair is a bit dark. You might be worth some as a bride, but not if I have a taste of you first." He took her chin as though coaxing a child with sweets.

He glanced up, referencing some plan. "We could take you west, to London. There are many whores, but none as elegant as a Venetian Courtesan," he proclaimed. "I believe we can market you now as a team to some of my wealthy friends who would love a double dalliance. This would require you to be in top form." He carelessly flipped open his fingers as he held his wine glass, grasping it with his thumb and forefinger like a gentleman, and glared at me. "I understand you have a weakened constitution, suffering from vapors and melancholia. Like any perishable good, I cannot have you rot before maximizing profits." He pressed his lips together with pride.

This was not the first time I'd been referred to as a *good*, and anger rose deep within me. But I would keep him from using my friend shamefully and resolved to sacrifice myself. "How would you like to proceed?" I brushed unseen dust from his lapel. "Perhaps we could whet her appetite and allow her to watch how the experienced enjoy each other," I coaxed. "As it's her first time, we want her as ready as possible."

He clasped my hand to his chest. "Aye, aye, I would like that very much. I want to see those mysterious eyes and the gold fleck shining for me as I ride you—hard."

I gave him a primed expression but was revolted by the image he painted.

Before I could consent, Asha interrupted again. "Shouldn't I be the one to see Carmine at his best? For it will take your skill, Renna, to bring him 'round again." She stepped in behind me, coyly peering at him around my shoulder.

Ready to argue, I noticed a cold blade press my back. It took all I had not to reveal my surprise. Asha's plan was coming to me, and thankfully, it had nothing to do with us using our bodies to delay. I pulled my free hand from Carmine's fingers while holding the wine glass, slipped it over my shoulder in an embrace of myself, and touched Asha's cheek. She kissed my fingertips, and I could put my hand behind my back in a bold stance. She held the hilt high within range of seizing the knife.

Asha and I couldn't have choreographed the next part. She stepped from behind me and gathered Carmine's face into a passionate kiss, leaving me free to strike. Swinging the knife around, I aimed for Carmine's back as he pulled Asha tightly to him.

Something in my movement alerted him. While holding Asha's face in one hand, he clutched my wrist with the other. Asha kicked him hard in the shins. As I pried his fingers free, I dropped the knife. Carmine squirmed in disbelief, and I bent to retrieve the blade. He snatched a fistful of my hair and yanked me down, my face at crotch level. My hair entwined in his fingers fell in patches past my cheek, blood trickling over me.

Asha was on him, clawing at his neck. Carmine belted her on the cheek, and she tumbled to his feet, unmoving. While he was distracted, I found the knife and stabbed at his foot. He wailed. I pulled it free and hit him again in the calf. He fell like a cut timber to the floor with us.

He snatched the knife still in my hand, and our bodies tumbled together. I lost grip on the blade. Carmine released me, clutching at his wounds.

Aching and stunned, I sought Asha. The thought of her dying here sent me into a panic. I stretched my fingers to her, discovering her mouth. Short bursts of air came forth, shallow but repetitive. The moment of concern was a mistake, for as I turned away from Carmine, a blazing scratch cut down the middle of my back. I screamed, and light at the edges of my eyes darkened.

With blurred vision, I spotted the knife between us. There would be no other opportunity. In a last burst of energy, I twisted to Carmine as he crouched to assess Asha himself. I pushed the blade long into his neck. He scrambled to defend himself, but it was too late. Carmine's energy seeped away, and he fell limp over my legs, pinning me down.

I slumped back, dazed, and struggled to sense if he was dead or alive. Holding my breath, I heard Asha steadily panting. Carmine emitted an awful gurgling sound.

The altercation scarcely settled when the door burst open, and Donovan tumbled into the room, shouting, "No!" He rushed down to us, cradling my head in his lap. "Renna, Renna, are you all right?"

I was surprised at my first comment, "You left." But my anger could not steal verve from the moment, and I collapsed entirely into his lap. From my position, I could not see the commotion of occupants as they tumbled into the quarters but took them in turn as they spoke—Camilla, Max, and Mother.

"Oh, God."

"Is she dead?"

"What have you done to my daughter?"

We waited as Mother dropped to the floor near Donovan and me. Although my back screamed from Carmine's cut, and I longed to tend to my wounds, I couldn't rip myself away from the stunning sight of Mother crouching by Asha and cradling her head in her lap, much as Donovan did mine.

I asked. "Your daughter?"

Her face clouded, and she knelt with Asha like a child rocking a kitten. "Of course. Why do you think I was willing to trade you? I've done all I can to protect her, and now, you!" She shot me a hateful stare. "Because of you, she is not safe."

Donovan pushed gently against my shoulder, sitting me upright to deal directly with Mother, seeming to know my disadvantage in lying on the floor. Camilla came to me, and Max knelt by my knees. Their presence bolstered me, although I knew Max longed to be by Asha, to be her protector. I ached where Carmine hit me. Camilla touched my back and showed me blood coating her fingers.

I looked to his thick, limp form sprawled at my feet, rolled onto his back, eyes wide and tongue lapping out the side of his mouth. Moments ago, he had designs of bedding me in front of my friend. Now, his bulbous body lay lifeless before us.

Max crouched next to me. "You are hurt, but it doesn't look deep."

A violent tremor overtook me, and I shook like I was possessed as I wiped the hair from my face to see Mother. "Why have you been unkind?"

"I told you. Asha's my child, and I've done everything possible to keep her safe, clean, and learned. That night I saw her in your room and realized you'd shown her *Aretino*, I knew you had to go." She stroked Asha. "And, of course, you simply remind me of someone I detest."

Donovan barked. "You bitch!"

Mother stiffened and stared at him. If she were close enough, I thought she'd hit him. "Bitch or not, I take care of my own."

Camilla interjected like a flustered bird, attempting to placate the escalating temperaments. "We must get you back, get you cleaned up, and then we will decide."

"Decide what?" Mother snapped. "She has tarnished my daughter, and I will not have her back. You will all leave!" Her voice roared.

Asha's voice cracked as she came around. "Daughter?"

Mother smoothed the hair from Asha's cheek and caressed her as Camilla had done for me so many times. "My dear. I'm grieved you found out like this, but yes, I am your mother." She leaned in and brushed her lips across Asha's forehead.

"Get off me," Asha grumbled. "You cannot be my mother."

I noticed Donovan's legs tighten. Max and Camilla froze at my side.

There was desperation in Mother's voice. "I am."

Their family riddle unraveled before me, leaving me feeling isolated and unjustly abandoned to the whims of fate. How could they discover their interconnectedness, but I was left floundering and alone? "If you're her mother . . ." I referenced Danielle and Asha. "And you're his mother . . ." I glanced between Camilla and Max. "Then what about me?"

Camilla caressed me. "Your mother is dead, dear. She died when you were three. She tried to kill you and your sister and suffered greatly after the incident."

A fog of disbelief enveloped me, and I shook my head at her words.

"You lie. No mother of mine would try to kill Felicity like that." I envisioned Felicity's burnt fingers pressed against the glass the first night we met.

Camilla gestured to Mother. "I know your story because Cassandra was our sister."

Donovan joined the disclosure. "You mean to tell me that all of you are related? Both of you have watched Renna—your niece—bear unspeakable travesty, and you are her kin?" Donovan's voice escalated with each revelation. He rose to his full height, his disdain shadowing his expression. Camilla scooted back, but he clasped the edge of her skirt. "You have been involved from the start, slipping her hints that she was safe, but never truly. Devising ways for her to be saved, but never completely."

Releasing Camilla, he retrieved the knife and wiped the drying blood on the edge of Carmine's shirt before tucking it into his waistband. He clasped me under my arms. "This is going to hurt, little love." He hoisted me up. The sudden movement made me retch on the floor. "And I have played a part in all this." Donovan tucked me tight into his chest like the two puzzle pieces we'd become. "Please forgive me."

Mother patted Asha, who rebuffed her. "You are all fools. Who cares who did what and to whom? This damned acquaintance needs to end."

Camilla accused Mother. "Why? Because maybe you participated in the fire?"

"Nothing provable." She glanced away.

Although I heard her words, I was still stuck on Camilla's involvement. "Did you know?" I gestured to her. "Did you know I was your niece when I came to you at the workhouse, when we moved to Harewood House, and when I met Father Thaddeus?"

Mother laughed inhumanly. "Is he still around?"

Camilla squirmed but didn't try to rise. "I knew Cassandra had become ill, had lost her wits. I was told she lit your family's house on fire, but that didn't seem correct. Danielle and I were sent here together after the house burnt. I was told to watch over her." Her voice quieted. "The voyage was terrible. All of your screaming." She seemed to plead for Mother's recollection.

"Don't make yourself the victim here. I'm the one who was jilted."

Mother's complexion darkened as she smoldered with rage. "I was in love, and Cassandra stole him. I burned the house down and let the blame fall on Cassandra." Mother's look settled solidly on me. "Why should I protect the spawn of my mortal enemy? Why shouldn't I profit from it."

Camilla bowed her head, flustered by the wave of accusations. "Danielle. She was our sister. They are your nieces!" She looked beseechingly to the rest of us to hear her out. "I became pregnant with Max without a husband, and Danielle had found a lucrative life in Venice, after San Servolo and Santa Caterina. When I heard Renna and Felicity were left to Bootham Hall, to the asylum, I had to go home." She crumpled in on herself. "But I am indebted. Danielle paid for Max and me to return to England and create a life in York."

Mother waved her hand at Camilla, signaling the recovery of her power. "Without me, you would have all failed. For you, leaving Venice meant survival, but only with my support. What do you think I sacrificed to provide that?"

I was struggling to accept their confessions. "And what of my father?"

"He was French." Danielle elevated Asha to a seated position, holding her back as Donovan had held me. "And he was my fiancé before Cassandra's, but she stole him. Fiend—she deserved what she received."

Max stepped between us. "How dare you?"

"How dare *I*?" Mother rose to her full height, leaving Asha leaning against her leg. "I let Camilla return." She nodded toward Max's arm. "I convinced the doctor to keep you, little beast. I am the reason you all exist!"

My rage roared with my awakening. "You killed her. You killed my mother. You burnt down the house. I have these scars because of YOU!"

Mother glanced at me, her look more tentative. "You can't expect a betrayal like that to go unpunished." She stiffened. "And you are a survivor. Remarkably, you managed to carry that little bitch of a sister out of the house with you. And all at the age of three?" She dared to reach out to me. "You were simply destined for a life of pain."

Her words hit me like a blast of frigid air, and I felt a rush of memories. Obviously, I was too young to know the whole story, but I could feel Felicity's infant body in my arms. I had struggled to hold her. Even now, I could feel my mother's hand in mine as we walked through blinding smoke. My body remembered it all. A sudden wave of sickness hit me, and I bent over, gagging and coughing on phantom fumes.

Donovan gingerly aided me, and my coughing subsided. I knew Mother's recount was correct. I had been there and somehow managed to pull my sister out. But that hadn't been enough, for Cassandra died months later in the asylum, and Felicity never left.

Fury awakened me, and I reached for the oil lamp on the table behind us. In a blind rage, I threw the lantern at Mother's chest. The glass shattered over her face and neck, and flames spread over her skin like oil over water.

She screamed and fell to her knees. Fire crawled up her face, neck, and chest, and the smell of her dress and burnt flesh choked us. Mother frantically slapped at the fire with her palms. "Help me." No one moved. We watched Mother writhe, attempting to suffocate the flames with her hands. The fire overtook her and alighted her wig like a bird's nest set aflame. She folded in on herself, her movements slowing like a de-animated puppet.

I couldn't let her die like that and pulled a shawl from Camilla's shoulders. Camilla stood stunned, mouth gapping as she watched her sister writhe. I hastily wrapped the shall around Mother. She collapsed beneath my weight. The heat of her body radiated through the covering.

Donovan tugged on the shawl, slowly revealing the fire's destruction. He bent to Mother, passing his fingers in front of her nose and causing her slumped heap to tip sideways. Her face was blistered and angrily red. There was little left of the hair on the right side of her scalp. She twitched and sucked in a breath. I held myself, numbed by the two bodies contorted before me, one stabbed through and oozing blood. I glanced at my hands, stained with the evidence of my actions. Mother lay near him, outwardly reflecting the monstrosity she'd always been to me, but she was alive for better or worse.

Donovan commanded. "We need to get off this ship. Carnival runs wild. Authorities search vessels for nefarious acts, which is exactly what they will find here."

Judge

Light Attributes: Managing with compassion
Shadow Attributes: Misusing authority

I clasped a warm mug and huddled near the fire in Alistair's workshop. Asha leaned against me, sapped of energy, her expression vacant, eyes transfixed on the floor. Camilla was at my shoulder, dabbing salve into my wound, while Benyamin, Donovan, and Alistair clustered around a splintered table to the far side, secretly devising their plans. Mother was huddled on a cot, bound like a mummy with wet bandages, occasionally groaning in discomfort. Although we'd cleaned her, there was an acidic, smoky smell wafting off her skin and hair.

We had brought her to Alistair's shop in the early morning instead of Benyamin's to throw off any police officials. Donovan had been reluctant to leave Carmine's body on the boat, for it would be easy for the authorities to connect him to the death.

I was pained as I watched him drain his third glass of whiskey, brooding over his options. He muttered to himself as much as to us, "I have to clean up that mess."

Benyamin patted his arm as he read a book on the table before them. "You will. But you know as well as I that nothing can be done until nightfall again."

My head was swimming with my revelations. I fixed on the smell of ink pressed into crisp news pages, which were noxious and intoxicating. It managed momentarily to mask the events from last night, rendering the affair a figment of my imagination.

I thumbed a stack of papers on a side table near me, noticing the title of an article: *Pope Signs Peace Treaty with France*. English newspapers, *Evening Mail, Telegraph,* and *The Times* had similar headlines. I read the first paragraphs from a few of them. They all had a contemptuous tone for Venice's current state of politics. It saddened me to think that this city would be degraded, although its influence had adulterated me. Venice now pulled on my heart in a way no man could.

The news of political change made me think of Ann and Henry. Were they off to Naples? A memory of their last image in the Piazza flashed before me, and I was envious of them moving forward with their lives freely while I cowered, fearful and uncertain in the Ghetto's confines.

Shaking off my longing, I questioned Alistair, sparking him to life. "Is this true? Are the French invading all of the city-states?"

He familiarly stroked the top of my shoulder. "There is great conflict. Bonaparte is battling the Austrians for dominance in the region. He has already taken Tuscany and Padua. Read how they describe the Venetian aristocracy," Alistair instructed. "They claim that we invite the French to 'liberate' its people from Venice's oligarchy. Do you notice no mention of the hostility in the streets?"

The articles said Venice had lost all sense of self and was open to French influence. "These articles have an air of French bias yet are printed by well-known English papers."

Alistair tucked a lock of hair behind his ear. A small smile played at the corners of his mouth. "I know you don't like Danielle to be right, but you have a bright mind. It is why I've loved you dearly from the first moment. You lack naivety."

"I think Mother would say otherwise. Isn't she the one who described me as 'missing' things?" I attempted to tidy the papers and conceded to leaving them in a crumpled heap on the table. Black smudges on my fingertips showed evidence of my musings. I rubbed my fingers in my skirt as Alistair approached me. I glanced at him, noticing his look, and watched droplets of sweat pearl on his upper lip. He wasn't with us last night and didn't know of the horror we'd experienced. If he had, he wouldn't dare search my face for an invitation now, one I was not open to give. Still, I stretched a hand to him and let my fingertips absorb the moisture on his face. He lingeringly kissed them.

Alistair leaned over my shoulder and whispered. "Who has captured your heart?"

I turned from him, glancing at Donovan. Then, promptly recalling Henry's serene gaze and slender form, I answered, "I don't know."

Max stumbled into the room with a bowl of steaming water and several rags slung over his arm as he struggled to manage the weight. He knelt by Asha and handed a dampened rag first to Camilla and then moistened one to perform his own ministrations of Asha, dabbing at her dirt and tear-streaked cheeks. Donovan and Benyamin watched as we all cared for each other.

"What do we do with Mother?" Asha was the first to name the truth we were all avoiding. She offered a reassuring look but said, "She is my mother. It feels very odd to say that. After all she's done to you, I couldn't think of a worse woman to be related to. We can't abandon her."

Camilla hovered around us, and I caught a whiff of her. Her sour stench revealed her anxiety and concern. "I'd like to suggest taking her back. Maybe we should all return to York. We could go back home and have Danielle treated by Father Thaddeus."

We stared at her. I had not thought of bringing her with us. I remember being on the boat deck when we set sail from Hull. I recalled my ache to return to Felicity, comfort her, and let her know she was not alone. That must have been Camilla's desire now. She, too, felt a duty to Danielle, bound to aid her when she could no longer help herself.

Asha pushed Max away and spoke to Benyamin. Her look narrowed. "Are you my father?"

I prayed the answer was yes. One of us should at least have a father.

"I am. Why do you think I demanded you take the knife with you? I thought something might happen." His look radiated loving devotion. "And then again, I am not. It was a plan Danielle and I devised to keep you safe. I met her when I was studying at Padua. She was traveling the region with her family. Do you remember Camilla? We were all young." Benyamin's appearance softened as he recalled their acquaintance.

Camilla sighed. "I remember."

"Danielle was beautiful. I would have gone to the ends of the Earth at her request, but she made it clear that she was betrothed to another man, a Frenchman."

"My father?" I asked

He looked at me. "Yes. Desmond Covert. He was a good man. But things happen. We often fall in love with those we do not intend." Benyamin bowed his head in sadness. "I wish Desmond and Cassandra had not met. We wouldn't be in this position now."

"And Renna would not exist," Max interjected.

Camilla answered. "Danielle met Desmond in her travels to Italy and France. They were betrothed, and Desmond quickly came to England to meet Danielle's family. Unfortunately, it was not she who enthralled him. Cassandra was young and smitten. When Cassandra and Desmond married, quite in secret, Danielle was utterly heartbroken. It changed her. Bitterness replaced the love and artistic sensibility that was our older sister." Camilla motioned to Benyamin. "I'd always known Benyamin cared for her. I sent for him when we knew she was pregnant."

I watched Camilla quizzically, struggling to put together what she was implying.

Donovan summarized first. "Let me put this right. Danielle was pregnant. Benyamin, you knew?" Benyamin inertly responded. "And she was in love with Desmond, thus presumably making Desmond Asha's father. Then that would make . . ."

Mother Shipton's words from her time in the asylum came to me: *three sisters, and now only two . . . of two, there are three.*

"That would make us sisters." My heart leaped out of my throat. All this time, our growing bond and love for each other and Asha was flesh and blood, not once removed through mere cousinly kinship. "The similarities . . ."

Asha looked at me, her expression sallow and haunted as she digested the meaning. "I think I always knew that."

I bent to kiss the top of her head. My back screamed in pain.

"Dear now, you must hold still." Camilla came to me with long strips of bandages. "Carmine wore a ring on his right hand, spiked at the palm. His seeming gentleman's slap inflicted lasting damage." Her voice cracked as she struggled with her declaration. "I am deeply sorry for the pain you've known. Your body is a true testament to the trauma you have endured. First, your lungs, for inhaling the burning smoke of the fire, and then your back. It is a cursed map of scars."

Donovan added. "If I'd known that fateful walk home from the Board Inn, when we heard that cry together, might signal something sinister, I would have taken you with me then and never allowed you to return."

I remembered that night and meeting Donovan, Henry, and Carmine. "Carmine. Did you know the kind of man he was then?"

"I knew he had connections with the British West India Company. He offered me a job not long after. I needed the work." Donovan came closer to the fire. His green eyes looked glassy from fatigue and whiskey. "God, how all the paths connect."

"Aye, and there was always Henry." Camilla kneeled on the floor. "He has always been part of the plan for you. Why did he take such interest in devising Harewood?"

Donovan clasped his head in his hands. "I was part of that too, sort of."

"Aye, but did he not suggest it and make most of the arrangements?" She stared at Donovan. "Somehow, you are present but never directing the course of action. I am sorry for the information you always miss. If you had all the pieces, then perhaps our effort," she seemed to plead, "would have worked better."

I could have lashed out at Camilla like a horsewhip. "Did you know Danielle would expect me to whore for her?"

"No, dear." Camilla touched my knee. "When you were taken to the asylum, I contacted Donovan, as I knew he was nearby. We said that you would need to leave York for a new life, for Father Thaddeus discovered the relation between you and Cassandra, and it would only be a matter of time before Max and I were brought into his suspicions. We couldn't leave you to such a fate after what we saw of his capabilities concerning Felicity." She looked to Max for reassurance, but he was absorbed with Asha. Realizing she must continue alone with her account, she answered, "I did not expect Danielle would make you sell yourself. I had written hoping you'd be the housemaid and I the housekeeper. Ann was the one with carnal experience."

"You knew of Ann's past?"

Camilla nodded. "She threw everything off when she made her own arrangements once we landed in Venice. Ann has had an ally this whole time. I'm not sure who."

My blood boiled as I thought of how Ann managed to complicate every aspect of my life since meeting her. "If I could wring her neck now, I would."

"Me too," echoed Max.

"And I," added Donovan. "I am the fool played in this game." Watching the man I'd deemed my rescuer bow his head in defeat was difficult.

There were still two facts unexplained. "Who gave me the locket? It was wrapped in burlap with British West India markings." I glanced between Donovan and Camilla.

They looked at each other, accusing the other of the secret.

"It wasn't them. It was me." Max said. "Father Thaddeus said our arrival marked a dark omen, and he was waiting for the evil within us to flesh out. The necklace was buried in the back of the church closet with the paper about Cassandra. I thought if you knew you were not an orphan if you had a real family, a wealthy one, it might keep you from being prey to Henry's plans. But Father Thaddeus only needed a scrap of evidence of your link to something he thought was nefarious. It's why I gave it to you in secret. If you kept yourself chaste and had a reason to endure a dull maid's life, maybe you could learn enough to escape them —all the men with their agendas."

I reached out to Max. He was my most beloved companion. "I love you." Releasing him, I asked about the room. "And what of Henry? Do you all know why he took Ann away, why she has woven through this tale unscathed?"

Donovan shook his head. "I met him while working for Carmine. The night in the Board Inn was one of our first interactions."

Camilla said. "I met him when he came to the workhouse the night before we left for Harewood." She paused briefly. "I hesitate to share this, but he left you a letter."

"What? Let me have it." Donovan's chair scraped across the floor, and he plodded toward Camilla as she pulled a letter from her apron.

Camilla withdrew. "I swore Renna would read it first. He said it could change her fate."

"Give it to me," I demanded. Camilla slipped a sealed letter into my palm. Breathlessly, I turned it over and inspected the emblem, the image of a lion stamped into the wax. I cracked the seal and turned the page so only I could see the writing.

> *My Dearest Renna:*
>
> *By now, I hope you are safely tucked away and not blazing across the Adriatic on some misadventure concocted by Danielle and Carmine. I am most sorry for abandoning you. I have another that demands my loyalty—Ann. I don't want you to mistake my relationship with her. She is my sister, and I must protect her, sometimes from herself. If this note finds you, hopefully still in Venice, I promise to return to you. I intend to claim you as my wife and return you to England for a respectable life.*
>
> *With unfailing intention,*
>
> *Captain Henry Abner Moore*

"Unbelievable," I murmured, absently tipping the page toward the fire. Here it was, the key to my fantasies. I reread the letter, and again, memorizing his declaration, *I intend to claim you as my wife.* I was baffled I could be more than a whore. My dreams of being someone's wife, have a family of my own—perhaps being a mother—were within reach.

Asha grabbed the letter and read it as Max peered over her shoulder. "No. You can't. There is something wrong with him," Max protested. "And he's Ann's brother. Do you understand what that would mean for you? Your life would be sheer torment."

Camilla took the note to Alistair, Donovan, and Benyamin. Each read it with a different response. "That explains the Harewood House suggestion."

Max asked. "What?"

"It was told Ann was listed in the Covent Garden registry as one of the best whores in London. She sought that life after taking to bed with a married man. The man's wife exacted revenge without regret, and Ann was ruined." Camilla turned to the room with an amused expression. "Henry, I understand, rescued her—must have changed her name and put her in Harewood House—where she was reinvented. Mrs. Brearcliff said Ann had scant references, but Henry insisted she take on a maid's position."

I could piece together what Camilla implied, for Ann simply was the worst of maids and did her best to avoid actual work, more ready to entertain Father Thaddeus or torment the patients at the asylum. "I can understand them as brother and sister, but what of Henry's offer?"

Camilla seemed eager. "Shouldn't it be considered?"

Benyamin addressed her. "It might be advantageous. Asha is her sister, after all. Perhaps it means a life for them both."

She nodded, reading his thoughts.

Alistair protested. "No. I won't have it. You cannot leave. You have to stay."

I was forced to tilt my head back to see his face. "Carmine was right. The tides are changing in Venice. All are absorbed in climbing to the top, like scum on a pond. What kind of life will we have if I am the tainted whore in a city writhing in French power and Austrian interests?"

Alistair resumed. "You can choose any life you'd like with your wit and perception. You could stay here with me. We could write about the real goings-on in the whole area."

I glanced at the stack of leaflets. "You don't run a newspaper, Alistair. You write snippets of information that are scattered on sidewalks, to which most never give a second glance." Although I didn't see his face, I knew I had offended him.

He was desperate. "I may not have the same prestige as a mainstay journal, but we can write here. You could express yourself any way you like. You could assume a pseudonym to share your perspectives with those who refuse to heed women's words."

Alistair's passions were noble, but I couldn't merely jump through life as a wretch, a maid, a courtesan—and then a writer. "Alistair, I think you reach too far."

"And what of me?" Donovan stepped in. "Don't I get a say in this matter? I have not intervened, over and over, to be jilted for another of Henry's schemes." His expression was most dear and pulled on me in a way neither Henry nor Alistair could.

Was it possible for me to love all three of them, to want a life with all or none of them? Mother Shipton's prophecy and my promises suddenly resurged:

To my mind: I promise to make choices with even measure, clear of lust or craving, and as protected against fear as I may—I promise not to make a permanent decision when my mind is clouded.

To my body: I promise I will keep you protected by my will or someone else's.

To my heart: I promise to know and love myself before I love another.

I considered my friends—my family. Each of them held deep connections, something I'd always dreamt of. I could stay here and make my own life. I could be with Donovan, but God only knew what that might bring. Or, I could wait for Henry, return to York, and claim what birthright I had.

Addressing each of them individually and collectively, I produced a reply. "It seems wise now to heal, breathe, and wait for the right answer to show itself."

15 MAY 1797

Liberator

Light Attributes: Freeing from beliefs
Shadow Attributes: Imposing tyranny

The Venice light was a healing rebirth and a foil for my years in Yorkshire gloom. The late spring weather wrapped us in protective comfort. I gladdened myself with mundane tasks and hummed in tune with a songbird as I hung the wash from a line in the midday sun. Francese perched on a pole and cleaned his feathers. Max sat nearby, handing up laundry pins in our balanced tranquility.

"It is good for you to return to England, Danielle. You will need the damp to soothe your skin." Camilla struggled with stretching a long blanket over a drying line.

Each time I looked to Mother, despite learning all she'd done to my family and me, I was run through with guilt at the horror she'd become. I stepped to help her, whispering, "She seems uncomfortable. Do you think she will manage the trip?"

"Come now. We need to finish these so the blankets can be packed, and we will be ready." Camilla shuffled to Mother and gently pulled a coverlet higher on her chest, touching her exposed cheek. "How are you feeling?" Mother squirmed away.

Mother sat in a wicker chair in the sun with her feet propped on a stool. A lemon tree shadowed her face and body. Bandages wrapped around the right side of her face, and a hat concealed the rest of her look, except for her left eye, which remained exposed. Despite the laudanum, she stared at us with cold penetration. She had lost the use of her right hand and seemed not to hear from her right ear. At this point, she didn't seem able to speak, uttering occasional grunts. This might have resulted from consistently applying laudanum to her brandy.

Since Mother's maiming, Camilla had regained much of her authority and was as commanding as I remembered her at the Cotton Workhouse. She turned to me with an assured look. "It will be a terrible journey for her, surely. But we can't leave her here. It is time to go home and put the pieces of our family together. I know you had a dreadful time at the asylum. I know you're vexed by the knowledge that Felicity is still there. And to answer your Carnival night question: I knew you were my niece when you came to me at the workhouse. Remember, no child under three is allowed without a blooded guardian. But I wasn't going to leave you to Bootham Hall. I am sorry I could not bring Felicity, but the fire damaged her, and she needed the nurses' support."

I froze with the power of her declaration. "Were you protecting or hindering me?"

She came to me for a familiar touch, and I allowed it. "Dear, always protecting. It was the least I could do for Cassandra and Desmond. Their betrayal was horrible to Danielle, but if you could have seen them." A light smile touched her face. "They were very much in love. It was unfortunate that Danielle met him first, for it was obvious to us that Cassandra was a more fated match."

I thought about that and considered how I could recognize the right match. Here, I had three suitors. That is, if I counted Alistair, if Henry was good for his word, and if Donovan ever returned from his errand of restoring the ship for our journey. How was I to know who was right for me?

We had sorted through the chaos of Carnival night, and Donovan removed Carmine's body and cleaned the ship. He sailed it to Triste to be gutted, repainted and renamed. Donovan claimed the vessel, which seemed like a justified payment.

Once the fear of being discovered about Carmine's murder had passed, we settled together in Benyamin's home. Life reminded me of time in the cramped Cotton Workhouse, but I was grateful for the kinship in close quarters. Although I felt safe, my nightmares were infused with Felicity, Mother, Carmine, and Mother Shipton's oracular warnings. I had agreed to return to England, for it seemed the right decision, but I was apprehensive about taking my friends with us. Jews were not well-received there, and I was concerned about Benyamin would get on in Yorkshire.

Asha approached in a hurry. "There you are. You two come with me now. There's something you must see." The temperature of her words radiated anxiety.

My heart thudded. "What is it?"

She panted with urgency. "You need to come to the gates. You aren't going to believe what is happening."

We abandoned our laundry and rushed with Asha through the campo to an alley leading to the Cannaregio neighborhood, the gateway out of the Ghetto. We sprinted through the paths toward the Ghetto gates. As we approached, loud clanging and a commotion rebounded against the walls.

Asha halted us with a flick of her hand. "Watch a minute, and I'll explain."

French soldiers pried at the bolts of the gate hinges, hammering free the pins, and the gates fell away from their moorings. It was mortifying that they would defile the city.

Asha clasped Max. "General Bonaparte has declared war on Venice."

I'd heard rumblings, but since deserting my life as a courtesan, I tried to bury my head in the sand like an ostrich when it came to worldly affairs. I kept busy with routine tasks and did not think about political upheavals.

"Napoleon has won. He is taking over the city—the whole Venetian Empire. Don't you understand what the soldiers are doing?" She was desperately enraged. "They are tearing down the gates. Gates that have separated us from the city for centuries."

We watched the French soldiers smartly dressed in their blue, red, and white uniforms, prying the gates off the walls and dragging them toward the walk adjacent to the canal. They quickly assembled the timbers into a high pyre. An overweight soldier dressed in a uniform angrily stretched across his breast, held a torch high, and touched the top of the wood, now covered in hay stalks, bringing the kindling to life. He repeated the process around the base, and soon the centuries-old gates groaned and cracked from the heat. Two other soldiers leaned against a wall and lighted cigars. One of them muttered, "*Vive la France.*"

Asha dragged us back the way we'd come. "Follow me. You have to see something else."

We drove after her, retracing our steps and dashing through the Ghetto Campo. Camilla still hung the line, and Mother reclined in the shade.

Our hurried pace drew Alistair's attention. "Where are you going?"

"Come with us," I shouted.

He was quickly at our heels.

Avoiding central alleys, we tore through crowded campos and packed bridges as a group. I clung to Max and Alistair to keep from being engulfed by people arguing or swallowed in the cacophony of hollering and pushing. We arrived slightly winded at the corner of St. Mark's Square, nearest the Basilica. A mass of people huddled together, their national affiliations signified by flecks of Venetian, French, Austrian, or English dialects.

Moving toward the middle, where we might blend in among the many, I heard:

"What does this mean?"

"*Bien sûr, cela se produit.*"

"*Sie verdienen das.*"

We found a position near the Tree of Liberty in the middle of the square. I turned to my companions and relayed the comments. "Why are the French saying they knew *this would happen*, and the Austrians stating *that we deserve this*?"

Asha spun me around to face the Doge's Palace. I looked to the four horses safeguarding the square and San Marco's Basilica for centuries. A tri-colored French flag flapped against the white marble. The site was unbelievable. The bronze horses, the French flag, and Venice's winged Lion were within the same view. Commotion atop the Basilica signaled a dozen soldiers working in unison with what looked like an attempt to take the horses down.

Alistair asked. "What are they doing?"

Asha's complexion was purple as she recounted her outrage. "Napoleon has decreed the city be remade to his liking. It's like the gates. The Ghetto is to be opened, no longer confining the Jews—no longer protecting us. I'm not sure he understands how vulnerable his act of *liberation* will leave us. And the horses, look at that!" She pointed to the Basilica again. "It is said he is a cavalier, and he wishes them placed outside the Louvre Palace, in the Tuileries Garden, a symbol of his horse mastery."

"You're quite informed," Max jested.

She poked at him. "You're not the only one who knows how to sneak around corners and learn of the world around us."

Although it was irrefutable now that they were blood-related, Max and Asha's bond only strengthened, sheltering each other's protective orbit. Their union sparked a feeling of jealousy in me, a sense of being an outsider. Since they both had at least one parent, I assumed they found allegiance in grieving the departed.

Alistair huddled close and asked, "Can we ever escape ourselves? I will always be a romantic and a writer and a Jew. Max," he gestured to him. "Sorry, friend, but you will always be lame."

A bit perturbed, I responded. "And what of me? I don't know who or what I am. Am I doomed to this life of chaos that befalls me?"

"No, that's not what I mean." He softened his tone. "Rather, we take ourselves with us, no matter where we go or what deliverance we experience."

A cry rose from the crowd, calling our attention again to the Basilica. The far-right horse rocked side-to-side as though riding out a tempestuous surge. The rocking picked up momentum, and soldiers on either side worked together to dislodge the horse. It teetered on two legs at a momentary standstill and came crashing down, emitting a thunderous echo through the piazza. I grabbed Alistair's hand.

"I told you this would happen." He squeezed my fingers but didn't offer anything reassuring before pulling away. "But I suppose you think this is none of your concern, right? You've learned that your destiny goes beyond this place."

"Yes, it does," came a deep voice from under the tree. I whipped around to find Henry leaning against the trunk, cleanly dressed in his uniform and posturing demurely to avoid attracting attention. He stood where I last saw him on Carnival.

I sank toward him. "You're here." I couldn't believe my eyes and had to touch him.

Striding from the tree, he met me partway and joined our conversation. "Things are going to change." He glanced from Asha to Alistair. "I believe the French way might bring balance to the society, where all can thrive, not just Venetian aristocracy." His speech was lost to me as I admired his polished poise. Henry eased close and brushed his lips past my cheek in a soft kiss. "I told you I'd come back for you." He gently collected my hand. "But this is not the worst of it." He spoke to my companions. "You must come with me. We must return to the docks if you want to see a real sight." Holding my hand tight, he dragged me after him as we disappeared into the crowd.

We funneled past women huddled together, prattling nervously. There was growing desperation amongst the people. I couldn't move fast enough. We ran down a side alley, hand in hand, Max, Alistair, and Asha a step behind. Our retreat brought flashbacks of two months ago when we left Carnival.

Henry slowed his pace and came to match me in stride. He clasped my arm, and I was grateful for his calm, firm grasp. "I don't like coming to find you in a crowd."

I squinted up at him. His expression was flat. "What do you mean?"

"It seems when I know how to have you in my life regularly, you slip away, and I must search for you again." He walked ahead without care. "The Harewood Christmas was disappointing. Then I find you at the Arsenal, only to discover you have changed again. Then, the Casino." He shook his head. "I can't explain my dissatisfaction when I met you at the Carnival with Donovan."

I wanted to rail against his assessment of the events but knew this was neither the time nor place. But his lack of compassion for my perspective was disturbing. Still, I bit at his bait. "What do you mean having me in your life regularly?" My heart thudded. Before giving him time to answer, a wave of anger focused my thoughts. "And what of Carnival? You left me there, spiriting away your little Ann. Do you know what happened?"

He avoided my accusations. "Let's say I've tried to make you mine from several angles. But at this point, I only see one way you will stay within my grasp and I prevent you from making foolish decisions." He dragged us around several corners, deftly moving through the city like a native.

I dizzied. "Why would you want me?"

"You are half English and half French, maybe a bit Italian. You are a true hidden treasure." He slowed his steps and looked at me, touching the locket resting atop my blouse. "I can't believe I missed it or to whom it belonged."

I rested a hand on my chest. "It was my mother's. But she's related to Camilla and Danielle. How are they important?"

"It's not them that interests me. It's your French heritage. I think you've worked out the entangled dependency of your English kin, but the French side, your father, holds real potential."

Alistair's footsteps echoed behind us, and I thought of how months ago he pleaded for me to use my voice how I saw fit—writing, living, learning, but with no certainty of the quality of life or the new political influence in Venice. Still, these were my friends. This had become my way of life. Family history or not, staying in Venice meant an unfettered opportunity but an uncertain future.

I wasn't sure what Henry proposed, but surely it would be different.

Before my friends caught up with us, Henry and I were enveloped in a crowd, bottlenecking at the Rialto Bridge. With each step, I desperately gripped his arm. As we approached the arch of the bridge, he pulled me aside. We watched the canal, packed and busied with boats of all sizes and makes, not the leisure Mayday of merchants moving their wares from one dock to another, but something hurried and frantic.

Holding tight to Henry's arm and the railing, I considered the people. It gave me a minute to notice the simplicity of my gown, nothing I would have ventured out in before. My fingers, still stained black from newspapers, poked through the crook of Henry's arm. I shamefully retrieved my hand from his coat and tried to brush away the smudges.

"You can be a nervous thing at moments. Strange for such a strong and intelligent being." Henry looked at me. "Unforgettable are those eyes, truly." He refocused on the commotion around us. "I have not figured out the details, but I've decided I can't allow you to escape me again. I will show you what I think will solidify your decision, and then I expect you to collect your belongings. We will return to England. I intend you to be mine." He turned away and went down the other side of the bridge.

Dashing after, I grabbed the crook of his arm. "Yours?"

"I assume you read my letter. I propose marriage. That is the only way I can ensure you are not taken from me or that you have the right to slip away. I can help you find clarity concerning your family." He gave me a side glance, his expression not cold, and thumbed the locket around my neck. "You don't come from nothing, which is why our union is justified."

I floated thrillingly in the wake of his proposition. As a courtesan, I'd never considered the possibility that I could be a wife. From my first bedding with Alistair I thought wholeheartedly that I would slowly perish as a whore. I had accepted that reality. Now, I dared to dream that Henry might mean a different life—and even love. I'd craved belonging in his world since the first sight of him at the Board Inn. Henry offered assurances. I wasn't sure at what cost to my autonomy.

We emerged onto the wharf, and I was deafened by the echo of boats knocking together and their loudly clanging mast bells. People clogged the walkway as they fought to get from one place to the next. Merchants hustled about with produce, shouting orders and screaming profanities.

I filed behind Henry and was grateful to see Alistair, Asha, and Max still on my heels. Without them, I feared I would continue to obey Henry and not speak my mind. We wove through the crowd like a serpent through reeds. I couldn't see much beyond the people and the boats. Nearing a clearing, I caught a glimpse of the ship that had brought me to Venice.

I searched the length of the vessel for Donovan. I spotted him hanging from one of the rope ladders, gazing long in the opposite direction across the lagoon to *terrafirma*. His loosely tied black hair flapped in the breeze. Maybe the bond pulled at us both, but he turned around. His focus seemed to narrow instantly, spotting me in the crowd. He descended from his perch, scampered over the boat's edge, and down a rope to the dock. Donovan pressed toward us with the stealth of a panther after spying on his target. I was worried he might grab me and spirit me away before I could understand the moment's revolution.

Instead, he plowed straight for Henry, fist sailing past a man carrying a hefty burlap sack, landing Henry squarely on the jaw. Henry's face jerked to the left. Speckles of blood dripped onto his white pants.

Donovan breathed over him with fury, his broad chest panting heavily as he sputtered: "Haven't you used her enough?" He continued assaulting Henry, pounding hard on his back.

I cried out at the violence. "Stop!"

He spun around to me, his face blazing with anger. "You can't have faith in him. Do you know how often he has tried to trap you into some service or another?" The anger faded, replaced by hurt. Donovan understood something I had refused to recognize. He offered his hand, neither demanding nor shaming me into taking it.

Since I'd listened to Alister's idea months ago and Henry's proposal, I went with Donovan to consider his viewpoint. He led me to a clearing on the dock and a sight attracting attention. We stood together near the water. He released me, giving me space but staying close enough for me to lean in. I shielded my eyes from the reflecting sunlight—my view adjusted and focused on the odd jaggedness of the opposing shoreline. An unbroken line of ships tied together like a great beast riding the tide.

"There must be a hundred of them," I exclaimed.

"More like 500. The ships will demolish this city if the Doge defaults on his agreement. Napoleon has won." Donovan closed the gap between us, still not touching me but holding my gaze intently in his. "Your eyes are glowing—that little fleck so bright." He grinned and sobered. "Things are forever changed in Venice. The *Serene Pearl of the Adriatic* has aimed to stay neutral during the revolution, but that choice is now gone."

This enlightenment bowled me over. Donovan was right. What did that mean for me if an Empire failed at neutrality and was forced into a decision? What fate was I to choose? Stalling, I might lose an opportunity, and one might be selected for me. I had yet to hear Donovan's version of what I should do and searched his expression for his plea.

He read my thoughts. "I won't tell you what to do. I am neither desperate for you like Alistair nor do I long to dominate you like Henry. If anything, you have me transfixed, and I am at your service, whatever that may entail."

He glanced over his shoulder, and I let my gaze follow. We watched Henry, Alistair, Asha, and Max stand agape as they studied the formidable French ships. He looked back at me. "That one wants you for his own. He will try to marry you and hide you in some corner of England. You will be cared for, but will you be loved?" Donovan then gestured to Alistair. "The other one wants you here, for change is coming, and he fears facing it alone. You will be exposed to all elements."

"And what exactly do *you* offer?"

He replied steadily. "What can I offer but myself? If you want to stay, we will stay. We can seek out your French heritage if you want to venture into Europe. I will support you and your sister if you want to return to Harewood. I own this ship and can take you anywhere you wish. I have no course except for the one we can make together."

That was tempting. My head dizzyingly spun as I weighed the options. Donovan was the obvious choice, but my heart could not let go of the possibilities with Henry. He'd always been out of reach, and now he wanted me.

My world spun—I couldn't breathe, couldn't balance myself. My vision blurred. As I retreated, my foot landed upon a slick black step. Donovan tried to snatch at me, shouting my name. I stumbled and lost my balance. Silvio's voice echoed in my mind: *Caution of the dark steps! They will send you for a swim.*

I smacked the water, and my loose clothing sucked me into the lagoon. I succumbed to the sea's power as it pulled me toward the seabed. My friends and my prospects stood united on the dock, watching my descent. All this time, I'd struggled to carve out an identity, to know who I was and where I belonged. Now, I was washed in relief. If I let the waters have their will, my struggles could vanish. I could sink into the Lagoon's embrace, away for the unfathomable events of the last two years—the workhouse, Felicity, the asylum, Harewood House, Mother Shipton, Danielle, Carmine, Venice.

The sturdy grip of my memories loosened as the water swallowed me. I watched Henry, Donovan, and Alistair peering at me from above as the waters towed me down. Who was the right one? If I stayed neutral, like Venice during this revolution, my choices would be made for me instead of me claiming them for myself.

My final promise came flooding back: *To my mind: I promise to make choices with even measure, clear of lust or craving, and as protected from fear as I may. I promise not to make a permanent decision when my mind is clouded.*

Mother Shipton's prophecies made sense now: *Your mind is your power source. It is tied to your heritage and will lead you to your future, but it is also your master of fear. When you are clouded, you will fall. Your body is your house of fear. Only when the mind and heart work together will you conquer your fear. Your heart is for love but is also for power. Only the heart can honestly know the difference in your motivation—love, fear, or power.*

The lagoon soothed my spirit, gifting me *acqua sanitas*, the sanity I craved.

Someone splashed into the water above. I couldn't tell who swam toward me, for the edges of my sight closed into a pinhole, squeezing out the world around me and leaving me in a floating abyss. The lengths of my dress gently pulled me toward the lagoon bed, and I wrapped my arms around myself like embracing a lover, longing for peace and solitude—only if I didn't fight back, only if I gave up my plight for a life of my own. After all I'd endured, I didn't know if there was any reason to go on.

I felt the sharp clasp of someone snatching at my wrist and their fervent tugging me in the opposite direction of the lagoon called. I still could not see who was fighting for me, and I didn't have the strength to help in that fight or the will to crawl back to the lagoon floor. Like so many moments in my life, I was adrift to the whims of fate, pushing and pulling me in one direction or another.

Slowly we rose through the waters, and I resurfaced, clapped back into awareness by the brisk air on my cheeks. Indiscernible noise and incomprehensible voices accosted my senses, and I wished for the water's silence. My rescuer hauled me up on the dock, and my chest collided with the cracked boards, knocking water from my throat. I curled in on myself, coughing at droplets that moments ago promised soothing sleep. My acidic hacking enflamed me with life, air, and clarity.

As the coughing subsided, I wiped at the hair hanging in my face, much like it had on that fateful night at the Board Inn. I looked at the faces of the men who each made me an offer—in some form.

Allister was shaking and staring. He clasped Asha and Max's hands like they prayed for a dying being but couldn't intervene.

Donovan sat next to me, dripping in water. His black hair draped around his face as his head hung. His shoulders heaved in an exhausted breath. I wanted to reach to him, to take him up in my arms and thank him for the countless times he'd pulled me from peril. But something prevented me.

Henry stood near but remained composed. I searched his expression for caring, for investment. He frowned and leaned toward me, extending a hand. "My dear. I believe it is time for us to go."

Without meaning to, I clasped his fingers and allowed him to haul me up. As quickly as I'd fallen into the lagoon, I was in step with Henry. I glanced over my shoulder at the life and the people I'd come to know as my own, and a deep pit of uncertainty filled my chest. I hoped that the world I walked into with Henry would give me what I always wanted—a family, opportunity, and security.

To this day, I couldn't say what made the decision—mind, body, or heart.

If only I'd made a different choice.

The End

Author's Notes & Acknowledgments

The Curse of Maiden Scars is a work of fiction intended to share the story of a young girl fighting for identity and opportunity in a harsh and unforgiving world. As an author and mental health professional, I know the exploitation of those struggling with mental illness, prostitution, and human trafficking are real and present today. This work of fiction is not meant to offend but to rouse thought around the experiences of victims of such traumas.

A trip to Venice sparked the idea for this novel. I was curious what kind of woman would appreciate—and fear—witnessing Napoleon conquer the Empire in four days in 1797. In my day job, I proudly support those struggling with grief and trauma. Starting the novel with the mental health history of the era seemed only natural.

My taste for literature has run dark since my teenage years. I was fascinated with the likes of Kafka, Poe, and Shelley and love Victor Hugo's *Les Miserables*. It is epic and poetic and indelibly speaks about love and suffering. The Georgian and Napoleonic eras were a birthing wave of change that came with great devastation. I hope my readers won't shy away as we explore timeless themes in old worlds with today's eyes. My stories are not intended to exploit or glamorize sensitive topics. I believe finding ways to look long and hard at suffering allows us to recognize and intervene when it transpires in real time.

Aretino's Diaries is mentioned throughout the novel and was a work I discovered during my English Literature studies, specifically a class on *Erotic Writing in the Renaissance*. I read Pietro Aretino's book the same college semester I became a mother. It was the first time I'd heard of the concept of a woman's life in trios—*Nun, Wife, and Whore*. Aretino's recount shocked me as much as motherhood changed me. When I was pregnant with my daughter, I later learned of *Maiden, Mother, and Crone*. A thematic overlap resounded to me, although admittedly distastefully.

I've always been fascinated by feminine history: our beauty, subjectivity, strength, and diversity. There is a common bond of fortitude, creation, and hope, often bread in sorrow and misfortune. I embrace these themes, along with the motto "life is difficult at its best", thanks to my spectacular mother, Hungarian-born and raised in post-WWII Idaho (a.k.a. the middle of nowhere) by my lovely and hardworking *Nagymama* and *Nagyapapa*. My father's family is compassionate and stoic. His Montanan upbringing somehow matched my mother's European values. Although my family is not of nuclear design, I'm extremely proud of my parents and their fortitude. I thank one for ADHD and the other for dyslexia. Somehow, the neurodiverse find each other.

I must thank my very patient Yorkshire-born husband for enduring my random interjections of inspiration. With his medical expertise, we share hours of stimulating conversation, and he's my favorite travel companion. My son and daughter are constantly motivating and have inspired almost all my educational and professional pursuits. I love you both. And—you're stuck with me.

This novel would not be as alive without the hours of detailed focus from my independent editor and dear friend, Candace Craig. She is a masterful wordsmith who understood the nuances of my dyslexic mind. She sweats love for imagery and literature onto every page she edits. Her brilliant philosopher husband, Dr. James Reid, generously read several versions of the novel and never gave false flattery when critical analyses prevailed. Tough love is the only way for me, and for them. Their writing and editorial work with Craig-Reid Editing is second to none.

I also thank my beta readers, like Eve Porinchack, who appreciated the intimacy of this gothic and tragic tale. To my family and friends who have put up with endless hours of brainstorming, reading, and listening to novel snippets and who were subjected to historical facts you never knew—and perhaps never wanted to know—I love you all. Get ready for more. Life-long learning means peppering conversations with random details and historical connections that will make their way into future novels.

REVIEWS ARE APPRECIATED

About the Author

Nicolette comes from a family of American and European storytellers, Montanan and Hungarian. From her earliest childhood playtimes, she was crafting stories. As a neurodivergent learner, writing those stories proved harder than creating them. Both nature and nurture fueled her spirit of determination. She pursued an English B.A. to learn how to write and worked at a weekly newspaper after graduating college. Motherhood came to her with complex circumstances, which inspired further education in twice-exceptional learners and counseling. She holds a post-Bac in special education, an M.A. in Education, and an M.A. in Clinical Mental Health Counseling. Nicolette's private counseling practice specializes in neurodivergent people, trauma, and grief. Storytelling has always been part of how she sees the world, including her Narrative Therapy counseling style. The Curse of Maiden Scars is her first novel brought to publication. She has previously published journalism and short fiction. When not working in her counseling practice or researching and creating her latest story, Nicolette shares treasured time with her family and friends, including her Yorkshire-born husband. She believes creation—in all forms—fuels contentment and personally pursues that through writing, cooking, hiking, traveling, and lifelong learning.

Follow the author at
www.nicolettecroft.com
www.thehistoricalfictioncompany.com/hp-authors/nicolette-croft
www.facebook.com/nicolettecroftauthor

www.historiumpress.com

Printed in the USA
CPSIA information can be obtained
at www.ICGtesting.com
LVHW041142080624
782685LV00030B/501/J